I0749329

NO PLACE

FOR

NAKED DOWSERS

Dot Ryan's

NO PLACE

FOR

NAKED DOWSERS

No Place for Naked Dowsers

ISBN:
978-0-9831197-3-9 (dj)
978-0-9831197-4-6 (sc)
978-0-9831197-5-3 (eBook)

Published by Checkered Swan Publishing, LLC

checkeredswan@att.net

dotryanbooks.com

United States of America

Library of Congress Control Number: 2012917818

To Sam

and

our loving family

Contents

PROLOGUE i

PART ONE

1 The Beginning of the End 1
2 Rome In Time of Carnival … 8
3 Memories and Loyalties 19
4 Be Careful of What You Wish For … 27
5 Time Was Supposed to Heal All Wounds 36
6 They is Gone to Texas … 42
7 Betrayal and Then Death, Isn't That Always the Way? 50
8 Drastic News Requires Drastic Measures 56
9 A One-legged Son-of-a-… the Confederacy 61
10 Kinship For A Fleeting Measure of A Day 69

PART TWO

11 A Strange Bond Among Social Disparities 79
12 This Ain't No Place To Tarry … 88
13 The Making of A Naked Dowser 101
14 In Company of A Nasty Old Man 114
15 Something Other Than A Fast Horse and A Poke Full'a Pesos 125
16 The Arrival 132
17 Let The Wimmen Do Wimmen's Work! 141
18 The Reunion 150
19 The Albatross Around Your Neck 158
20 Friend or Foe? 165
21 Miracle or Mishap is a Hard Call Sometimes… 179
22 What Was the Price of Them Kids? 192
23 That's My Damn Horse! 206
24 Enemies Must Join Hands, Señor 219
25 'Pears to Me Like Georgia Done Come to Texas 234
26 Which Was He, Despot or Ignoramus?" 248
27 Was He a Man Driven Crazy? 257
28 A Hanging, A memory, and A Bitter Decision Renewed 264

PART THREE

29 Rain 281
30 What Are You Up To, 'Actually,' Ella? 289
31 A Night of Twin Storms 296
32 The Morning After … 308
33 A Dowser, a Killer, and a One-legged Ghost 317
34 Justice 331
35 Superstition or Intuition? 339
36 We're All Naked Dowsers, of a Sort… 349
37 A Stink Worse Than Death 357
38 Burying Things 363
39 My *Cuchillo* Had a Very Large Target, Señora 376
40 "Good as Gold" 384

PROLOGUE

GENTRY GARLAND STOOD ON THE BLUFF overlooking Greenpoole plantation, his sunburned face void of emotion, and his black eyes unreadable. Only the rapid drumming of fingers against his leather-encased thigh gave away his turbulent thoughts: The time had come to tell his wife that the Georgia home she so revered was not for him. He was a cattleman, not a farmer. Cattle were his business, not cotton. Ella's dream of restoring Greenpoole to its old splendor had become his nightmare, and he was tired of pouring good money after bad. Lately, the vast open ranges of Texas beckoned him more and more. He wanted to go home.

Gentry lit a thin cheroot and tossed the match over the bluff into the wind. As beautiful as Ella's ancestral property on the Savannah River still was in many ways, the scars of war and poverty were everywhere. The end of slavery meant the end of prosperity to planters such as the Corrigans, an end to 'the old days' that Ella, and others like her, spoke of with such longing.

Ella's sharecropping adventure with her freed Negroes, trading crops for labor, was a failure that she refused to acknowledge. Her share of those crops was never enough to pay the bills. Blind to reality, she and fellow planters refused to see the hopelessness of their efforts. Southerners all across the South were starving on a new diet of higher and higher taxes; their land, animals, and goods of all types confiscated for nonpayment. Disenfranchisement—men stripped of their voting rights—left Southerners no voice. Without the vote, there was no sane way to fight the injustices taking place, nor could peaceful-minded Southerners halt the radical and violent societies springing up in nearly every Southern community.

Gentry wanted no part of this postwar turmoil. He had fought for neither North nor South, and like many Texans who clung fiercely to their independence, he considered his isolated land a perfect divide from both arguments. There, he and his little family could be lost from the rest of the world if that's what they wanted, and he could concentrate on trailing his vast herds of longhorns to distant markets in answer to the renewed demand for beef. He needed to go home and take care of his business—*permanently.*

He'd returned to Texas four times in the past two years to sell off more and more of his land—all to keep Ella from losing Greenpoole Plantation. With each brief appearance at his ranch, his *vaqueros* and their families eyed him with unspoken questions, undoubtedly wondering if he had gone *loco.*

His love for Ella was not diminished by his mounting disgust for her delusions about Greenpoole. It was his *spirit* that had been diminished, leaving him with a feeling of cravenness that he had never before experienced; his reaction to it was silent anger, and with each passing day he struggled harder to restrain that anger.

His foul-mouthed old friend back in Texas, Hempstead Grouse, said he was the worst kind of "whupped" that can happen to a man. "And out of respect for your lady, Gent, I ain't saying the part of her anatomy that's got you so golldamn whupped."

Had any man other than Hempstead Grouse made such a remark, he would've landed on his back in the dirt while spitting out a mouthful of bloody teeth. But Gentry knew that if he struck the wiry old former Texas Ranger—who dressed like an undertaker, swore like a demon, and armed himself like a cutthroat outlaw—odds were he'd just have to go ahead and shoot him, for the bad-tempered old cuss would've done his best to shoot *him.*

Anyway, Gentry doubted if Hempstead, a hard-bitten, sworn bachelor *"in loathe of female situations,"* would understand his reasons for pampering Ella. Five years ago, he had made love to her beneath the moonlit oaks alongside Corrigans' Pool, and then beat a hasty retreat out of town first thing the next morning. It wasn't exactly that cut and dried: He had left a letter telling her that his father had been shot and he must go to him. He wrote that he loved her, and would be back as soon as possible. But she never got that letter because the love-sick, sorry-excuse-for-a-preacher, *Timon Pledger,* destroyed it before it could reach her hands. Bitter and heartbroken, she married a brutal man who, after systematically stripping the joy from her life, had tried to kill her.

Gentry dropped his head, feeling a fresh surge of his old guilt. Without having read that letter, what else could she have thought except that he had callously used her, and then jilted her? Four long years later, on the day he and Ella finally wed, he silently vowed to do all within his power to heal her so completely that not one memory of Victor Faircloth remained. An old misogynist like Hempstead Grouse would never understand loving a woman that much.

For the most part, he had succeeded in making Ella happy, but he did not fool himself that the gladness in those beautiful blue-green eyes was as much for Greenpoole's resurrection as for the newly rekindled love between them. He was almost ashamed of his secret pleasure when another batch of sharecroppers didn't work out as she planned, or when it rained too much or not enough, and her cotton crops perished. Glad, even when it was his money being plowed under, every dollar of land and cattle revenue he provided swiftly gobbled up by that hopeless dream of hers. *There's something mighty sad,* Gentry thought, *about folks who live so much in the past that they can't get their feet moving toward the future.*

Gentry's jaw tightened. He'd once thought he was a man like his father: Kiel Garland had been fierce in his beliefs, unyielding in what he knew was either right or wrong. Maybe he should do what Kiel did over thirty-five years ago when he rode silently into the Irish settlement of San Patricio and carried his bride away while her clueless parents slumbered in the next room. But Kada Garland had been a willing conspirator, full of determination and knowing every minute what and whom she wanted. She was a woman whose heart, once set, had never changed. Was Ella's heart set? Gentry wasn't sure. He was certain of only one thing; he had a rival: *Greenpoole Plantation.*

Gentry gazed at Greenpoole's tree-lined acres and the beautiful old Savannah River that rippled past between shimmering walls of vine-hung foliage; but he did not see any of it. Instead he saw a vast, rolling prairie, spattered with oak motts and knee-high prairie grass that melted into infinite fields of bluebonnets, sunflowers, Indian blankets, and buttercups. A vast herd of wild horses thundered into his vision, and beyond them hundreds of long-horned cattle stepped warily from a wide patch of Mesquite brush to graze upon the peaceful open range.

After a moment, Gentry sucked deeply on the cheroot, and then spewed the smoke from between his tight lips as if he had tasted something foul. Slowly and steadily, there came into his black eyes a look more reminiscent of the 'old days' and the old Gentry Garland. He took another drag from the cheroot before tossing it over the bluff's edge into the river. He'd wait until this last crop was in, and then he'd tell his wife to pack their duds, because he was taking her and his son *home* to Texas.

Part One

1

The Beginning of the End

THE LOOK ON ELLA'S FACE WENT FROM COOL TO HEATED. "What do you mean, Honor, 'when we've packed our bags and gone from this place'? Explain yourself, please." Ella almost whispered the words, and then stared at her younger sister. *Surely, Honor could not be serious!* If so, the girl had no more sense now than when she was a giddy fifteen-year-old girl all too anxious to wed her irrepressible beau, Andy Kearney. *One would think that motherhood would have matured her,* Ella thought, and then looked at their grandmother, fully expecting Beatrice Corrigan to be as shocked as *she* was at Honor's silly remark. However, no sound came from the woman, not even a derisive hoot!

Ella continued to eye the elderly woman whose owl-like eyes, like the steely orbs of an aloof wizard, continued to gaze elsewhere. Surely she would say something upon hearing such twaddle. The Beatrice Corrigan Ella knew had a rejoinder for every conversation within hearing range, invited or not.

Finally, Ella gave up and leaned forward to face her sister, determined to speak softly, knowing that if she let her emotions escape, the colossal empty room would echo her words like stones striking the walls of an iron well. "I'm waiting, Honor. What did you mean by that ridiculous statement? Surely the notion that we would leave Greenpoole must have come from *somewhere.*"

Honor glanced fearfully at Ella then at their grandmother, who still ignored them both. Suddenly nervous, Honor quickly shifted her attention to the small girl draped across her lap and began poking nervously at the girl's blond curls. The child immediately slid into a sitting position on the floor and scooted on her tiny rump until she was out of her mother's reach. When Honor motioned for her to return, the child entangled her fingers in her curls and stuck out her bottom lip. Honor giggled. "She thinks I'm gonna comb her tangles out."

"Honor ..." Ella persisted.

Honor again looked to their grandmother, but Beatrice stiffened her chin against her high lace collar, as if to say, *"You got yourself into this, young lady, now get yourself out of it."* Honor sighed. "I only meant that maybe ... *someday* ... we might all just move into Grandmother's lovely home in Savannah like she keeps inviting us to do." She hesitated, and then blurted, "Grandmother says we'll never be able to turn this place around because God and those hateful politicians in Washington won't let us!"

Ella stared at her for a long interval and then settled back against the hard wooden chair. "You and Andy may go whenever you wish. I won't abandon Greenpoole to the sharecroppers. How would the work get done without Gentry and me encouraging them? Besides, I have to consider Hannah and the others. She and old Baker Ben said they will never leave, nor will Cricket and the twins," she said, pausing to note that neither woman was looking at her. She continued in a matter-of-fact tone, "And since Meshach was unable to abide the North and has come home, I intend to make him Greenpoole's overseer. The crops are bound to improve." She waited for her two companions to agree. When neither spoke, she went on. "Meshach and the others love Greenpoole, just as I do." She glanced up from her sewing and looked sternly at first one, and then the other. *Just as the two of you should love it,* she wanted to say, but instead said, "They love it just as Father and all Corrigans before him loved it, none of whom would have left simply because life got a bit harder."

"A bit harder, you say?" Beatrice finally spoke. She took a sip of tea, then balanced the cup in her free palm, her sour expression deepening as she looked around the room. "I know the tables are gone—firewood for General Sherman's army in '64. What was left was later sold by *you* for Greenpoole's upkeep—but have you not another *chair* on which to set our repast?" Apparently knowing the answer, she continued. "You know very well, Ella, that Hannah and the others, except for old Baker Ben, would gladly follow you to town or anywhere else. Tis *you* who refuse to leave."

"That is the very truth," Honor chimed in, nodding in agreement, as she jerked her attention from Beatrice to Ella and then back to Beatrice. She was apparently expecting the usual fireworks between her older sister and their grandmother, but Ella spoke softly.

"You have so many lovely old tables and other treasures in your attic, Grandmother. Seems to me you would have sent them out here to Greenpoole by now, knowing our need."

Beatrice sipped at her tea, her weathered cheeks tightening with a smile as she gazed over the cup's rim. "You and your sister may divide my property between you, dear girl, when I am dead and buried. Until then, I shall keep my treasures where they are."

Honor leaned far out of her chair to deliver a hurried pat to Beatrice's knee. "In that case, Grandmother, I hope those lovely pieces of furniture stay where they are for a very, very, long time ... even if we do need them terribly, and your poor, little great-grandchildren would be so much more comfortable if the house wasn't so bare."

Beatrice glowered at her, and then switched her gaze to Ella. "Your husband tells me that Greenpoole's taxes have increased and are due weeks before the harvest ... a harvest that will not be sufficient to pay them, just as last time."

Ella set her cup firmly in its saucer. "I'm surprised to hear that Gentry spoke to you of that matter, Grandmother. I've never known him to complain."

"He was not complaining. And why shouldn't he speak to me, his elder, and his friend? Anyway, he is a cattleman, not a planter. Perhaps he sought wiser council than has been his privy of late." She ignored Ella's sudden frown. "As a former planter and eternal realist, I advised him to the best of my awareness and experience."

"May I ask what advice you gave him?"

"I suggested that he follow his heart ... as long as it did not bog him down in a quagmire of malcontent."

Ella smiled. "Thank you, Grandmother, because my husband does, indeed, follow his heart. I am most fortunate that his heart is with *me* and here at Greenpoole, where it will always remain. There is no 'quagmire of malcontent' here," she added, ignoring that the two women glanced briefly at each other.

~

At dusk Ella stood on her balcony watching the red sun sink into the river, and waiting for Gentry to come home. In the back of her mind was her grandmother's insinuation. Had Gentry disclosed feelings to Beatrice that he had yet to reveal to her? Oh, but he would never do that! If Gentry was thinking of moving them into town, he would have said so by now. Besides, he knew they couldn't run Greenpoole while residing seven miles away in Savannah. Even with a reliable overseer like Meshach in charge, they'd constantly need to be here.

The stunning sunset shimmered across the river like liquid rubies, but Ella turned her back to it and pressed her knuckles to her lips. She had little time for sunsets these days. She hurried back into her room, her mind racing. Gentry was in Savannah more than usual lately, mailing instructions to his employees back in Texas, and checking for mail from them or his mother. He seemed so restless at times. Some days his moodiness made her so uncomfortable that she purposefully forced her thoughts elsewhere, because there were just so many *crucial* matters to ponder that she did not have time for …

Her concentration turned automatically to the new tax notice in the bureau drawer. She'd have to ask Gentry for more money. Oh! How she wished Beatrice had not come to visit today!

Ella frowned, and glanced sidelong at herself in the mirror, wincing at the plainness of her dress, the severity of the way she now wore her long hair in a tight bun on the nape of her neck. She looked so plain … almost angry. Did Gentry find her unattractive? Subconsciously, she loosened the bun and let her thick blanket of pale hair fall to her waist. Was he glum because she no longer went out of her way to make herself pretty for him? But when did she have time to preen her feathers when they both worked themselves to the point of exhaustion each day? Or was he sullen because she neglected him, falling asleep as soon as her head hit the pillow, sometimes so tired she pretended to be asleep, ignoring his touch until he gave up and rolled away from her?

She jerked the cover from her huge copper bathtub, lamenting only briefly over how General Sherman's men had taken the tub's beautiful rococo base when they occupied Greenpoole. The twins, Sunbeam and Moonbeam, kept six large buckets of water filled for her bath, and she emptied them into the tub. After rummaging through several drawers for a forgotten pouch of coveted bath salts, she peeled away her sweat-soiled garments and sank gingerly into the cool, spicy water. While lathering her hair and body, she tried to remember the last time she added fragrance to her bath, but could not recall. Lying back, she slipped beneath the water to swirl the soap from her hair, staying under for as long as she could hold her breath.

Upright again, she lifted her hands and examined her dirt-rimmed nails, and then thrust them back into the water to soak. "Hard work and success go hand in hand," she mumbled, repeating the axiom she had heard for years. She wondered who had first voiced that bit of truth. Whoever had said it, she was sure it was truer now than ever, and with a little cooperation from her doubtful family, Greenpoole's success would happen a lot sooner rather than later. It was up to her to convince them, but ... *first things first.* Tomorrow she and Gentry would go to town and pay the taxes.

She towel-dried her hair, patted her body dry, and, ignoring her nightgown hanging on a nearby hook, slid between the linens to await her husband. She had neglected him too long.

~

Sometime later, she lay with her head resting cozily on Gentry's shoulder. The full moon, unusually bright, hung over the balcony like a giant lantern, splashing a transparent blanket of silver over their bodies, and setting Ella's pale, bare skin aglow. A whispery breeze from the open windows and French doors toyed gently with the mosquito netting that hung from a tall mahogany frame attached to the ceiling over their bed. As usual after making love, they had settled snugly against each other.

Ella stroked Gentry's forehead with the softer back of her hand, and ran her fingers through his jet-black hair, her lips brushing his cheek from time to time, as she chatted casually about the unfairness of the Yankees being in command of everything now. Laughing lightly, she repeated the gossip that Judith Ashville had passed along about Cleta Harris' affair with a married Yankee, "the affair having started long before she divorced her husband—the low-brow drummer she had run away with during the war, thereby disgracing her socialite family to no end!"

She laughed softly again, and then, after a short pause said, "I'd like to go into Savannah tomorrow, Gentry ... just you and me. We can pay the new taxes they have so unfairly levied against us, and if you like, we can dine at the Savannah Hotel afterward." She paused, waiting, but he was silent.

She wiggled closer. "It'll be so much fun getting away for a few hours, and then we'll have a leisurely ride home in the moonlight. I hope the moon is like it is tonight, don't you?" She continued to stroke his forehead, waiting for his response, but none came. Disappointed, she was about to conclude that he was fast asleep and she would have to wait until morning to repeat herself, but then his low laughter jarred her. She sat upright, trying to see his face in the shadows. Stunned, she watched him roll out of bed, pull on his trousers, and busy himself with the buttons.

"Gentry...?"

"Do you know what they call a woman who sleeps with a man for money, Ella?"

"I didn't!"

"You did. And I might as well tell you, we're leaving for Texas just as soon as your cotton is picked and we've settled with the sharecroppers—you and I and our son." He finished buttoning his pants and took his coat from the bedpost.

"But Gentry, we don't have time for a visit to Texas. After the crops are in, the land will have to be plowed ... readied for the next planting, and ..." Something made her hush, as he strode to the door, and then turned to observe her for a long moment.

"Not a visit, Ella. We won't be coming back to Georgia ... except maybe for a short holiday someday in the far-off future."

"What? But I can't!"

"We've tried living your way, Ella."

"What about *Greenpoole?* What about my *home*?"

"You can sell it, give it away, or burn it down, which I wish to God Sherman had done, and saved us both a lot of headaches."

Ella jumped from the bed, pulling the sheet around her, her eyes ablaze and brimming, not knowing whether to scream her rage or sob her despair. Before she could do either, he stepped silently from the room and closed the door; the finality of it stunned her anew.

2

"Rome in Time of Carnival ..."

"TESSIE PECKENPAUGH, IF YOU DISHONOR YOURSELF in that beggar's line for charity, I shall never speak to you again!"

"Beatrice!" Tessie shrieked, jumping as if a long-feared ghost had sprung up in the street to accost her. Standing in the charity line on Bay Street with a hundred or more other Savannahians, the *'old maid of Savannah'* was as shabby as any. Her faded bonnet, with a fresh camellia japonica pinned to the side, was like a wilted rag on her head, albeit her frayed garments were of the finest cloth. Beatrice had been sharing her home with Tessie ever since Sherman and his army vacated Savannah three years ago. His departure had been followed a few days later by a hellish fire that destroyed half the downtown area before sweeping into adjacent residential sections and burning homes—one of them, Tessie's.

Twittering, Tessie immediately abandoned the crushing line. Her shoes, broken open at the arches and split across her bunions, glared from beneath her swaying skirts as she stepped off the sidewalk and rushed into the street to lean against the ancient barouche in which Beatrice Corrigan sat, rod-stiff, and scowling down at her. Before the war and famine had arrived, the luxurious old barouche and the bony-backed mule harnessed to it would have been a laughable spectacle on Savannah's streets; but no one was laughing at such sights these days. Atop each of the two plush back seats was a stack of cherry wood chairs, six to a stack. On the floorboard between them, a small cherry wood tea table lay on its side.

"Please don't be angry with me, Bea," Tessie cried. "I have not tasted sugar in ages, and today they are adding a *beautiful* sack of flour and a *glorious* pound of sugar to our weekly ration! Heaven only knows when they will be so generous again!"

"Shame on you, Tessie Peckenpaugh! Tis Yankee charity," Beatrice spat. "I would rather starve before I put a drop of their begrudged offerings in my mouth." She jerked her arm from Tessie's grip, glowering at her, swishing the hand back and forth as Tessie tried unsuccessfully to recapture it.

"Next you will disgrace us both by opening our doors to that despot Sherman should he visit us again!"

A woman, identified as Northern by her handsome new attire, and with a small daughter clinging to her skirts, eyed Beatrice with hostility from the sidewalk.

"Excuse me, madam..." the woman said, her eyes steely with indignation, "General Sherman and our armies did naught but their loyal duty when they divested our land of its bands of rebellious revolutionaries—or *rebels,* as you are commonly known. However, it seems their lot persists, and my husband has brought me into a most ungrateful nest of them."

Beatrice bristled. She jerked her head at the woman, her flat little straw hat doing a dance atop her silvery bun. Her lips spread into a tight smile. "I am a *'rebellious revolutionary,'* eh?" Her eyes narrowed. "Well, I am most pleased to agree with you, madam. But lest you assume too much, I shall inform you that I have always been a rebellious revolutionary, as were my ancestors who fought to *'divest'* this country of *English* tyrants. If you knew your history, madam, you would know that this country of yours and mine is a land that was indeed created by *rebels,* and would not exist were it otherwise."

The woman's uniformed husband stepped away from his sentry post alongside the charity line and quickly escorted his wife and child away.

Beatrice scowled after them, content, like most Southerners in the aftermath of losing the war, to believe that the abolishment of slavery was not the North's only intention as they systematically destroyed the prosperous South. "War," the Southerners said, "had been the only way the North could dismantle a superior financial system—riches gained through the South's independent trade with Europe." That the "radical government in Washington" had simply used the Abolitionists to implement their goal was, to Southerners, a belief as irrefutable as the Bible itself. Deep down, Beatrice knew better; but she was angry at the destruction and, mostly, the indignities that followed. Paramount of those indignities were the bread lines.

Two of Beatrice's old *'tea and cakes brigade'*, Bethel Pruett and Prudence Hornden, abandoned the line and approached, shouting Beatrice's name and waving their arms in greeting; one clutched an empty basket, the other an old bucket, just as empty.

"Look at those two," Beatrice said to Tessie, growing even more hostile as she watched the pair approach. "Begging bread from the Yankees! I never thought to see the day when my own kind would…" Silenced by Bethel and Prudence's unsuccessful attempts to embrace her, she raked up a handful of newspapers from the seat and shook them in their faces.

"Have you not read these?" she cried, glaring. "They are Northern papers, every article gloating over their victory and ridiculing the South's hunger, chiding us for accepting their charity! Here! Read this!" She shoved a paper into Bethel's stunned face, but then jerked it back. "I shall read it to you," she snapped. "This," she wagged the paper, "is the *New York Times* describing one such spectacle right here in Savannah, and which is taking place this very instant!" She pointed at the needy crowd.

"Listen to this, you people; here is what the Yankees enjoy about our misery!" She stood in the carriage and began to read, her voice loud and resounding, carrying to the heart of the hungry-eyed crowd:

> *"Rome, in the time of carnival, can exhibit no such spectacle. There are two doors to the store, one on Bay and the other on Barnard Street, affording entrance and exit."*

Beatrice pointed at the Bay Street door at which the long line waited to enter.

> *"Several hundred persons of both sexes, all ages, sizes, complexions, costumes; gray-haired old men with canes, with bags, bottles, and buckets; old "Uncle Neds" who just before death gives them delivery from hardships and suffering are made freedmen by the mighty march of events; well-dressed women, wearing crepe for their husbands and sons who have fallen while fighting against the old flag, stand there with pale and sunken cheeks, patiently awaiting their turn. There are women with tattered dresses—old silks and satins which were lain aside as useless, but which have become valuable through destitution."*

Bethel and Prudence tugged at their attire as if such smoothing action could transform the rags into their old elegance.

> *"There are women in linsey-woolsey, demi-white women wearing Negro cloth, Negro women dressed in gunny cloth; men with Confederate uniforms, men with butternut clothes. There is a boy in a crimson plush jacket, made from what was once the upholstering of a sofa. There are old men in short jackets, little boys in long ones—the cast-off overcoats of soldiers, the rags which have been picked up from garrets—wearing the boots and shoes which have been kicked off and thrown aside, down at the heel, out at the toes, open on the instep. There are old bonnets of every description, some with white and crimson flowers, some with ribbons once bright and flaming but now faded and worn."*

Beatrice paused to draw a deep, ill-tempered, breath. Tessie, Bethel, and Prudence's eyes were upon her, sad with reminisces.

Several women in the crowd wiped their cheeks with tattered shawls; one dropped her basket and moved slowly away. Beatrice continued:

> *"There are Shaker bonnets, Sugar scoops, coal scuttles, hats of every description, size, and shape worn by both sexes—women wearing men's hats of palm-leaf or felt, men wearing stove-pipes battered and bruised, felt slouched and torn, ventilated by accident and not by patent ventilators. There is one which had no crown, worn by a man who had red hair, reminding one of a chimney on fire and flaming out at the top."*

Beatrice's voice rose in studied fury with the next.

> *"It is the ragman's fair rather than the ragman's jubilee and day of rejoicing, for Charity, like a kind angel, has suddenly stepped in to ward off the wolf which is howling at the door."*

An angry male voice interrupted from somewhere in the line. "The Northern dastards feign to feed us, yet rejoice that we starve!"

Beatrice's old mule shied backward a few steps before she ferociously jerked him still, her voice rising with increased fervor.

> *"There are teams in the street—old, dilapidated wagons—weak, broken-down horses and sorry mules with rope harnesses."*

Beatrice nodded wryly at her own sorry mule.

> *"It is a collection of odds and ends. It is literally a distribution of the bread of life. In no profane sense, but in truth and reality, it is a sacrament, given freely, and I doubt not gratefully received. The recipients, at any rate, are eager to partake of it—so eager that the sentinels at the door at times are compelled to present their bayonets to the crowd to keep the passage clear."*

"Damnation upon them!" a woman's voice cried as she threw off her stained slouch hat, shoved past the Yankee sentry, slung her empty basket at his feet, and stomped away. Beatrice nodded her pleasure, her eyes falling quickly back to the newspaper.

> *"There will be some who fail to receive the aid they need—persons who have never known want who will suffer silently*

rather than mix in the crowd which throngs at the door. Others will obtain provisions when they have abundance at home."

Finished, Beatrice crumpled the paper into a ball and hurled it into the street. Tessie capped her old friend's tirade with loud sighs of agreement. Then, jerking at the tattered shawl that hung from her bony shoulders like a frayed strip of gauze, she imitated Beatrice's hostile gaze at their two companions.

"I just *never!*" Prudence said, her layered chins jiggling, her round face growing even rounder in furious but speechless defense of herself.

Bethel patted Prudence's twisting fingers, then bustled closer to the cart. "Beatrice Corrigan, how dare you judge us, when for the past two years you have had your granddaughter's new husband providing for *your* needs! Most of us are not that fortunate!" She raised her bosomy chest in a manner that could only be seen as confrontational. "As for our tolerating the Yankees and thereby keeping *'the wolf from the door,'* I have bequeathed to our veterans and youthful hotheads any wasteful bitterness I might have harbored, for only *they* will live long enough to nurture it! *I* shall not live that long, Beatrice Corrigan, and neither shall *you!* Come Pruddie, old Mister Habersham is holding our place in line."

Beatrice slashed the mule viciously across his rump and jolted into the street, causing a rickety wagon to swerve from her path, its sway-backed horse showing a spurt of energy by rearing his front hooves a few inches off the sandy thoroughfare.

Tessie, running alongside and struggling to keep up, finally halted. "I shall be home soon, Beatrice! See you at tea time?" she called out and, after a moment, added, "Where on earth are you taking those chairs, Beatrice?"

Without looking back at her eternal house guest, Beatrice slapped the mule again, not bothering to reply that she was on her way to Greenpoole and would be gone overnight—a command appearance, of sorts.

That Bethel! Even without Gentry's generosity, no Corrigan would ever please Northern detractors by showing neediness! *Indeed not!* Nor would her own Cuthbert lineage, all of whom had sold their property and left for England soon after the war started.

Suddenly Beatrice was glad that she had refused the horse and buggy Gentry wanted to buy for her, keeping instead the oddly stunted mule that wandered onto Greenpoole's property one day. Meshach had mended the fancy old barouche that she and her dearly departed husband had purchased in their youth. The Yankees had evidently not wanted it when they stripped Greenpoole of its vehicles and every animal on the place, including the four slow-moving plow oxen, all of which they had promptly roasted and eaten. Never one to seek favors, Beatrice was proud of her transportation. The old mule and barouche allowed her the *respectability of equality* among her peers—Savannah's genteel citizens of society whose two-hundred-year fortunes had washed away beneath a relentless tide of blue-coated avengers too massive in number to turn away.

On the outskirts of town, Beatrice tapped at the ache behind her bosoms, and then yanked at a dangling thread on her last lace blouse which was in no better shape than Tessie's sad-looking old shawl. *And when, for God's sake, is the woman going to discard that disastrous hairpiece bun?* Even before the war, it was no more than a snarled ball of mousy brown fuzz, and now it looked as if a family of mice had actually made it their home—*starving mice, no doubt.*

~

Baker Ben, his black face as stoic as ever, slowly made his way across the dining room toward Beatrice at the head of the table. His long, thin hands, sinewy beneath skin the color and texture of old leather, gripped an elaborate silver tray atop which sat a small, two-layer cake without frosting or sauce. The tray and silverware had been salvaged from the cave beneath Corrigans' Pool where Meshach and Cricket had hidden them from Sherman's men in '64. The servants that remained at Greenpoole after the soldiers departed laughed at how the Yankees, finding no silver in such a magnificent plantation home, had dug up half the property looking for it. Ella did not laugh; they had found plenty else to cart away.

Baker Ben sat the cake in front of Beatrice, and she eyed it grimly.

"Don't tell me it's that time of year again," she said, and glowered at the old servant. "I thought you were getting so old and feeble you would forget all this silliness."

Honor laughed, and gazed fondly at the old servant who had pampered and spoiled her throughout her childhood. "How could Baker Ben forget your birthday, Grandmother, when his very own birthday is on the same day? As many of those cakes as he's baked over the years, I bet he even knows how old you are."

"I doubt it. How old am I, Baker?"

"You is eighty-two, Miz Bea," he replied, and then added haughtily, "and I is eighty-four, aiming for a hundred and four."

Gentry, Andy, and Honor laughed, but Ella, having chosen to sit between her son Adam and Honor's little Elizabeth, could only manage a smile. She ate very little of the chicken and dressing Baker Ben prepared for the occasion, and now she scarcely heard the drone of voices and light laughter of those around her. *Oh, but surely Gentry didn't mean it!* He was just angry; frustrated, as she was, with the slow progress at Greenpoole. But if he would just be patient!

A moment passed before her shoulders slumped. *He meant it. Meant every word of it!* Suddenly, she stared at her hands in her lap, pain alerting her that she had been wringing her perspiring fingers like a piece of wet laundry.

Beatrice executed her dominion as matriarch of the family by tapping her spoon against her glass, signaling that all should follow her into Greenpoole's sparsely furnished parlor, where they would have their tea and cake. She had parted with the dozen chairs and the matching tea table, but her sofas, settees, and other fine household items—collections from over the past sixty years—were still in the attic of her Savannah home, all covered with sheets or packed away in crates and boxes. Gentry and Andy helped Moonbeam and Sunbeam lug the much-needed gifts across the massive marble-floored entry hall and into the parlor, where the small tea table already sat.

Ella, purposefully avoiding Gentry, sat on the floor reading *Two Doves and the Owl* to the children—until she got to the part where the naughty old owl came along, killed the mother dove, and then flew away with the two baby doves in his clutches. She closed the book, suddenly remembering how she had detested that story as a child and cried when Grandmother read it to her. Adam and Elizabeth, unable to sit still, jumped up and darted out into the entry hall, their shrill screams and laughter soon echoing through the house and drowning out the adults. Hannah, unhampered by her girth, chased the unruly duo into a corner, and then marched them off to bed.

Later, after Honor and Andy departed for upstairs, Gentry politely excused himself. When he kissed Ella's forehead and she neither spoke nor responded, Beatrice's eyebrows shot upward. She waited until Gentry disappeared through the doorway.

"The last time I saw you ignore your husband like that, you were married to Victor Faircloth."

Ella closed her eyes. A moment later, she was sobbing quietly into her hands.

"The honeymoon lasted a lot longer than I thought it would, you being so stubborn about leaving this place," Beatrice drawled.

"You knew he wanted us to go to Texas and didn't tell me?"

"It was not my place to tell you ... none of my concern."

"It's none of your concern that he wants to take me and your great-grandson away, far away, to a God-forsaken place so far from home that you may never see us again?" She arose from the sofa and marched to the window. "Or has he convinced you to sell out and come with us," she said, her disgust evident.

"Ha!" Beatrice retorted, not trying to hide her amusement.

"I thought so," Ella nodded, turning. "I don't want to leave my home any more than you, Grandmother."

"But you will leave it." It was a factual remark rather than a question.

"He is willing to wait only until the last crops are in," Ella said. "That's little more than a month from now." She turned to face Beatrice, her expression miserable. "How can I leave behind all that I've loved and cherished my entire life?"

"It is your husband that you should 'love and cherish'," Beatrice said sternly.

"I do! But ... I never dreamed he would want me to leave my home, my family ... *Greenpoole.*" She did not attempt to silence the next burst of sobs. "How can I leave? How can I?"

Beatrice patted her shoulder. "You will do better than you think."

Ella jerked away. "No, I won't, and I don't want to." She wiped angrily at her eyes. "I pray to God something happens to stop us!"

"Be careful of such prayers, my dear, because..."

"Because I just may get what I pray for? I hope so!"

"Ella, except for me and Honor, the family you speak of is dead and gone. Honor and Andy will soon find another way of life, one they are eager to undertake. I am certain that Greenpoole will always be in Honor's memories, but she will not allow her feet to be frozen to Greenpoole's soil in a useless search for the past."

"For heaven's sake, Grandmother," Ella protested. "It isn't the past I want to preserve; it's Greenpoole's future! Honor never cared about Greenpoole the way I do, and Andy couldn't care less! He cares only about running off to town every chance he gets, to curse the Yankee soldiers when their backs are turned ... he and his friends plotting revenge they could not possibly accomplish without being caught and hanged!"

"I don't condone Andy's kind of bitterness. It will only cause him trouble. But aside from his hatred of Yankees, he and your sister have sense enough to know that life, as we knew it, is finished and will never return, Ella. Your sister has the good sense to know that her obligation is to Andy and little Elizabeth, not to a dead past."

Ella clutched Beatrice's hands, shaking them with each word. "But if we work together, we can turn a profit at Greenpoole, Grandmother. I know we can. Greenpoole is our *home!*"

"Gentry and little Adam should be your only concern, Ella, not Greenpoole."

"My son and husband *are* my concern, but so are you and Honor. This land has been the pride of Corrigans since Great-great-grandfather began building it in 1735, and ...! Oh, Grandmother, I thought you, of all people, would understand."

"I do understand," Beatrice said, and Ella was surprised to see her grandmother's eyes glisten for a moment before she continued speaking. "I was my happiest *ever* in this beautiful old house with your Grandfather, raising our son then watching my grandchildren being born here. I looked forward to each new day, and I never wanted those days to end." She paused. "However, to expect life to go on and yet remain the same was quite foolish of me, indeed." She drew her shawl around her shoulders. "After your mother's horrible accident, and I became your teacher of all things vital, I should have made certain you possessed the vision to see further than the *always fleeting* present. I apologize for being remiss," she said, with a heavy breath. "I am going up to bed. Try to attain that vision now, on your own, won't you? It's never too late."

After Beatrice went upstairs, Ella stood on the veranda, staring into the dark night and thinking of her grandmother's words. She should attain v*ision* to see *what?* Vision to see herself living out the remainder of her life in a strange land, tales about which made her cringe. In a few short weeks, she would be forced to desert her beloved home and to reside, like a trapped animal, in a place she knew she would hate. *If only something would happen to make Gentry change his mind!* Beatrice was wrong—nothing could be as bad as leaving Greenpoole!

3

Memories and Loyalties …

ELLA WATCHED SUNBEAM AND MOONBEAM transport a heavy cauldron of scalding water from the coals to the wash tables behind the kitchen house. They inched along, their chattering in contrast to their alert movements, both sets of hands gripping an end of the hickory pole on which the iron pot dangled by its handle. Sunbeam's daughter, Belle, followed, dragging a small bundle of dirty linens, which Ella knew would be twice as soiled by the time she reached the tubs. She gazed silently at Belle, then at the child's mother and aunt. What would these faithful servants do when she was gone from here? She had been through so much with them during those terrible years at Moss Oak plantation. Victor Faircloth's cruelty had touched them as well as her. She would be pleased if they stayed on at Greenpoole, collecting their wages, taking care of the place and old Baker Ben, until...

She did not like to think of Baker Ben dying. He was a part of Greenpoole, a part of her happy childhood memories when her father was alive. But he was dying. Recently, the obstinate old servant had marked his place off in the Negro cemetery behind Greenpoole's old slave quarters. He had served her family faithfully, even after her father freed him before the war. She worried even more about dear Hannah. The woman had raised her and Honor, had nurtured them, spanked them, loved them as if they were her own children. Hannah said she would never leave Georgia and "go to that wild Texas place what Miz Ashville's maid say ain't hardly got no genteel folk like we gots in Savannah."

Ella's chin began to tremble. How could she just walk away from those who had come to mean so much to her? She gazed at Moonbeam and Sunbeam hovering over the washtubs, still chattering back and forth, one scrubbing, and the other rinsing. Despite her sadness, she smiled gently at the pair. She learned during the hard years with Victor that affection grows between those who struggle together, who depend on each other for survival. She thought of the day she found Sunbeam near death, beaten and raped at the hands of Brunot, Victor's brutal slave driver. How could there not be a bond between her and this remarkable pair? The three of them had saved each other's lives, had hidden in terror together, comforted each other, laughed together, and all too often, had cried together in mourning. Did Gentry understand that she would be leaving behind much more than Greenpoole Plantation when he took her away?

After a while, Ella moved absently toward the stable to search for a broom to replace the one she had busted on the window sill when she swatted at a family of raccoons about to enter.

She turned when the boy Cricket called out to her. He came bounding down the back steps, a huge bundle of dirty laundry clamped atop his head.

"Miss Ella, can you wait up, please?" He hurried to the washtubs, dumped his bundle on the ground, and then raced up to her. He stood there smiling, not knowing what to do with his empty hands, his grin stretching almost ear to ear, the same energetic smile he'd had as a babe. He was twelve years old; no longer short for his age, but thin as a willow switch. His long arms and legs were ever ready for action it seemed, for he could not stand still for more than a few seconds.

"Did Mister Gen'te tell you, Miss Ella ... I is going to Texas with you all? I gonna be a *vi'karo* Mister Gen'te say, and I gonna have my own hoss—a fine, fast hoss that Mister Gen'te say I can pick out for my own self from all them hosses he gots in Texas. I gonna look for one just like Princess Gaia what belong to you before the Yankees took her off the place." He paused, his smile slowly disappearing. "What the matter, Miss Ella? Ain't you glad I is going?"

"I don't want to go, Cricket. Greenpoole is my home, not Texas."

He shuffled his feet in the dirt. "I ... I shore don't know what to say about that, Miss Ella ... 'cept, you is going, ain't you?" He caught his bottom lip between his teeth, sudden worry dulling his expression.

Ella finally nodded.

Cricket's smile returned. "That real good, Miss Ella. I go help them gals with them tubs now," he said, and hurried away.

Ella's gaze traveled the cavernous stable that once held her father's prized thoroughbreds; it was empty now, save for a lone black horse that stood like a peculiar novelty amid a long line of vacant paddocks. The horses Gentry brought from Texas at the end of the war were sold long ago for Greenpoole's upkeep—even the beautiful silver gelding he had gifted her. To Gentry's consternation, she had sold the horse to buy cotton seed while he was away in Texas raising more capital. She had also tried to sell the little mare, in foal, that he had gifted Honor; but when the buyer came to Greenpoole to collect the animal, Honor screeched like a wild woman. She'd plopped little Elizabeth on the animal's bare back, wrapped her arms around the mare's neck, and cried: "You'll damn well have to sell me and your niece with her!"

Ella had sent the man away empty-handed. But then, just a few weeks later, she and Honor had stood for hours, sadly enwrapped in each other's arms, as they watched Meshach struggle to pull the dead colt from its mother's womb. The mare had died in agony moments later, her blood rushing from her ruptured insides like a waterfall. As sympathetic as Ella was for the grieving Honor, her foremost thought was of the money she had lost in not selling the animal when she had the chance. A flash of guilt had preceded that cold reflection; but war and its cruel aftermath had forced her to a more practical nature when it came to surviving the new order of things. Very rarely did sentimentality triumph over reality.

The only other horses on the place, besides Timon Pledger's old horse, Blackie, were Gentry's buckskin and a pair of carriage horses, the latter three grazing peacefully in the small meadow accessed from the stable's open back doors. Old Blackie preferred his paddock most of the time, "likely in hopes of getting someone to pet him," Gentry once said, while obliging "Pledger's old pet-of-a-horse" with a vigorous rubdown.

Today, Ella ignored the animal as he stretched his long neck around to watch her, his gray-streaked muzzle twitching expectantly while his dismal excuse for a tail twirled like that of an exuberant colt. "You big baby," she muttered at him. "You're as ridiculous as was your master, that sneaky thief, Timon Pledger."

She had conflicting emotions about Timon, in that she felt both anger and pity toward him. He had likely paid a thousand times over for stealing Gentry's letter to her and then destroying it. *Poor Timmy.* He had silently loved her so much and for so long that it was entirely possible that desperation had driven him to that terrible deed—a desperation that he was not equipped to handle. He'd had no experience at all with the emotions of love, with jealously, or with the helplessness of hatred. Gentry told her how emaciated Timon looked when he'd seen him in New Orleans a year before the war ended. Timon had been on the street, preaching to a crowd of ragged, escaped slaves that had flocked into the city when New Orleans fell to the Union. Despite his godly mission among those displaced slaves, he had taken to "women and drink."

"The sorry cuss deserves all the misery he makes for himself," Gentry said, and it was obvious that *pity* was not present in his attitude toward Timon Pledger.

In recalling her and Timon's childhood together—his shy demeanor, his constant blushing and stammering—Ella could not imagine him sinking to debauchery and drink. She wondered absently where Timon had disappeared to after stealing Gentry's prized stallion, Red Man, from the Yankee officer. No one ever heard from the disgraced preacher again after that.

Ella rested her head against Princes Gaia's empty stall, and let her tired mind escape to pleasanter times before the war, when she would be mounted on her beautiful golden filly, and would canter through the woods, trails, and back roads of Greenpoole Plantation.

She started upon hearing Meshach call her name, and she turned to see his giant frame silhouetted in the wide doorway.

"Miss Ella, them Yankee soldiers from Savannah what you done sold that firewood to is 'bout through cutting it down. They chop three wagon loads this time."

"Did they pay you?"

"No'sum, they say they be 'long soon to pay up to th' rightful one."

"I'm sorry, Meshach. I told them the last time that they could pay you."

"Don't reckon they cotton to it, Miss Ella." He pulled his frayed straw hat from his head and rolled the brim between thickly calloused fingers. "Seem like to me, we Greenpoole folk could be cutting and selling that wood our own self to them townsfolk what need it. That lumber be getting a mouty big price now."

Ella nodded, her eyes absent with other thoughts. Meshach took up a broom and began to sweep the dirt floor, glancing at her from time to time, waiting, it seemed, for her speak.

"I know my husband has told you of our departure next week, Meshach."

Meshach politely set the broom aside, and studied the tips of his brogans. "Yes'sum."

Ella turned away lest he see the sudden trail of tears on her cheeks. "And he offered you an extra share of the crops to keep the house in order?"

"Yes'sum. I gonna be sending ten cents on th' dollar to you and Mister Gen'te. I gonna be keeping th' rest for to pay the workers and my own self."

There was a long silence while she waited for the tightness in her throat to subside.

"We ... we won't be back for a long time, Meshach. But I will return someday. I will. I won't sell Greenpoole, and my husband will continue to pay the taxes." She kicked a clump of hay, her mouth tightening. Gentry had forced a compromise; he would prevent Greenpoole's foreclosure indefinitely, and she would pack off to Texas without further ado. She pressed her face to the stall and wiped uselessly at the increased stream of tears.

Meshach snatched up the broom, the dust flying around him in choking puffs, as he averted his eyes from Ella's misery. The old horse, Blackie, nickered as if in sympathy for her, and then stretched his long neck around to nudge her shoulder until she absently stroked his persistent nose. Meshach came to her rescue, cupping the animal's muzzle in his giant hand and slapping gently at Blackie's neck until he backed away.

"Mister Gen'te done teach me a lesson about hosses with this old Blackie, here," he said. "Mista Gen'te say if a hoss got heart and his legs ain't sprung, he don't need much else to do heself proud, no matter how he put together." He looked Blackie over, shaking his head. "I ain't surprise at all that Mister Gen'te keep this old black hoss after what they done been through together. Just the same, it 'pear to me Mister Gen'te sure miss that big red hoss what he leave in New Orleans with them Yankees."

"I suppose," Ella said.

"I asked Mister Gen'te if he miss that red hoss, and he sayed, 'Meshach, a man that don't pine after a good horse or a good woman ain't fit for neither." Meshach laughed softly, his bass tone unobtrusive in the stillness of the stable. "Mister Gen'te tell you about how that old Blackie save him from drowning in th' ocean after that Yankee boat sink?"

Ella sniffed a "yes," her face still averted.

"I never forget how Mister Gen'te come flying cross that pontoon on this ole hoss. You 'member that, Miss Ella? Dat was th' night them ten thousand Confederates and mor'n half Savannah done cross that bridge just ahead of them Yankees what coming over th' hill at us."

"I remember," Ella said, regaining composure.

Meshach nodded at her, almost fatherly in his manner, and then he nodded again as if in affirmation of what he would say next. "And after that, I ain't never seed you so pleased as when you and Mister Gen'te get married. Mister Gen'te a fine man, Miss Ella, a rightly fine man, if I ever knowed one."

Ella turned to gaze out at the last cotton crop, ripe in the field.

Meshach laughed low again; anxiously, it seemed, as if he felt she needed further cheering, and continued, "… and I ain't ever seen a hoss eat bananas like this old Blackie do … when even a *mule* won't eat one. Mister Gen'te bring a stalk about every week. O'course, that Cricket and them chil'n eat most them bananas ... even before th' green is off'um." He glanced at Ella. "Cricket say Mister Gen'te gonna take him to Texas and make a cowhand out'n him. I sure glad something gonna be made out'n him long last." He laughed again. After a while, when Ella remained silent, he scratched his ear and took to sweeping again, this time without stirring the dirt.

Ella glanced at Meshach's unique face, which was now sad. He knew how much she would miss her home—the people, Negro and white, that had been a part of her life since birth. She wondered if he knew that she would miss him, her trusted protector throughout those hard years with Victor. In town, she witnessed strangers scurry to the opposite side of the street at the sight of this hulking ex-slave, his frightening maroon-colored eyes and treacherous demeanor being all they encompassed before hastily judging him as someone they should fear. But Ella knew that within this man was a thoughtful, intelligent human being, one with compassion not only for his own race, but for many of those who had enslaved him. That she had witnessed him kill Victor's cruel Brunot did nothing to dampen her belief in Meshach's humanity; there was a time when *she* would have killed Brunot *and* his master, had she the strength.

"Well lookie there, Miss Ella ... Miss Honor and them chil'n climbin' up th' hill," Meshach pointed to the bluff overlooking the river. "Miss Honor look like she carrying a big basket of vittles."

Ella smiled at the sight of Adam, Elizabeth, and Sunbeam's little Belle, skipping along. She smiled again when her son grasped his little cousin's hand and led her carefully along the path. The pair was more like brother and sister than cousins. *How terrible it will be for them when separated by thousands of miles,* she thought sadly.

"Yes, Meshach," Ella replied, "they are going to picnic and watch the last of the cotton being brought in from the field below." Her smile faded as she spoke. She closed her eyes to the sight, thinking, *and in another week, we will leave Greenpoole forever!*

"Why don't you go on along with'um, Miss Ella? You look mouty tired. You done worked most hard today, you and Mister Gen'te. Why, he out there picking that cotton so fast you'd think his heels was on fire … lot faster than them sharecroppers is a'picking."

He's on fire all right! Ella thought bitterly, as she clenched her eyes against the fresh sting of tears. *On fire to pack us off to Texas!*

4

Be Careful of What You Wish For …

HALFWAY UP THE PATH, on her way to join her picnicking sister and the children, Ella paused to look around. Like always, she ignored the scars of war, evident in the shattered tree trunks and great chunks of earth gouged out where shell and cannon had struck. She saw only the gentle ripple of grass on the hillside, and the arrowheads that floated gently along the river's edge. Closing her eyes, she tried to remember the sweet scents from the orchards and the rose gardens that once drifted on the breeze up to the bluff. She had thought to replant the destroyed gardens soon. Meshach reported that there were young fruit trees on abandoned property hereabouts that he could easily dig up and transplant at Greenpoole. Rose bushes, too. She closed her eyes tighter. She could smell them now—the roses, the peach, orange, and lemon trees in blossom—delicious fragrances that she could almost taste.

The loud splat of a whip against a mule's rump in the cotton field jerked her back to reality, and now only the river's unremarkable conglomeration of odors—fish and vegetation, coupled with the scent of plowed dirt—reached her nostrils; even these she relished.

Growing sadder, she continued her examination of the land she would soon leave behind. The grass-covered levee still snaked its way along the river's edge, and then disappeared into a shadowy stand of mulberry, bay, long leaf pine and oak trees. Now, many of those beautiful old trees leaned, split and broken, their dead tops folded down over their scarred trunks like aprons. However, to Adam and Elizabeth's joy, Gentry and Meshach had rebuilt the pier, along with the ancient replica of a ship's crow's-nest that had towered there for generations. The children loved playing on the old make-believe ship, just as had five generations of Corrigans before them. *Soon, Corrigans at Greenpoole would be no more,* she thought, as she stopped to gaze dejectedly at the crow's-nest.

She joined Honor on the blanket near the bluff's edge, where they could watch the goings-on below. For the first time, she dreaded the sight of cotton shrubs picked nearly clean of their growth. By sundown, the wagons would be full, and the stems would be bare of all but their green leaves. She looked away, and then frowned at the children as they darted among the scarred trees and clamored over fallen trunks, shouting and playing soldiers.

"Don't scold them, Ella, they're just having fun," Honor said. "Andy says there's no harm in a child playing *war*, now that it's over, as long as they pretend our Confederates won." She offered Ella a slice of green grape pie, then took a bite of it when Ella refused. "Andy and I are all packed and will be moving in with Grandmother tomorrow," she said. "Gentry said you will spend your last night with us in Savannah before you leave for..." she trailed off, afraid, it seemed, to finish.

"Leave for Texas, Honor. You can go ahead and say it, since, unless I get my miracle, Texas will all too soon be my home."

Honor scooted closer and grasped her hands. "Oh, Ella, please don't be sad. I have been trying my best not to cry, but you are about to make me bawl my eyes out. Andy says we can visit you soon, maybe next Christmas. We'll bring Grandmother, if she'll go. So, you see, it won't be so lonesome there," she said, the puddles in her own eyes silently spilling over.

Ella did not respond, and that is likely what caused Honor to cry out enthusiastically, "I know what we'll do when we get lonely for each other, Ella. We'll stop whatever else we're thinking, and think only of the great fun we've had together! Think only of things that made us laugh. Things like..." she began to giggle, "like ... remember when we were on the pier and saw old Picklepuss Faircloth coming up the road, and we dropped down into the river in our Sunday finery; clothes, hoops, hats and all, to hide behind the arrowheads?"

"I remember," Ella replied, still sad.

Honor let out a squeal of delight. "The minnows were after us like crazy, and frogs were hopping off the arrowheads onto us, remember? Our skirts kept ballooning up around our chins, and we started laughing so hard we lost our balance and went under and then came up sputtering and laughing like it had never happened!"

Ella smiled slightly.

"Oh Ella, you looked so funny with your new hat all wet and hanging around your shoulders ... mine was, too. Then, lo and behold, we looked up and there sat old Picklepuss Faircloth in his buggy, just a few feet away, staring at us, and his face like a stone. Without a word between him and us, we ducked down behind the arrowheads again and waited for him to drive away. We were giggling like mad and couldn't stop no matter how hard we tried. Remember?"

It was difficult for Ella to laugh when reminded of Victor Faircloth, but, in this instance, the memory was all too funny to prevent it, and so she did. After a moment, she smiled at her exuberant little sister, and Honor continued.

"We'll remember the great talks we had, Ella. You were always laughing at something I said—and it wasn't always because I was so dumb, either."

"You were never dumb, Honor; *I* was." She looked down, absently plucking at leaves that had blown onto the blanket.

"That's not a bit true, big sister. You were always smarter than me, but I didn't mind. I was really quite glad. It seems that so much worry comes with being smart." She flicked a finger at one of the leaves. "I suppose smart people keep secrets better than most—something I've never been able to do. If ever I've had a secret, the thoughts in my head are like a toothless old hound forever gnawing at a bone. I just can't forget it and let it lie."

Ella glanced up at her, amused. Honor was being Honor. "Want to tell me your secret, Honor?"

"See! You know what I'm thinking. You always have." She laughed, then grew serious. "All right, I'm gonna tell you at last. My secret is ... I sort of knew the day little Adam was born that he wasn't Victor's child. I wasn't entirely sure, of course, but … I sort of knew."

Ella smiled. "I think I 'sort of knew' you knew. So, see? You haven't been harboring a secret after all," she said. Then, as if in her own defense, she added, "I didn't' know I was with child when I married Victor, Honor."

"Oh, I know that, too," Honor said, then dipped her head, and looked quite guilty. "And Ella, don't get mad at me, but the rest of my secret is ..." she paused to bite her lip, and then blurted, "I told Grandmother! I suppose I told her 'cause I wanted to shock her ... give her a good *jolt* because she disliked my Andy so much, and thought Gentry was the next best thing to peach cobbler! But she came right back at me, like she always does, and said, 'Surely, child, you don't think for one minute that *you* knew something that *I* did not know?'" Honor looked exasperated for an instant before adding, "Grandmother said she knew who little Adam's father was long before he was born … and so did Father."

"*Father* knew?" Ella whispered, her eyes rounding. She stared silently at Honor for a long moment before she finally uttered, "Oh, what does it matter, anyway? The past is over. Father and Mother are dead, and Victor is burning in hell. It's the future that threatens me now."

"Please don't feel that way, Ella. Going to Texas may not be so bad. Why, you just may like it after you get used to it. I think I could be happy there, but—don't tell Andy—I still have a yen to go abroad to England and France someday. I'm hoping Andy and I and Elizabeth can live in England, maybe a year or two, before coming back and settling down. Grandmother's Cuthbert kin from Hilton Head moved to England when the war started, you know, and I'm sure they'd love to have us visit."

Ella did not look at her, still unable to understand how her sister could care so little about Greenpoole.

"Ella, you'll be with Gentry, and I know you love him enough to want to be where he is, always. That's how I feel about Andy."

"Yes, I love him, and I'll go. But Honor, I will hate that place! I will long every day for every part of Greenpoole … for this very spot we are sitting on … especially our beautiful Corrigans' pool. Our entire family … our *ancestors* of more than a hundred years ago … are buried here, Honor!"

"I know Ella, but who's to say what they would have done if the war had happened to them like it did to us?" Honor said, then clutched her sister's hands harder, and spoke rapidly. "Look, Ella, I'll make a promise. If Andy's new job at the lumber mill doesn't work out, I'll insist we come to Texas. Elizabeth wants to go right now. She's gonna miss Adam so." She paused to look lovingly at the children as they ran past, and then she giggled. "Why, she actually stomped her little foot and said, 'I go with Adam, Mommy … now!'"

Ella tried to smile. "I'll be the happiest woman alive the day you show up in Texas, Honor, but I'm afraid I'll always yearn for home."

Honor was not listening; her eyes were on the children. "Come back here, you two! Look at them, they see the Yankee's lumber wagons coming to the house, and they're running to meet them, the scamps!" She jumped to her feet and tied her shawl around her waist. "You stay here and rest, Ella, I'll go after them." She took off down the bluff, beckoning to the children, yelling for them to wait for her, the long tails of the new paisley silk shawl—upon which Andy had foolishly spent his first civilian pay—floating on the wind behind her like a pair of colorful wings.

Ella lay on the blanket, gazing up at the bank of feathery white clouds that drifted slowly across the sky, her mind agonizing on Greenpoole and her lost dreams for it. Engulfed by silence, except for the distant squeak of wagon wheels on the circle drive, she turned over in her mind fresh appeals that could possibly make Gentry change his mind about dragging them off to Texas. There has to be *something* that would sway him...

Moments into her gloomy ruminations, the renting scream of a child propelled her upright, followed by another scream, and then another, paralyzing her for an instant as the terrified sounds blasted, like a mortal warning, into her very soul.

Scrambling down the steep bluff, she saw Gentry sprinting from the cotton field toward the house, saw the line of wagons in the drive, saw the blue-coated drivers and the large, mounted escort of Union soldiers jump to the ground and run to an obscured spot behind the wagons.

Screaming her son's name, Ella scrambled down the bluff, half-running, half-sliding, falling, and picking herself up—all the while her terrified eyes searching for sight of the children, but seeing neither of them. Suddenly, an ever-haunting scene passed before her dreaded mind's eye as another precious son—tiny and defenseless little Seth—slipped beneath the choppy waters of the river. *"No, God! No! Please! No!"*

She ran harder, screaming little Adam's name until she saw him clutched safely in Hannah's arms ... saw Sunbeam with Belle, and saw little Elizabeth, kicking and crying in Moonbeam's arms, as the three children were carried into the house. *But who...?*

She stumbled toward the cluster of Yankees at the rear of the last wagon, heard a chorus of hard masculine grunts as the rear of the wagon was lifted, then almost instantly lowered again. She pushed through the workers who had followed Gentry from the field, tearing at their sleeves, frantic to know why they stared so miserably at the wagon!

Gentry sat on the gravel, one leg curled beneath him, and with Honor cradled like a baby in his arms, her head in the crook of his elbow. Baker Ben knelt beside her, her small hand held tightly between his trembling palms. Ella stared at them, her mind so fractured, so broken by what she saw, that she dared not fully comprehend it. A bright color next to the dull lumber wagon drew her eyes to it, and she recognized Honor's pretty shawl, half its length wrapped tightly around the wheel, the other end encircling Honor's small waist.

"I promise. I promise, sweetheart," Gentry was saying, his voice unrecognizable in its hoarseness.

As if in a nightmare, Ella dropped to her knees and slid her arm beneath Honor's head alongside Gentry's arm. Honor's chest rose and fell, each breath like a rapid wind shuddering through her. Ella clutched her sister's slender white hand and pressed it to her lips. Honor's massive brown eyes glistened up at her.

"My legs, Ella ... I can't feel them," she whispered.

A cry tore from Ella, as she glanced down at Honor's skirt and watched it slowly transform into a shiny red blanket as blood soaked through the layers. Suddenly she was aware of Gentry ripping at her skirt and petticoat; as he tore them into strips for bandages, one of the Yankee soldiers peeled back Honor's bloody garments.

"Oh, Lawd! Oh, Lawd!" Baker Ben moaned at the same time Ella cried out again at the sight of her sister's injuries: Jagged white bone protruded from one of her thighs, a constant gush of blood bubbling from it, more blood seeped through her clothing well above her hips.

"Bring her inside! Bring her inside," Ella screamed, jumping to her feet, her eyes frantic upon Honor's ashen face.

"We can't move her until the bleeding's stopped," Gentry said, encircling Honor's bloody thigh with a long strip of petticoat. Ella saw only a flash of blue sleeve as someone rushed up and handed Gentry a short stick to tighten the tourniquet.

Honor's wide eyes continued to stare up at Ella, the puddle of blood beneath her deepening as it flowed, unstaunched, despite efforts to stop it.

Ella's frantic thoughts screamed. *She's dying! Oh, Honor ... please! Don't do this, Honor! Please!* She clutched Gentry's sleeve. "Do something! Do something!"

Gentry shook off her grip, and spoke to the second Union soldier. "Press both your hands into the stomach wound. Keep pressure on it, or she'll bleed to-!" He hushed, and suddenly Ella realized that the wagon had passed over Honor at an angle … injuring much more than her leg!

"Move back! Give us room," he ordered of her and Baker Ben.

Ella stood, and took a halting step backward, her agony shining in her eyes like a silent scream, as she clung to Baker Ben's trembling arm. Suddenly, she bent double, rocking back and forth, her wail only stemmed by her fist pressing hard against her mouth, as Beatrice's words of warning echoed inside her head, *"Be careful of such prayers, my dear …"*

Only Honor calling out to her made her force composure, and she fell to her knees at Honor's side.

"Ella, you'll be ... my Elizabeth's mother, won't you?"

Ella struggled to speak calmly. "*You* are her mother, Honor. *You* will raise her. I will take care of her only until you get better." A sob tore from Ella, and she could no longer control her terror. "Oh Honor, try! You must try!"

"Tell my Andy ... goodbye. Tell him ... be good. You know ... how he gets ... sometimes. His temper ..."

Ella cried harder. "Oh, Honor, please, hang on! Don't do this! Don't give up! Honor! Please! You can't!"

"Gentry will look after my Andy, too … will take him and little Elizabeth to Texas … he promised me," Honor whispered, barely audible, and then she tried to smile. "Do you think … I'll see Father and Mother … and your little Seth?"

"Honor!" Ella cried, grasping her shoulders. "Don't talk like that! You can't give up! *Honor!*"

"I ... I bet I do ... see them," Honor whispered, as her eyes closed, and her breathing hung on one deep breath, her chest suspending for a long moment before it fell.

Ella stared down at her, waiting to see her sister's tiny bosom rise... waiting to hear the soft draw of another sustaining breath. Moments later, she fell across Honor's still body, her agonized screams echoing across Greenpoole's vast acres.

5

Time Was Supposed To Heal All Wounds

DESPITE GENTRY'S INDIFFERENCE TO IT, dawn appeared on the horizon, as usual. Standing in front of the Pulaski House, he watched a lamplighter become smaller and smaller as he moved further and further down the sidewalk to snuff out the long row of gaslights that lit the street. A dilapidated buggy rolled by, followed by another with a half-dozen children in the back, all dressed in the shabby finery of their church-going clothes. He had forgotten it was Sunday. He watched a steady procession of wagons, carts, and buggies roll pass, and then shifted his attention to nothing in particular. Where would a man, who had just buried the young wife he worshiped, go?

Andy couldn't go to his family; there wasn't a Kearney left in Chatham County. His father and most of his brothers were killed in the war, and his mother had gone to her Missouri kinfolk after the Kearney plantation was destroyed. Ella had tried to console Andy, but the pair only added to each other's misery.

For days, Ella's sobs echoed through that empty old mansion, each tormented wail tearing through him like a spear in his gut. When he told her to forget about going to Texas for the time being, she stared at him as if he had slapped her, then collapsed, sobbing bitterly. "It's my fault she's dead! It's my fault!" she had cried, and nothing he said convinced her otherwise.

Conversely, as much as he wanted to find Andy, he was relieved that the young hothead wasn't in town. There were too many Union soldiers in Savannah, and Andy's hatred for what he called "the vile Yankee presence in the South" could boil over, especially now. His bitterness toward the government had driven him into organizations that preached white supremacy from the podium and an all-white Heaven from the pulpit; Honor's death would likely intensify Andy's involvement in that craziness if someone didn't talk some sense into him.

Finally, close to sundown, Gentry headed for Greenpoole. At the fork in the road, he stopped, and then turned off toward the one place he had not looked—the deserted Kearney plantation.

Once, the Kearney property, like Greenpoole, had been a showplace of Southern opulence. But now, scattered heaps of brick and ash were the only reminders that it had existed at all. Where a barn and stable once stood, there lay only piles of charred rubble. All that remained was a row of slave's cabins toward the rear of the property. Gentry rode up to each cabin and, without dismounting, looked into the open windows. The freed occupants had left long ago, and only chunks of broken pottery and old rags remained. A horse neighed behind the last hovel, and Gentry slid from the saddle as Andy called out.

"I ain't hung myself, Gent ... if that's what you come to find." He sat straddle-legged and leaning against a hickory stump, a small campfire at his feet, a bedroll laying open nearby. His wife's pretty shawl was looped around his neck; one end draped across his shoulder, her blood still on it. He tossed Gentry a bottle. "Have yourself a nip or two. I got another in my bag."

Gentry flipped the cork away and turned the bottle up. "I worked up a hell of a thirst looking for you, my friend."

Andy's bloodshot eyes rolled away to stare at nothing. Gentry squatted on the ground across from him and took another drink before handing the bottle over.

"Ella and Miz Bea are worried about you, Andy. It won't put you out none to show up at Greenpoole today, if only to make them feel better."

"Those goddamn Yankees!" Andy spat, then drained the bottle and threw it into the fire, sending sparks and embers swirling up into the smoky twilight.

"It was an accident, Andy. Those men were sickened by what happened ... still are. They tried to save Honor's life," Gentry said, then poked the fire with a stick, and watched Andy pull the cork on another bottle. "Come home with me, Andy. Your little girl's been crying for her mother. The child needs you now more than ever."

"Okay! Okay!" Andy's face reddened, and he looked past Gentry rather than at him. "Look, Gent, I 'bout got this place sold. I can't keep up with the taxes anymore." He looked this way and that, as if taking a final inventory. "Not much left of it, but there's good pine woods back yonder, and my buyer wants it. He's coming in the morning. I'm waiting so I can show him around the place. I just want to be by myself 'til then, understand?"

Thinking that the last thing his brother-in-law needed was to be alone, Gentry reached over and took the bottle from Andy's hand. "I'll go, but mind if I rest a bit first?" He took a long swig of the whiskey, and when Andy remained silent, he stretched his long legs out toward the fire and leaned back to rest on one elbow.

Andy ran his hands through his cap of wiry, blond curls. "Man, did she love to dance!" His voice grew hoarser. "Why, just that same morning, before those Yankees ..." He gritted his teeth, trembling. "Just that same morning, we danced all 'round that big old empty house, laughing, chasing each other. Dancing like there was no tomorrow...." His head fell to his chest, his shoulders shaking. "She was real special, wasn't she?" he choked.

"Yes," Gentry replied softly, thinking of the young girl he had loved like a sister almost from the day they'd met. Even with her mischievous air, her words, her thoughts, her actions, had been as open and honest as a saint's. Honor never wasted a minute crying over the past. On the other hand, Ella seemed incapable of emulating her young sister's eagerness to face a changing future.

He glanced at Andy, seeing in the young man's eyes a brooding rage that surpassed the grief that had been there moments earlier.

"How 'bout I keep you company tonight, my friend? I haven't camped out under the stars in a long time," Gentry said.

Without looking up, Andy shook his head, and waved him away. "I don't want any company, Gent. Not tonight."

Gentry, not one to interfere with a man's wishes unless the man's actions were intolerable, arose, paused long enough to squeeze Andy's shoulder, and then left.

~

The next morning at dawn, Gentry sought Ella out in Honor's room, from which she rarely emerged nowadays. He found her at the window, her eyes shadowed, but tearless at last. He rested his hands on her shoulders, and pressed his lips lightly to her crown of platinum hair. He, too, gazed out the window at the headstones that stood in neat rows at the end of what was once Greenpoole's rose garden. He knew her thoughts, and it pained him to see her torturing herself, reliving Honor's death, her parents' deaths, and that of her and Faircloth's son, the little boy she often spoke of, as did Adam.

"Are the children still asleep?" she asked.

"Like kittens."

"Did you find Andy?"

"He's at his family's old place, waiting for a buyer. He's selling."

"Selling? Today? But that Union sergeant came yesterday and paid for the wood they forgot to pay for when …" she clenched her eyes a moment, "and he told Meshach he and his wagons were going to the Kearney place this morning. He said they had contracted with Andy to clear ten acres of timber. Why would he do that if he was selling?"

Gentry tried not to hurry. He said maybe Meshach had misunderstood, and then he kissed her cheek and left.

~

At the fork in the road, Gentry saw fresh hoof prints and three sets of wagon tracks leading off toward the Kearney place. He kicked his mount into a crazed run.

Around a bend in the road, he saw the wagons five hundred yards ahead, and heard the distant squeaking of wheels mixed with the low drone of Negro voices bantering back and forth as the entourage rolled onto the Kearney property near the old slave quarters.

Then, as speedily as an ax splits a piece of kindling, a blood-chilling yell exploded above the clatter as Andy burst from the cabin, pistols blazing, his mouth open in that eternal scream of battle reviled so by Northern veterans of the war. Almost in that same instant, a dozen rifles and pistols cracked in rapid succession… until their target lay, bloodied and still, his body half-hidden in a gently rippling patch of wildflowers.

A soldier on one of the wagons clutched his bloody arm while the man next to him, the driver, slumped lifelessly over the dash.

The Sergeant who had helped stem Honor's bleeding stepped from his horse when he saw Gentry.

Gentry jerked his mount to a halt and dismounted, thinking that the Sergeant was about to approach him; but the man took only one step before slumping to his knees and then falling onto his face, obviously dead. Men from the third wagon jumped down and ran from body to body.

"Six dead, including one nigger who didn't hit the ground fast enough," one of them cried.

"That son-of-a-bitching Confederate bastard makes seven," cried another.

~

With Andy's gory body wrapped in a canvas provided him by the Union soldiers, Gentry rode home to Greenpoole with his small brother-in-law cradled in his arms like a child. Andy's crazed plot to kill Yankees was testament to the madness of a war that, though ended, still raged in hearts and minds on both sides, more so in the South than anywhere else. The notion was that *time* was supposed to heal all wounds, but Gentry had a feeling that the wounded face of humanity in the South would show its ugly side more and more, rather than less.

As Gentry steadied Andy's lolling head against his shoulder, he tried not to think how many long months must now pass before he could finally gather his little family and leave this senseless existence behind.

6

"They is gone to Texas ...!"

DESPITE GRIEF AND HARDSHIP AT GREENPOOLE, Ella found time for company when the town ladies visited in hopes of cheering her by providing the latest gossip. Somehow, the tittle-tattle was not as enjoyable as in the old days, when she and her cousins, the lively Sutton triplets from Hilton Head, had "stirred the pot of bubbling secrets." But Honor had been among them back then, and without her eager smile and mischievous brown eyes flashing at them as she spoke, nothing was the same, and never would be again. The little group's world had turned too serious. All three Sutton cousins married soon after the war began. Maureen and Nouveen moved to distant towns. Poor Vestal remained in the area, but died in childbirth a short year after her marriage. Conversations with friends that remained were mostly chronicles of hardships, deaths, and the tragic outcome of the war on just about everybody she knew. Most times, after wrenching emotions were laid bare and the ladies departed for their homes, Ella collapsed in fresh mourning for the little sister whose death had left her crushed by loss and guilt.

Clutching a dust rag, Ella stood at her bedroom window, gazing down at the rose bushes that Meshach had planted among the tombstones. The lovely Apothecary's Rose over little Seth's grave had thrived during the summer months, but now, in the chill of November, it was naturally dormant. Come next season, its lovely, pale-red blooms would brighten the entire area. Its fragrance would drift across her balcony and through the open windows like a gentle greeting. She crossed her arms against the cold and gazed at the garden's newest plants. Prior to the war, folks had ridiculed old man Thropeshire for growing acres of roses instead of cotton; but were it not for that prissy old man's neglected acres since his passing, Meshach would have had small pickings on his frequent forages around the countryside. Thanks to Meshach, many useful items left behind by neighbors that had given up and left were finding their way to Greenpoole; among them, *beehives*. Honey was a blessing now that sugar was scarce, and too expensive to buy at five dollars a pound.

Subconsciously, Ella wiped her cheek with the dust cloth while wondering if Gentry was having success in New Orleans. He had gone there to collect money owed him for cattle that his men in Texas had shipped there by boat upon receiving Gentry's word to do so. Quite a bit of money, she hoped. She missed him and wondered if he missed her. He'd not mentioned Texas since Honor's death. Lately, with time crawling slowly by since that heartbreaking day six months ago, she sometimes wondered what Gentry was thinking, but she dared not ask. Why start a conversation she was not willing to have?

~

Ella knotted her hair into its bun and continued her chore of putting the house in order. This morning, since Baker Ben was feeling poorly again and had taken to his cot, she would help Hannah prepare the meals. Miffie usually helped Hannah, but she had recently married a Negro Union soldier and moved to Washington. Since then, Baker Ben, jubilant in a crabby sort of way, abandoned his old room attached to the outdoor kitchen house and moved into Miffie's vacated room adjacent to the manor's rear entrance.

Ella headed downstairs clutching the dust rag that had become so much a part of her lately. She paused along the way to polish the once-beautiful mahogany banister. Sherman's men had showed little regard for the masterful piece of woodwork as they carted away the upstairs furniture, while scratching and knocking chinks in the wood as they went: She remembered how much she had loathed the Northern invaders as she watched them stoke their campfires with Greenpoole's magnificent furnishings.

On the landing, Ella pushed open the cracked, stained-glass window and gazed out at Beatrice's old barouche and sorry mule coming up the drive.

Ella scarcely had time for a greeting when, to her shock, Beatrice announced that she had come for Sunbeam and Moonbeam, saying that she needed them, since her "well-paid but ungrateful" servants—except for old Bootsie—had "moved on to greener pastures via a train going North." Then she added, "Besides, I pay the twins their wages. I have every right to expect something for my money."

Ella's face reddened with anger. "I know what you are up to, Grandmother! First, you wanted to take Honor and Andy away. And now you are taking Moonbeam and Sunbeam only because they are so much help to me!"

Without a shred of shame for her intentions, Beatrice looked Ella squarely into her accusing eyes and admitted it.

"You are absolutely correct. However, my original plan was foiled when our sweet Honor died so senselessly ... and then that foolish husband of hers orchestrated his own demise. With Moonbeam and Sunbeam no longer a part of your dwindling crew, I pray that you will come to your senses. Then, my dear, you and Gentry can orchestrate *his* original plan, and leave here."

With those remarks still ringing in Ella's ears, Beatrice commanded the sobbing Sunbeam and Moonbeam to gather their belongings.

Sunbeam's child, Belle, was dragged out the door kicking and screaming between her mother and aunt, both of whom had a firm but reluctant grip on the child's tiny arms. After that frenzied scene, Adam and little Elizabeth refused to kiss their adoring great-grandmother goodbye.

~

Gentry came home the following week. After a quick meal with Ella, Adam, and little Elizabeth, he went into Savannah to bank his money. Ella did not ask the amount, but hoped it would be enough to pay the taxes and their creditors. She had not told Gentry that the last batch of sharecroppers had left, and she wondered if he noticed their absence when he arrived.

She waited impatiently until he was well on his way to the bank, and then summoned Meshach and Cricket, gave them a dollar each and a large sack of vittles, and sent them on the long journey to Macon, where Meshach said a family of Victor's ex-slaves had gone and were now in dire straits, and needing work. Afoot, Meshach and Cricket would likely be gone a few days. Though uncomfortable that she hadn't told Gentry that she intended to hire new sharecroppers, she forced the guilt aside.

That evening, as dusk fell and the children slept, she pulled the new tax notice from her apron and laid it atop her bureau. She would not tell Gentry about it just yet—in a few days, perhaps, but not tonight. Even before he left, they had scarcely had a conversation these past months that hadn't involved money, and she regretted it. Gentry was so kind to her, so understanding of her moods. Yet, sometimes, when she glanced at him and caught him looking at her, she saw something intangible in his black eyes. Was it sadness? She would rather see anger in them ...or resentment ... anything but sadness.

Had she made him doubt her love? Had she been too busy with her constant efforts to save Greenpoole to notice changes in him? She loved Gentry as much as ever! Did he know it?

At the sound of his footsteps in the hall, she quickly smoothed stray wisps of hair from her face. Forgetting all about the taxes, she rushed to the door and pulled it open. The look on her face must have pleased him; his eyes gladdened, and he smiled.

"I've missed you," he said, taking both her hands in his.

"I've missed you, too, Gentry … so very much. I was just so worried about Greenpoole … and … I miss Honor so." Tears welled in her eyes, as always, when she thought of Honor.

"I know," he whispered, and put his arms around her. "But Honor wouldn't want us to mourn forever, my darling." He touched her cheek with the back of his long, tanned fingers. "She'd want us to get on with our lives."

"I want that, too," she said, and rested against him, pressing her head to his shoulder. "You're so good to me, Gentry. I love you so. You know that, don't you?"

She waited for his reply, then leaned her head back to smile up at him, expecting to see his eyes warm upon her face. Instead she saw that his eyes were trained on the tax slip atop her bureau. *Oh... but that's not why,* she wanted to say, but instead she grabbed his hand and led him through the French doors to the balcony.

"We haven't watched the sun disappear into the river in a long time, Gentry. Look at it. Isn't it beautiful?"

She watched him turn his back to the sunset. He leaned against the balcony post and crossed his arms over his chest. *As if to keep me away,* she thought, fighting a strange panic. Suddenly, she knew what he was about to say and there was no way to stop him.

"It's time to leave here, Ella."

The firmness in his voice made her shudder. She gripped the railing and stared into the glittering twilight for a long while before twisting her head in the opposite direction, away from him.

"Please, Gentry ... don't make me go. Not yet. I ... I can't."

"Leaving Georgia has always been the plan, Ella. Honor's death won't change that. We're through here."

"No!" She fairly screamed the word at him, and then, reddening at her outburst, whispered, "Not yet, Gentry. I need more time."

When long moments passed and he did not reply, she turned and discovered him gone. She had not heard a sound. He had left as silently as a shadow moves. From the balcony, she saw their bedroom door shut behind him.

Fighting the panic his words revived, she shakily went into their bedroom, sank onto the bed, and cried.

~

She awoke in the night as the lamp at her bedside flared and Gentry sat down beside her. Silent, he slipped his hand beneath her hair to the back of her neck and pulled her gently forward until his lips pressed against her forehead. After a long moment, she dropped her head back to look at him, then clenched her eyes shut against the sight of his own. Those mesmerizing black eyes that had always thrilled her with their boldness, their promise, their sureness, were filled with sadness—a sadness unmistakable now in its intensity. With a soft cry, she threw her arms around his neck and kissed him hard, clung to him, frantic in her desire to remove that sadness.

His response was immediate, his lovemaking carried out with a slow urgency that soon carried her away from the stress and worry that had become so much a part of her. When at last they lay silent in each other's arms, she felt infinitely peaceful, and great sense of relief filling her: Did Gentry's silence mean that he had thought it over and decided they did not have to leave for Texas just yet? *Yes!* That was it! That is why he came to her tonight, so sweet, so filled with desire for her. He was weakening! She could sense it! With a little more time, she would convince him that her cherished Greenpoole should be their permanent home.

She snuggled against him and slept sounder than she had slept in months.

~

She did not know when he awoke and left their bed. During the night, she had roused only once to glance sleepily at his shadowed face. His eyes had been closed, his chest rising and falling gently in sleep; but when she tried to roll away to a more comfortable position, his arms tightened around her, and she had quickly fallen back to sleep. Now, wide awake, she pulled herself up on her elbows and looked at the haze of cloudy sunlight visible through her windows. Smiling, she slid from the bed. She was still smiling as she washed her face in the icy water on her washstand, donned her clothes, and combed her hair, while pausing occasionally to listen for Adam and Elizabeth. Thinking they must be playing outside, she stepped onto the balcony to search the grounds. Seeing no one, she retreated inside as the frigid wind whistled eerily though the trees and around the house, setting her teeth to chattering. The morning was too cold for the children to be outside, and it looked like rain. Strange that they hadn't come running to wake her, bouncing on her bed and making enough noise to wake every soul on the plantation.

For the first time she noticed that the fireplace, usually stoked and blazing by now, was cold. She opened the door and called out to Hannah, then went back to light the fire. Done, she paused, frowning. The house was quiet. *Too quiet …*

Possibly because of the eerie silence, she tiptoed to the railing and looked down into the colossal foyer where the children could usually be seen playing when the weather prevented them from going outdoors. She called out to them, only to be greeted by more silence.

Whirling, she ran to the children's rooms. Both were empty! Frantic, she dashed back to little Adam's room and threw open the wardrobe that held his clothes. *Empty!* The drawers ... *empty!*

She stumbled down the sweeping stairs and, unmindful of the cold marble beneath her bare feet, stood sobbing in the center of the gigantic entry hall, crying out her son's name, and then screaming for Hannah.

"They is gone, Miss Ella," Baker Ben said from the back end of the entry hall. He stood, his frail body leaning against the doorframe as if that was all that held him up. He pointed at the front door, and then waved his arm in a fashion meant to encompass the world.

"They is gone to Texas … that ol' Hannah woman, too. Her was right unhappy about going, but Mister Gen'te, e'say Miss Honor's chil' and his boy gonna need her more'n ever ... since theys Momma done 'side to stay put in Georgia."

Ella felt her legs weaken. She glanced about for something to hang on to, but her feet held her prisoner.

Baker Ben drew a feeble breath, clutching tighter at the door as if he needed its assistance to stand. "I was wondering last night why Mista Gen'te come home in a rented buggy, and a'pulling his hoss 'hind it. Guess dat buggy how he done took'um off to th' boat what's taking 'um to Texas."

The color drained from Ella's face. Trembling uncontrollably, she dropped to her hands and knees, and screamed, "Gentry! Gentry! You bastard!"

7

Betrayal and Then Death, Isn't That Always the Way?

LIGHT MIST FELL as Beatrice sat in her old barouche in Greenpoole's driveway and stared at the deserted-looking house. Strange that the place was so quiet, and there were no sharecroppers in the fields or along the river as she passed. Nor did their offspring play on the old ship replica at the end of the pier, as they often did, rain or shine. Where was everybody? Usually when rain kept workers away from their chores, they could be seen dragging trotlines in the river, hoping to catch the gigantic mud cats and soft shell turtles. Both of those creatures were plentiful this far upriver, as would be the hordes of overgrown mosquitoes after this rain stopped, were it summer instead of winter.

She pursed her lips and wagged her head, her little pancake straw hat doing its customary bobble, as it dawned on her that Ella's sharecroppers were, indeed, gone. Gone like all the others before them. Who could blame them? Even now, with a share of the profits, sharecropping was too much like the drudgery of slavery for many freedmen. Thank heaven Gentry had ended Ella's attempt to resurrect the tidal rice lands that the family had wisely abandoned ages before the war started! The steaming rice swamp was drudge work, an ex-slave's least desirable way of making a living, and Ella's workers had abandoned the swamp in droves. Aside from backbreaking labor, there slithered beneath those marshy acres of twisted undergrowth denizens of venom and sickness of a kind that the newly freed Negroes—now able to choose how they lived and died—were little inclined to embrace. Ella's tempting offers of land, to be deeded families willing to work in the rice marshes for five years, had no effect on their decisions to leave.

Beatrice nodded in confirmation of her thoughts. Maybe when *all* of Ella's sharecroppers followed their predecessors into the cities, she would see the hopelessness of this scheme to prosper from the soil 'like in the old days,' and she and Gentry could be on their way to Texas, as was the plan before sweet Honor's death.

Beatrice continued to look around. Where were her great-grandchildren? Adam was usually the first one out the door when she came for a visit, with little Elizabeth always close behind. She tightened her collar against the cold drizzle, and then shifted on the buggy seat to gaze fore and aft again. Several times this past week, she had wondered why Ella had not come into town on Saturday as usual, nor had Gentry.

She tapped at the pinching sensation in her chest, annoyed that her indigestion came and went with much greater ado than usual lately. She fished in her reticule for a sprig of mint, and was about to pop it into her mouth when stopped by a screeching, rasping sound—like heavy iron scraping against a surface that was just as unyielding. Groaning with the effort that it took to climb down from the barouche, she ascended Greenpoole's twelve slate steps as speedily as her lumbago allowed.

The metallic screeching grew louder as she crossed the veranda and approached the massive double doors, one of which stood slightly ajar. Was no one interested in keeping out the cold? She swung it open, and then stared, her face transforming into a mask of shock. Her hand flew to her chest, and then to her gaping mouth, as she gawked at her nearly unrecognizable granddaughter.

Ella, her tall frame bent nearly double and one arm stretched far behind her, laboriously dragged an iron cot across the colossal marble-floored entry hall. Stunned silent, Beatrice continued to stare. Ella looked as if she had been sloshing around in a swamp hole! Her sleeves and skirt were heavily anchored with caked mud, grass, and twigs ... her long, dirt-streaked hair swung heavily back and forth in front of her as she tugged her burden forward. *What on earth…?*

Ella raised her head, and for a brief instant before she lowered it and continued her task, Beatrice stared into a stranger's eyes. Ella's face was pale and thin, as if she had not eaten in days. *Dear God, she looks positively demented!*

The cot screeched along the floor as Ella continued dragging it toward the wide front doors.

"Ella! What has happened to you? What are you doing?"

Ella stopped, but did not look up.

"What has happened, child?" Beatrice repeated, managing to sound calm.

Ella released the cot and straightened. "Betrayal, and then death, isn't that always the way now?" she said in a low, bleak voice.

"Tell me what has happened, child."

"You know what has happened, or you *should* know, you being my husband's confidant, his friend and adviser." She turned back to the cot. "You know what's happened," she repeated dully.

"I do *not* know what has happened, Ella. How would I?"

"Didn't Gentry stop to tell you goodbye, Grandmother, after he stole my son and Honor's child and took them to that terrible place?"

"Do you mean that he ...?"

"Yes. He stole my son and crawled away in the dead of night like the snake that he is! Hannah, with him. She betrayed me."

"Oh, Ella!"

"Baker Ben said Hannah went because she didn't want Adam and Elizabeth to be frightened, but she should have told me he was scheming against me!" She wiped at the mud on her cheek. "I trusted Hannah. All my life I trusted her." She slumped against the cot's iron foot post. "They both betrayed me," she murmured.

The flatness of her granddaughter's tone was as alarming as her appearance, and Beatrice reached out and stroked away some of the mud in Ella's hair. "Oh, my child, I would not have encouraged Gentry to such an act. Surely you know I would not," she said, then suddenly gasped, as her gaze locked on the lengthy form that lay wrapped in a patchwork quilt atop the cot. A long, thin foot, encased in a red woolen sock, protruded from the end of the blanket.

"Oh my, our poor old Baker Ben is gone," Beatrice whispered, not realizing that she had spoken until Ella said yes, then snapped her wet hair from Beatrice's fingers.

"He died four days ago. I couldn't bury him because of the rain... ground too wet to dig a grave." She tightened the blanket over his exposed foot. "It's been unusually cold, and he hasn't begun to..." She paused. "I finished digging last night or ... close to daybreak." She pressed her dirty hair away from her face, then slid her palms down her drenched skirt, as if to dry them. "I pulled a tarp over the grave, should it rain again ... staked it down with boards and scraps of old plow heads from the barn."

"You poor child," Beatrice whispered, touching Ella's shoulder tenderly before she lifted the blanket from Baker Ben's face. A moment passed before she nodded, not surprised at how composed he looked.

"You are as unperturbed by death as you were by life," she whispered, patting his bony shoulder, and noting that he was neatly attired in his "burying finery"—the bright red coachman's garb with braided epaulets that he wore fifty years ago when driving her and her husband around Savannah in their luxurious old barouche.

"I am glad you dressed him in these," she said to Ella.

"It was his wish. He reminded me of their purpose more times than I can remember. I'm burying him in the rose garden near Father and Mother. He wanted to be buried in the Negro cemetery near the quarters, but it's too far away … too wet. I'm burying him beside Honor. She loved him so."

"Yes, and he spoiled her rotten. I dare say she was the only soul on earth he ever truly cared about," Beatrice said, and nodded her approval. "But … is there no coffin for him?"

"No, there's no coffin being built. Meshach and Cricket are in Macon looking for sharecroppers. The others left."

Beatrice nodded. "I am certain old Baker would put up a hellacious fuss about it, but the blanket will have to do." She removed her hat and short black jacket and rolled up the sleeves of her lacy white blouse. "Between the two of us, we should be able to carry him."

But she was weaker than she cared to admit, and Ella's strength, like her spirit, was spent. They eased Baker Ben's narrow mattress to the floor and dragged him on it to his final resting place, careful to maneuver him gently down Greenpoole's twelve steps.

Thunder rumbled in the distance as they hauled the tarp aside, lowered him atop his mattress as gently as possible into the hole, and began the chore of covering him. An hour later, they were exhausted from wielding the heavy shovelfuls of soggy earth, and oblivious to the fresh drizzle that pelted them without letup.

Ella dragged the tarp back over Baker Ben's grave to keep the fresh mound of dirt from melting away in the rain, and then dropped to her knees beside Beatrice, who was asking God to give old Baker Ben his place in heaven:

"Lord, I have always believed that a good Negro's soul shined as brilliantly in the hereafter as any man's did. It is especially true of this old man," she said, adding, "Indeed, he was grumpy, and indifferent to this world, but inside he was as sweet and gentle and caring as any heavenly bound child of God had ever been or ever will be. Amen."

Ella's eyes burned, as she nodded her amen. Rain merged with the hot tears streaming down her cheeks, as she mourned yet another loss—the old ex-slave who, alongside Hannah, had nurtured her and her sister since birth. She closed her eyes against the drizzle, seeing Baker Ben as clearly as she had seen him beside Corrigans' Pool that day long ago when he casually revealed the pool's secret cave to her, then smugly explained how Victor's slaves escaped without a trace. *"I ain't lied, Missy—them Moss Oak niggers what escape ain't* on *the place, they is* under *the place."*

Before helping Beatrice to her feet, Ella gave the tarp a final, gentle pat, her sad thoughts skipping from memory to memory, as she looked around at the other graves. Her parents, Honor, Andy, and her precious little Seth—all of them lay nearby. Greenpoole continued to slip away from her, death by death, soul by soul.

She had thought never again to feel the sorrow, the bitterness, the rage she had felt while in Victor Faircloth's cruel grasp during the war years, but she felt it rising in her now as intense as ever as she stumbled away from the tarp-covered mound and moved among the gravestones. *I'll get my son and little Elizabeth back, and when I do, I'll make Gentry Garland suffer for what he's done to us ... I swear on my very soul I will!*

8

Drastic News Requires Drastic Measures

BEATRICE DARED NOT RETURN to Savannah. Fear for Ella kept her at Greenpoole. When Meshach returned, she sent him into town to fetch Moonbeam and Sunbeam, thinking to please Ella with their return; but their presence made little difference to her state of mind. Just the same, Beatrice was grateful that the watchful pair stayed at Ella's side at every turn.

Ella's anguish was unrelenting. Not since the loss of precious little Seth had Beatrice seen in Ella this tearless combination of grief and acrimony. Beatrice cringed at the sound of her granddaughter's dry-eyed ravings "As soon as the next crop is in, I'm hiring the Pinkerton Detective Agency to find my children and bring them home!"

"The Pinkertons?" Beatrice cried. "For Heaven's sake, Ella, they spied on the Confederacy during the war!"

"I don't care if they spied on Jesus Christ! I'd enlist Sherman himself, if I could!" She stared accusingly at Beatrice and added, "We could manage much easier if you would sell your house in town, Grandmother. You don't need it, and I want you here at Greenpoole where you belong ... here with Adam and me and Elizabeth, when I get them back," she said, as she glowered at

Beatrice. "I could get them back a lot sooner if you'd sell. We need the money. If you love us, you will do it."

"We shall see," was Beatrice's only reply, forgiving, for the moment, her granddaughter's uncommon rudeness.

Meshach and Cricket had returned from Macon with a new family of sharecroppers. Beatrice could only watch and worry, as Ella worked tirelessly around the house and grounds, in the stable, and in the gardens and orchards, all of which Meshach and the others labored tirelessly to restore. When Ella wasn't scrubbing floors, she was pulling weeds from the graves in the rose garden, digging for their roots even before they broke the surface.

In all Beatrice's years, she had never seen anyone in such a state of mental and physical undoing. Ella scarcely ate, and was so thin that Beatrice worried she would collapse. Soon, Beatrice could not bear to look into her granddaughter's eyes, for Ella's anguish was ever evident in them, her tormented thoughts constantly flickering in their depths. Something had to be done, and quickly!

Beatrice daily pondered a solution while wandering through the old mansion, something she had not done in years. Greenpoole Manor, once exquisitely furnished with the collected treasures of five proud generations of Corrigans, was now simply a collection of cavernous, mostly empty rooms, its deterioration echoing in every hollow footstep across its bare floors. Like the whole of Greenpoole Plantation, the house was beyond the frantic efforts of one thin, angry young woman bent on restoration. *Even if this old house were refurnished, what good would it do?* Beatrice wondered.

One morning, soon after one of Ella's heart-wrenching outbursts, Beatrice stood wagging her finger at Cricket on the stairs, as he toted firewood up to her room.

"Why, it would take the entire inventory of my attic just to furnish the downstairs rooms of this monstrous old mausoleum," she mumbled to herself while looking straight at him.

"Huh?" Cricket said, his eyes rounding with attention.

"Don't 'huh' me, young man! Put that wood where it belongs and find Meshach. Tell him to bring round one of the cotton wagons. We are going to town."

Perhaps Ella will calm down in the midst of a few comforts, Beatrice thought to herself a half hour later, as the three of them—she, Cricket, and Meshach—headed for Savannah. Besides, if she decided to sell her stately home on the corner of Bull and Taylor streets, she most certainly was not selling her treasures along with it.

~

With most of the downstairs cozily furnished and Beatrice's promise to sell the house in town as soon as she found a buyer, Ella seemed better ... until a cold day at the end of February when she stumbled, sobbing, into the parlor. She had been down at Corrigans' Pool for hours, and now she ran toward Beatrice, her eyes swollen nearly shut from crying, her nose red and dripping.

"Grandmother, I am with child! I am going to have a baby!" she screamed, then dropped to her knees beside Beatrice's chair, her eyes filled with disbelief. She buried her head in her arms across Beatrice's lap, deep sobs convulsing from her as if she were choking.

Beatrice could only pat her shoulders and stroke her hair. The thought of Ella giving birth at this time, when food was so scarce and Ella's health, not at its peak, worried her as much as it horrified Ella. Even so, perhaps this unwanted baby was the miracle that would jolt Ella back to her senses. She would forget about hiring those Pinkerton detectives, and would realize that her place was with her husband and son in Texas.

However, when weeks passed and Ella's determination only intensified, Beatrice decided that drastic news required drastic measures.

~

Ella wondered why Beatrice suddenly went into Savannah "on business," Beatrice had said. What business could she possibly have in town? None of her old friends had recently died, and like most Southerners who refused to sign the oath of allegiance to the Union, the Yankees had padlocked her office on Factor's Row, taking possession of the Corrigan warehouses and shipping business. All she owned was her home across from Monterey Square. She had been enraged to find her old pew at Christ Episcopal Church occupied by two Yankee women, and rather than slide in beside them, she and Tessie Peckenpaugh tromped home, and immediately accompanied old Bootsie to the colored Baptist Church on Franklin Square. Later, she railed to Ella that the sights in Savannah had so eroded with Yankees that she would not go there again ... unless obligated to do so by the death of a respectable citizen of long standing—"as long as they had not signed that Yankee oath of allegiance!"

Nevertheless, she had gone, closed-mouth, and in no mood for questions. Even more surprising, she enlisted Cricket to drive her—she, who, for all her years, insisted on doing her own driving. Ella watched as her grandmother offered him the reins in complete silence, remaining mute, even when he let out a happy whoop and thanked her repeatedly for the honor.

"I'se driving us to town in style, Miz Bea!" Cricket cried. "That ol' mule too old to pull this fine 'rouch anymore," he said, then added, "It shore was nice of Mista Gen'te to take that ol' Blackie to Texas with him and leave us these fine carriage hosses."

As the barouche pulled away, Ella's eyes flashed: *Nice? There's nothing nice about Gentry Garland!*

~

In the following weeks, whether consciously or because nature induces a woman to eat when her body hosts another life, Ella regained her appetite. By the end of May, her cheekbones no longer stood out sharply beneath the covering of her alabaster skin. Still, nothing lessened her agony over the loss of her son and Honor's child. Her every waking thought was of them. Her dreams were of them, and with each dream, each thought, her sorrow and anger grew. How could the man she had loved so completely, and who said he loved her the same way, have done this to her? As much as she abhorred what he had done, and loathed him for it, she mourned the loss of the love between them.

Despite her misery, Ella laughed along with Beatrice the day Judith Ashville rode out to Greenpoole and gave Ella her blue shawl. Both women knew it was the same shawl Judith had worn to conceal her twelve pregnancies—all of which had occurred in rapid succession, and which only ceased when her tyrant of a husband—an ex-Confederate official—was sent away by the U.S. government to Castle Williams Prison on Governors Island in New York. Fortunately for Judith, he had not returned. His departure was another of God's miracles in disguise, Beatrice quipped.

Ella laughed dryly again, when, sitting on the veranda with Beatrice, she added more folded paper to the insides of her shoes.

"I remember before the war, Grandmother, when we sat on this very spot and lamented over the poor crackers across the river … and you said, '*there*, but for the grace of God, go any of us.' How right you were! But I'll bet even you and that old fortune teller of yours, Bootsie, never guessed that I'd marry twice … end up deserted, pregnant, and," she violently stuffed the other shoe with paper, *"barefooted!"*

Beatrice did not look up from her sewing. Not that her mind was idle, but the moment was not yet right in which she should put her long-thought-out plan into play. However, time was not her ally. She glanced at Ella's swollen stomach outlined beneath the blue shawl. Her plan had to be executed soon. Ella's future depended on it.

9

"A One-legged Son-of-a-... the Confederacy"

ELLA DID NOT CARE that Beatrice had stopped inviting her along when she went into Savannah to get supplies. A prisoner behind Judith's blue shawl, she would not have gone anyway. Surely everyone in Savannah knew by now that Gentry had abandoned her, abducting his son in the process. She could just hear the gossip about his farewell gift, which no shawl could conceal.

Thinking of her friend, Judith, she recalled past remarks of Savannah's elite *tea and cakes brigade* each time they discovered their youngest member was about to bring another little Ashville into the world, "Good Lord! I just saw Judith, and she is once again prisoner of that awful blue shawl!" No telling what they were saying about *her*. She wouldn't put it past any of them to decide that someone other than her husband had gotten her into this fix—especially since her dear friend, Jack Kearney, was back.

She was sitting in her awkward position on the veranda the day he rode up astride a mule, his one leg dangling almost to the ground.

She did not recognize him at first, and so would wait until the last minute before expending the energy needed to rise from the comfort of her chair. If he were someone looking for work, she would call out that there was none. Even if this decrepit-looking one-legged man were starving, she wouldn't pay a stranger for work she expected her sharecroppers to do. She was saving every cent to pay taxes and the Pinkertons she planned to hire.

She eyed the approaching stranger moodily. Perhaps she'd spare a couple of biscuits and a saucer of molasses, and that was all ... maybe a bowl of Meshach's catfish stew, if there was any left.

But as he jerked the mule up at Greenpoole's bottom step, she saw a familiar glint of green eyes beneath the circle of a once-grand brown beret. Her hand went to her throat as she tried to gaze beyond the tangle of beard hiding his face. He slid from the mule, slapped a pair of crude wooden crutches beneath his armpits, and hopped, painstakingly, up Greenpoole's many steps.

Ella came to her feet, images racing across her mind like pictures in an old kaleidoscope she had lost long ago and now suddenly recovered—the brightly colored elegance of the Kearney brothers, ever cocky, and primed for fun—especially this one, as he waltzed Savannah's belles around every ballroom floor in the county. "The best dancer in all of Georgia," the girls claimed, she among them. How poised, elegant, and carefree she and her dear childhood friend, Jack, had been as they whirled!

Before she could regain her speech, he was before her, leaning on his crutches and eyeing her up and down, the same as she was doing him.

"Oh, Jack..." was all she could manage to whisper, suddenly heartbroken for them both. He had been her dearest comrade, her confidant, and as he often teased without meaning it, a beau after her own heart. Now they stood facing each other at the worst possible time in their lives—he, without one of his legs, and she, nearly in rags, and without her old charm and beauty to bolster her. She released her shawl, and, with a cry, all but threw herself into Jack Kearney's arms.

"Hey! Hey!" he yelled, struggling to stay afoot, "Have a little mercy on a one-legged son-of-a- … the Confederacy," he said, grinning.

"Oh, Jack, I'm sorry about your leg!"

He pressed her at arm's length, looking directly at the obvious hump beneath her skirt. "Now I'm thinking, would it be proper for me to extend my apologies for your condition?"

She blushed, suddenly reminded that she wasn't as pretty as she used to be ... being so heavy with child. She gathered the shawl tighter around her, and then tried to poke a long wisp of hair back into the careless bun on the back of her neck. "I am a mess, aren't I?"

"Yes, but the prettiest mess I've seen since the last time I treated myself to your company." He bowed, extending one crutch and wobbling on his single leg. "I stand, if ever so unsteadily, in awe of your messy loveliness."

She laughed, the first genuine laugher in a long time, and caught him to her, again taken aback by the feel of him, how thin he was, how easy it was to support him. He grasped her shoulders, letting his crutches fall away, and now they both swayed, laughing at their clumsy efforts to buoy each other. He rounded his eyes and made a game of nearly falling, gasping in exaggeration each time she shrieked and clutched him harder.

Suddenly they could not stop laughing, swaying in mock peril, each pretending to keep the other from crashing to the floor. Her mouth ached from doing things it had not done in ages. Merriment, pure and unrestrained, had control of her. How good it felt!

Jack's face, lined now where there had been no lines before, was still the most beautiful sight she had seen in ages. She stepped back to feast her eyes on him, her heart quickening with adulation; how priceless their friendship ... how precious the memories they shared. Finally, they gazed silently at each other.

"If I had two good legs, I'd be after you again, Ella," Jack said, breaking the silence. "I'd marry you and take care of you and the baby." He quieted, in frustration it seemed, before continuing. "Damn it, Ella, when I got to town this morning and heard that Garland took off and left you, I got so mad I started to get drunk."

She smiled. "I'm glad you didn't."

"Only because I don't do that sort of thing anymore," he replied. "A man in my condition has to stay sober on his feet ... *foot*," he corrected, as if trying to elicit another smile from her.

"I'm not looking to marry, Jack, and I won't, ever again, after I've divorced Gentry Garland," she said, then smiled. "And, Jack, for the sake of honesty, you were never after me or any other girl." Her smile widened. "You made it quite clear to every belle in Georgia that you never intended to waltz any of them into matrimony, ever."

"And now it's too late, isn't it?" he said softly. "The die's been cast, and I sure enough can't waltz anymore. But I'll do anything for you that's within my power, Ella." He looked around. "Jesus, this place needs some work. Just tell me what to do. I still have two good hands. I'm busted ... couldn't buy a pair of bloomers for a gnat, but I'll buck up against anybody that gives you trouble." He gazed fiercely at her, and then away. "I've always loved you, you know."

Ella laid her head on his shoulder, tears filling her eyes. "You are my dearest friend, Jack. The one thing that hasn't changed in our lives is our love for each other, and it will never change."

Later, as they stood beside Honor and Andy's graves, he draped his arm around her shoulders. "I'll never forget the day that brother of mine came tearing into the house to tell Mamma and Poppa that Mister Corrigan said he and Honor could get married. He was one happy runt. But ..." his voice broke, "damn that crazy temper of his! I never could beat it out of him, nor could any of our brothers. No one could." He dropped his head.

Ella put her arms around him and clung tightly, just as she clung to all the pure, sweet memories of her past. Jack was loyal. He understood her dreams for Greenpoole. Moreover, his lost limb would not stop him from helping her get her son back, if that is what she asked him to do.

~

The following weeks in Jack's company brought enlightenment to Ella that saddened her anew: Jack's cheer was only a well-practiced performance. His old exuberance, his shining spirit, had been blown away with his left leg, and was not to be restored. Aching inside, Ella mourned yet another loss. Somehow they had switched roles, and now *she* tried to cheer *him*. In one of his dark moods, he confided that he often thought of ending his misery, even dreamed about it, and the thought had become more appealing lately.

She angrily admonished him. Didn't she have enough to worry about without having to worry about him, she asked.

Horror struck her the morning she sought him out in the barn and found him sitting on the ground, his musket balanced between his good leg and the stump of the other, the barrel tight beneath his chin. She screamed and kicked the weapon away, and then sank to the ground beside him and wrapped him in her arms. Sobbing, they clung to each other through the long afternoon, each babbling their own personal misery, their anger, their frustrations, and then at last, promising each other to *live* despite it all. Ella did not tell him that she never had dreams of dying—only of revenge.

She was pleased that her grandmother now showed Jack the regard that she had never shown him or his brothers in the old days—nor Andy, until he married Honor. Even so, only Andy's death got him the full measure. Jack, however, seemed as close to her now as any person ever was. When Beatrice discovered that Jack lived in the old slave quarters on his family's destroyed plantation, she demanded that he stay at Greenpoole. Ella marveled each time she saw the odd pair share a pot of tea, their heads together, chatting privately. It seemed that they always hushed immediately upon her approach, which made her a bit uncomfortable. She was soon to discover why.

~

Cricket found Ella at the washtubs with Moonbeam and Sunbeam and said, "Miz Bea want you, Miss Ella. Right now, her say."

He was oddly serious, which prompted her to ask if he knew what Miz Bea wanted; but he darted away without answering.

Ella dried her hands on her apron as she hurried toward the house. Grandmother had not looked well lately. It was probably only her digestion, since she kept those sprigs of mint in her cheek worse than Grandma Kearney used to dip snuff. They'd go to Savannah in the morning and see old Doctor Boales. She'd insist.

In the parlor, she was not surprised to find Jack, as unsmiling as her grandmother, leaning on his crutches behind his new friend's chair. Ella surmised that they had stopped conversing the moment she opened the door. Worried anew by her grandmother's pallor, she studied her a moment.

"Are you ill, Grandmother?"

"Probably," Beatrice growled, "but that is not the reason I summoned you. Jack has something to tell you, and so do I. You first, Jack."

Ella looked quizzically at him, half-smiling. "My, my, how glum the two of you look. What has happened? The sharecroppers abandon us again? I wouldn't be a bit surprised. If so, we'll simply get …"

"I'm leaving in the morning," Jack said, interrupting her. "I'm going to Missouri."

"Missouri?" Ella's confusion showed. "But Missouri isn't your home, Georgia is. *This* is! For heaven's sake, Jack, have you a fever?"

He pulled an envelope from his pocket, and Ella glanced quickly at the other envelope in her grandmother's lap, and thought how ridiculous it was that they both had envelopes.

"This letter is from Ma's sister, Aunt Nellie, in Springfield. She said my little sister and Ma are sick. Aunt Nellie's husband and sons died in the war—just like Pa and my brothers. Now Aunt Nellie has my two little brothers, my ailing ma, and baby sister on her hands … plus a widowed daughter-in-law with three little mouths of her own to feed. They need me. I'm all they got left."

"But, Jack, I was going to offer you half of Greenpoole just to stay and help me run things. Don't you want that? We'll send for your family. Missouri isn't your home. How can you call a place that you weren't born and raised in *home*? For God's sake, Jack, don't leave me! Not *you*!" She paused, then blurted: "I ... I'll marry you when I'm free, if you want!"

"Ella!" She heard her grandmother's angry bark, but did not take her pleading gaze from Jack.

"I can call Missouri my home because I've got blood kin there, Ella. A man's home is where his family is—a woman's, too." He gazed meaningfully at her, and she felt her face flame. *So that's what they've been up to. They've been plotting against me!* She glared expectantly at her grandmother.

Beatrice drew a deep breath through her nose, held it, then noisily released it through her mouth—a sure indication that a task, unpleasant but unavoidable, weighted her. She smoothed the long envelope in her lap, then raised it. "I have had this in my possession for some weeks, knowing it was the only thing standing between you and freedom."

"Freedom? *My* freedom? Have you both gone daft?" She stared at the envelope. "What is that?"

"A declaration, in my own hand, stating what I have done, and also a letter you can present at Planter's Bank."

"Oh, Grandmother, you sold your house in Savannah!" Ella cried, her mood improving. She would miss Jack terribly, but now she would be able to pay the taxes and the Pinkertons much sooner than she thought.

"Yes, Ella. I have sold *all* my properties—Greenpoole Plantation, among them."

Ella stumbled back a step, slowly moving her head from side to side. Jack, obviously afraid that she would collapse, swung close to bolster her, but she threw up a hand to keep him away.

"But you can't do that," she finally whispered, her voice so croaked by her emotions that it seemed she could barely get the words out.

"Greenpoole was mine, child; surely you knew."

Ella sunk to the sofa, staring at the floor but seeing nothing, as Beatrice continued.

"Had your father lived, Greenpoole would have been his after my death, and then yours—but not yet."

Ella stared silently at her for a long time, letting the shocking realization sink in, and then finally cried out, her pain glowing in her eyes. "How could you be so cruel? How could you? Greenpoole is all I've ever wanted! It's all I have left of my life! It *is* my life!"

Beatrice stiffened, her abrupt anger widening her owl-like eyes into a frightening stare. "You stupid woman! Your husband and your son and the child that you carry, is your life! *This...*" she swept her arm out, indicating their surroundings, "is not your life! It is the rotting albatross around your neck! Around all of our necks! And you must escape before you rot with it!" Grimacing, she pushed up from her chair, surprising Jack, and now he swung to her side. She stood over Ella, trembling with her rage.

"So help me God, You *will* leave this place! You will go to your family! You will go if I have to hire those Pinkertons to drag you there every step of the way!" She swayed, her mouth freezing in its open position, her rigid fingers going to her chest. Jack caught her, his crutches clattering noisily against the bare floor as he fell backward onto the sofa with her.

Ella dropped to her knees beside them, screaming for Meshach. Then, as Cricket tore into the parlor, she cried out to him, "Take the fastest horse and get Doctor Boales Hurry! Hurry!"

10

Kinship for a fleeting Measure of a Day

WAR AND ITS AFTERMATH had absolutely no impact on the social structure that had for generations separated the white classes in Savannah and across the South. The high notion of blue-blooded superiority persevered among Chatham County's elite like an irreplaceable old heirloom. Persons of gentility remained aloof to anyone other than their own class; even though they were now as poor as those from whom they and their ancestors had segregated themselves. There were but two events that could bring these white classes, high and low, together in one large, shoulder-bumping crowd—*politics,* or the death of someone respected by both castes. Therefore, an unusually high regard for Beatrice Corrigan drew the disparate throng to Greenpoole for her burial. "Kinship for a fleeting measure of a day," Beatrice had once uttered at another such funeral.

Before sunrise on the day after Beatrice's death, men from town arrived to construct the long plank board tables that would accommodate the copious amounts of food soon to arrive with nearly each mourner, no matter how poor. The men placed the tables beneath the least-mangled oak trees a short distance from the rose garden. *Just like in the old days,* Ella thought listlessly, as she watched from her bedroom and reminisced about the days when Greenpoole hosted barbecues and elaborate balls. The strains of a sweet waltz began to play in her aching head. Her father always hired the very best musicians, she recalled. After a long interval, she clenched her eyes shut, silencing the music. When she opened them again, she saw Tessie Peckenpaugh rushing across the lawn, her arms piled high with a stack of table linens.

Tessie had arrived the prior evening with Judith Ashville. Sniffing and crying, and after occupying the chair next to Beatrice's simple oak casket for hours, Tessie insisted on showing Ella the contents of the huge trunk she had brought to Greenpoole. Inside were the never-before-used delicate linens, napkins, and doilies she had made for her very own trousseau some twenty-five years ago, and which would now be initiated at her dear friend's funeral feast, just as her beautiful never-before-used wedding dress had adorned Ella on the day of her wedding to Gentry.

Ella had wanted desperately to leave poor Tessie to her bouts of tears, but that was not to be.

"You know, my dear child, when our dear Bea sold her house to Banker Treadwell, he agreed that she and I could reside there until her demise, but..." she glanced sadly at Ella, then blew her nose into a worn, lacy-edged handkerchief that Ella recognized as one of Beatrice's, "I shall have to move out right away now." She glanced at Judith Ashville across the room. "Our sweet Judith has offered two rooms of her lovely home; but Mister Ashville is back from the Yankee prison, and is not at all pleased that she offered. He was quite discourteous to us both on the drive out here today."

Though she felt little like answering, Ella was obliged to do so. "It is Mister Ashville's way, Miss Peckenpaugh. Just ignore him."

"I cannot abide the man. I would be quite miserable under his roof."

"It's hard to believe that Grandmother didn't make provision for you, Miss Peckenpaugh—her permanent houseguest, and friend."

"Well, I ... I believe she did," Tessie said, then glanced warily at Ella. "I am not a brave woman, my dear, but I ... I would very much like to accompany you to Texas."

Stunned, Ella stared at her. "You must be joking."

"Oh, no, I would never joke. I think it quite vulgar for a lady to do so," she replied, before continuing. "I know Texas is said to be a terribly wild place, but when I think of going, the thought indeed suggests an excitement which I cannot explain." Her dark-blue eyes sparkled with sudden anticipation. "A new place ... a new life, and perhaps I might even find ..." She reached out, her trembling fingertips touching lightly at her trousseau trunk before she jerked the hand back and squeezed the fingers tightly in her other hand.

Ella continued to stare at her. Had Grandmother planned this? Had she known she was dying and planned this? Ella's expression grew grim, as she allowed a fresh swell of anger at her revered elder. Of course, she knew! She always knew everything!

"I intend to buy back Greenpoole, Miss Peckenpaugh. I intend to use the money Grandmother got for her properties for that purpose. I'm sure Banker Treadwell will not decline such a profit, seeing as he will have gotten Grandmother's house in town for nothing."

"You can't."

"Oh, but I can."

"No, my dear, you cannot." She hesitated only a moment. "Immediately after the sale, Bea sent the money to your husband."

"What?"

"Yes. She left only enough for our steamboat passage—for the boy, Cricket, also, and for provisions on the way—food, water, lodging, and such. So you see, you cannot possibly buy this place back. I suppose poor Bea knew you would try." Suddenly, the ever-meek old maid of Savannah seemed almost defiant.

Ella's shock turned to rage. *"You,* Miss Tessie, aboard a steamer? Why, the only body of water you aren't terrified of is in your bathtub! You've never set foot on a boat, remember? You wouldn't even cross that pontoon bridge to escape the Yankees, remember *that*? If you go with me, there could be a terrible storm, and we'd be on a deep, dark sea, tossed by giant waves and howling winds. Aren't you afraid you'll drown or get eaten by sharks?"

"I ... I am doing it for Beatrice. I promised!" Her gloved hands shot to her splotched cheeks, and she gazed worriedly across the room, her mind no doubt on the horrors ahead. In a moment, she was boo-hooing and poking fretfully at the pins protruding from the pitiable fuzzy bun at the back of her head.

Ella's shoulders slumped. *How could Grandmother have done this to me? I would have gotten back my son and little Elizabeth, and brought them home! But now Greenpoole was gone, and the money with it!* She burst into bitter tears and ran from the room, pushing past the reaching arms of Beatrice's tea and cakes brigade that had gathered at the foot of the stairs and were sadly consoling each other.

Sometime later, Ella laid aside the cool wet cloth she had been pressing to her red, swollen eyes and went downstairs to accept the mumbled condolences from the vast number of mourners as they filed by the casket. When the last of them had passed by, Ella did the same; her heart conflicted by both love and anger, as she gazed down at the chalky white face that little resembled the once-exuberant Beatrice Corrigan.

Years ago, Beatrice had left instructions as to the type of funeral service she was to have; therefore, after a few short prayers offered up in the parlor by the new minister from Christ Episcopal Church, the burial procession descended Greenpoole's twelve steps behind the men carrying Beatrice's casket, and headed for the far side of the rose garden to the spot where Beatrice was to rest beside her long dead husband. As they moved slowly along, a single voice began to sing *Amazing Grace*, a hymn that had comforted mourners—as well as slaves suffering their lot and dreaming of freedom—for almost a century. Ella glanced over her shoulder to see that Tessie, hands folded angelically under her chin, was giving the song her all. Her shaky but loud soprano modulation was soon joined by others of Beatrice's old *tea and cakes brigade,* and then everyone present joined in. As the casket was placed on ropes to be lowered into the grave, more prayers were said, and then *Old Rugged Cross* was sung as the mourners filed by one last time, some of whom tossed roses onto the lid, a few of the ladies tossed prayer cards.

Ella was last to drift away from the burial site. The men with shovels waited patiently while she stood silently over the open grave, tears streaming down her cheeks. The loss of Beatrice Corrigan was as shattering to her as was the loss of Greenpoole, for Ella had felt for as long as she could remember that the land and Beatrice Corrigan were one in each other, just as *she* and all Corrigans were a part of Greenpoole. *Why did you do it, Grandmother? Oh, why did you do it? How* could *you have sold our home? You were wrong! Wrong!* Brokenhearted, she joined the others on the lawn where the tables of food had been uncovered and were now being consumed by the vast crowd.

"I love Southern funerals," said the Northern woman Mrs. Fenwick, as she balanced a chipped, French-made *Sèvres* china plate in one hand and shoved a shrimp patty into her mouth with the other. As she chewed, she gazed about the yard at the conglomeration of mourners, swallowed, then explained, "I love Southern funerals because there is always such a diverse mix of you people. Wonder what your grandmother would say about this huge crowd—especially us *Yankees* showing up to pay our respects?"

"Probably that the lot of you were drawn by the smell of good Southern food," Ella replied, and guided the surprised woman and her near-empty plate back to the loaded tables.

Just then, Cricket handed Ella a note. She thanked the Northern woman for coming, and then turned aside to read Jack's message.

Are you too mad at your old friend to tell him goodbye? Hester and I are waiting at Corrigans' Pool.

Stronger than her earlier feeling of betrayal was the fresh well of sadness that suddenly swept over her. She slipped the scrap of paper into her pocket and slowly made her way through the crowd.

She saw Jack leaning against the mossy boulder that fed ancient Corrigans' pool, his fingers playing with the steady trickle of water that cascaded down the slick, rocky surface. Hester grazed nearby, her bony rump loaded with the same raggedy bedroll that had been there the day Jack arrived. Silent, Ella sat on the cracked marble bench at the pool's edge and stared into the blue-green depths. Jack watched her a moment, then jabbed his crutches beneath his armpits, swung to her side, and sat down. He gazed at the pool and then at the gigantic oaks that surrounded the entire area in a misty, sun-flecked haze. The sweet chirping of a robin broke the silence, and Ella wondered how it dared sing on this saddest of days.

"We sure had some good times here—talking, soaking our feet, laughing—didn't we, Ella?" When she didn't answer, he caught her chin in a crooked finger and turned her face until their eyes met. "I'd be highly flattered if that's what you were remembering right now."

Ella nodded, but it was not Jack and the times they spent together as children, and later as best friends, that filled her mind this minute. She closed her eyes, trying to blot out that moonlit night over six years ago when, to Gentry Garland's urging, she so willingly surrendered her virtue to him. It crossed her mind that she had been more than willing, but she quickly pushed the uncomfortable thought aside. That foolish night was the beginning of her misery, and now, after he'd convinced her that he'd never allow her to anguish over anything ever again, he had done his worst. Better had he slit her throat than steal her son!

Jack nudged her. "If you're remembering our good times, you sure don't look too pleased," he said, grinning.

"I miss those times, Jack. I miss … everything."

"I know, but we can't go back to those days, Ella. We aren't those people anymore ... never will be again."

"If we aren't, then who are we? I can't seem to think straight. We can't go back, but what's to become of us? I'll never believe that Greenpoole was a hopeless cause. I've tried to imagine the future … tried to capture that *vision* that Grandmother said I lacked, but all I can see is what has passed. I am a part of that past! I can't be anyone other than myself! But now, I'm expected to be different … to be someone else!" She stifled a deep sob. "I'm so scared, Jack!"

He pressed his forehead tightly to hers, and she felt him tremble. "Me, too," he said, pausing for a long moment before continuing. "I only know that everything that once bound us to Chatham County, Georgia has fallen away, and I think—maybe for the first time in our lives and for the rest of our lives—that what becomes of us is up to us. It might not be what we think we want, but for the moment, it's all we've got." He pressed a quick kiss to her forehead, then pulled back to smile mischievously at her. "As for myself, I'm accepting it. I'm going to Missouri, where I suspect Aunt Nellie's got her widowed daughter-in-law convinced she's duty-bound to take me on."

Ella sniffed. "About time you married *somebody.*"

"Yeah," Jack drawled. "Looks like I'll have myself a plump, homely wife who'll cook my meals, have my babies, and consider herself damn lucky to have a one-legged scamp like me."

"She *will* be lucky," Ella said softly, as she brushed a lock of reddish brown hair from his eyes and smiled sadly at him.

"Aunt Nellie writes that the girl is kindly and has a great personality, which means that she ain't much to look at, and she talks a lot."

Ella could not laugh, even knowing he was trying to make her do so. "I wish we had married, Jack. You once said that friends make better alliances than lovers."

"With you always thinking of me like a brother, it would have been like incest," he said, and chuckled. "On the other hand, with me knowing full well we *ain't* brother and sister, I wouldn't have been all that religious about it, myself."

This time, she chuckled with him. He gripped her hands.

"Ella, Poppa used to tell my brothers and me that no matter how many bad things happened to us, if we thought real hard on it, we'd see that good lessons were learned from each mishap. Think about it,

Ella. Think real hard." He slipped an envelope into her hand and kissed her goodbye. "Remember, Ella ... if we can learn from our mistakes, we can maybe learn a new way."

With tears glistening on her cheeks, she watched him tie his crutches to the bedroll on Hester's rump, then he belly-flopped across the animal's back, swung his leg over, and sat upright. He tipped his brown beret and then, as if to extract a last laugh, cocked the beret between Hester's ears as he rode away.

When he was gone, Ella eased her tired body onto the cool grass between the pool and the marble bench, and tore into the envelope. Inside was a map, crudely drawn, but to the point. High in the corner Jack had drawn a dilapidated old mansion, unmistakably Greenpoole. From there, he had drawn a line along the coast and into the Gulf of Mexico, at which point the line took a sharp turn inland and stopped at the outer rim of a large circle. Inside the circle were scrawled the words, *"A New Way."*

A 'new way?' she thought bitterly. Jack could be optimistic about his 'new way' because, unlike her, he wasn't going to a place he dreaded. And what did he mean by 'if we can learn from our mistakes'? Gentry Garland had made the mistake, not she!

She crushed the paper in her palm, laid her cheek against the cold marble, and cried.

~

The next day, Ella left Greenpoole Plantation with only her grandmother's old Jenny Lind trunk and a small carpetbag holding her worldly possessions; but the weight she carried in her heart was heavier than any dozen trunks she could have filled in better days.

Tessie followed so close on Ella's heels down the steps that she had to stop repeatedly to jerk her hem from beneath Tessie's shoe. Cricket, fidgeting, and obviously eager for Meshach to drive them to Greenpoole's pier, sat on the edge of the wagon bed, his legs dangling, and his sparse bundle squeezed tightly under his arm. Ella tried not to cry as she said goodbye to the sobbing Moonbeam and Sunbeam, but the tears kept coming.

In the distance, sitting high in the water, *The Swan,* a paddle-wheel steamer that plied the river between Augusta and Savannah, waited. In Savannah, they would board another steamer for the journey along southern coastlines into the Gulf of Mexico, and then to the port of Indianola on the Texas coast.

At sight of *The Swan,* Tessie squeaked like a squeezed mouse and leaned far back in Meshach's grasp as he helped the trembling woman onto the wagon seat.

Ella touched Meshach's sleeve. "I'm glad you are staying on at Greenpoole, Meshach ... and will be watching over the place, along with Moonbeam and Sunbeam."

Suddenly Ella could say no more. She turned her miserable gaze to the rose garden and the tombstones visible between the rippling bushes. Little Seth's Apothecary's Rose was in full bloom, swaying in the breeze, as if waving goodbye to her; she could not suppress the sob that tore from her. Meshach quickly looked down, his eyes watering, but his deep voice did not give him away.

"Yes'sum, I'se glad I'se staying, too, Miss Ella. That what Banker Treadwell say Miz Bea want when he asked me to stay on. So don't you worry none, 'cause I gonna take good care of them roses and them that rest there. That garden a might pretty place to lay when the Lord call a soul to glory." He looked at her now, frowning slightly, but his maroon eyes were as gentle as a child's. "You gots to be happy now, Miss Ella. You gots to try real hard to be happy."

She grasped his large, work-scarred hand with both of hers. "Thank you, Meshach, for all you have done for me and my family all these many years." Memories of the perils they had faced together flashed through her mind—the cruelties at Victor's Moss Oak Plantation, the vicious slave driver, Brunot, the murderous white trash Shipleys—and that terrifying night in Savannah when looters rampaged in advance of Sherman's army.

A startling blast from the ship's horn ordered them to hurry, and he helped her onto the seat before himself boarding. Ella stared straight ahead as Meshach slapped the reins against the horse's rump and drove her, for the last time, through Greenpoole's ancient avenue of oaks to the pier.

Once at the dock, Ella shook Meshach's hand, her shoulders slumping as she turned toward the gangplank. Tessie's eyes, as large as the big blue buttons on her old woolen jacket, seemed about to pop from her head. Glancing irritably at her through teary eyes, Ella grabbed the woman's elbow none too gently and hustled her aboard. Cricket, his own eyes as large as Tessie's, grabbed the quaking woman's other arm and held on tight.

~

To stand on the paddle wheeler's deck and watch her beloved Greenpoole growing smaller and smaller in the distance was completely defeating to Ella. When a bend in the river blocked her cherished home from view, she gripped the rail and leaned forward, but was not to see her Greenpoole again. She began to tremble, feeling as if the well of utter hopelessness that flooded her insides would stop her heart before she could take her next breath. If she'd only had the money to…!

She thought of Jack's parting words, and her eyes glittered. If her *"mishaps"* had taught her anything, it was that money, and the independence attained by it, was paramount to a woman's survival in this world. As soon as this baby was born, she'd let nothing stop her from attaining both. She'd get her children back … and Greenpoole, too. Gentry Garland nor anyone else would stop her!

Part Two

11

A Strange Bond among Social Disparities

ELLA'S APPREHENSION DEEPENED with each stop along the coast. Having to contend with the frantic Tessie only intensified her stress, *and* her irritability. Tessie, ever horrified by the sight of deep water, scurried into the staterooms of each vessel they boarded, faced the wall and looked neither left nor right. Each time Ella entered one of the cramped compartments, she'd found the woman pale and petrified.

Finally, after four days of changing ships along the Southern coastline, Ella allowed her better nature to prevail; she sat down beside Tessie and silently patted her skeletal clenched fists. However, conversation proved to be impossible, for Tessie's replies consisted of sharply gasped epitaphs of impending disaster, her dire predictions interrupted only by the terrified rolling of her eyes if the ship creaked or rose on a swell of rough sea. For that reason, Ella had spent most of her time on the windswept decks.

They boarded the *Mary* in New Orleans. Ella struggled to keep the gusty winds from whipping her cape back and forth like an untethered sail, as she looked around for Cricket. She wanted to send him to the lower deck where a five gallon barrel of fresh milk nestled in a huge crate of rapidly melting ice. The milk was available to passengers for five cents a quart. She found Cricket segregated with other Negroes at the far end of the steamer, and gave him the three empty jars she had purchased at a cost of one cent each from the man who tended the milk barrel. Cricket went right away to get the milk. It was not the discomfort of her huge belly or the threat of the steep stairs that discouraged Ella from fetching the milk; it was the very cows that provided the milk that kept her away. Their tethered rear legs, and the brass knobs on their sharp horns, did nothing to prevent them from gouging away at one-and-all, often sending less wary passengers sprawling across the deck. Fortunately, Cricket's experience with Greenpoole's stubborn old milk cow made him quite the skillful horn-dodger.

After handing her the milk, Cricket pointed to the man in charge of the cows. "Miss Ella, that man tell me we ain't got far to go. He say we be in Galveston 'fore we know it. Then he say we gonna have to get on another boat that will take us to our last getting off place. I sho is happy to be getting to Texas, Miss Ella!"

"I'm glad you are happy, Cricket. I wish ..." She stopped herself from saying that she wished she was happy, too. *Her* happiness would come only when she and her children were back in Georgia.

As they docked at Galveston, Tessie seemed to calm a bit, but it didn't last. When it came time to leave the boat, she whimpered like a motherless pup. Finally, holding onto Ella's sleeve, she emerged from the cabin to tiptoe across the deck as if the slightest pressure from her shoes might send her crashing through the boards and into the sea. As Ella tugged the exasperating woman along, the gale-like winds glued her skirts to her huge belly and whipped her hair so hard against her face that her eyes stung from the lashing. Sick, angry, and feeling dozens of stares upon what must be a wildly hilarious spectacle to the curious onlookers, Ella gave the fleshy part of Tessie's arm a twisting pinch that elicited a painful shriek, as well as sped her along.

Soon, the three of them stood sweltering on Galveston's wharf downwind from a stench comparable only to a pig sty. The dock was so crowded with unwashed humanity of all persuasions that to identify the odor correctly as belonging solely to the four-legged passengers was impossible. Sweat-drenched stevedores, black and white, toted long planks of lumber, crates, and barrels across the gangplanks of two ships; Ella wondered which of the two she was supposed to board for the last leg of her journey two hundred miles down the Gulf. However, she soon discovered that both ships were sailing up the East coast.

Weary of waiting, Ella looked up and down the dock, and then out across the open bay at the slowly disappearing *Mary* as it headed for the its next stop, Mexico. *Where is our boat?* she wondered. The bay, as well as the horizon, was empty of other ships, save for a small fleet of fishing boats surrounded by drifting seagulls. Among them inched a dilapidated-looking flat-bottom sternwheeler, no more than thirty feet wide and sixty feet long and which, by the sounds coming from it, had been converted into a cattle boat. Ella pulled away from Tessie's grip and approached a man who stood nearby giving orders to a group of stevedores.

"Sir, we disembarked the *Mary* hours ago and were told by a crewman that another vessel would take us to the port of Indianola. Can you tell me if our transportation will arrive soon?"

Frowning apologetically, the man removed his hat. "Why, ma'am, that crewman must have been new on the job. Indianola's on the *Mary's* route." His quick glance took in her condition, then he smiled kindly. "I'm afraid, ma'am that you should have stayed put on the *Mary*."

Fighting the impulse to scream her frustration, Ella stared up at him. Finally, she thanked him in a small, shaky voice, and turned away. He stepped in front of her, his hat still in his hand.

"Ma'am, if you're not in a hurry, the next steamer comes in three days. If you *are* in a hurry," he hesitated, "that boat yonder ..." he pointed at the cattle boat that had caught Ella's attention moments earlier, "is leaving for the Port of Lavaca, just this side of Indianola, as soon as those cattle are unloaded. It mostly just travels 'twixt here and there, and it's low-draft enough to get through the shallows without folks having to change boats in deep waters."

Ella wiped her sweaty cheek with the back of her hand, her tired eyes focusing on the rickety-looking boat moving toward the dock, the anxious bawl of its four-legged passengers getting louder and louder, the smell of their droppings getting stronger and stronger.

Ella silently dismissed the option of boarding the cattle boat—she was sick enough already. She turned to the man. "Sir, have you heard of a town called Victoria?"

"Sure have, ma'am. It sits just north of Port of Lavaca and alongside the Guadalupe River." He smiled suddenly. "Is Victoria where you're heading?" Without giving her a chance to reply, he grinned as if quite pleased. "Well then, be glad you missed the *Mary*. Port of Lavaca's a lot closer to Victoria than Indianola ... about thirty or forty miles closer, I'd say. Too bad the railroads were mangled during the war... or wouldn't be far at all by rail."

She refocused on the approaching boat, realizing that it actually was her only option if she didn't want to spend days waiting for another vessel. She gave out a forlorn sigh. *Am I to get this far only to end up sinking in the Gulf of Mexico amid a sea of floating cow patties?*

The man continued, "Just as soon as the deck's sloshed clean, them folks yonder are boarding, and maybe a dozen or so others." He pointed at a shabby, hard-faced elderly woman who was grimacing while ferociously scratching her armpit. A man, who looked nearly as old and disgruntled as the woman, slouched next to her. A few feet away from the pair, two small boys and three ragged little girls huddled silently together in a tight cluster. The eldest of the girls looked no more than twelve.

Ella stared at the twelve-year-old, abruptly stunned by what she saw. Though hunched deeply into a tattered, oversized, man's coat, the stark protrusion of the solemn-faced girl's belly left no doubt that she was heavy with child. As Ella gaped, the girl's sullen eyes met hers and then abruptly widened into a look of helplessness that brought a lump to Ella's throat. There was a time in distant memory when she would have quickly turned away from this hapless girl of obvious low station, but now, without knowing why, she allowed the slight beginning of a smile to erase her look of dismay. The girl's mouth appeared to struggle with a timid grin, the attempt quickly squelched by the clench-jawed man's rough poke to her shoulder. Then the lot of them moved off down the dock. Ella watched them, puzzled by her concern for this scruffy girl. Oddly, it was as if, in that transient moment of awareness between them, they had formed a bond.

She abandoned the thought, feeling quite foolish, and thinking it was this insufferable heat that had her so mush-headed. She dragged a soggy handkerchief from her sleeve and mopped her brow. *The only bond between that poor child and me is the size of our bellies ... and possibly our misery!*

She jumped when the man cleared his throat, nodded at the untidy group and ran his finger down the list on the clipboard.

"That bunch goes by the name of Barton," he said, with a measure of disgust, and then tapped the clipboard as if in affirmation of words left unspoken. "They'll be onboard, but there'll be others more like yourself, ma'am." He pointed at a family of six coming toward them—a mother, father, and four children, one of whom was an infant. "The Englemore family is boarding, and a few others, soon as the deck's sloshed clean," he added again, as the boat bumped the dock and the biting stench of fresh manure further soured the sultry, fishy breeze.

An hour later, Ella leaned weakly against the upper rail of the top deck while tugging at her suffocating collar and wishing the little vessel would depart. The lower deck had been "sloshed" clean, but the smell lingered; several half-grown calves had been herded aboard, replacing those that had been unloaded, though not as many. Tessie immediately disappeared into the tiny, makeshift stateroom with the well-attired Mrs. Englemore and her children, while Mr. Englemore stayed on deck. Ella looked around for the grubby Barton family and the girl, spotting them in the bow of the boat, where they had obviously opted to isolate themselves. Cricket and a lone Negro man sat on the deck near the stern.

Still tugging at her collar, Ella watched absently as a crate that contained two small, squealing pigs was rolled aboard. Behind them ambled an exceptionally tall, slightly bow-legged old man leading a fine saddle horse—*likely much too fine an animal for the man in possession of him,* Ella thought, unable to shake her irritation at the heat, and life in general. Just the same, she continued to watch him. His body was oddly straight for an old man, wiry rather than muscular. Just the way he moved about the deck made him a curiosity—purposely stiff-legged it seemed, chest raised, arms relaxed at his sides but fingers slightly curled, as if to say, *"Stay out of my way, or you'll wish you had."* He wore a dusty but formal long coat—much like those worn by *morticians*—black in color, as were his trousers, vest, and high-bowled, wide-brimmed hat that shielded most of his face in a cavernous shadow. She watched him strip off his coat and toss it atop the crate of squealing pigs, cursing them as he did. In two swift moves, in which he unbuckled the horse's cinch strap and swept the saddle off, he backed the animal to a spot alongside the crate of squealers, and then yelled at them to "Shet up, you stinkin' *sons 'a—"* he paused to take a long look up at Ella on the upper deck, then pointedly finished his sentence with a loud *"boar hogs!"*

Ella shivered under his attention, but could not help but stare back. The sun glinted off a thick buckle that held two long-barreled guns low on his hips. She shaded her eyes with a hand, deflecting the glare, while thinking that a man who needed two guns strapped to him was likely as dangerous as he was peculiar.

Standing no more than fifteen feet above him, she could see his patchy gray and black whiskers and slashes of thick, spidery eyebrows above steely, light-gray eyes—eyes so pale as to be startling; or was it their hardness that made them so frightening? His face was unusually thin, his long nose rising like an eagle's beak from the bridge between his eyes. Ella released an embittered breath.

A face like that could only belong to a criminal—likely, one of many such felons where I'm going! She was the first to look away, hesitating only a moment before retreating into the stateroom.

She sank to a narrow cot near where Mrs. Englemore was nursing her baby. Tessie, obviously relieved to see her, sprang to her side and helped remove the suffocating high-collared jacket, and then hovered there while Ella eased onto a stack of pillows. For the past two days, she had felt increasingly awkward, heavily burdened by her swollen body and the overwhelming heat; so much so today that she did not protest when Tessie began to fan her vigorously with a huge rattan fan streaked and stained with the grime of countless passengers gone before. Knowing that she must eat to keep up her strength, Ella ate from the warm jar of beans and boiled pork she had purchased before boarding.

Slightly comforted by the swooshes of hot air from the fan, Ella forgot the scary old man on the lower deck and the poor girl huddled in the bow. With the realization that she was only a few hours from her destination, an onslaught of worrisome thoughts and questions flew at her like vultures tormenting crippled prey. The knowledge that she would soon embrace her precious son gave her unaccustomed joy; but when she envisioned her husband's disturbing black eyes probing her, her elation melted. Gentry Garland was not a man to be cowed by anyone or anything. She knew him well enough to know that he thought himself justified in doing what he did, and he would not be sorry for it. She wiped fitfully at the sweat trickling down her arms. What did it matter whether he was sorry or not—she was there for her children, not apologies.

She must be calm, must calculate her every move. Hannah would deliver this baby just as she had delivered Seth and Adam. After that, she would concentrate on regaining her strength, and then she'd find a way to return to Georgia with her children.

What seemed like days later but was actually less than two, a loud rap sounded on the door, and then a male voice called out,

"Port of Lavaca! We'll tie up in ten minutes." The voice hesitated and those inside the cabin heard the shuffling of papers.

"Port of Lavaca?" Tessie screamed, the very word sending her into a fit of nerves as she jumped to her feet and clamped her hands to her cheeks. "Isn't that where we ...?"

The voice outside the door continued. "Miz Garland, and the Englemores, best get your party together. Your gear's on deck."

Tessie's second scream joined the abrupt, loud, brassy tooting of the ship's horn, followed by the persistent clanking of a bell. The calves bawled, the pigs squealed, and the Englemore children laughed, waving teasingly at Tessie, as their scolding mother herded them out the door.

Ella stumbled to her feet and waited, motionless, for the unexpected wave of dizziness to pass so that she could get dressed. Tessie's trembling hands were more of a hindrance than a help, but at last the chore was done. Tessie's eyes were glassy with fear as she watched Ella knot her hair into its bun, and then she put a stranglehold on Ella's elbow and did not let go until Ella stripped her hands away, finger by finger, like one peels a banana. With much effort, she tugged the terrified woman to the door and opened it to discover Cricket, eyes as wide as Tessie's, staring at her.

"We'se here, Miss Ella! We is home!"

Ella flinched at the word. *No. Not home. Never home!* A great longing swept over her and she passed a shaky hand over her glistening eyes, wiping away all visible traces of pain that thoughts of Greenpoole evoked. Silent, she handed Cricket her valise, then stepped out of the musty stateroom and onto the deck.

She swayed as her gaze swept past the rows of landing docks and boats to the harsh, unfamiliar land—sand, and mounds of windswept dunes. Beyond that, a vast prairie began, with just a spattering of buildings before continuing on and on with nothing but faded blue sky above and scorched prairie grass below, the grass squirming madly with each erratic puff of sultry gulf wind.

She wondered when rain had last nourished this desiccate patchwork of unending browns and grays and dirty yellows. The few trees that stood some distance from the beach appeared malformed in that their thick canopies were bent in a permanent arc away from the wind. *Tormented things,* she thought, as she gazed at their odd patterns of twisted branches.

Quite unexpectedly, her hand flew to her mouth, and it was all she could do to suppress the rising fullness in her throat … followed by the sour taste of beans and pork.

12

"This Ain't No Place to Tarry ..."

TWENTY-FIVE PASSENGERS, in addition to the Englemores, Ella, Tessie, Cricket, and the ragged girl and her family, crossed the low gangplank that led them onto a long pier laid with railroad rails. A line of small railcars waited to haul passengers and cargo to the wharf. Ella and her companions rode the very last little railcar, pulled along the track by two young Mexican boys in faded baggy pants and blouses. Somewhere in the distance, far down the pier, Ella heard the fractious squeal of pigs; but the black-clad old man was nowhere in sight, nor was the girl and her scruffy family, both having been the first to grab a railcar.

After a slow ride up the pier, with the metal wheels clacking noisily on the rails, Ella struggled out of the cart with help from Cricket and Tessie. She moved toward their trunks, which the boys had loaded into a two-wheeled handcart. One of the boys put out his palm, smiling agreeably. Ella dug in her reticule and handed him two pennies. He immediately nodded to the other boy, and the two of them maneuvered the cart across the wharf, its wooden wheels bumping and clunking down the steps to the sand. Cricket, excited to be on Texas soil, fairly bounced down each step. Tessie hurried close behind him, the immediate prospect of finally being on solid ground evident in her wide-eyed exuberance.

Ella hesitated, feeling the need to rest before maneuvering the short flight of stairs. She shuddered as the taste of sour beans and pork suddenly burned the back of her tongue again. One of the Mexican boys looked up at her with concern and pointed toward a scattering of buildings rising from a long bluff above the beach.

"Port of Lavaca, Senora, she not far," he said. "You like I ride you in the cart?"

She thanked him but shook her head. She could see now that the town was of some size, and mostly made up of wooden and *crete* buildings—concrete made from lime, sand, and oyster shells—much like the simply constructed dwellings in countless seaside towns along the Southern and Northern coasts. A broad street banked by one-, two-, and three-story structures appeared to be the town's main thoroughfare. A few buildings were brightly painted; others stood gray and unadorned.

Ella started down the rough wooden steps but grabbed the railing when, for the third time today, an unexpected wave of nausea weakened her. She rested a moment, and then was about to move on, but instead gave out a startled cry at the feel of her elbow captured in an overly firm grasp.

"You sure as hell ain't no seaman's lady, are ya ma'am?" a raspy voice chortled. Without choice, she was suddenly being ushered down the remaining steps, then onto a wide trail of packed sand.

"Just stand still here on the flat earth 'til you get your land legs under ya."

"Thank you, sir, but I can manage …" A small gasp ended the sentence as she glanced up into the frightening visage of the old man's face. Up close, he was even uglier than she had assumed from a distance on the boat, his pale gray eyes even colder. His was possibly the meanest-looking face she remembered ever seen. His cheekbones were like anvils, and what she had earlier mistaken for skimpy facial hair was actually a short beard riveted by a crisscross pattern of long, hairless scars down each leathery, sunken cheek. In embarrassment of her rudeness in staring at him, her eyes batted downward. He grinned, as if from some secret pleasure.

"I … I will be quite all right, sir." She kept her eyes averted. "But I do thank you for … for your kindness."

"You're thinking I'm as ugly as a baboon's ass, ain't you, ma'am?"

Ella's face reddened at his language, but she snapped, "Certainly not!"

"The hell you ain't," he said, and chuckled.

Tessie rushed up to cling to Ella's free arm, and Ella watched the man's daggerish eyes crawl over Tessie with merciless scrutiny. Then one of his leathery cheeks clenched with disgust as he gave a final shake of his head before tightening his grip and ushering Ella away from the docks. She thought she must have cried out because he stopped abruptly.

"Ain't time yet, is it?" he asked gruffly.

"I don't think so," she answered weakly, still aghast at the wild-looking old man with a tongue as horrid as his looks. She tried to step away from him, but his firm grip on her arm prevented it.

"Sir, I assure you I can walk without assistance! I am neither faint nor weak."

He glanced down at her. "Yup, I can shore see you're about as strong as a tow-sacked kitten in a suck-hole creek."

"Sir!"

"That there's a nine-month belly, if I ever seen one," he muttered wryly. Under Ella's newly open-mouthed stare, he swung his head around to glare at Cricket, who immediately halted. Tessie had not stopped gasping, and now she was twittering like a frightened bird and had almost stopped the circulation in Ella's other arm.

"The golldamnest thing I ever did see," he growled, appraising first Cricket and then Tessie with fresh disgust. He gave poor Tessie twice the repulsive stare as Cricket before turning his penetrating pale-gray eyes back to Ella. "Been watching you two all the way from Galveston where I hitched on. What in hell you doing here without no man … just a scared-ass little nigger to tote your gear and," he observed Tessie again, "a pinch-faced old woman, ugly as me, and with some kinda dead pelt pinned to the back of her head and about to blow away in the wind."

Tessie's hands shot upward like exploding missiles to grasp the wildly flapping hairpiece just as it came loose. The rescue of her fuzzy bun and firm recapture of Ella's arm was executed in a blur of speed that made the old man give out a low cackle before resettling his steely gaze on Ella.

"What in hell kinda man you got, if you even got one," he said. "Ain't nobody here to meet you, I can shore see that." He waved his arm about. "Ain't you got a husband or a pa? He must be a real sorry sort to let a young woman like you travel in that kinda fix." He eyed her stomach with disdain.

Ella's eyes blazed. It was bad enough that this crazy old man had insulted her, and had terrorized poor Tessie Peckenpaugh to the unfathomable point of speechlessness; but she would not allow him to demean her dead father! Angry tears sprang to her eyes.

"You shut your dirty old mouth, you … you …" she raked him over with her enraged stare, "you nasty old man! I will not have you insult my dead father, a dear, sweet man … gentle and kind for all of his life! *You*, sir, would not have been fit to shovel manure on my father's plantation back in Georgia!" she cried, and could not contain her next thought: "My God, what have I come into?"

He grinned while rubbing the bristles on his long cheek. "So it's a Southern Belle you are, eh? A Georgia peach, at that. Well, pardon me, Your Highness," he mocked, doffing his hat. "As to not being fit to shovel manure in your old man's barn, I ain't never shoveled poop for any man, not even myself." He laughed that low laugh again. Then, as if he'd had enough banter, pulled her hands away from her face and thrust a crumpled, grayish handkerchief at her. She recoiled from it and snapped up the one that Tessie offered and pressed it to her nose.

"That'll be enough of that bawling, ma'am. Squalling females irritate me mor'n a patch of body critters. I'm just trying to help, so spill it out. What you two and that black boy doing here, and where you heading?"

"That is none of your business, sir," Ella said, forcing composure with a sniff, as she pulled her blue shawl tightly around her shoulders. "If you truly wish to help, please direct us to a stable where I can rent a buggy and obtain directions."

To her dismay, he shook his head, then grasped her elbow again and began pulling her along. She sputtered her protest, but he kept going.

"Tain't a far piece from here. Keep your dignity, ma'am. You wouldn't want the good folk of this town to wonder at your bad behavior, would ya?"

"*My* bad behavior? Let go of me, you … you old …"

"Sons-a'bitch?"

"I do not use such language, sir."

"Bet you're thinking it, though, ain't'cha?"

"Nor do I befoul my mind with such thoughts."

"Ha! Females is such liars. Why don't you just go ahead and spit it out, ma'am. I'm sucking wind just dying to hear from your own genteel lips what you're so golldamn ready to tag my tail with." He gave her a sidelong glance. "No? You can't think of nothing else?" He eyed her longer this time. "Well, that just goes to show how much you need my help. A woman who can't speak her mind is about as helpless as a fly in a slop jar out here—especially one who ain't got no man in tow. Got any money?"

Suddenly aware of Beatrice's leather pouch, drenched with sweat between her breasts, Ella's eyes slid suspiciously to him before looking straight ahead. "No. I have no money."

"Give it to him!" Tessie cried, her voice trembling with obvious fear of being murdered.

"How much," he prodded.

"I … I'm not sure. Enough to get us where we're going is all." Other than Tessie's outburst, Ella didn't know why she answered him. Perhaps she did so, thinking he would not be so quick to rob her if he thought there would be no profit in it.

"No need lying like that, ma'am. I ain't never taken a peso off a female, but I sure as hell shelled out plenty. 'Course, that was back in my younger days, mind you, when I still had a young man's faults and urgings … and more than a vague memory to bargain with."

Tessie's gasp nearly drowned out the sound of waves crashing on the distant beach.

Ella dug her heels into the sand, refusing to budge. *"Mister …!"*

"*Grouse,* ma'am. Hempstead Grouse," he said.

"Mister Grouse! I do not know what you think, sir, but not in all our days have Miss Peckenpaugh and I been disposed to tolerate such foul-mouth utterances!" She glared at his hand that gripped her arm. "I suggest you release me this instant or we shall scream loud enough to wake the dead in this God-awful place!"

"And what do you suppose would happen to you and," he tossed a discerning scowl over his shoulder at Tessie, "*Miss* Peckenpaugh, there, should you do that little thing, ma'am?"

"Unless we've truly reached the end of civilization, you will be arrested and tossed into jail for assault, both verbal and physical!"

"It'd take a lawman to do that, ma'am, and I sure as hell ain't gonna toss my own rear-end into no hoosegow." He chuckled beneath his breath as he flipped over the dusty lapel of his coat and flashed a small badge at her so quickly that she did not have time to read the engraving.

Her eyes widened in disbelief. Was this rank old man—a despot if she ever saw one—an example of "law and order" in the state of Texas? *Surely not!*

"Let's get moving," he growled. "It's hotter'n sizzling spit on a campfire out here, and I ain't in no mood for mollycoddling a couple'a hysterical females."

Ella pulled back, her hair coming loose from its bun as she struggled to break free. Cricket, trotting nearby, scrambled to pick up her combs as they hit the ground, but he made no effort to get close enough to hand them to her. She knew, by the look on his face, how frightened he was of this ugly old white man in the dusty, long-tailed *undertakers* black coat … who now had her firmly in tow and was forcing her down a narrow, sandy trail that led onto an equally sandy street.

"I've got to get to Hannah," she groaned, more to herself than to anyone else.

"Where's this Hannah at?" he demanded.

While Ella only glared at him, and struggled anew to free her arm of his grasp, Cricket called out:

"Hannah is Miss Ella's ol' mammy! Ol' Hannah done birth two babies for Miss Ella, and Miss Ella been saying all 'long that ol' Hannah gonna birth this new one for her, too."

Hempstead Grouse halted. "I asked *where* in hell is she, not *what* in the hell is she," he growled, setting Cricket back several more steps with his cutting eyes. "Clear the molasses out'n your golldamn fuzzy head, boy, and answer my question … since it don't seem like the lady's gonna."

"Hannah live on Mista Gen'te Garland's ranch somewhere here in Texas … that's where we is going," Cricket blurted, almost too fast to understand.

Hempstead Grouse stopped abruptly, his eyes narrowing.

"Gent Garland? Well, I'll be a cross-eyed sap sucking sons-a'bitch!" His eyes shot back to Ella and then down to her stomach.

"That his'n?"

Ella flushed crimson. "Do you know him? Can you tell me how to get there?" Her hands went to her swollen waist and then, in another rush of embarrassment, fluttered up to brush the wildly blowing strands of hair away from her face. Then she grabbed at her heavy woolen skirts as the hot gulf winds inflated them like a balloon and then glued them to her huge, round belly.

He ignored her questions and continued to stare. "Bet the hell it is. I'll be a damn pussy-footing, prissy-pants she-man if it ain't his'n."

"Oh! For God's sake, Mister Grouse, please answer me!" Ella closed her eyes for a moment, exhausted by this old delinquent of a lawman.

"You married to Gent Garland, ma'am … or come out here for a belated wedding?"

"How dare you! I am his wife, and have been for almost four years."

"Yup, I knowed him," he drawled. "Mighty strange, though. Gent's been back in Texas a few months now, came home trailing two motherless youngens and a sour-pussed old Negro woman. By the dark look of him, he was just a'daring anybody to ask who, what or why," he said, and squinted at her. "And *now*, sudden-like, a wife he ain't ever mentioned shows up carrying the seed of his loins low in her belly … and *him*, not here to meet her or send someone else to do it. You know why that is, ma'am?" he finished, and then spit out a wad of tobacco that drilled a little brown hole in the sand.

"It is a long, complicated story, Mister Grouse, and I neither have the time nor the desire to explain my personal business to you. Your position as sheriff or marshal, whatever it is you are, gives you no right to bully me or insult me the way you've been doing since you so crudely forced your company upon us. I am not a criminal. I wish to be on my way immediately."

"You ever hear of the Texas Rangers?"

"Of course."

"Well, to answer your question, I used to be one. I'm now a deputy constable, and doing my job is what I'm about, ma'am, not *bullying*," he said, then laughed. "Hell's bells! I could see on the boat that you was skeered whiter than a fish's belly. Yup, green as cow's teeth in a weed patch, ain't'cha? Bet you ain't ever been out of Georgia and away from the old plantation before now, have you?"

"You are quite mistaken. If I seemed apprehensive to you, sir, it is due to my condition. I did not want my baby born aboard that boat, nor do I want it born *here*." She fought back tears. "Please ... I must have transportation. If you feel duty-bound to help me, then please direct me to a stable where I can rent a rig, and then be so kind as to tell me how to get to my husband's home. The boy, here, can drive me, she said, pointing to Cricket. "Please, sir!"

As if he had not heard a word she said, Hempstead Grouse hustled her across a vacant lot that led to the street with all the buildings she'd seen from the pier. With his hand still gripping her, she could do nothing but go along. Tessie grabbed her free arm and clung there, faintly whimpering as she tripped alongside.

Stepping onto a sidewalk, Ella looked warily at two men moving slowly toward them, both in long leather chaps, big crumpled hats pulled down over their eyes, and pistols strapped to their hips. Ella caught her breath as they neared, thinking that the pair looked almost as dastardly as the man hustling her along. Suddenly, she wondered if they would fall upon her and take what little possessions she and Tessie had. She wondered also if Hempstead Grouse might happily join them. To her relief, the two men stepped aside to let her pass.

"Afternoon, Hemp," one of them said, and then they both tipped their hats, and in a quieter tone they both added, "Ma'am." A second "ma'am" went to Tessie.

"Afternoon, Alvin ... Baldy," Hempstead Grouse said, without slowing his pace. Cricket, apparently forgetting his fright, jumped to his side.

"Mister, is them gent'mens *cowboys*? I gonna be a cowboy soon as Mista Gen'te teach me how."

"Ha! Reckon he better be a miracle worker if he's planning on making a wrangler out of a skinny-assed little pup like you," he said with a brief chuckle, and then mumbled just loud enough to be heard, "Yep, they's cowboys. D*ead* cowboys if I ever catch 'em doing what I think they been doing."

Cricket's eyes rounded. "What them cowboys been doing, Mista Grouse? What they been doing, huh?" he asked excitedly.

Hempstead Grouse stopped abruptly and gave Cricket such a withering look that Cricket immediately dropped back to walk well behind the Mexican boys and their cart.

In front of a large wooden building that emitted the strong odor of horses, hay, and damp manure, Ella jerked her arm free and peered inside. Hempstead Grouse stalked past, and with an authoritative quirk of his bony wrist, motioned for her to follow.

No attendant was inside, only two gray-muzzled old horses whose burdens should have been long past. Nearby, a lone wagon stood with one wheel leaning far inward on its axle and ready to collapse. Ella stared at it, determined not to cry. But she wanted to cry, wanted to cry and scream, wanted to slap the wall in a fresh surge of despair. What was she to do now? Still miles from her destination, she was stranded … and deathly afraid of Hempstead Grouse … who had spun around and was coming toward her from the opposite end of the stable! She drew in her elbows, fully expecting him to grasp her again, but he stomped past as if she were invisible, and went outside.

She stood motionless, frowning, trying to think, but hindered by an overwhelming weakness. Wiping perspiration from her forehead with the back of her hand, she waited for strength to return, and then slowly made her way to where Hempstead Grouse sat on a bench against the stable wall. She glanced up and down the empty street and sidewalks, wondering at the absence of people.

"I wish we hadn't left the *Mary*," she finally said. "Surely the town of Indianola would have been more accommodating than this place." She swayed, feeling weak and terribly sick to her stomach again. Tessie rushed up and latched onto her arm again.

Ignoring them both, Hempstead Grouse produced a small, stained pouch of tobacco from his pocket. Holding a thin square of paper between two ridiculously long, bony fingers and a thumb, he leisurely jiggled tobacco from the pouch and into the paper. With his cigarette rolled, licked, and lit, he leaned far back and took several deep drags before scowling up at her.

"If you'd stayed on the *Mary,* you'd damn well be on your way to Mexico by now."

"We would not be on our way to Mexico, Mister Grouse. We would be on our way to *Indianola,* the *Mary's* next port. There, I would have rented a carriage to take us to my husband's ranch."

"Golldamnit woman, I said you'd be on your way to *Mexico.* There's yellow fever in Indianola. The *Mary's* sure as hell gonna be waved off by a high-flying Yellow Jack. Likely the same quarantine flag is flapping over Corpus Christi, and maybe on down the coast to Brownsville. Then, quicker'n you and that ol' gal, there," he tossed a scowl at Tessie, "could squall your objections, you'd be on your way to Mexico." With that, he arose and walked off down the street.

"Mister Grouse ...?" Ella cried out to him, suddenly afraid that he had decided against helping them. As frightening as he was, he appeared to be their only hope ... and he knew Gentry.

Without turning around, he yelled, "Gonna find out why in hell the town's deader than an old maid's ..." He coughed over the last word. "It can't be yeller fever, or they wouldn't let us get off the boat."

"You are coming back, aren't you?" she called.

He spun around as if agitated. "Now do I look like the sorry kind of sons-a'bitch that'd leave two ladies in dire straits?"

Tessie spoke for the first time. "You certainly do!"

He guffawed, and continued down the street. "I'll rustle up a team and wagon to take you on down the road to the town of Victoria. You can rent a buggy there and get directions to your husband's ranch that's further north."

Ella watched him until he disappeared around the corner. *Further north? How much further north!*

An hour later, he sped right past them, whipping two large white mules harnessed to a flatbed wagon with green sideboards painted in large red letters, *GROSBECK & SONS FREIGHT.*

"Gonna get my hoss and pigs!" he yelled over his shoulder.

Ella stared after him. Did that mean he was leaving without her?

"Oh, Ella, what are we to do?" Tessie cried. "He is surely gone, and I don't see a soul we could ask for assistance!" She craned her neck to gaze inside the empty livery stable, then turned to stare frantically at Ella.

"We are going to wait," Ella replied. "If he doesn't come back, then we'll worry about what to do." Exhausted and still queasy, she sank onto the wooden bench, laid her head back and closed her eyes. Tessie crowded up against her, her arm looped tightly around Ella's arm. Cricket and the Mexican boys squatted nearby.

A half-hour later she opened her eyes, and like Tessie, wondered what they would do if he didn't come back for them. Suddenly, she felt like standing in the middle of the street and screaming for help.

Before she could ponder yet more, Hempstead Grouse, still atop the wagon and whipping the mules ferociously, rounded the corner. His fine horse was tied to the back, the crate of snorting, grunting, squealing, little pigs taking up half the wagon bed.

"Get aboard, ladies, and don't dawdle." He swung down and growled at Cricket and the Mexican boys: "Load them parcels and do it *muy pronto*, golldamnit!"

Ella struggled to her feet, then fluttered her hand before her nose. "I am not ungrateful for your help in getting us to Victoria, Mister Grouse, but must you take the pigs? I'm feeling quite ill already, and their odor is nauseating."

He glowered at her as if she had just asked him to cut his own throat. Clearly, he did not intend to leave his pigs behind.

"Get in the wagon, golldamnit! Us, and them pigs, is gonna hightail it on outta here. Ain't you noticed the town's locked up tighter'n a tick in a hound's ear? This ain't no place to tarry. It's yeller fever! The 'black vomit' is coming this way sure as flies on a pile of ..." He coughed. "That's why ain't no hosses or vehicles left to rent—most the town folk done headed for the countryside in 'em, thinking to escape the sickness that usually flares up first in these seaside ports. We gotta shed this place before the quarantine's posted. I ain't going to Victoria, neither. The man I borrowed this wagon from says it's killing folks there left and right."

"Oh, my God!" Tessie screamed, and then slapped her hand to her forehead as if testing for a fever.

After Cricket helped Ella and Tessie onto the seat, Hempstead ordered him to get aboard and take the reins. Then he mounted his horse, came up next to the wagon, and snatched the whip from Cricket's hand.

"You handle them traces boy, and I'll set the pace," he said, snapping the whip hard above the mules' ears.

As the wagon lurched away from the sidewalk and headed out of town at top speed, Ella and Tessie held on for dear life. "If we survive, it will be a miracle!" Tessie cried. Ella swallowed back the bitter taste of sour beans and pork.

The mules' pounding hooves scattered the dust and anything else in their path. Bits of paper swirled up; a little square piece stuck to Ella's sleeve. Retrieving it before it could again take flight, and struggling to hold it steady, she read the words written on it in perfect penmanship:

T. Pledger's Divine Dowsing Service
If Water is below, We will know
Will Travel Texas and Beyond

Frowning, she read the words again. Surely, the T. Pledger in that advertisement was not *the* Reverend Timon Pledger—the engineer of her ill-fated marriage to Victor Faircloth. No, it couldn't be him. What in the world would a man like *Timon Pledger* be doing in *Texas,* of all places?

13

The Making of a Naked Dowser

TIMON PLEDGER HELD THE FORKED ENDS of his dowsing stick close to his groin. He stepped gingerly across the desiccated patch of crinkly brown grass, grass so short that only a persistent goat could pry it loose from its crust of dry, crete-like earth. He glanced over his shoulder at the McCarthy family—a man, his wife, and their five children. They were watching him with a fascination usually reserved for circus freaks. *That* was against the rules. Timon shot his well-practiced warning stare over his shoulder and they looked away—except for the youngest three of the McCarthy's rowdy-looking, giggling, red haired little urchins.

"Más Alto, Sandoval!" Timon hissed to the old Mexican man limping along directly behind him. He was holding up a big, colorful blanket that was supposed to shield Timon from such humiliating exposure as had just happened. More often than not, when the old man performed his boring chore, his consciousness slipped, lower and lower, into its own private orb, and the blanket followed.

"Más Alto!" Timon repeated, and then glanced around at him. "Looks like there may not be any water to find on this place, Sandoval," he said.

"You are not concentrating, my son," Sandoval replied in his kindly voice.

"Neither are you. Can't you keep that blanket up?"

"In God's eyes, it is not wicked to be naked. It is only wicked in the eyes of mortals."

"*And* funny," Timon mumbled.

"I myself would go naked each day and always," Sandoval said, "for it is the way God intended before the great sin of Adam and Eve. But, then I would be shot. It is bad enough to be *Mejicano* ... far worse to be a *naked* Mejicano."

Timon nodded. The old man's statement was droll, but true. He personally had seen Mexicans shot since coming to Texas. Some deserved it. Most didn't. A naked Mexican limping around the countryside would last about as long as it took to take aim.

Timon glanced appreciatively at his partner, marveling again at how he and Sandoval had survived their backlog of liabilities.

The McCarthy children laughed louder; someone threw a rock that missed, and then Timon heard a loud *slap,* followed by a kid bawling. Timon swore under his breath. He had a good mind to put on his clothes and go home! He'd been dowsing the McCarthys acres all morning, starting out close to the house, where Mrs. McCarthy said she'd prefer the water to be, and then he'd circled the barn and outbuildings, with no better luck.

But no, he would not give up until McCarthy waved him off. Giving up was not part of the deal he'd made on the day his water witching gift was revealed to him—the day he became *"the naked dowser."* He was remembering it now as he trudged along the McCarthy's property, waiting for his dowser stick to speak to him.

He'd been on his way to Laredo with a fine string of yearlings sired by a stolen horse—the stolen horse belonging to a man he'd made his worst enemy long before he turned horse thief. Timon winced, hating it whenever Gentry Garland crossed his mind.

Anyway, the stallion *Red Man* was his now, and he had ridden him all over Texas, just as on that memorable trip to Laredo, when he and old Sandoval, strangers at the time, found themselves in the same unsavory kettle of soup. At dusk, he had camped down in a gully, and hobbled the yearlings and Red Man nearby in a mesquite thicket. They were well out of sight of the road he had been traveling all the way from San Antonio. Tired, and confident that a rough, deep gully was the best cover for a lone traveler, he laid out his bedroll and encircled it with several coils of rope to keep the rattlesnakes off him. To his knowledge, the ropes had never been tested, unless of course he'd been asleep when the snakes were deterred. Anyhow, the ropes were a comfort, and he would not *siesta* on the ground without them. His feet itching, he shed his boots and sweaty socks, and then lay down to dream, as usual, of Ella Corrigan. It seemed that every night, as he faded from consciousness, his last drowsy thoughts were spent wondering if his dreams of her would ever cease.

He was in mid-fantasy when a sharp poke, something hard and cold dug into his cheek, and a sickening smell of rancid sweat and other things foul to the senses invaded his space, choking off his breath.

"Arriba!" the intruder yelled, jerking Timon to his bare feet and kicking him in the small of his back toward more shadowy figures coming forward to rummage through his camp. The horses whinnied, and Timon knew he was about to lose his valuable horses and, likely, his life.

Rather than kill him, his captor cracked him across the forehead with a pistol, hogtied him and threw him like a sack of corn across the back of a shaggy mustang that smelled almost as bad as its owner. After pulling on Timon's boots, the assailant mounted Red Man, grabbed the reeking mustang's reins, and jerked the animal into an excruciating gallop. Timon's bleeding head bounced so hard against the animal's ribs that he felt his neck would snap. They caught up to the whooping gang of horse thieves, and the lot of them plowed through the darkness as if they knew where they were going.

Just past sunup, they rode through the gate of a Spanish *rancho,* and then through another gate into a courtyard surrounded by high adobe walls. The ropes that had him plastered across the mustang's back like a sweaty saddle blanket were roughly jerked loose. Half-conscious, and with his head throbbing, Timon slipped into a kneeling position in the dirt and then pressed his forehead against the animal's flank to keep from toppling. A big moccasin-shod foot kicked him over onto his back, and Timon got a first look at the assailant. Long black hair, brittle looking even in its greasiness, hung like curtains around a puffy, brownish-red face. Small slits of close-set eyes, beady like a gopher's but light brown in color, looked him up and down. Atop his head was a faded and lopsided stovepipe hat, banded with a thin animal pelt entwined with red and green beads. Around his neck, a calico bonnet hung like a necklace from its strings. Timon rubbed an eye, trying to focus more closely on the odd yellow strip hanging from the bonnet; but was suddenly jerked to his feet and surrounded by maybe a dozen other aggressors in various states of dress and partial dress, including the ugly man wearing his boots.

He'd seen such men as these since coming to Texas—*Comancheros,* they mistakenly called themselves, said the old Texican he'd met in San Antonio and who'd sought to take the green off him:

"They are half-breeds, either Comanche or Apache or other Indian tribes, mixed with Spanish, white, or Mexican blood," he said. Originally, in the early years, Comancheros were Mexican traders in northern and central New Mexico that made their living by trading with the nomadic plains Indians, often wandering far into Texas. "Primarily harmless," the old Texican said, "but not *all.*" Their dynamics had changed in the last century, producing another branch of Comanchero—"an indigent and rude class"—progeny of Mexican, Anglo, and Negro women stolen in Indian raids, raped and impregnated by their Comanche, Apache, and Kiowa enslavers. Some Indians were more tolerant of half-breeds than whites; but those half-breeds not accepted by full-blooded Indians grew up in a world laced with cruelty, the consequence being "too many cur litters of thieves, murderers, plunderers and *weirdies*. Them's the scum-of-the-earth kinda Comanchero," said the old Texican.

The "scum-of-the-earth-*kinda* Comanchero" was what Timon now stared at. His wide eyes refocused on the yellow strip attached to the slatted calico bonnet around the snarling Comanchero's neck—long, wavy blond hair, hair that no doubt had once been shaded by that calico bonnet: With recognition, a mouth full of vomit shot from between Timon's clenched teeth and ran down his chin, eliciting uproarious laughter from his captors.

If he thought that the biting ropes on his bloody wrists were being cut away because these heathens had decided to allow him a bit of ease before they murdered him, the notion was quickly amended. In a matter of seconds, a blur of hands tore, like steel hooks, at his clothing until he stood buck naked … and shielding his genitals from the pokes and jabs aimed specifically in that direction, until he squatted and attempted to protect the area.

Above the unfamiliar languages grunted and screeched at him, Timon heard an English-speaking voice coming from the shaded *porche* of the hacienda—an accent-free voice of a white man, unseen behind a tangle of thick vines.

"What have you brought me, *muchachos?"*

The bunch stopped laughing and one of them—runty, and looking half-white—pointed at Red Man and the string of horses. *"Hola, Jefe!* We have brought you many fine animals, and …" he pointed at Timon while clutching his crotch in mocking translation, "one gringo *pendejo*—a hair of the nuts!"

Knowing that he would soon be dead, Timon railed back, "I know what that means, you godless trash heap, and it don't mean *that!"*

"It mean what I say it mean!" the godless trash heap cried as he kicked Timon in the head, sending him into a deep, black sleep.

~

He woke in the dead of night in a low chicken coop, still naked, hogtied, and lying on a solid scab of dried chicken manure. Bright moonlight seeped through the wide cracks in the coop, revealing a hunched, shadowy form in the opposite corner.

"You are awake, my son?" asked the shadowy form.

Timon thought he was still dreaming—it was the second time in his life someone had called him *'son.'* Was he being visited by a ghost? If so, it would not be his father, the senior Reverend Timon Pledger, for the man had never uttered the word, neither in kindness nor in anger. That terrifying zealot would never rise up from the grave and finally acknowledge his son with affection. It could only be the ghost of Ella's father, the gentle but tragic Adam Corrigan, come to escort him into the unknown.

The huddled form repeated the question, and Timon came fully awake. The thick Mexican accent was nothing like Adam Corrigan's soft, Southern drawl. The Mexican leaned forward, and Timon saw that he was *old,* and with a thick shock of white hair that touched his shoulders.

"Yes. I am awake," Timon said.

"I am Sandoval. I am to die with you."

"What have you done ... that they would kill *you,* an old man?"

"The same as you. *Nada.* My attempted crime was foiled." He arose stiffly and untied Timon's hands and feet, then he removed his woolen serape and draped it around Timon's bare shoulders.

He and old Sandoval talked quietly through the long night. The rancho had belonged to the old man's great-grandfather, and Sandoval lived and worked there for more than forty years. He had lost his parents there in a cross-fire between bandidos and Texas Rangers, lost his wife when she stole away in the night with his three sons and returned to her home high in Mexico's Sierra Madre Mountains. She was a Tarahumara Indian, not Mexican like himself, he said.

"It is only because I slapped her that she took my *bambinos* and left," he said, adding, "I only slapped her because of her sharp tongue."

"A man shouldn't strike a woman," Timon mumbled. "You should have told her you were sorry and asked her to forgive you."

The old Mexican opened his hands and shrugged. "I did so, *every time,* but always she refused to listen. I did not go after them," he said, "but stayed to protect my property. My father said a man's property is more valuable than a woman, and it is better to miss one's sons than to lose one's property."

"I don't see it that way," Timon murmured, pulling at the dried blood and grass sticking to his head.

Timon listened as the old man talked on. Indians carried his sisters away one day when they went down to the creek to catch a turtle to make *sopa de tortuga.* His relatives went back to Mexico after that, but he refused to leave his land. His stolen sisters would be old women by now, if they had lived, he said.

"I will get no dying wish, but if so, I would go see my sons before I die." With that, he became quiet for a long time. Timon asked about the white man he had heard but not seen, and Sandoval said the voice belonged to a gringo the others called "El Jefe," meaning "*the chief.*" *El jefe* and his "pendejos" came to Sandoval's rancho two weeks ago. They spared Sandoval to cook their meals, but he had yet to see *el Jefe's* face.

"You were useful to them. Why will they kill you now?"

"I cooked El Jefe a pot of my special frijoles, but he made a Negro *bandido* eat them first. The Negro died."

Timon frowned. "It's hard to see how eating beans could kill a man."

"Have you not heard of the Castor bean, my son? I ground a few of them into a fine powder and added them to *El Jefe's* bowl of my tasty frijoles. I do not know why he made the Negro eat them. Perhaps he was growing suspicious of me. It was hard sometime to hide my hatred for this man. He gave the order to kill many, two of them my nephews when they innocently came to visit me one day. I have seen it."

"You should have left him to God. I can understand why you poisoned those beans, but it ends with your own death," Timon said.

Sandoval shrugged. "He was going to kill me anyway, I know this. He wants my land ... this *rancho* ... my *hacienda*. This, even though the well is dry and there is no water for forty miles."

Sitting upright and hunkering beneath the serape, Timon wrapped his arms around his knees. "I should have known better than to set out for Laredo on my own. I should have waited for the freight wagons that make the trip."

"*Si*, you should have waited, my son. These pendejos would not attack so many wagons and men with guns."

Timon nodded, while silently acknowledging that he had always done things on impulse, hindsight preceding regret—like the day in Miz Bea's parlor when he stole Gentry Garland's letter, read it, then ripped it in half before hiding it between the pages of his Bible. He then joined the Confederate Army. Afterward, he'd settled in New Orleans, and for the first time, experienced wickedness with wine and women.

"Yes, I should have waited. Better yet, I should have stayed in New Orleans," Timon finally muttered.

"A man's fate is not changed by his location on this earth, my son."

"No, old man; his fate is changed by the evil doings of others. In my lifetime, I have been that evil. I was an ordained Minister of God, but there was a fire inside me that drove me to sin. I guess I deserve dying this way."

"*Es no bueno dar la bienvenida a muerte*—is not good to welcome death if there is evil on your soul. I am not a priest, but if you like, I will hear your sins."

Timon almost smiled. "No, thanks. I'm afraid life will be too short to hear all that I would have to confess."

"You make a joke. That is good, Preacher Timon."

After a long silence, Timon realized that Sandoval was asleep, and while he wondered how a man about to die could relax enough to sleep, he began to nod off as well. At some point, a recurring dream he'd had for years—other than those of Ella Corrigan—filled his subconscious mind. Perhaps old Sandoval's lament about his dried-up water well induced the familiar dream.

In his dream he was a small boy, scurrying to keep up with his grandfather, a tall, wise-faced man with a long, bushy gray beard. He was clutching a forked stick to his groin as he tramped slowly and steadily across a field. When the stick began to bounce lightly up and down, quivering, as if some great source was forcing it downward … downward … his grandfather marked the spot with a wooden stake. He then called Timon over to hammer the stake deeper into the earth with the wooden mallet he had handed him earlier. Afterward, Timon watched his uncles dig all day at the spot, shoring the deepening hole with big timbers … until water seeped up and filled it. He'd watched his *divining* grandfather find water dozens of times all across the county.

Timon awoke with a start, a pain in his side where someone had kicked him. Rough hands jerked him to his feet and then shoved him from the coop. Panicked, and trying to cling to the safe image of his grandfather dowsing for water, he didn't resist as rough hands dragged him across the courtyard. His only struggle was mustering enough spit to moisten his mouth that had suddenly gone as dry as ashes. He'd felt close to death several times the past few years, but never feared it until now, when it was imminent.

He managed to twist his head enough to see old Sandoval hustling along behind him.

Suddenly, the serape was jerked away, and he was naked again. A hard kick to his backside sent him to his knees. Sandoval landed on his face nearby, and then scrambled up to kneel beside him.

El jefe, still unseen, yelled out from the shade of the hacienda: "I'll give you a minute to say your prayers, pendejos."

Sandoval leaned close and whispered in Timon's ear, "Preacher Timon, unless God strikes them dead, they will slit our throats. That is their way to kill a man."

Timon began to tremble, his thoughts so scattered that he did not realize that he had thrown his hands high over his head and was waving them in the air and yelling—yelling at the utmost timbre of his voice!

"Jefe! Jefe! I can fill a well for you! I can find water! This *rancho* is no good to you without water!"

There was a long silence, and then laughter all around. The killer's knife poised closer to his neck. Panic rose in Timon's throat and then spilled out in a Biblical roar:

"I am a man of *God!* I have … I have a gift! A *power!"*

"Then use it against my men to free yourself," El jefe called out, and chuckled.

"It isn't that kind of power! It is a power that allows me to find underground water!" He had fallen back on a tactic of mistruths many times in recent years, but never one like *this*—a lie gleaned from the memory of last night's dream. If they let him try to find water, maybe he could escape into the wide mesquite thicket that lay two hundred yards beyond the gate.

"You have nothing to lose in letting me try! If I succeed, I would like my horse and … and Sandoval. You can keep the yearlings."

El Jefe's laughter rose even above the roars from his men.

Timon yelled louder. "Not an unreasonable request for a well full of cool water in a place that has not seen rain since God knows when!" He waved his arms in a sweeping circle.

Another long silence. Then El Jefe called out: "The old man must sign his land over to me."

At Timon's urgent nodding, Sandoval finally said, *"Si."*

"All right. But how will you do your water witching, preacher?" El Jefe laughed again, evidently enjoying himself. "You'll need a dowser stick, or maybe you're planning on using that *pequeña ramita* between your legs."

Relieved, Timon darted a quick look around for a hickory or willow tree, but saw only Mesquite. But what difference did it make? There was not a chance in heaven or hell that he could find water.

He'd tear off a forked mesquite branch, go through the motions of dowsing, and look for his opportunity to escape; hoping old Sandoval could do the same.

"I will need my clothes."

"No. Give him back his boots, Tito," El Jefe said to the evil-looking man wearing them. "We don't want his bare feet so stabbed with goathead burrs that he can't concentrate on his *powers*."

The boots struck him hard in the stomach, and Timon sat down on the ground, pulled them on, then jumped to his feet, brushing red ants from his backside.

"I will need Sandoval to follow me with a few stakes … for when I find the water."

"Just holler when you find it. Tito won't be far behind you. He'll have your stakes … and a close bead on your shiny ass should you try to get too far ahead of him."

Timon knew despair as Sandoval was tossed back into the chicken coop. He found a forked mesquite branch, and Tito hacked it free with a big machete that looked sharp enough to lop off a man's head. Clutching the forked ends, Timon lowered it, level, well below his waist, the same as he had seen his fully clothed grandfather do—and began divining around the courtyard.

The slower he walked, the faster his life passed before his eyes. He would be dead soon, one way or another. Tito would kill him if he tried to escape, and El Jefe, obviously already aware of his lie, would kill him when he grew tired of humiliating the stark-naked '*pendejo*' wearing only his boots and a look of panic.

In desperation, and even while knowing the hopelessness of this crazy endeavor, Timon tried to focus on his grandfather—the expression on the old man's face as he worked, the terrifying intensity of his eyes, the way he insisted on complete silence.

"How did you find that water, Grandpa?" the boy Timon had asked one day after witnessing a find.

"The water talks to me."

"I didn't hear anything."

"It don't talk out loud like you and me are a'talking, boy. It and me got a connection. I reckon I could dangle a watch chain or just about anything over it and it'd talk to me ... long as I was listening just to *it* and nothing else."

"But if it don't talk out loud, Grandpa ... how?"

"When I get close to it, it starts talking to me like a chill wind feels when it hits your face. It comes up at me through the sticks, into my hands and into my belly way down low ... a chill that shrivels my innards. The bigger that underground vein of water is, the tighter that chill shrivels my innards. That's how I mostly find them good wells, and don't pay no mind to the *little* breezes that don't shrivel much—them little shallow veins will play out after a while."

"Can I find water, Grandpa? Will it talk to me?"

"You can if you concentrate on nothing else ... and if you got the *power*."

The next day, Timon took his grandfather's willow stick and sneaked out back to the family's water well. If he had the power and he concentrated, he'd feel the chill.

But it never happened. He even climbed up on a crate and held the dowser stick directly over the open well, and it did not happen. Earlier, Grandma had said that God liked Grandpa better than He liked most folks, and that's why Grandpa had the power. Timon gave up and ran into the house—a bit sad that he had not inherited God's fondness for his grandpa.

Timon waved a fly from his nose with the mesquite stick, unable to get his mind off that boyhood day when he tried his hand at dowsing. *"Concentrate on nothing but the water,"* his grandfather had said. But the boy, Timon, always hungry in those days, had concentrated *mostly* on his empty stomach that morning.

Suddenly, Timon settled the mesquite branch lower on his groin, did a slow about-face, and trudged back toward the *hacienda* to the spot where he had started out. The Comancheros lounging about the grounds yelled obscenities at him then laughed.

"What the hell you doing, *pendejo*?" El Jefe growled.

Briefly wondering why El Jefe hid from sight and spoke only from behind the scrolled iron lattices around the *hacienda,* Timon yelled back:

"I respectfully request that you quiet these men! If I am to find your water—that you desperately need if you are to live here for long—I must have complete silence so that I can … concentrate my powers."

El Jefe laughed, and then barked out an order that resulted in a dead silence.

Timon glanced at the chicken coop and saw Sandoval peering through the slats at him. Then, staring straight ahead through half-closed eyes, he moved off across the courtyard, the two ends of the forked stick held tightly in each fist … the fists held tightly against the soft tissue of his groin well below his stark white hipbones.

He made turn after turn around the courtyard imagining … concentrating … trying to converse with … *water*. Soon, his mind seemed to go someplace else, and it was as if a wall had settled around him and he heard nothing of the outside world. Suddenly, he pictured water. Water *dripping*. Water *gushing*. Water *flowing*. Water rising higher and higher until his brain had filled with it! He could *feel* it there, *see* it with his mind's eye, *smell* it with his senses, and then … he *heard* it! The dowser stick quivered then pulled downward … downward … to bounce atop his shockingly erect penis! It was all he could do to keep the mesquite stick from ripping from his hands! Then, '*the chill*' his grandfather told him about sped up through the forks and blasted into his groin, tensing his innards. He let out a stunned cry, his eyes going huge with the shock of discovery.

He fell to his knees on the spot and drew a circle with the Mesquite stick. "Your supply of water is … *here*," he called out to El Jefe, jabbing the stick into the earth, "and it's a big one!"

He and Sandoval had to dig the well before they could leave; it took them a week, and then the water flowed. Sandoval signed over the deed to his land, but if Timon thought he would learn *El Jefe* identity at the signing, he was wrong; the grantee was left blank, no doubt to be filled in later if question of the land's ownership ever came up.

That was how he came to be the naked dowser. At the threshold of a gory death, and in a Godforsaken place fit only for snakes and scorpions, he'd discovered his purpose in life. Repeatedly after that, he'd tried it fully clothed, but it never worked. Maybe the humiliation of nakedness was meant to be a reminder that *blessings* had nothing to do with obtaining forgiveness for past sins, such as he'd committed in Miz Bea's parlor that time—he still needed absolution, but not from God.

Then again, maybe his necessary nakedness was punishment for the murder he'd committed after El Jefe allowed him and Sandoval to ride away from the rancho, both astraddle Red Man and glancing over their shoulders at Tito following close behind them.

"Tito will escort you off my property," said El Jefe with a chuckle, as he waved goodbye to them from his hiding spot behind the lattice, and then addressed the grinning Tito. "A mile or so should be far enough, amigo," he said.

Sandoval leaned forward and whispered in Timon's ear, "Tito is going to kill us and bury us, my son. Do you not see the shovel he tied to his saddle? El Jefe will not allow this magnificent animal we are riding to slip through his hands."

"They kept my gun," Timon whispered, trying to keep this new fear from showing in his voice. "It was in the sack of vittles they robbed me of."

"Aw!" Sandoval hissed in disgust. "A man should wear his weapon on his person, not in a sack!" He glanced over his shoulder again, waited a few seconds, and then whispered, "Almost a mile from here, there are a few trees. When we have ridden to them, shove me from the horse and curse me, and then run away as fast as this animal will go. I will kill this Tito as he passes me by to chase after you."

"But how? That's impossible!"

"Unlike you, my son, I keep my weapon on my person, and it is sharp. I buried it in the chicken coop until I found need of it. It will fly from my fingers like a bullet."

"I … I don't know. What if you miss?"

"Then you must keep running. *Este caballo es muy rápido.* Your fine animal will carry you away from this foul man. While he is chasing you, I will hide where he cannot find me."

"No. No. It's too risky."

"Then you must tell me *your* plan, my son."

Timon bowed to the old man's sarcasm, and they rode in silence, urged to a full trot by the impatient Tito. Finally, the trees were visible in the distance.

"There aren't but four skimpy saplings up there, and not one low thicket, Sandoval—not enough cover for hiding if your knife misses its target."

"Bueno," Sandoval shrugged. "I am an old man. I have nothing left to do but die."

But the plan soured shortly before they reached the trees and Tito ordered them to dismount. Timon stiffened as he felt a length of something cold against his back, and then realized that Sandoval had slipped a distressingly long knife down his belt!

"Take the opportunity when I give it, my son," Sandoval whispered, as the two of them slipped to the ground, at which time the old man's legs seemed to go rubbery. He quickly pressed his two hands into the dirt to steady himself, arising slowly to face Tito, who had also dismounted and was coming toward them.

Timon had come to believe that men did unfathomable things mostly by accident rather than by an awareness of what they were doing. He was wrong. They did them out of fear. He knew it the moment Sandoval threw his two handfuls of dirt into Tito's unsuspecting eyes, yelling, *"Apuñalar le! Apuñalar le!"* and he had obeyed, stabbing Sandoval's dagger deep into Tito's chest.

They dug two graves and buried Tito in one of them, hoping that when he did not return to the rancho, El Jefe would think Tito had killed them, buried them, and then, after deciding to keep Red Man for himself, rode off to parts unknown.

Timon urged Sandoval to escape to his relatives in Mexico, but Sandoval declined.

"You will need someone to stay awake while you sleep, my son."

Another sarcasm of truth, Timon thought, as he bowed to the old Mexican's sharp observation.

The pair had been together ever since, with Timon earning a good livelihood by dowsing for water all over Texas, and studding out Red Man along the way. Old Sandoval brandished his colorful blanket to protect Timon's dignity, and his sarcasm to keep Timon alert—a good edict to follow in a land historically dangerous to innocents like the former Reverend Timon Pledger of Christ Episcopal Church in Savannah, Georgia.

When Timon discovered that he could find water only when fully disrobed, then said it was too humiliating and he wouldn't do it anymore, Sandoval had answers.

"It is God's way to make you humble, my son. It is the way a man must be if he has sinned and he wants to see heaven."

"Going naked in broad daylight with people staring at me doesn't make me humble, Sandoval, it makes me mortified."

"What is this '*mortified*'?"

"*Humiliated,*" Timon answered.

Sandoval thought a moment. "Your humiliation must be what God is charging you for the power He let you have." Then Sandoval went on to assure him of the importance that a man's willingness to be "mortified" plays when God chooses him to be one of his earthly messengers—in Timon's case, a *diviner* ... a water dowser ... a very much *naked dowser.*

Having once been a preacher, albeit a sinful one, Timon believed in heavenly gifts. How could he not believe? His dowsing worked. He could find water. Pinpoint its exact location. Doing it in the nude was a small price to pay God for such a gift, he decided. He, in turn, was paid plenty by the appreciative cattlemen and farmers, like the McCarthys.

The McCarthys yelled with delight as Timon, now fully shielded behind Sandoval's outstretched blanket, pulled on the shirt and pants that had been draped over Sandoval's shoulder. He strapped on the six-shooter Sandoval handed him. He'd been wearing his weapon on his body for some time now, and had even learned how to use it.

Dressed and still frowning at the McCarthy children that had begun giggling again, he motioned for Mr. McCarthy to bring the stakes.

"It's a big one," Timon said to McCarthy, as the man handed him a fistful of United States greenbacks.

14

In Company of a Nasty Old Man

"GOLLDAMNIT, WOMAN!" Hempstead grouse railed at Tessie, as he leaned from his horse to crack the whip hard against the wagon's dashboard. "Like I been telling you the past thirty miles, there *ain't* no houses we can stop at on this here route, and I'm getting tired of your asking! I'm taking Miz Gent Garland straight as a crow flies to her husband before she ups and pops that kid out on me. Now climb on back there and see to her!" He wagged his head backward, motioning to where Ella now lay on a crumpled tarpaulin in the wagon bed.

"How dare you, Mister Grouse! I will not lift my limbs to climb over this seat!"

Hempstead snickered. "Bet you ain't never lifted a 'limb' on nothing, have ya, Miss Pecken-*what-ever-your-name-is*."

"Mister Grouse!"

Grumbling, he ordered Cricket to halt the mules.

Tessie, oblivious to all but getting down from the wagon—and perhaps to show youthful agility—hopped to the ground, and immediately let out a piecing scream.

"Ow! Ow!" she cried.

"Well, I'll be a-! What'd you, do?" Hempstead yelled. "Break your damn foot? That's all I need!"

"You just never mind!" she yelled back, and then gave out a little sob as she clutched the side of the wagon, and began a slow, one-legged hop to the rear. Moaning with pain, she crawled past the trunks and pig crate to Ella's side.

Mumbling, Hempstead dismounted and tied his horse to the tailgate. He flopped heavily onto the driver's seat and stripped the reins from Cricket's hands. Cricket immediately jumped over the seat to sit atop the pig crate.

"Get back up here, boy," Hempstead gruffed, "unless Miss Pecken-*whatever-her-name-is* ... says you gotta sit there and suffer them pigs a'sniffing at your black ass."

"Mister Grouse, you are beyond crude!" Tessie cried. "And my name is *Miss Tessie Peckenpaugh*. Unless you can address me properly, do not speak to me at all!"

"I damn well wish I didn't hafta *look* at you at all, woman."

"Well, why don't you just turn your head around and stop looking at me then?"

"I ain't lookin' at you, gollda-!"

"You *were*!"

"You must be as blind as you are tetched!"

"My eyesight is perfect, thank you very much!"

"Well, count your blessings, *Miss* Tessie Peckenpaugh—I guess you ain't no total mistake of nature, after all!"

"Oh! Why don't you just shut that nasty old mouth?" Tessie's voice cracked on the last three words.

Ella, having lain quietly for miles, finally cried out to her squabbling companions. "For heaven's sake, please stop your bickering!" They did so, and she closed her eyes, giving in to her complete exhaustion.

Sometime later, Ella wakened to a star-filled night, the sounds of the squeaking wagon wheels intermingling with the distant howl of coyotes and the lonely hooting of an owl somewhere out on the moon-washed prairie. Tessie lay snoring softly on the canvas beside her. Ella struggled up on her elbows and was immediately surprised by how heavy her head felt.

"Mister Grouse, is it much further?"

He laughed, as if she had made a joke. "Well, lemme see," he drawled. "From Port of Lavaca to Gent's place, I'd say it's about seventy-five miles—a little mor'n a day and a half more of me staring at these mules behinds, is my guess."

"What?" she gasped.

He pulled the mules to a halt, slipped a watch from his vest, and tilted it to the moonlight. "It's two o'clock. We been on the go 'bout twelve hours, at not-too-fast a clip, account of your condition, Miz Garland. You and the old gal's been sleeping through most of it, and giving my ears a mighty nice rest."

Ella stared at the back of his head. "A whole day and a half *more?"*

Tessie rose up and rubbed her eyes. "Where are we? What time is it?"

"Which answer do you want first?" Hempstead asked, and without waiting for an answer, continued: "We're still in Texas, and the time is crawling."

"I need to ... walk about a bit," Tessie said in a hushed tone.

"Why don't you just say you need to do your personals? We all do it, you know ... ain't no way around it. There's a little patch of low bushes yonder," he said, pointing.

"Stop there, then," Tessie said frostily.

"I'm gonna do that, woman. I got the urge myself. I'll just step behind the wagon whilst you're gone. You might watch out for them seven-foot rattlers when you find your spot, *Miss* Peckenpaugh," he added with a chuckle."

"You are a cruel man, Mister Grouse," Tessie said.

"I ain't kidding you this time," he replied.

Ella, feeling her own need, crawled behind Tessie to the end of the wagon. Tessie, still grimacing with pain, immediately leaned on her.

"Oh Ella, I am so miserable. My lumbago has me in terrible agony and now my ankle," Tessie mumbled, as they pulled up their profusion of petticoats and skirts, and then squatted behind the fullest bush. Ella felt so unwell that she could not muster an ounce of sympathy for Tessie's discomfort. Then, as she stood and shook her skirt and petticoats into place, she suddenly bent double, the urge to vomit constricting her stomach. The taste of soured beans and pork coated her tongue, but even after repeated heaving, nothing came up.

Finally, after helping Tessie back to the wagon, and lying exhausted on the canvas, Ella snapped at Hempstead, "Were you telling the truth about the distance, Mister Grouse, or were you having more sport with us, as you seem to enjoy so much."

"When we cross the Guadalupe River, it might be three hours, more or less."

"How many miles to the river?"

"'Bout thirty-five. We might make five miles per hour … mebbe three, going this here pace," he said. "You might just as well sit back and concentrate on not having that kid yet, and I'll concentrate on making this here ride as gentle on you as possible."

~

After several stops to rest the mules, Hempstead glanced over his shoulder, and mumbled: "You want a long-shot view of the Guadalupe? It's showing up pretty good in the moonlight."

Ella pulled her sweat-drenched collar away from her throat, and with great difficulty, sat up to peer over the seat as the wagon reached the top of a hill.

"There she is," Hempstead growled. "She's only half her banks, without no rain to speak of in nigh on three years. Still, low as she is, she's a welcome sight to man and animal. We'll be on Garland land in another few miles."

The river, glistening in the distance, reminded Ella of Gentry's description of his ranch lands—miles of gently rolling hills that lay between the Guadalupe River on the north, and the San Antonio River on the south.

"In my husband's boasts about this insufferably hot place, he said his land was between *two* rivers; where is the other—or was his brain permanently damaged from living so long in this heat?"

Hempstead laughed. "The San Antone's thirty miles that way." He pointed south. "Your husband owns mor'n a few little city blocks that can be took in with a short gander, ma'am—although he's sold some outer pieces of it in recent years, but I'm sure you know all 'bout that," he said, and laughed again. "After we've crossed that there Guadalupe, we'll be twix both rivers, even if ya can't see t'uther."

Tessie, sitting on the wagon bed with her back purposely to Hempstead Grouse, twisted around to stare. "Cross that river? No! I am not crossing that river in this thing!" she cried, and slapped the floorboards, as she loudly exclaimed: "*Drown*! We shall *drown! Drown! Drown!* I will not do it! I will not do it!" She burst into tears.

"Christ-all-mighty, woman!" Hempstead glowered at her, and then addressed Ella. "A body can just wade across in some places, and that's another reason I come this way. The Guadalupe's low as a cow's belly in this here spot cause of the god- ... golldamn drought."

Tessie grabbed Ella's arm. "We cannot be sure it is that low, Ella. It looks deep. Very deep!" She let out a series of long, mournful whimpers. "And look how steep the bank is!"

Ella was surprised when Hempstead Grouse's only response was to click his tongue at the mules as he pulled them around to travel in an angular path alongside the river rather than fording it.

"What are you doing? Where are you going?" Tessie asked, her hands gripping the backrest of the seat as she stared up at Hempstead, her eyes so filled with fear they appeared unable to blink.

"Going a mile outta my way just to please *you, Miss* Tessie Peckenpaugh ... a place in the river so dry, you could choke on it—if my luck was to take a good turn and you truly *was* to choke."

"You are a rude, rude, man, Mister Grouse," she huffed, then added, "I pity your wife … if you have one."

He let out a string of hiccupped laughter. "No, I ain't married, *Miss* Peckenpaugh, but you can forget it."

"Forget what? Oh! If you were the last man on earth, Hempstead Grouse, I would not …"

"Well, let's say I *am* the last man on earth. I'm turning you down."

She glared up at him, her thin lips twisting on a tornado of silent words; but when Ella weakly touched her wrist, she ducked around, obviously deciding to end their banter.

The creaking of the wagon, joined by the distant howling and yipping of coyotes, kept Ella from further rest. Nevertheless, she was tired, the kind of overwhelming fatigue a woman feels *after* childbirth; but she was feeling it *now*, and with her pain steadily increasing. Would she have her baby on a dirty wagon bed, next to a crate of snorting and snuffling pigs, and in the presence of the foulest old man she had ever met—and with only the twittery, jittery Tessie Peckenpaugh to help her?

She hung her head over the side of the wagon each time the urge to vomit struck her, but like each time before, nothing came up. The breezeless night, even without the sun burning down on them, was stifling. She became increasingly dizzy. Lying flat on the tarp, she looked up at Tessie sitting next to her. The distraught woman had rolled her sleeves high, and in the moonlight, Ella could see the sweat glistening on her stark white skin, as she madly fanned herself with her handkerchief. Cricket had not uttered a sound since ordered from atop the pig crate to sit next to Hempstead Grouse. Plainly, he was petrified; she had to admit that so was she, a bit.

Caught in another wave of dizziness, Ella dropped a wrist over her eyes, wondering if she was dreaming. Traveling so close to the river, she smelled familiar river smells like, when back home at Greenpoole, wood smoke, mixed with the excessive piquancy of plant, animal, and fish, drifted over the road.

Wood smoke? She pulled herself up on her elbows again, looking left and right. Were they at the end of their journey? Had she actually fallen asleep and slept through the river crossing and the miles that Hempstead Grouse said would follow?

"Stay down," Hempstead said, "'til I see who's cooking on that campfire up ahead. Looks like a bunch of 'em." Without another word, he handed Cricket the reins, slipped both six-shooters from their holsters, and then crossed his arms casually across his knees, holding the guns low.

"Do you think we could be in danger, Mister Grouse?" Ella whispered weakly.

"Who knows what kinda off-shoots of the human race is up there," he growled. "For a long spell in these parts, life was mighty cheap, and death even cheaper—some folks still think so."

Tessie, huffing in fear, scrunched her bony body closer to Ella, as if she were trying to burrow beneath her. Ella, remembering the many disturbing stories she had heard about the wildness of Texas, dropped an arm heavily over Tessie's trembling shoulders. Had they come all this way only to be murdered, and in an area so remote that their bodies would be bleached bones by the time someone found them, if ever?

"Aw, hell, it's just them damn Bartons," Hempstead growled, holstering his six-shooters. "We ain't stopping," he added. "They're about as friendly as a nest of badgers. I ain't ever cottoned to 'em or any of their kin —'specially them we done hung."

As the wagon rolled past the camp, Ella and Tessie rose up at the same time to stare at the Bartons—the hard-faced old woman, her male companion, the two small boys and three little girls—all of whom stood watching them. When the pregnant girl wearing the shabby long coat saw Ella, she broke away from the others and ran alongside the wagon. With one small hand holding onto the wagon's side-rail and the other pressed to her massive belly, she stared into Ella's surprised eyes.

"Air you all right?" she asked, in a twangy accent more *Arkansas* than Texan, and as if they were old acquaintances.

"I ... am. Are you?"

"I reckon so. What's your name?"

"Ella. I'm Ella Gar..." A harsh cry from the camp interrupted her.

"Molly! Get on back here! Air you a'asking for another whupping?"

"That's *me—Molly*. Molly Barton," she said to Ella, and smiled. She let go of the side-rail, and Ella watched her turn and walk briskly back to the camp, her little hands clamped beneath her big belly as if carrying a great burden.

"Got the nerve of a dimwit, that one—comin' up to you like that," Hempstead growled.

"She's no dimwit, Mister Grouse. Just a poor child in an unspeakable situation."

"I'd say you're right. But don't be planning on feeling sorry for her. You don't want nothing to do with that bunch. They're crazy worthless. We just hanged her grandpa and uncle down in Galveston for stealing a man's horses, killing him, and then setting his house afire before hightailing it back down here. I arrested the sorry scum and took 'em both back to Galveston to get their necks stretched."

"Surely that poor girl was not to blame for what her relatives did?"

"Nope, and none of them with her tonight; but they's all trash from the same heap. They was in Galveston to watch the hangings and see to the burials. That's how come we all ended up on the same boat coming back."

Ella could not hold back her sarcasm. "I thought you might have gone there to buy yourself a couple of little pigs."

He cackled. "You ain't too sick to be contrary, are ya? I'll have it known them two little shoats ain't no ordinary *American* pigs. They is *French* pigs ... come all the way across the ocean from France. A right good friend of mine in Victoria ordered 'em for herself from her homeland. Gonna raise a few hogs to sell, as a *sideline*. I plan on delivering 'em two little French squealers to that sweet little *Mademoiselle*," he said, chuckled, and added, "just as soon as I know there ain't no more yeller fever in Victoria. She's a mighty fine squealer herself after a few shots a'good whiskey. Fact, there's always five or six of them fancy little French gals in her fine *parlor*. Mayhap she'll invite you two ladies over for tea if you visit Victoria for a little culture."

Ella rolled her eyes, ignoring him, refusing to allow him the satisfaction of thinking he had succeeded in shocking her again; it had finally dawned on her that he enjoyed himself at her and Tessie's expense. She twisted onto her side and drew up her legs as another pain throbbed slowly through her lower spine. Her labor had begun in earnest, and in four or five hours at most, she would have this baby.

Tessie was gazing up at Hempstead. "Mademoiselle has a tea parlor, Mister Grouse?" She gave out a forlorn sigh. "I would so enjoy a cup of tea in a nice cozy parlor," she said, then glared at him as he guffawed.

Sometime later, Tessie hovered on her knees to gaze over the seat. "Look! There's a big house up there, Ella," she cried, and pointed. "It is a beautiful house ... so large. Look at those pillars! Why, it looks like one of our Savannah homes. Is that *it*? Is that Gentry's home?"

"Nope," Hempstead replied. "That's the Rawls place. They're cattlemen now, as well as the planters they were before the war—cotton, cattle and corn, and ain't doing too good at nary one in this drought—like all the rest here 'bouts."

"Oh my, how inviting their home appears. Will we stop there for a rest, and perhaps some tea?" Tessie asked breathlessly.

"Yup, you'll be getting all the tea you can handle, I reckon."

Weak with pain and feeling the sour contents of her stomach racing up her throat and then down again, Ella swallowed hard at the bitterness. "How much farther to my husband's home, Mister Grouse?"

"Three or four hours, I'd say, going this slow. If we stay on that trail straight ahead, it'll lead us right smack-dab to Gent's front gate a little ways after we cross the river."

"Then we mustn't stop. I need to keep going … because …" she waited for the stab of pain to subside before continuing, "because I don't think I am able to … to leave this wagon."

"Oh Ella, of course you can," Tessie cried. "Won't you please allow us a small respite from this dreadful bouncing and bumping? I would so much like a cup of tea. Besides, my sprained limb is swollen, and in need of a poultice."

"No, Tessie. You can have your poultice when we get to Hannah. Mister Grouse said we will be there soon, and I need to keep going."

"Oh, Ella!" Tessie gave out a loud wail of disappointment.

"You'll get your golldamn tea and poultice, woman. We're sure as hell gonna stop at the Rawls," Hempstead growled. He glanced over the seat at Ella, and added, "A wagon ain't no place to birth a baby, Miz Garland. I'll go in and tell Miz Rawls to get a bed ready."

Although suddenly filled with frustration at this coarse old man's indifference to her wishes, Ella did not have the strength to protest. She closed her eyes and firmed her mouth—this time in anger rather than pain. She wished she could be rid of him *and* Tessie—now that she knew she was on the trail that would *"lead us right smack-dab to Gent's front gate"* … and to Hannah whom she knew would deliver this baby just as she had delivered Adam and Seth. Hannah would know what to do about this terrible sick feeling … would cure her the way the old servant had been curing her and Honor's ills since they were babies.

As the wagon stopped in front of the Rawls house, Ella struggled up on her elbows. She watched Hempstead help Tessie down, and then she watched their receding backs as they passed through a white-washed gate. Hempstead cast a long look over his shoulder at her.

"Me and this boogered up old gal will wake the house, Miz Garland. Soon as them folks inside has changed out'n their night clothes, I'll damn well guarantee Miz Rawls and the whole damn house will rush right out to you a'clucking like a bunch'a hens over a fresh-hatched batch of chicks."

"Oh yes, Ella dear," Tessie cried out. "They will get you right into a nice soft bed." Then Tessie sweetly addressed Hempstead: "Do you think they will have lemon, Mister Grouse? I do like fresh lemon in my tea."

"If the drought ain't stunted 'em, Miz Rawls got lemons big as oranges. Grows 'em her own self," Hempstead said. "While you're a'sipping your lemoned-up tea, I just might bend an elbow myself, but not with no damn tea."

No sooner had the door closed behind the pair, Ella whispered to Cricket. "I can't stay here. I need Hannah …"

"Yes'sum," he whispered back, "but what we gonna do? Miss Tessie bound on having her tea, and Mista Grouse act like he all for it."

"Untie Mister Grouse's horse from the wagon and shoo him away."

"Huh?"

"Hurry!" she said, and then fell weakly back to the canvas.

Cricket stared at her only a second before hopping to the chore, obviously happy with her plan to leave the scary old white man afoot, even if it also meant leaving Miss Tessie behind.

As Hempstead Grouse's horse galloped off in the direction they had just traveled, Cricket leapt onto the seat and slashed the whip down hard on the mules' rumps, and then spent the next hour glancing fearfully over his shoulder.

15

Something Other Than a Fast Horse and a Poke Full'a Pesos

HEMPSTEAD GROUSE HAD LIVED ALL HIS LIFE without feeling obligated to anyone other than himself. He was a hard man doing a hard man's work, and doing it since the age of thirteen. Not once, during those fifty-two years of selective embroilments, had he done one damn thing he didn't want to do—except for tonight.

Hempstead's thoughts meandered from place to place as he rode along on a borrowed horse looking for Stonewall. Were it not for this peculiar turn of events, he'd be back there sipping old man Rawls' good whiskey, and making the old fart and his Missus cringe at tales of his rangering days with the likes of old friends, Jack Hays and Bigfoot Wallace. However, like Jack and Bigfoot, he was a man of duty, and duty was calling him to finish what he'd started, even if he was as galled about it as a peed-on hornytoad about having to hunt for his horse. Anger aside, he had never "beat the devil around the stump" and he wouldn't do it now: No sirree! He'd been called a lot of things in his life, but never a shirker.

'Tweren't no toss-up to who he'd go after first—his horse or Gent Garland's wife. A good horse like Stonewall was a value that disappeared real fast in these parts if a man didn't keep a peeled eye on him. He'd had to hunt down one damn horse thief already who'd taken Stonewall from in front of Mademoiselle's parlor in Victoria last New Year's Eve. He caught the bastard just this side'a Cuero over in DeWitt County and hung the sons-a'bitch on the spot. Damn thief tried to say Stonewall followed his heated mare out of town. A man who couldn't tell a gelding from a stud hoss was too damn stupid to live.

Hempstead spied Stonewall near a clump of oaks. The animal didn't move as he approached. Groaning, he hefted himself into the saddle. He was damn stoved up from bouncing on that wagon seat hour after hour. He was an *equestrian;* not no damn mule whacker. Astraddle a horse, a man could relieve himself upward by way of his stirrups every now and then, taking the pressure off his bone-and-hide rear-end. Tit for tat, riding an easy-gait horse beat the hell out of bucking on a hard wagon seat for any length of time—especially with *Miss* Tessie Peckenpaugh harping in his ear the whole damn way!

"Gent can send somebody after the old Peckenpaugh gal in a few days, but it ain't gonna be me," he muttered, as he led the borrowed horse into the Rawls' barn.

Soon, he and Stonewall followed the wagon tracks.

~

In the bright moonlight, Hempstead saw the wagon stuck in the shallows of the river, and the Negro boy out front tugging on the mules' harnesses. Even as he noticed the two trunks broken open and the ladies' personals scattered in the muddy water, he saw that his French pigs were missing from their crate.

He nudged Stonewall into a slow walk, coming up on the scene without a sound. Cricket yelped at the sight of him, and then his face went slack with relief.

"Glory to th' Lawd! You has found us!" For the first time, he gazed at Hempstead with emotion other than fear. "We's got stuck in the mud, Mista Grouse, suh … and something bad done happen!"

"Shetup! You wanna wake the whole damn countryside?" Hempstead hissed. "We got three kinda folks in Texas, boy—the good, the bad, and them that ain't decided yet. Can't never tell just which one might hear your caterwauling and come a'running."

"Them bad ones done been here, Mista Grouse!"

Hempstead nudged his horse up alongside the wagon and peered down into the flat bed. She lay on her back, her damp hair sticking like wet coils to the dirty canvas. Her eyes, queerly glazed, blinked up at him, as her dry lips moved with silent words. Her jacket was missing its buttons and gaping open. Hempstead leaned from his horse and squinted for a closer look at the red scratches on her neck and half-exposed bosoms.

Cricket stared at Hempstead through stricken eyes. "Miss Ella was getting sicker and sicker as we go along, but she tell me to keep going and don't you stop for nothing!"

Hempstead slid to the ground, walked to the rear of the wagon, and dropped the tailgate. Reaching in, he gripped one of Ella's limp arms, slid a hand beneath her knees, and pulled her crosswise to the end of the wagon. Cricket clutched the side rail.

"We was doing just fine 'til we start to cross the river and got stuck in the mud. Then, three men come riding up, and Miss Ella, sick as she was, was sure glad to see 'em, thinking they was gonna help us." He drew a deep breath, and wagged his head as if to say how wrong she was. He pointed across the narrow stretch of river to trees near the bank.

"One of them bad men stayed over there behind them big trees whilst the other two come right up to us. They was laughing and talking in a way I couldn't make no sense of. They was dressed might strange, too."

"What'd they look like?" Hempstead said, while glaring at his empty pig crate.

"One of 'em wore a tall hat like the fine gent'mens back home used to wear 'fore the war. He had a woman's bonnet round his neck wid some long yellow hair hanging on it. He was *bad! Real bad!* He jump in back with Miss Ella and tear her dress open and find her money pouch she got hid!"

"If the skunk had a scar down his chin like somebody had split it wide open, he's a rotten Comanchero called Rabbit Jack—an offshoot of the worst kind," Hempstead growled.

"He had a black streak painted down his chin," Cricket said.

"That's him." Hempstead pressed a palm to Ella's forehead. "The sons-a'bitch traveled a fur piece from his home ground, coming this far north of his territory. What'd the other two look like?"

"I was too scared to see much, 'cept the one that scatter Miss Ella's and Miss Tessie's trunks in the mud wudn't no white man. He wudn't no black man, neither… was more like that Rabbit Jack. The third one always keep 'hind them trees." Cricket paused to nod, as if confirming his thoughts. "*He* was *white*."

"He was white? So you did get a look at him," Hempstead said, as he removed his palm from Ella's forehead.

"No suh, I didn't see him, but he *sound* like he was white. When Rabbit Jack come at Miss Ella wid a big knife, she holler out and sayed her husband is *Gen'te Garland* and he gonna pay good money for his wife and unborn chil'! Then that white man holler at Rabbit Jack to leave her be."

"That wouldn't do it," Hempstead said. "They would'a took her with 'em if they wanted ransom, unless they knew Gent well enough to be damn scared of him."

"I thought that there Rabbit Jack was gonna kill us anyhow, but that white man sound like he getting real mad, and holler again, 'Leave the woman and her nigger alone!' he say. 'If you gots to cut something, slit them pigs' throats and bring 'em along. I'm hungry for some good ol' pork ribs.'"

"Son-of-a-bitch!!!"

"Miss Ella seem a might more sick after they is gone. She sayed she can't swaller, her mouth so dry. That Rabbit Jack done take our water jug, so I gots to walk a ways down yonder to find water that ain't mud and carry it in my hat. When I get back, she done pass out." He paused to point at Ella. "She been like that ever since."

Hempstead took a canteen and blanket from his saddlebags and, as he went back to the wagon with them, he drew a wicked-looking pearl-handled knife from under the tail of his dusty black coat. Cricket made a defensive sound and dared grab at Hempstead's sleeve.

Hempstead shook him off. "She's burning with fever, and no wonder, dressed in that damn getup," he said, ignoring Cricket's startled cry, as well as the look of relief on the boy's face after he sliced away everything except her chemise and three layers of long, dusty, white petticoats. He sheathed his knife, then he rolled the blanket into a pillow and slid it beneath her head.

"There. That's all can be done for her 'til we get someplace else," he said, as he emptied the canteen over her.

"She dead, ain't she, Mista?" Cricket sobbed. He was still clutching the side rail, letting go just long enough to wipe his nose with the back of his hand.

Hempstead let out a string of curse words.

"She sure enough is, you sniveling, wobbly-eyed saphead! She's deader'n a door nail! That there's why I wasted a whole canteen of good drinking water by pouring it on her dead carcass! Then I stuck my one-and-only winter blanket under her cold, dead head, thinking I'd likely enjoy freezing my bony ass off this winter!"

He grabbed Cricket's collar and ran him toward Stonewall.

"Listen good, boy! Up ahead, there's a fork in the trail that goes left! Take it! Three miles, and you'll be in the town of Goliad. Fetch the doc, and be quick about it! Anyone in town can tell you where he lives. Tell him Hempstead Grouse said to get to Gent Garland's place, *pronto!*" He tossed Cricket into the saddle, and Cricket was gone on Stonewall even before Hempstead could slam his raised hand to the horse's rump.

No doubt Cricket heard Hempstead's raspy bellowing as he flew down the eerie, moonlit trail to Goliad. "… and if you don't come back with my hoss, I'll hunt you down, strip the hide off your black ass with this here Meskin toothpick … and then, by damn, I'll feed ya to the stinking coyotes!" He cupped his hands around his mouth. "You do know which way is *left,* don't ya, boy?"

Without looking back, Cricket waved his left arm over his head.

Cursing even more at getting his boots soaked, Hempstead tromped around in the water while gathering up the womens' scattered clothing. Then he set about stuffing them under the wagon's bogged wheels—they'd need traction if they were to roll free.

Before he climbed onto the seat and gathered the reins, Hempstead studied Miz Gentry Garland's face closely for the first time. *A damn pretty female,* he decided, *even in her present state of peskiness.* He had a feeling that Gent would want him to get this woman to him alive and kicking, and he was damn well gonna oblige him, *God willing and the creek don't rise.* And he'd bet money that the Almighty wasn't gonna let the creek rise ... since He'd already proved Himself stingy enough with His rain to damn near make fossils out'n nearly every damn frog in the state.

Anyhow, he'd been thinking of paying Gent a visit. Gent had made him a tempting offer of employment a few weeks back, and he'd been chewing on the prospect. Being a lawman nowadays wasn't what it was cracked up to be; too damn much politicking involved, too damn much paper work ... too damn many fat-assed judges and town bigwigs bucking his means ... their fancy laws getting stuck in his craw. In the old days, when Indians, Mexican bandits and mean-assed white men threatened life and limb in these parts, a lawman or a Ranger like he was in them days was pretty much his own boss. He dealt out justice the best way he saw fit—hanging a few, jailing a few, shooting a few, letting a few go with a good scolding, and then going on about his business. Nowadays, he had to fill out a damn report on everything from wife beating to whizzing off the sidewalk—neither of which was worth the waste of time and paper, in his estimation. Hell's bells! He was busy enough writing up murderers, horse thieves, and cattle rustlers, without interfering with a man's *personals.*

Miz Gent Garland groaned, and he glanced over his shoulder at her, relieved that there was no sign of child birthing … yet. "Christ!" he muttered, remembering once seeing a Comanche squaw give birth. The sight had set him to *"airin' his paunch"* worse than a puking buzzard. If she could hold out another hour, he could lay this female in Gent Garland's lap where, no doubt, the trouble had started in the first place … and which now had *him* playing nursemaid in a matter damn disgusting to him.

As he slashed the mules' rumps, he glanced again at Miz Gentry Garland lying unconscious on the dirty canvas. Then, for the first time in a long time, Hempstead Grouse said a quick prayer for something other than a fast horse and poke full'a pesos.

16

The Arrival

GENTRY GARLAND PUSHED ASIDE the stack of papers on the roll top desk and leaned far back in his chair. He had no stomach for the figures that glared up at him from the worn ledger, nor had he been able to concentrate on them any other night the past few months. He owed money, lots of it; but South Texas was in the clutches of a cattle-killing drought that had kept him from paying it back.

Taking an angry swipe at the sweat trickling down his cheek, Gentry scowled. Funny, he thought, how a man could prosper for decades ... then, in a couple of bone-dry year, face losing it all when rain stopped falling and grass stopped growing. The water well that supplied his house and the Mexicans on his place was nearly dry, slow to leave the pump for months now—a sure sign of future disaster, since it was the only supply of water that didn't come from the rapidly receding Guadalupe River. He knew it was bound to rain someday, but would it be soon enough?

Despite the need for water, he had one last chance to reverse his bad luck moneywise: He had contracted to trail fifteen hundred head of his longhorns to New Mexico Territory for sale to the U. S. Cavalry. The money earned from that drive would stake a much bigger drive to Abilene, Kansas; but *time* was his enemy. He had to get that herd moving out of South Texas before drought and starvation left them too weak for a thousand-mile trek up through North Texas and across the Red River into Indian Territory, and then on up to Kansas. He'd already sold hundreds of the worse starved longhorns to the Hide and Tallow factory in Rockport, but he preferred to market his cattle the way his father had marketed them—long drives to distant markets that offered top dollar for good beeves.

Gentry poured whiskey into a tall glass, pushed away from his desk, and stood at the bottom of the stairs, listening. Silence told him that the children and old Hannah were sound asleep. Six-year-old Adam no longer woke in the middle of the night crying for his mother, nor did little Elizabeth; but both tykes insisted that old Hannah sleep with them. The Corrigans' old servant was as protective of them as a momma bear with cubs … and *still* as hostile as ever toward *him*.

He strolled out onto the porch, set his whiskey glass on the railing, lit a thin cheroot, and then peered intently around him. In the moonlight, the sun-bleached outbuildings and long bunkhouse glowed fancifully as if doused with whitewash. A lambent glow spread over his land, giving him a clear view for miles in all directions. A stretch of the Guadalupe River, though shallow because of the drought, shimmered like a diamond-studded snake in the far distance. The rolling prairie and its scattering of oak motts lay before him as if painted on an iridescent canvas of muted silvers and grays, the trees like spreading pools of ink in a pale, rippling sea. All around him, the miles of rain-starved prairie grass glowed like an ocean of golden wheat, gently swaying in the hot winds … hot winds that would only starve their roots more completely if rain did not come soon.

To Gentry, there had always been incomparable beauty in the sights before him. Even when standing in the unenhanced light of day, with the drought's ravages touching everywhere, he felt the same.

But tonight, he eyed the colossal Texas sky with a scowl. No clouds meant no rain. What he wanted to see was a cloud-filled sky, black as pitch, and a raging thunderstorm that lit the night with flashes of lightning, followed by a gully-washing downpour that rushed, with healing wetness, down into the widening cracks and crevices of his wilting land. *That's* what he wanted—not all this damn illusionary, moon-drenched, imagery.

He took a deep drink from his glass, then winced more from his anger than from the sting that followed the whiskey down his throat.

If he didn't make some money soon, he'd have to sell off more land. He wondered what his father would do if he were alive. Kiel Garland had said many times that a man with a *powerful intention* could do anything he set his mind to. Kiel had held onto his land by any means necessary when, back in the old days, land-grabbing neighboring ranchers tried to take it from him … tried to force the upstart half-breed to accept his low place among them. Kiel Garland—three quarters Irish, the rest French and Narragansett Indian on his mother's side—came to Texas from the North at a time when *white skin* was the only qualifier in most men's eyes, but Kiel had equalized himself by outshooting, outfighting, and outthinking his foes. He'd taught his only child the same skills, installed in his son that same *powerful intention to* survive. But, in this day and age, it wasn't the haters or the land-grabbers that Kiel's son had to whip; it was the weather—more dangerous to a man's livelihood than any human force; a man's *powerful intention* wasn't much use against it.

Gentry's resolve was as strong as ever, but a hard test was upon him, and it weighed mightily on top of the bitterness that accompanied him from Georgia. Shock had been his reaction upon coming home and discovering his wealth gone and parcels of his land up for sale due to non-payment of taxes; but none of it compared to the guilt of discovering his mother gallantly traveling all over Texas selling horses to pay *his* debts. The consequence of his tardiness struck him full force the day he returned and saw Kada Garland standing in Victoria's town square, wearing his father's old hat and coat, and hawking her four-legged merchandise like a seasoned horse trader. From his vantage point a few yards away, he had watched her brandish the animal's good points with a flurry of hands and glib tongue, passing over the animal's bad points with a wary eye on her customer, as he did his own examination and then dickered for a better price.

That improbable sight would have been amusing to Gentry had it not been for the expression on Kada Garland's face when she glanced away from the object of her argument and saw her son watching her. That staunch face had almost crumbled then, as he had not seen it crumble since his father's death. At that moment, he felt shame that he had been away so long, shame that he had disassociated her from the ravages of war, had never allowed himself to think that she might be in need of him.

But he *had* thought of it. He had thought about it for two long years before finally regaining his senses and coming home. He just hadn't acted soon enough, and that reality stunned him that day in Victoria's town square when he saw how his mother had changed. Her skin, once white and only softly wrinkled despite her age, was now sunburned and leathery from too many days in that same blistering Texas sun she'd once avoided as if it carried the pox. Her gray hair previously coiffured in the latest styles and with never a hair out of place was now cropped short around her ears, the hot, gusty winds whipping it into ragged little wings of disarray all over her head.

By the time they made their way toward each other, her expression had become familiarly adamant. Even so, her blue eyes alternated between relief and joy as she grabbed him to her. She laughed as he swung her off her feet.

"You young devil! I've never been so glad to see any…" Her gaze locked on his wide-eyed companions, and then jerked back to him.

"Well, son, what have you got hanging around that neck of yours to shock your mother with this time?"

"Nothing shocking, Mother. You knew I had a wife and had made you a grandmother," he said, smiling. "His name is Adam, and this beautiful child," he said, as he mussed little Elizabeth's blond curls, "is Elizabeth, my dead sister-in-law's child that I swore to raise as my own." He turned. "And this is Hannah, the woman who's cared for their needs since birth, and will continue to do so."

Hannah had time for a hurried curtsy before Adam and Elizabeth clutched her billowing skirt and hid their faces in the heavy folds.

"The boy's mother?" Kada inquired, looking around as if expecting to see her.

"Still in Georgia," he said, his bitterness evident in his voice.

"She'll be joining you soon, of course?" she asked.

Gentry knew she'd read his face, as usual, and already knew the answer, but he replied anyway.

"I don't know, Mother."

"What kind of mother would agree to be separated from her own child?" she hissed, her eyes going piteously to her grandson.

"A wronged one! Dat's whut kind!" Hannah retorted. "And Miss Ella didn't agree to no such thing!"

Kada frowned at Gentry, and then she shifted her attention to Hannah. "A wronged one, you say?"

"Yes'sum! My missy don't know Mista Gen'te gonna take this boy and Miss Honor's chil' and leave Georgia! Lawd! To think I kept my mouth shut and went 'long with that bad thing Mista Gen'te done." Hannah slapped a handkerchief to her mouth to smother her wail.

"Quiet, Hannah," Gentry said softly. "You'll get them to squalling again." He took his mother's arm and led her a distance away.

"What Hannah is saying, Mother, is that my wife never would have allowed herself to be separated from her child. In fact, she'd have done anything to prevent it, which is partly the reason I didn't tell her I was taking him and coming home, where we belong." His eyes hardened. "If she wants her son and niece, she'll have to come to them. If she wants to keep them, she'll have to stay. Otherwise, it'll be her loss, not mine."

"Oh, Gentry, so callous?" Kada whispered, touching his arm but gazing at the children still clinging to Hannah.

"He's as much mine as hers, Mother. So is the little girl, even though I'm not her father. Like I told you, I made a promise to the child's mother," he said, then frowned at her. "But let's talk about *you*, Mother. At first glance a while ago, I thought you were that old horse trader, Sally Skull."

Kada gave out a small laugh. "We're in the same business lately, that's for sure. Sally and I have an agreement; we don't sell horses in the same town on the same day. Other than that, we are good friends. She visits me regularly at the Strip."

"I told you the last time I was here that I didn't want you going back to the old ranch," he said. "Without father or me there, it's still too dangerous along the Nueces. It's too far away from civilized folks."

"The Nueces River land is my home, Gentry. The new house you forced upon me here in Victoria is a grand place, but it isn't home. Even so, to please you, I stay cooped up in it most of the year. But when it's roundup time, I go home where I belong," she said, adding, "Your cousin, Luther, comes by the ranch often, always ready to help out."

Gentry frowned at the mention of his cousin, Luther Garland. "You've got plenty of Mexicans working on the place, Mother ... you don't need *Luther* hanging around."

"Gentry, you two aren't boys anymore, and it's high time you forgive and forget." With that, she had wanted to know more about Ella, but he repeated only what he had said before—if she wanted her son she'd have to come for him, if she wanted to keep him, she'd have to stay. Finally, his mother had studied his face hard and accused him again of being callous, saying that she could see in his eyes that he had changed, and not for the better.

Tonight, standing on his porch and gazing at his moon-drenched land, Gentry's eyes were as brooding as his mother claimed they were that day in Victoria's town square. He took another drink, and then held the cool glass to his chest. His mother was right; he'd returned to Texas with a giant-sized chip on his shoulder. He felt mean, and it showed. He'd thrown himself back into ranch life, starting work hours before sunup and not quitting until the prairies were so black on moonless nights that he'd had to give his horse full rein to find his way back home. He stayed out of town as much as possible, knowing that the slightest provocation, a remark or a look, would uncap the bitter anger inside him. The carpetbaggers that strutted around playing their political games under the protection of coercive local officials were only a part of his malcontent; he was lonelier that he had ever been in his life. He was able to deny his powerful ache for his wife in the light of day, but too often he awoke in the middle of the night painfully aware of that loneliness ... wanting to see her face ... longing to look into those bewitching eyes. Once, he'd dreamed that she was dead, and he saw her lying cold and chalky white, her arms folded across her chest, and those mesmerizing blue-green eyes closed to him forever.

He tried not to imagine what was happening to her. He had hoped for months that she would give up on Greenpoole and follow him and their son to Texas. But in three months, a year would have passed since he left Georgia. She would have come to him by now if she was going to come. Had Beatrice Corrigan gone too far in selling Greenpoole and sending him the money, all done in the hope that Ella would come to her senses? The thought that Ella might not love their child because *he* was his father enraged him. *If that's true, she isn't worth…!* But he knew she loved their son. He knew also that he'd had no other choice in what he had done. *She should have kept her word and come with him!*

With anger creasing his forehead, he turned toward the familiar sound of jingling harness and squeaking wagon wheels coming faintly from out on the prairie. He make out the silhouette of a wagon pulled by two white mules, the mules shining ghostly silver in the moonlight. A lone figure hunched on the driver's seat. Not one of his wagons, Gentry knew. He'd sent Flaco to Goliad for supplies this morning, but the old man always spent the night with relatives before starting home come sunup the next day. Gentry stepped off the porch and waited. Besides, he didn't own a set of white mules.

When the wagon passed slowly beneath the arched gate, he recognized Hempstead Grouse and shook his head, thinking that the old badger had decided to accept the job offer after all. It was typical of Hempstead to show up when least expected, and long after a normal man his age would be snoring in a comfortable bed somewhere.

"Evening, Grouse. Come all the way out here for a reason, or just out pleasure riding?" He motioned at Hempstead with the glass of whiskey. "Get down … I'll pour your breakfast."

"Ain't pleasure riding, Gent. And I'll have the drink later," Hempstead said. Then, as if spurred by an agitated after-thought, he added, "And when in hell you ever seen me riding atop anything but a *hoss*?"

"You're a man of habit, Grouse—no argument there," Gentry said, and grinned.

Hempstead tossed a glance over his shoulder to the wagon bed. "Got something for you, and the quicker you take her off my hands, the better I'll feel. I just weren't meant to be no damn nursemaid. Sayed she got an old mammy out here what can help her. Reckon I know who *that* is," he said, and grimaced.

Before Hempstead half-finished, Gentry had dropped the glass and tossed away the cigar with one startled jerk of his wrist and was bending over the side of the wagon. A sickening wave of fear shot through his chest and his dark face paled as he stared down at the still form lying death-like on the canvas. She cried out so faintly that it could have been the distant mewing of a kitten. Then she lapsed into incoherent mumbling, as her tongue ran across dry, swollen lips. He whispered her name as her shadowed eyes opened enormously to stare up at the sky. Gentry knew by the vacant glassiness in those blue-green depths that he was not a part of whatever she was seeing.

"Had a skeered little Negro with her, and a crazy old white woman uglier'n me. Nagginest woman I ever had the mishap to acquaint. Left her at the Rawls' place, and sent the black boy to town to fetch the doc," Hempstead said, pausing to spit a stream of tobacco juice, some of which snagged on his mustache. He stripped it away between thumb and forefinger and slung it into the dirt, then added, "but that doc mor'n likely won't get here before high daylight."

Gentry thrust his hands downward, one beneath her head, the other to her waist; but that hand jerked back, his eyes darting to where it had touched. His dark face went slacker as he stared at her pregnant belly. While he stared, it quivered, and then bulged into a small, tight knot beneath the damp petticoat. His hand went down again, almost testily to the spot, to rest atop the gentle movement beneath his palm.

"Damnit, Gent," Hempstead muttered, "I ain't sure, but looks like she may have the fever, as well as being ready to foal. Yellow Jack's crawling the coast. 'Pears to me she just might die. I stopped the wagon several times back yonder thinking she had gone ahead and give up the ghost," he said. "I sure as hell didn't want no dead woman on my hands, especially one that sez she's your…"

"Shut up, Grouse!" Gentry growled, as he gathered Ella up in his arms. She moaned softly, her hands going low on her stomach just before her head fell back over the crook of his arm and her hands slipped slowly away to dangle lifelessly.

"Goddamnit, Grouse! Get down from there and open the door!" Gentry shouted as he bounded across the yard to the house. He was fumbling helplessly with the door latch when Hempstead clomped onto the porch, pushed his hand away, flicked the latch, and shoved the door open.

"I'll help my own self to that drink, Gent," he said.

17

"Let The Wimmen Do Wimmen's Work"

THE BURNING DAYS AND SMOTHERING NIGHTS passed in a kind of delirium, alternating between flickering lights of consciousness, and gloomy pits of darkness. At times, Ella was aware of spinning dizzily in a long, hollow tunnel. A woman's voice, moaning, sometimes crying out in an indistinguishable rant, echoed peculiarly from the spiraling walls. Lost in the sweltering passageway, Ella was surrounded by darkness one minute and in the next, immersed in a luminous shaft of light that seemed to move in a gentle, calming circle above her. She reached for the light, and just when she felt within grasp of it she began to slip back ... back into the swirling tunnel. The woman's cries eased, replaced by slow, hard breathing. *That poor woman!* She sounds like Honor's beautiful little mare, lying spent, trying to foal but dying. Soon, the raspy breathing would stop, and Meshach must burn the carcass.

It was then she opened her eyes to see the angel of death hovering over her in the form of a looming shadow. It was he, *death*, who gripped her so tightly and kept dragging her down ... down into that terrible, dark place. Suddenly, she heard a different voice calling out to her—a man's voice—telling her to "try ... try!"

Who was that? Did she know that voice? Too tired to care, she slid back into the tunnel. The light disappeared, and she heard the woman breathing hard again. Good. She had not died. She was fighting to live. Ella wished that she had the strength to do the same.

~

Standing in the hallway, Hempstead Grouse did the unthinkable—he opened the door and peered inside.

"Thundering hell!" he muttered, then clicked his tongue against the roof of his mouth. It was hardly a sight a man of his salt could abide. Caught in the orange glow of the lamp held high over the bed by the sniveling old Negro woman, the heretofore unflappable Gent Garland hunched over his unconscious wife *crooning low to her like he was talking to a baby, for Christ's sake!* It was damn right embarrassing to watch.

Hempstead pulled his head back into the hallway, and then, grimacing, stuck it back around the door.

"Come away from there, Gent, and let her old mammy tend her," Hempstead urged, his voice unfamiliarly low. "Hell man, you can't do her no good. 'Pears to me, you're getting in the way. Let the wimmen do wimmen's work."

"Where's that doctor?" Gentry growled, as he swung his head around to glare at Hempstead. "If he doesn't get here quick …!" His enraged voice collapsed into a groan. He pressed his haggard cheek against his wife's wet hair.

This time, Hempstead could only gulp at the sight.

The woman, Hannah, sniffed as she set the lamp on the bedside table. "You better be calling on somebody a lot closer to you than th' Lawd, Mista Gen'te, if you wants to help my poor baby!" She wiped her face on the collar of her bright-blue night robe and continued, her voice growing louder as she spoke. "Th' Lawd ain't ever gonna listen to you and me no more after what we done. I knowed something bad was gonna happen to her. I been feeling it in my bones ever since you tol' Miss Ella she gots to come to this Texas place, *or else!* I hear Miss Ella tell Miss Honor before she get kilt that you don't care how she feel 'bout nothing! She say you is a wild man what gotta have your own way in this world, no matter what!" She stifled a loud sob, and mopped her face, but she wasn't finished.

"Miss Ella ain't able to take no more suffering, Mista Gen'te. She done loss her folks and our Miss Honor, and weren't nothing worse on her than that crazy Mista Vic what cause her sweet little boy to drown in that river! Then, after all that, we done stole her last chil' from her, and Miss Honor's baby too, and run off from her!"

"She's here with me now," Gentry growled, "and that's all that matters."

Hannah drew a loud breath. "She ain't come here to see you, Mista Gen'te, she come to fetch her boy home."

Hempstead nodded, always glad to have things cleared in his head. So, the little mamma came to Texas to retrieve her stolen property, eh? No wonder Gent never offered nobody a "what-for" for having them motherless little scamps with him when he came back.

"Yes'sum, Mista Gen'te," old Hannah sobbed, "the Lawd punishing us now, you and me! She can't birth that baby you done give her. He gonna make us watch her die!" She wrung her hands and paced back and forth beside the bed, then stood over Gentry to peer into Ella's white face.

"Lawdy, Mista Gen'te, I done held Miss Ella in my arms since the day she was borned … why you make ol' Hannah help you kill dat sweet chil'?"

The moan that came from Gentry was more than Hempstead could tolerate. He stomped so forcefully toward Hannah that she took a step backward, her heel striking the washbasin and overturning it, the water splashing across the wide plank floor.

"Shetup, you mean-mouthed old hellion!" Hempstead yelled. "There ain't nothing on God's earth more vicious-tongued than a golldamn female, black or white!"

Hannah grabbed a towel from the washstand and hurried to mop up the water.

"Leave it be!" Hempstead ordered. "Get to the kitchen and boil me some mustard seed 'til the water's near black. Get it up here, and bring me a spoon, damnit! And don't tell me there ain't no mustard seed in the house, 'cause if there ain't, I'll have to do this the hard way."

"Do *what?* What you gonna do to that chil'?" Hannah asked, her eyes rounding.

Hempstead raked her with his steely glare, figuring he'd have to answer her question before she'd skedaddle and get the hot mustard water.

"It just may be that she ate something bad on that there boat and got poisoned by it. Boats is a bad place to get a good feeding. If she can be made to give it back up, it may do her some good." His stare shifted to Ella. "If not, she got the yeller fever and likely gonna kill off the whole damn house with it—'cept me. I had it once, ain't never been bothered with it since."

"Oh, Lawd!" Hannah cried.

"Get that mustard seed, woman!" Hempstead ordered. "I ain't anxious to go poking my finger down her throat and getting the damn thing bit off."

When Hannah returned, Hempstead pried Gentry away. "You're in my way, Gent. Get the hell off the bed and quit acting so undignified. If you wanna keep watch, do it from over yonder." He jerked his head toward a chair beside the empty fireplace across the room. "Get drunk like any self-respecting man would do … and I'll try like hell to forget I ever seen you acting like you was wearing a pair of lacy drawers."

He waited for Gentry to obey, then went about his chore. Ella twisted her head aside and clenched her teeth against the brackish liquid that Hempstead tried to spoon between her lips, and which she promptly spewed back at him. He swore, and then clamped her cheeks hard between finger and thumb and squeezed unmercifully. She let out a cry that brought Gentry charging to her side.

"Damn you, Grouse," he bellowed when he saw what had hurt her. "I thought she was having the baby!"

"This stuff stings worse than toad piss!" Hempstead screeched, as he ducked his head to wipe a smarting eye on his raised shoulder. "Get down here, Gent. Put your hand where mine is! Hold 'er tight. Don't let her close her mouth 'til I'm done getting it down her."

"Hurry up!" he screeched again when Gentry hesitated to stare down at his wife's ghostly face.

"Are you sure about this, Grouse?" Gentry asked, as he clamped Ella's cheeks.

But Hempstead did not reply. He was busy rapidly spooning the warm liquid from pan to mouth. After each forced swallow, she gagged, and her breath heaved loudly from her lungs. Seconds later, as Gentry and Hempstead watched, her glazed eyes flew wide, then, taking them by surprise, her arms shot upward to thrash away at them. Hempstead ducked and then cursed, as half of his potion sloshed from the pan onto his trousers.

"Hold her! Hold her!" he yelled to Gentry and Hannah. "You two got locked bones all a'sudden?"

They obeyed, and after a moment, Ella grew still. Gentry edged onto the bed and placed a forearm across her chest. At Hempstead's command, he then grasped Ella's cheeks hard between fingers and thumb again.

Hempstead pinched Ella's nostrils shut with one hand, while the other commenced spooning the liquid. When her mouth was full to running over, he sat back and waited—the spoon reloaded, poised and ready. She tried to struggle free, her wide eyes rolling upward and then from side to side; but Gentry's strong hold on her jaws held her head perfectly still, so that not a drop of mustard water escaped her wide-open mouth.

"She can't breathe," Gentry murmured, watching her face. "Let go of her nose, Grouse!"

Hempstead ignored him. Hannah, restraining Ella's legs, divided her rapid stares from one to the other of the men.

"She can't breathe, Grouse!" Gentry repeated much louder this time, as he watched Ella's pale face slowly tinge with purple.

"She'll breath when she swallers her dose," Hempstead grunted, and then he leaned forward and blew in her face. No sooner had he done so, than she swallowed, then coughed.

"See?" Hempstead said, and guffawed. "Now … again," he said, and Gentry and Hannah automatically repositioned themselves.

Thrice more Hempstead forced the mustard water down her throat, and each time she fought them, refusing to swallow until she nearly turned blue for want of air. After the last spoonful, she began to wretch so violently that Hempstead barely had time to pull her onto her side to the edge of the bed and shove the washbasin against her cheek. A foul-smelling mixture of fermented beans and pork shot forth with a force so powerful that the bed shook.

Suddenly, Hempstead thrust her at Gentry, slapped his hand over his mouth, and sped from the room, obviously looking for a place to "air his paunch."

Soon afterward, the doctor arrived, and gave the hovering Gentry an ultimatum: "Get on out of here, Gent … or you can deliver the baby yourself."

~

Thinking they were both deserving of a few stout drinks, Gentry and Hempstead slouched in huge leather chairs in the oak-walled parlor, drinking liberally from the store of liquor bottles Hempstead had lined up on the mantle of a massive rock fireplace.

Hempstead yawned, then scratched his scruffy cheek. "I told you, wasn't nothing wrong with her that a good puking wouldn't fix."

"No you didn't. You damn well scared all hell out of me by suggesting she had the fever," Gentry drawled, then took a deep drink from his glass before continuing. "In the first place, aside from food poisoning, the site of your ugly puss couldn't have been too soothing a sight for her."

Hempstead cackled. "Well, the ol' gal traveling with her wudn't all that pleasing to *my* eyes, either, Gent. I ain't had no choice but to leave Miss Tessie Peckenpaugh at the Rawls' place. She had a sprained ankle and yacking-mouth disease—neither one making her fit company for traveling."

"I'll send someone to pick her up."

"You don't mean you're gonna let her live here, do you?"

"I know the lady well, Hemp. She's a fine woman, and with a heart as big as your muddy vocabulary."

"It gets a lot muddier around that ol' gal. She *gen-u-winely* chaps my hind end."

Gentry refilled their glasses. ""I can guess what she thought of you."

"Well, lock her up when you see me coming down the road, won't you?" Hempstead growled.

Just then a slight noise, like a distant cry, came from upstairs. Gentry jumped to his feet, his startled eyes raised to the stairway.

"Settle down, Gent," Hempstead urged. "Ain't fixing to don them lacy drawers again, are ya? Wimmen was made to have babies," he offered, "just like cows and mares and ewes. Hell! Wimmen is tough! That's what chaps me 'bout 'em when they go acting all helpless and delicate-like." He snorted, and then nodded approvingly when Gentry slowly sat back down. "Wimmen is fakers, don't cha know. Blood and guts don't faze 'em a bit—they just don't admit it cause it'd peel the sugarcoat right off 'em, and that's what they use to fool us with—all that damn sugarcoating." He took a quick drink. "Oh my! Oh, my goodness! I do believe I feel faint," he mimicked in a teensy voice.

Gentry laughed for the first time tonight, and Hempstead continued.

"Take ol' Sally Skull what run the freights with us to Mexico and back during the war—that there's a *real* woman. She probably kilt more Indians and Mexican bandits before she was fifteen than you and me put together. Sally can do anything a man can do. That there is my kinda woman."

Gentry grinned. "I heard another one of her husband's died a sudden and unexpected death while he and Sally were out on the prairie together. So, why don't you pop the question … grab her up while she's still free, Hemp?"

Hempstead glared at him. "That ain't even funny, Gent."

Gentry laughed again, slid low in the thickly stuffed leather chair, laid his head back, and spread his long legs wide to rest on his boot heels. After a moment, he rubbed his shoulder.

"That bullet hole ain't still bothering you, is it," Hempstead asked.

"Not much. I was lucky it didn't hit bone."

"Oh yeah, Gent. You are *real* lucky," Hempstead scoffed. "You ain't been shot at but *twice* since you got back from Georgia. 'Pears to me somebody didn't want you coming back to Texas. If you ever figure out who in hell wants you dead, we'll put the quietus on the sons-a'bitch."

"I'll handle it myself when I find out. So far, he's been pretty good at sneaking in those shot without anyone seeing him."

"*Sneaking* …" Hempstead drawled. "I'm wondering how come your cousin Luther comes to mind when I hear that word."

"Luther thinks too much of my mother to want me dead; if she found out, she'd take him out of her Will," Gentry said jokingly, and chuckled, while thinking that Hempstead had been a lawman so long it had jaded him.

"He wants your mother's land someday, you know … 'cause it joins his."

"I don't want that Nueces Strip land mother owns, Hemp. She knows that, and she's leaving it to Luther."

"Okay. But you know he never was worth a hill of beans—not even as a youngster. He might be trying to figure out a way to get this place, too, right along with you mamma's land. Who knows what the rascal's got up his sleeve.""

"I'll keep that in mind, my friend," Gentry said, and then laid his head back, thinking that Luther Garland was the least of his problems right now.

"That's it … relax," Hempstead urged. He glanced toward the stairway. "She'll be all right. She made it just fine the first time, didn't she?"

"I guess. I wasn't there."

Hempstead shrugged. "Well, 'pears to me everything went hunky-dory. Counting her sister's child, you got two fine, strapping youngsters, and is fixing to have another. The boy looks just like you, and that's the purtiest little gal child I ever did see," he said. Then, peering over the top of his glass, he drawled, "That boy wasn't a hit and run like this last one, was he Gent?"

Through half-closed eyes, Gentry gazed back at Hempstead over the top of *his* glass. "Old man, did anyone ever tell you you're a pain in the …"

A powerful scream spread through the house, and Gentry was abruptly on the move, thundering up the stairs and down the hallway.

He burst through the door just in time to witness the infant, supported by the doctor's steady hands, as it gradually slid from between Ella's spread legs.

18

The Reunion

HOW GOOD TO LIE IN THIS STRANGE BED and blink appreciatively at the glorious light of day streaming through the open windows, and realize she was alive, Ella thought. Though weak, she felt surprisingly like her old self, except that memory failed her when she tried to remember the hours before this waking moment. She recalled everything right up to the terrifying attack in the muddy river; after that, all was a blank—except for the dream that Hannah was bending over her. In the dream, she had clung to her old servant's hands ... just as now.

"Hannah," Ella said softly, "how long have you been sitting there?"

"Praise th' Lawd!" Hannah cried, coming up out of the chair where she had been dozing off and on. "He done sent my baby at last!" Then she immediately looked sad. "You gonna forgive ol' Hannah for what I done, Miss Ella? I knew them two babies gonna need ol' Hannah when Mista Gent say he leaving with them chil'n but you was stayin' behind. That's why I done it."

"I know that's why you did it, Hannah. I was angry at first... near out of my mind until I came to my senses and realized you would be cuddling them when they cried ... would take care of them the way you took care of Honor and me."

"Praise th' Lawd," Hannah repeated, and sighed with relief.

Ella sat up and patted the old servant's arm. "Now please get my son. I'm sure he's as anxious to see me as I am to see him, and little Elizabeth, too."

"He ain't here, Miss Ella. He visiting his grandma."

"His *grandma?*" Ella said incredulously. She had never thought of *her* son having kin in Texas, other than the thief who had stolen him away from her!

"Why, yes'sum, Mista Gen'te's mamma, Miz Kada. Her name is Miz Kathleen, but everybody call her Miz Kada."

"I suppose little Adam sees a lot of this woman," Ella said, reddening with the sudden wave of jealously that swelled up through her throat and tightened her lips.

"Yes'sum. She right fond of him ... little 'Lizabeth, too."

Ella slapped at the covers, as if attempting to straighten them, her frown clearing only when the tiny bundle in the crib beside her bed let out a sharp squawk.

"Give her to me, Hannah. She's hungry."

"I go get Fat Lupe. She got a bottle." She yelled out: "Lupe!"

"For Heavens' sake," Ella said, frowning. "Give me my baby. I'll nurse her."

"No'sum. You can't nurse that baby. Th' docta say you gots to wait, cause you milk was bad from that food poisoning you had and what near kilt you. Her been having goat's milk these past three days." She called out for Lupe again.

"*Three* days?" Ella was stunned.

"Yes'sum, going on four. Sick as you was, that ol' doc says you lucky to be alive. But don't you fret, 'cause he sayed you can start nursing that baby in the morning if you feel like it."

"Who is this *Lupe*?"

"Her is *Fat Lupe*, what work for Mista Gen'te. We gots two more house gals working in th' house—only don't ever call 'em *house gals*, 'cause they don't like it. They is Francisca and Manuela, and twix them two and Fat Lupe they got so many chil'n they could fill three wagons plum full." She turned, and bellowed again for Lupe.

Fat Lupe sailed into the room. Smiling like a child with a new toy, she scooped up the baby.

"*I'll* give her the bottle," Ella said, putting out her arms and beckoning with her fingers. Fat Lupe paused just long enough to glance over her shoulder, and then scooted out the door. Ella stared after her, and was about to voice her annoyance when Hannah interrupted her intention.

"Miss Ella, honey, this am a wild place fulla bad folk. They ain't all bad, I 'spec, but you can't hardly tell by looking."

"Oh, yes, one can easily tell by looking, Hannah," Ella muttered, remembering quite clearly the vile man who attacked her in the river.

"Ol' Miz Kada am the onliest *back-home* kinda folks I seen here. Miz Kada sayed they's plenty God-fearing folk in Texas, but I 'spec you'd hafta ride quite a spell to go visit'um. I ain't seen nobody as gen'teel as you and Miz Bea, though."

"Grandmother died, Hannah."

Hannah bowed her head. "I right sorry to hear it. Miz Bea was a mighty force on this earth. I reckon heaven gonna has to be on its toes from here on out."

"Baker Ben, too … soon after you left," Ella said.

Only then did tears leap into Hannah's wide eyes. "I knowed that ol' fool wudn't gonna live forever, but even bad-moufed as he was to this ol' Hannah, it make me mighty sad he gone." Sniffing, she went across the room to straighten and then re-straighten the curtains, all the while emitting mournful little groans. Finally, she wiped her face on her apron, and returned to Ella's bedside.

"I 'spec th' chil'n gonna be here soon. Some of Mista Gen'te's cowhands went to fetch'um home. Th' chil'n doan go nowhere without a whole mess of Mista Gen'te's hands riding 'long side."

Ella frowned. "My children need *bodyguards* in this place?" she cried, while thinking it all the more reason to get them away from here as quickly as possible. Her face must have shown her anger, for Hannah wagged her head the way she'd wagged it for years when the look on Ella's face alerted her to something.

"Now Miss Ella, you ain't got no business fretting like that." She tried to press Ella back into the pillows. "You gots to rest 'til you feel a might more perky."

"I'm likely as perky as I'll get until I can gather my children and leav-" She caught herself, but Hannah's big kerchief-clad head whipped around, again reminding Ella that very little escaped her old servant.

"What you thinking, chil'?" Hannah sounded almost cross.

"Nothing," Ella replied, then closed her eyes. "You may go about your chores, Hannah. I'm going to take your advice and rest.

"Today is Sunday. Ain't got no chores on Sunday, 'less I want some. I reckon I just gonna set a spell and watch you rest." She eased into the big rocker beside Ella's bed. After a moment she said, "I 'spec Mista Gent gonna be coming home directly."

Ella's darkly circled eyes hardened as she opened them. "I suppose he will be quite surprised to discover he's a father again."

"Lawd, chil', Mista Gen'te done know all 'bout that baby. He scoop you up from that wagon what that bad mouthed ol' Mista Hempstead done brung you in. Mista Gen'te carry you up here to his bed. He done sit right there 'side you holding you in his arms like you was a little chil'. He didn't leave 'til th' docta make him leave."

Ella blinked angrily. Had she been conscious, she would not have wanted him anywhere near her!

"Seem like you gots a little better after Mista Hempstead feed you that mustard water and make you throw up all ober the place."

Ella shuddered, suddenly remembering the bitter taste of soured beans and pork that had raced up and down her burning throat all the way from Port of Lavaca.

"You would'n push no more to have the baby, and that was bad. When you faint, like you was doing off and on, Mista Gen'te go white as them bed linens thinking you was dead."

"I doubt my death would matter all that much to him," Ella said.

"Now Miss Ella, don't talk like that. I ain't never seed Mista Gen'te so shook."

"I'm sure it was only *guilt* he was feeling, if that's possible for him."

"Miss Ella, the pain that come with birthing ain't man's fault. The pain of having babies am a woman's lot, not man's. You know what the Bible say 'bout it. It the sin of Eve when she temp Adam in the garden."

Ella's face reddened. She hadn't *tempted* Gentry—she had only wanted to erase that awful sadness from his eyes ... "I was not talking about childbirth, Hannah. He stole my son and ..."

She was silenced by the sound of running feet on the stairs, accompanied by the scintillating laughter of children. She barely had time to sit up straighter before the door flew open and little Adam bounced onto the bed and into her outstretched arms.

She clutched him to her, her heart pounding, her tears now tears of joy. He wound his arms tightly around her neck, and she rocked him, unable to speak. This precious moment could only be ended by words, and she wanted to hold him close forever, never let him out of her sight!

When she opened her eyes at last, the breath again caught tightly in her throat, for peering up at her from over little Adam's shoulder were two massive brown eyes, framed in a radiant halo of shiny, yellow curls. How often she had looked upon that happy cherub's face in another time and place as she and Honor were growing up. Little Elizabeth's countenance, like her mother's, was one of angelic beauty and shining innocence. With a cry, she pulled Honor's perfect image into her arms alongside her own child, buried her face between their small heads, and cried.

Hannah stood nearby, her great shoulders heaving, her apron clutched up around her fat cheeks.

"Momma," Adam cried, "bet you can't guess what Daddy gave me? He gave me a horse! 'Lizabeth got one, too!"

"A big, *big* horse," Elizabeth said, spreading her little arms wide, and then giggling happily.

"Oh my darlings, how wonderful," Ella said, pretending to be excited while bitterly thinking: *He's buying them, giving them anything they want and hoping his gifts will make them forget me!*

Suddenly Hannah mopped her wet face one last time and gently pulled the children from Ella's grasp. Ella started to protest, and Adam yelled his own objection; but Hannah's hands grew firm as she rolled her eyes toward the open doorway.

Ella did not have to look in that direction to know who was standing there watching her, but she did anyway.

"Run along, my darlings," she told the children. "You can come back soon."

Possibly it was the hushed tone of his mother's voice that made Adam take little Elizabeth's hand and follow Hannah out the room. All the while, Ella's eyes remained locked with the infamous coal-black ones—eyes as unwavering now, in whatever he was thinking, as they had always been.

"Welcome to Texas," he said.

"I've *already* welcomed to your state, Gentry—I was nearly murdered."

"Hempstead told me," he said, and she thought his tone dismissive. "If your grandmother had written about the baby, Ella, I would have returned and tried to convince you to come back with me."

"Grandmother didn't write to you because I made her swear she wouldn't. This one time, at least, she respected my wishes. Anyway, you would have wasted your time," she said, staring coldly at him.

He had been holding his hat in his hand, and now he tossed it onto a nearby rack of deer antlers on the wall. "At any rate, I would have tried," he said.

"How could you have taken them from me?" she said barely above an angry whisper, and fighting to stay calm when she wanted to scream at him. "Didn't you care that they were all I lived for ... all that mattered to me?" Unwanted tears burned her eyes, but she fought them. Even as outraged as she was, her heart ached with loss. She had loved him so … and he had ruined it.

"I'm sorry; I thought all that mattered to you was *Greenpoole,*" he said flatly, as he kicked the door closed.

"That isn't true!"

"Even so, you were determined to bury yourself in the ruins. I wasn't about to allow my son and Honor's child to be buried there with you."

"You had no right to take them!" This time the entire house could have heard her. She swiped vehemently at her stinging eyes.

"As the boy's father, I had every right. As for Elisabeth, you were there when I promised Honor I'd raise her as my own, and that's what I intend to do."

"I made that same promise, and you made me break it!"

"But I was the only one capable of keeping it." He leaned forward, bracing both hands on the bed beside her, and his voice was softer when he continued. "You weren't able to care for yourself, Ella, much less two small children."

"I took care of myself quite well after you left," she lied, knowing that if not for her grandmother she would've had to ask friends—whom themselves had nothing to spare—for help. "I would've found a way to make my children's lives much better," she added.

"You've found it. You're here. You can keep that promise to Honor now … raise Elizabeth and our children *here,* with me," he said, then added, "I'll be leaving on a drive to New Mexico Territory in the morning. My absence will give you time to get used to the place, get reacquainted with the children without me underfoot." He paused, and she thought for a moment that his black eyes were almost pleading. "This is *home,* Ella. *Our* home. *Yours* and mine."

She stared at him, her eyes drying, as she slowly shook her head. He would never understand her love for the only home she had ever known or would ever want to know. With a grimace, she raised a foot and pushed his hands from the bed.

"I won't be here when you return. I'm leaving as soon as I'm strong enough to travel, and I'm taking my children with me."

He stood up, and strolled to the door. Once there, he turned, and it was as if a thundercloud had dropped over him. A muscle in his cheek twitched as his glinting black eyes raked her.

"Go whenever you like, but you go alone. I love you, Ella, and I want you here, but not if you don't want me." He slammed the door so hard behind him that the room shook.

Ella turned her face into the pillows, enraged beyond tears this time. Was it was possible to loathe someone and yet love them at the same time? He had hurt her deeply! If he loved her, he could not have taken her children and deserted her! Suddenly, the memories of those dark days at Greenpoole were as real as if she were still there—the loneliness, the misery, the longing for her son and never knowing if he was safe. Lastly, the panic of watching Greenpoole's once-luscious fields go fallow … the nightmares in the dark of night when the old house began to talk to her, her dead loved ones whispering their ghostly sorrow in every creak and groan.

She threw aside the covers, and shakily made her way to the window nearest her.

This time, she could not prevent the tears that flowered faster and faster down her cheeks as she stared out at her husband's vast, uninviting land. She could make Greenpoole beautiful again, for she knew its potential; but this dismally unnourished place—with its huge puffs of dust-filled wind, wilting trees, and grass that protruded from the ground like brown straw—could *never* be her home!

19

The Albatross Around Your Neck

IF GENTRY PLANNED TO LEAVE, something had changed his mind, because early the next morning he sauntered into Ella's room, his tanned face showing no trace of yesterday's rage.

After quietly closing the door, he turned and greeted her with a quick flash of white teeth, the gesture briefly transporting her back to happier times between them. She frowned and looked away; but not before she noticed that he was freshly shaven and wearing a handsome light-gray coat and breeches, and his black hair trimmed neatly to his collar.

"Hannah's bringing coffee," he said. "Or would you prefer tea?"

"Coffee is fine," she replied coldly, but her expression softened as she returned her attention to the baby nursing at her breast and discovered her asleep. She could feel Gentry watching as, careful not to disturb the baby, she closed her gown and settled the sleeping infant more comfortably in her arms. She glanced up at him to make certain she had not imagined his amiable mood. He was still smiling and, as he settled into the chair beside the bed, she decided she would say nothing to wipe that smile from his face. Just then, Hannah entered with a tray, filled their cups, and then reached for the baby, but Gentry waved her away.

"I'll hold my daughter for a while, Hannah," he said, as he took her from Ella's arms and settled back into the rocking chair. As Hannah left the room, she paused at the door, rolled her eyes toward Gentry, and then gave Ella a little nod. Ella frowned at her, thinking; *Don't tell me she's been taken in by him!*

Ella watched him draw out a folded handkerchief from his breast pocket and dab away the trail of milk running from the corner of the infant's pink mouth.

"My mother sends her apologies for not coming out here to meet you just yet," he said, still smiling down at the baby, "but she's gone to her place along the Nueces to round up horses to sell. She goes there against my wishes, as usual; but she's a woman who does as she pleases."

"I thought you were leaving," Ella said, ignoring his remarks, but thinking how little she cared to meet the woman her son had constantly and exuberantly referred to as "my Grandma" all afternoon yesterday when he and little Elizabeth played in her room.

"What are we naming her?" Gentry asked, still studying the baby.

"Didn't you hear me? I said I thought you were leaving."

"I heard you."

"Well?"

"I'm leaving, but we need to have an understanding first."

"I agree. I want you to understand that I want to leave here as soon as possible, my children with me."

"I understand that's what you *want*, Ella."

"I won't object to you visiting them any time you wish," she said, and waited for him to reply. After a long wait, she continued. "It wasn't fair of Grandmother to send you that money, Gentry. Knowing it is *Corrigan* money, perhaps you will give it back to me. I'll need it for the children when I get back home to Georgia." Noting that his black eyes had narrowed, and he was no longer smiling, she was unable to keep the sarcasm out of her voice as she added, "That is, if you haven't spent it by now." Instantly she wished she had not said it. What if he'd changed his mind and was willing to let the children go? She quickly softened her tone. "You owe me for what you did to me, Gentry."

He stood and placed the sleeping baby in her crib, then sat back down and leaned forward, his hands on his knees.

"Ella, don't you remember how hopeless things were for us in Georgia?" he said softly.

"Only *you* thought it was hopeless. *You* and my own Grandmother," she murmured, her heart sinking at the realization that he had not changed his mind.

"Cricket told me Miz Bea died," he said. "I'm sorry. She was a great lady." He reached out to touch the blanket of pale hair that fell across her shoulders. "Your grandmother was wiser than you know, Ella. She sold Greenpoole because she knew the place would eventually break your heart."

Ella wrenched her shoulder aside. "*Greenpoole* didn't break my heart! *You* did that! You and *her!*"

"I'm sorry you were hurt, but I'm not sorry for bringing my son here. When your grandmother sent that money, she wrote that Greenpoole was a rotting albatross around your neck. She was right. It was the rotting albatross around *all* our necks, its useful days over and done with, the same as all plantations so big that they couldn't operate without slave labor."

"Who were you to proclaim that Greenpoole was over and done with? You *wanted* it to go to ruin! You hated it! I don't doubt that you influenced Grandmother's thinking! You never gave it a chance!"

"I gave it too many chances," he said, then gently grasped her hands. "I never hated it. I only hated what it was doing to you … to us."

She yanked free, and he leaned back in his chair. He studied her solemnly before speaking again. "At any rate, what you wanted wasn't possible anymore."

"It was possible until Grandmother gave you money that should have been mine. With it, I could have made Greenpoole a thriving cotton plantation again."

"The kind of Greenpoole you want died with the Emancipation Proclamation, Ella, just like the rest of the old South," he said; his mounting disgust for the conversation evident in his voice.

"That isn't true. The old South may be gone, but cotton is still king, and the South will always be its ruler."

"Mebbe so, but it'll now come from hundreds of smaller farms. Big plantations like Greenpoole existed only because of slave labor, or have you forgotten just how many enslaved Negroes it took to keep that place going?"

"I haven't forgotten *anything*!" she retorted, glaring at him meaningfully.

He drew a tired breath. "No, and you *won't* forget, will you? You'll hold on to your anger at me until it chokes you. Go ahead; but you'd best get over Greenpoole. There wasn't anything we didn't do in trying to make it work. Who knows why the sharecroppers never stayed? Maybe sharecropping reminded them too much of slavery. Maybe they just wanted to rest a spell. Who in hell knows?"

"Give me back my money, and I'll show you how wrong you and Grandmother were." She managed to sound calm. "We don't have to fight, you know. You can visit the children any time you want." She paused, and dropped her eyes. "We … we can still be husband and wife." When she looked up he was smiling, but this time the smile was not amiable. She hardened her expression. She knew what he was thinking, but it wasn't true—she had not slept with him only for the tax money!

"Anyway Gentry, Hannah tells me that you leave this place for months at a time with those cattle of yours. The children should have at least one parent with them when the other is gone for long periods. Their *mother* should be the one to guide them, not Hannah, and not your Mexican servants. From what I've seen, those women have enough children of their own to worry about."

"I'll make it short, Ella. You're not taking Adam and Elizabeth to Georgia, or anywhere else—this one included," he said, nodding at the sleeping baby. "Texas is their home now. If you want to mother them, stay here and do it."

"They are not safe! For God's sake, Gentry, I was almost murdered only a few miles down the road!"

"They're safe, I see to that—and I'll see to your safety, if you stay. Texas is a better place to be than anywhere else in the South right now," he said, leaning forward again. "We've got cattle and horses and nothing between the towns and settlements except miles of open grazing land. This drought can't last much longer. Someday, our children will own this ranch. They'll have something to inherit rather than a crippling memory of a dilapidated old plantation in Georgia." His black eyes left no doubt of his determination. "If you leave here, you go alone. I'll give you boat fare," he said, adding, "As to what I did with your grandmother's money, it's put aside for Adam and Elizabeth when they're grown—that's how Miz Bea wanted it."

Ella threw back the covers and jumped from the bed, her fists clenched at her side.

"You can't stop me from taking them!"

He rose from the chair. "Save yourself the effort. You'd never get past that gate with them," he said, pointing out the window. "Every set of eyes on the place will be watching you, and they are loyal to *me*. Like I said, go if you want; but you go alone."

Before she knew she had done it, she struck him across the face and tried to do it again, but he caught her wrists and forced her arms to her sides. He stared hard into her eyes before releasing her and strolling to the door.

"Yes, go on!" she cried through gritted teeth. "Get out! I despise the sight of you! I was a fool to marry someone like you!"

This time, he closed the door with hardly a sound.

She whirled to stare out the window at the parched land that would become her prison if Gentry Garland had his way. She pressed her hands to the window sill and dropped her chin to her chest. "You won't stop me! You won't!" she whispered.

She raised her head to see a band of mounted men trotting leisurely beneath the gated arch—some in big Mexican sombreros, and others in the common clothes of the cowboy. All were armed with guns and rifles—their horses lathered and snorting, as if they had traveled a long distance and had only now slowed their pace. Suddenly, she heard the door open, and Gentry poked his head back into the room.

"I think I'll name my new baby girl after me ... *Gentalee,* spelled with a *G,"* he said, as if that had been the topic of conversation all along. He was grinning, but then he slammed the door so violently she jumped.

The sound, as loud as a gunshot, must have carried, for when she looked out the window again, the riders, with pistols in hand, were charging toward the house! Without being told, she knew these men were her husband's *"loyal"* employees ... a part of his force against her.

Little more than an hour later, noises again drew her to the window, and she watched Gentry and his mounted men lope away, the dry earth puffing up around them like powdery, brown clouds. A big canvas-topped wagon, with Cricket and another Negro on the seat, followed.

Hannah entered the room and stood beside her at the window, gazing out at the dusty procession.

"Bandits from Mexico steal some of Mista Gent's cattle sometime back. Today, he done learn where they was took, and he going after'um ... then he going off far away for a time."

Ella sighed with disgust. He'd run off to hunt a bunch of stupid cattle and then go off the New Mexico Territory with more of his longhorns, but had never given a thought to hunting down the men who attacked her! He had not even responded when she mentioned it, other than his bland reply that Hempstead had told him about it, nor had he shown one bit of sympathy. He hadn't even said that he was glad her throat wasn't slit!

"Sure hope Mista Gen'te don't get shot again, like th' last time."

"What?" Ella murmured, and was a bit stunned to hear that he had been injured. She had never imagined that something bad could happen to Gentry … that he could die. *Oh, why couldn't he have lived safely at Greenpoole with me?*

"That was the second time somebody done shot at Mista Gen'te since we been here," Hannah continued. "The first time, they miss, but this last time they got him in the shoulder … but it weren't no bad wound," she said, and chuckled. "I think Mista Gen'te gots th' Lawd's angels flying 'long side him, much trouble he gets in and out of."

Ella scoffed. "I recall a day when it was the *devil* flying alongside him," she said, remembering the morning she awoke and found her son gone. She switched her attention back to the yard below. "What is Cricket doing on that wagon?"

"That the cook wagon. That black boy a'driving it is ol' Pewee Hines. PeeWee calls it a *chuck wagon.* PeeWee cook for all them cowhands. Mista Gen'te say Cricket can learn how to be a *vi'karo* on the way to New Mexico."

"He'll get Cricket killed, that's what he'll do," Ella said.

Hannah glanced sidelong at her. "Ain't no telling how long they be gone. Fat Lupe tell me one time Mista Gen'te 'bout gone a whole year on one of them drives. Fat Lupe say that was 'fore he went off to Georgia and was gone way too long for his own good. Uh … that what Fat Lupe say, not me," she said when Ella gave her a look. Then she stared silently out the window for a while, just as Ella was doing.

However, she soon grunted, and cast another sidelong glance at Ella. "I gots to tell you, though, Miss Ella, from the look on Mista Gen'te's face when he walk out th' door, I 'spec he gonna be gone a long time *this* time, *too.*"

20

Friend or Foe?

WEARING TESSIE'S SHAWL and a tunic called a *"quéchquemitl"* that belonged to Fat Lupe's thinner sister, Ella hesitantly followed her laughing son and niece across the unending ranch yard. She needed clothes badly; thanks to that awful Hempstead Grouse, every article of clothing she owned, other than her undergarments, were shredded under the wagon's stuck-in-the-mud wheels. Hannah salvaged her shoes and corset from the wagon bed, and had managed to restring the corset she had worn loosely over her swollen waist, but her ripped jacket—already threadbare—was beyond mending. Fortunately for Tessie, she still had the clothes she'd worn when left behind at the Rawls'. In addition, Tessie now had a trunk full of Mrs. Rawls deceased sister's clothes.

Aside from squirming uncomfortably in her peculiar costume, Ella's first venture outdoors was proving to be nerve-wracking. Every sudden sound or move made her jump. No doubt her experience with her knife-wielding attacker in the shallows of the river created most of her uncommon nervousness, she thought, as she glanced over her shoulder at Tessie standing on the bottom step and shading her eyes from the glaring sun with both hands. Tessie had arrived a few days ago, courtesy of Hempstead Grouse. Surprisingly, Tessie settled in as if she actually belonged here.

Ella gave her traveling companion a sour look, thinking how the motherless, husbandless, homeless Tessie's acquiescence to new surroundings was nothing new, the woman being fully accustomed to the charity of others. For years, the old maid of Savannah depended on two spinster aunts for home and sustenance. When they died, leaving Tessie their house and enough money with which to survive, she *still* rotated among the residences of her fellow *tea and cakes brigade* members, staying with each family for days at a time. Apparently frightened to be alone, she scarcely spent a night in her own domicile. Ella suspected that Tessie felt quite fortunate when her inherited home burned to the ground and she instantly became Grandmother Beatrice Corrigan's permanent houseguest. Ella shot Tessie another unfriendly look, thinking that *now* Tessie had latched onto *her … possibly for the rest of my life!*

"Come back inside, Ella dear," Tessie cried from the porch. "It is too hot out. I promised Bea I would look after you, you know."

Ella ignored her.

Adam and Elizabeth called out, beckoning with exuberant swings of their arm. She followed them, still gazing around as she went.

Adjacent to the barn was a huge, empty corral, its earthen floor deeply chunked and chopped by hundreds of hoof prints. Nearby, unpainted outbuildings of various sizes dotted the grounds, along with a row of long chicken coops surrounded by broad wire pens, one of which contained dozens of chickens and a rafter of turkeys, the gobblers strutting about with their feathers quivering. In another pen, a parade of extravagantly tailed peacocks exhibited their spectacular feathers to a small harem of distinctly less attractive and disinterested peahens. Wire fencing covered the top of each pen, protection from night prowling wild animals, just as such wire protected Greenpoole's pens in the days before the war. However, she could make no other comparisons between Greenpoole and this raw place in the middle of nowhere. The very air was different … the smells … the sounds … the winds that blew in wild gusts or blew not at all.

The thought of her beautiful Greenpoole plantation made Ella turn and stare at the plain, unpainted, two-story structure that was Gentry's home ... and which would be *her* home until she figured out a way to get her hands on enough money to sneak her little family back to Georgia.

She shaded her eyes as she surveyed Gentry's huge, old house. In the sun's glare, it stood grayish white; its smooth, hard cypress wood reminding her of a weather-beaten old rock that had defied years of nature's pelting. The architecture of the two-story domicile was rectangular–a smaller rectangle sitting atop a larger rectangle. The house's first story roof gradually sloped downward to form the low overhang that shaded the porch. An open-air passageway, called a dog run, split the first floor into two sections. Standing where she stood and peering dead center through the dog run, she could see a distant spattering of shacks, a small village it seemed, that housed the Mexican families that worked for Gentry.

Ella eyed the house's porch with disdain; it went no further than from one end of the house to the other end. *She* preferred a porch to circle an entire house, that way one could find shade and a breeze any time of the day. *Breeze?* This place has no breeze ... only a hot wind that carried sand and grit. She patted at the perspiration trickling down her neck as she gazed up at the smaller second story. Its roof slanted downward to shade a wooden-railed balcony.

She was already familiar with the old house's interior. The "day rooms"—as Hannah called them—were to the left of the open air passageway, and consisted of a wide hall with a staircase, a parlor and a rather plain dining room that led into an even plainer and larger kitchen ... that smelled of garlic and spices no matter what was being cooked on the big, wood-burning stove. To the right of the passageway were two large guest rooms, a smaller parlor, and Gentry's office with a massive roll top desk next to another stairway. The family bedrooms were upstairs.

At one end of the stone-floored kitchen, a long oak table that must have been twelve feet in length was banked on one side by a long wooden bench, the seat of which was shiny from use. On the opposite side stood eight wooden chairs with cowhide seats and backs—*hair* seats mottled with patterns of wavy grey, black, brown, and white—hair like that on the gigantic longhorn bull whose hoarse, loud bellowing had brought Ella to her bedroom window yesterday. Fascinated by the animal's length of horns that appeared to spread three feet on either side of his massive head, she watched him paw the ground beyond the corral and then trot off to a herd of other such animals in the far distance toward the river. Hannah quickly enlightened her about the extraordinarily-horned bull.

"That ol' Mean Daddy. He musta lost one of his cows and he looking for her," Hannah said nonchalantly, as if knowledgeable of the bull's objective.

"*Mean Daddy?* You mean they actually name those wild beasts?"

"Some of 'em, I reckons," Hanna replied, then added, "Lookie here, Miss Ella; doan you never go out there waving your apron thinking to run ol' Mean Daddy off from th' house, though. He mor'n likely get all red-eyed and slobber mouthed, and come running at you like th' wild, mean thing he am," she added, and Ella guessed the old servant was speaking from experience.

No sooner had Ella left her sickbed, than Hannah explained the order of things: Three women—Manuela, Francisca, and Fat Lupe—shared the household and cooking chores. Hannah minded the children, sometimes cooking when she felt like it. Old Flaco milked the cows, fed the pigs, and tended the vegetable garden. Little Adam and Elizabeth fed the chickens and other fowl. "But don't talk to Manuela, Miss Ella, 'cause she can't speak no English … or she *acts* like she can't. Just say something she don't like though and she talk well enough with them mean looks she give."

Hannah said Miz Kada told her that the house was built to the specifications drawn up by the old Irishman who had, years earlier in 1820, taken a Spanish wife, daughter of a Spanish general in Mexico. Being Catholic, the Irishman qualified for a Spanish land grant. Through politics and nepotism, his acreage grew until one could not ride from one end to the other in less than a week. After Spanish rule was ousted from Mexico, many of the original Spanish grants were recognized by the new Mexican government, and that is when Gentry's father—already owning land along the Nueces River Strip— bought the land for five cents an acre from the disheartened Irishman after a rattlesnake bite killed his oldest son. Before that, another son, no more than four years-old, got drug off by a big panther. The Irishman and his ranch hands had followed the tracks until—miracle of miracles—they heard the screech of *two* panthers down in the creek bed. The child-stealing panther had dropped the boy and, refusing to share his supper with the other panther, was fighting him. The boy, crying, and holding his bloody arm, sat only a few feet away from the battling animals. The Irishman rushed in, grabbed up his son and ran home with him.

"Fat Lupe say that big cat walk 'long in that creek with that boy cause he smart and knowed he being followed, and he ain't about to give up his dinner. If it weren't for that other panther showing up, that little boy would'a been ate up, for sure," Hannah had said, adding, "He would'a been ate up anyhow iffen his papa hadn't showed up when he did."

"How horrible!" Ella had cried.

Ella shivered. "Oh, I despise this place," she muttered aloud, glancing quickly at the children as they stopped on their way to the barn to play with a litter of puppies that had been nipping at their heels. She halted abruptly to wipe at the tears that kept spilling down her cheeks. She hated how much her eyes watered lately.

"*Madonna*, do not cry. I will clear the path for you."

With a start, she looked up to see old Flaco, his wrinkled face odd with concern, hobbling toward her clutching a small shovel in one hand, and dragging a tow sack from the other.

He gave her a timid bow before shoveling up the large pile of horse manure at her feet and dumping it into the sack.

"It is not such a bad thing, Madonna," he offered, pointing to her foot. "The feet can be washed, but the way of the horse cannot be denied," he said, and smiled meekly. "Do not cry."

"You think I was crying over …? Don't be ridiculous!" she huffed, then was sorry that she had possibly hurt the old man's feelings. As Flaco limped away, she called out to him. "Thank you, Flaco … I thank you very much for … for doing that."

Flaco turned briefly, gave her a soft smile and a receding bow, and then continued on his way.

The children called out again, and she followed them into a massive barn. Adam and Elizabeth ran to a row of wide pens that contained several small colts. Ella watched as both children climbed into one of the large pens and opened a gate that led out into the corral, then shooed the colts into the sunlight.

Jostled from behind, Ella spun around just in time to deflect the graying muzzle of a familiar black horse.

"Blackie!" she cried, as *Timon Pledger's* old pet-of-a-horse insisted on pressing his nose into her open palm. She stepped to his side and stroked his mane, finding it silky from regular currying. She didn't wonder why Gentry had brought him along to Texas. He was fond of the horse that saved him from drowning in the Atlantic shortly after Timon Pledger had lent the animal to him—despite the two men having no use for each other. Confederate gunboats then sunk the Union boat on which Gentry had hitched a ride, and Blackie swam ashore with Gentry clinging to the saddle horn.

Ella gave Blackie an affectionate slap on the neck just as her attention was drawn to a small colt trembling in the far corner of the stall that had held all the colts. *That's strange,* she thought, and wondered why he had not bolted away with the others.

She had little time to ponder further because Blackie, also, suddenly became jittery. Ella reached out to stroke his nose, but he tossed his head aside and backed away, his eyes rolling from side to side. Suddenly, his whinnying scream competed with the deep, throaty growl that came from somewhere high above.

A paralyzing chill shot through Ella as she looked up into a pair of large, yellow eyes that stared evilly down at her from the loft.

The animal was huge, too huge to be a cougar of the type she had seen in Georgia. And he was *black!* Black all over! Before she could muster another thought, his thick, ebony paws curled over the edge of the loft, and he pounced!

It happened so fast! The loud gun-shot … her knees buckling … the giant black cat thudding lifelessly to the hay-covered floor just shy of the terrified colt … a whiff of burnt gunpowder, and then a burst of boyish laughter coming from the open barn door. Ella stared at the slight boy standing there, two smoking pistols in his hands.

Little Adam and Elizabeth burst in from the corral.

"Hi, Dan!" Adam cried, throwing up his arm in greeting. "Gee! Is that old *Demonio Negro* you shot?"

"No, it ain't. This one's too small. Looks like a relative of his, though," the shooter replied, as he grasped Ella's elbow and helped her to her feet.

"Howdy, ma'am. I heard in Goliad that Miz Garland was here from Georgia. I reckon you must be her. Pleased to meet'cha. I'm Dan Meaney from East Texas a ways off yonder." He flung his arm in no particular direction. "I come visiting over these parts and decided to ride out and see if Mister Garland could use a top cowhand for a spell before I head back home in a year or so," the boy said, then nodded as if proud of something. "Gent done tried me out before this. I was here on the place most all winter, then I left for a short visit home to see my ma."

Ella accepted his outstretched hand, noting his confident manner, as he physically tried to stop her hand from trembling with his own firm grip—an unusual gesture for a boy that obviously was no more than thirteen or fourteen years old.

"That panther wasn't gonna jump you, ma'am. He was after the colt," he said reassuringly, smiling as if he had just given her a polished apple.

"I thank you, Dan Meaney, as does the colt, I'm sure," she said, allowing herself to laugh lightly despite her shattered nerves. She examined him more closely as she withdrew her hand from his powerful grip. In spite of his timely arrival, the *two* 44 colts and the rapid fire way he had used them, contradicted every charitable thought she tried to have of this boy. He was slightly built, even for his young age. He was hazel-eyed, had tanned cheeks, and thick auburn hair framing a face as pretty as a girl's. He dressed like someone much older, and was impeccably clean in his striped brown breeches, green shirt, and tight leather vest. He wore high-heeled, knee-high boots like those worn by all the "cowhands" she'd seen so far. Without the boots, garb, and attitude, he would have looked like an innocent schoolboy. However, in the time it took to shoot the panther and then help her to her feet, she had witnessed his young face metamorphous from a look of cold-eyed determination ... to one that was almost angelic: *What a strange combination,* she thought, watching him guardedly.

He strolled over and stuck a boot between the animal's legs. "A male," he drawled. "This one's only half-grown. For sure he's a son of old *Demonio Negro—Black Devil,* the Meskins call him."

"If he's only half-grown, I would surely hate to encounter the full-grown father," Ella said, grasping Adam and Elizabeth by their shoulders and drawing them away from the animal.

Dan Meaney laughed. "They say Demonio Negro is actually the offspring of a couple of spotted leopards brought to America from Africa in a ship that was wrecked somewhere on the Louisiana Coast. They say the pair swam ashore, mating as they migrated into Texas. That was quite a many years back."

As he spoke, he lifted his pistols, one by one, reloaded them, and then twirled them back into their holsters. "Anyhow, Miz Garland, it'd be a good idea to keep an eye on Adam and little 'Lizabeth here when they're outdoors. Lately, them cats just been killing young cattle, horses, goats, and fowl; but if they get the chance for an easy meal, I doubt they'll be choosey."

Ella's contempt for her husband's domicile suddenly intensified. Further conversation between her and Dan ended with a noisy invasion of Mexicans from the house and grounds, followed by a wide-eyed Hannah and Tessie; all proclaiming they had heard a shot and then all going silent as they gawked at the dead panther. Without hesitation, four small Mexican boys dragged the animal away "to be skinned," said Flaco. "The dogs will eat well today," he added. "The dogs" being the vast number of mixed breed canines that lounged around the Mexicans' *haciendas*, many of which could be seen with ropes around their necks and being pulled along by the frolicking children. Even little Adam and Elizabeth owned a pair of these gentle curs, both dogs constantly underfoot when she ventured across the house's dog run where they lay in wait, night and day, for their little masters.

"Visitors coming...," Hannah called out, as she retreated to the house a good distance behind the ashen-faced and twittering Tessie. Hannah paused to toss a warning stare over her shoulder at the boy. "You best behave you'self this time, Mista Dan," she warned with a scowl before trudging on.

Fat Lupe, looking especially angry, paused to glare and shake her finger at Dan before she followed Hannah.

Dan Meaney grinned, and the crowd of Mexicans, laughing as if memory had just served them up a delicious morsel, dispersed.

Ella could not resist. "What on earth did you do when last here, Mister Dan Meaney? I assume it involved Lupe?"

"Well, ma'am," he said, and pointed at the privy, with a cattle brand burned into the unpainted wood over the door, a few yards from the bunkhouse.

Before he could say more, he was suddenly distracted, as was Ella, when the squeaking of wheels drew their attention to the huge tarp-covered wagon nearing the gated arch.

On the wagon seat, and snapping the reins against a double team of sturdy horses, sat an elderly woman in a calico dress and a faded cloth bonnet. A rider, astraddle a big white horse, traveled alongside the wagon. Far to the rear of both rider and wagon rode a band of men so disparate in appearance that Ella's eyes—like those of a child visiting a zoo for the first time—shot from one to the next. Most of them were Mexican, several were Negro, the remainder a race impossible to determine, and each man wearing a conglomeration of leather, cloth, and hairy hide, most with Indian-type loincloths worn over long pants. *Indians?* Although unseemly in appearance, she thought them not near as malicious-looking as the men who attacked her by the river.

Her gaze went back to the rider next to the wagon. Sitting on that big, white horse, he was as noticeable as a grimy smudge on white linen. He wore a dusty black coat, striped vest, black breeches, and high-crowned hat with what appeared to be a big flower pinned to the side. Despite his manly attire, there was something indistinctly *feminine* about him, which made him even more of a curiosity.

"Oh-oh-oh," the boy Dan Meaney said, then laughed as the wagon rolled beneath the gate. "You're about to meet a real Texas lady ... and another one so far from it it'd take an act of heaven or hell to gentle her—*that* one wrongly accused my Pa of stealing a horse from her one time," he added, suddenly looking like he did when he shot the panther.

As the visitors pulled up a few feet away, Ella's gaze remained on the rider she had mistaken for a man—and now the rider suddenly squinted threateningly back at her.

As fast as eyeballs can move, Ella abandoned her critical observation of the creature and swung her attention to the elderly woman on the seat. Before Ella could utter a word of welcome, little Adam and Elizabeth, screaming with delight, jumped up and down beside the wagon, crying "Grandma! Grandma!" Both sets of little hands clutched for the woman as she climbed down.

A familiar twinge of hostility struck Ella, and she could not make herself smile a welcome to the woman who had obviously captured Adam's and Elizabeth's affections. She watched silently as Gentry's mother stripped off her bonnet, then bent to administer hugs and kisses to the pair.

"Grandma," Adam said excitedly, "Dan shot a big old black cat like *Demonio Negro* in the barn."

"Good! We'll hang his old black hide on the barn wall," she cried in grandmotherly enthusiasm for anything a grandchild may utter.

Upright again, she observed Ella as closely as Ella was observing her. *She looks like someone chopped off her hair with a dull knife,* Ella thought, and then instantly felt the sting of her mother-in-law's own critical observation.

"You look ridiculous in that get-up, young woman."

"This 'get up' is not mine by choice, I assure you, ma'am," Ella shot back, noting the woman's slight Irish brogue.

"Well, every stitch you'll ever need is in this wagon, as well as a chifferobe and a chiffonier in which to store them."

Taken aback, Ella glanced at the tarp-covered wagon.

"There's also a piano in there," the woman added dryly. "Because I haven't seen my grandchildren in over a month—not since *your* arrival, my dear—I assume they will no longer be taking piano lessons at my house in Victoria?" She did not wait for a reply. "I have instructed Monsieur Fasset to come out here the first Monday of every month to teach them … unless, of course, you wish to teach them yourself?"

Ella continued to stare at her. They'd not been introduced, and yet this woman was already making decisions for her and her children! That anyone would dare choose an entire wardrobe of wearing apparel for her without knowing her preferences was astonishing, as well as infuriating! *Has Grandmother's ghost followed me to Texas and taken over this woman's body? As for the piano, there would be no children here to play it,* she thought hotly.

However, Ella concealed her emotions, and extended her hand.

"You must be my husband's mother."

"Correct. I'm Kathleen Garland, but I prefer that you call me Kada," she said, then pointed to the dire-faced woman on horseback.

"This is Sally Skull, a friend from these parts here-about. I just this morning traded her that fine animal she's riding, and nothing would do, she had to ride out here with me just in case someone tried to waylay me and my wagon of goods. That's her hired hands out there," she added, pointing to the divergent horsemen keeping their distance outside the gate.

"Mrs. Skull," Ella acknowledged her, nodding politely.

"No-o-o …" Sally Skull drawled, still looking hostile. "It ain't *Miz* Skull. I got divorced and got rid of the Miz part long time ago. Kept the *Skull* part—liked *it,* but not the man."

"I understand, Miss Skull," Ella said, trying to be cordial to this intimidating woman. "You were given your freedom from marriage in a court of law."

"Ain't nobody *give* me nothing, Miz Garland. I claimed it for myself, damnit-to-hell! Not just 'cause I didn't like the *Miz* part screwing up a tolerable name neither, but 'cause he was a son-of-a-bitch from the get-go," she growled, then jerked out a massive handkerchief from her coat and loudly blew her nose into it, adding, "Call me *Sally,* Miz Garland, just *Sally.*"

Even before Ella could reply that Sally Skull could call her *Ella,* Sally said, "I heared you nearly got your gullet split down by the river."

"I was quite fortunate that I did not … get it split," Ella replied.

"You sure as hell was, lady. Rabbit Jack's a killer, a rustler, a kidnapper, and a defiler of women and children—an animal so bleak of human traits I doubt he has a soul," Sally said. With that, she ended the conversation by plopping a sliver of stick in her mouth and chewing it vigorously while gazing about.

It was then that young Dan Meaney stepped from the shadows of the barn, leading his horse.

"Morning, ladies," he said, doffing his hat.

"Howdy, Dan," Kada Garland greeted, giving him a quick smile before turning all her attention back to the children.

Sally Skull spit the flayed stem from her mouth and gave Dan a long, squinty look. "That there's a mighty fine hoss for a boy to be riding," she drawled. "Where'd you get him, Dan Meaney?"

He smiled, but his hazel eyes were anything but courteous. "Got him from the big mustang getting place out on the flats before I come moseying on down to this part of the country."

"That ain't no full-blood mustang," Sally insisted. "The momma of that hoss got mated with a good blood hoss somewhere other than the prairie, I'd guess."

Dan Meaney smiled while petting the horse's neck. "Well, mebbe that 'good blood hoss' got loose '*somewhere,*' then trotted out on the flats where he met up with this fine animal's mustang mamma," he said, and gave her a slow wink. "Was my lucky day, is all I can say about it, *Miz* Skull." He continued to pet his horse. "Fact is, *Miz* Skull, that's this horse's name—*Mustang Momma.* I call her Momma, for short."

"It ain't a name I'd favor," Sally said. "I don't reckon your mamma's too flattered by it."

"I don't reckon you even know my mamma, do you? She likes it just fine."

Ella watched them. This handsome but abruptly dangerous-looking boy and equally threatening woman were chatting easily enough, she thought, but their mutual hostility hung in the air like the filmy dust that never seemed to settle in this cruelly stifling place. *Hot winds and hot tempers,* she thought, as a gust of sultry air whipped a loose strand of hair across her mouth. She spit it out, along with the gritty dirt that accompanied it.

Sally Skull drew a long leg over her saddle horn and slid casually to the ground. Immediately Ella saw that the *black trousers* were actually a heavy woolen skirt that the woman obviously wore tucked tightly around her legs when astraddle her horse. Sally walked to the rear of the loaded wagon, and Ella watched her as she dropped the tailgate. Speaking in a surprisingly soft and rhythmic tone this time, she reached into the wagon and appeared to pat something. Ella wondered if Kada Garland was about to bestow another pet upon Adam and Elizabeth? The place was already overrun with dogs of all size and age. *The woman would just have to take that one back where it came fr-*. The thought ended abruptly, as Sally stepped aside and an abnormally thin girl, with a curly mane of jet-black hair framing a face as pale as chalk, scooted from the wagon, and then stood motionless while Sally gently slapped and patted her pretty yellow skirt into place.

With Sally's guiding hand grasping the girl's frail arm, the pair moved slowly toward the house. As they passed, Ella stared at the girl's colorless eyes that were as milky white as her skin. Adam and Elizabeth each took one of the blind girl's hands and silently strolled alongside her. Ella turned to Kada Garland.

"She is Adeline LaPonte. We call her Addie," Kada offered, before Ella could ask. "I took her in after her mother was murdered and Addie was shot in the temple and left for dead. She was only eleven at the time. The bullet blinded her. We aren't sure if she is deaf, or if she can speak. She's never shown signs of wanting to do either one."

Ella's piteous gaze followed the little procession as they mounted the steps to the porch.

"The girl's mother was a relative … or a dear friend?"

"I knew the woman only in passing," Kada answered.

Ella's feelings about Kada Garland softened a bit. "I admire you, Mrs. Garland. It takes a special person to take on the responsibility of another woman's child, especially one like Addie, when it was not your duty to do so."

"Duty and responsibility fly into one's life on many wings, my dear girl … 'tis not always the angelic dove that brings it or the saint that accepts it."

Ella glanced sidelong at Kada Garland. *The last thing on earth she needed right now was a Texas-style Beatrice Corrigan.*

21

"Miracle or Mishap is a Hard Call Sometimes..."

After Sally Skull consumed a pot of coffee, a large bowl of frijoles, a half-dozen tortillas, and a hunk of fried beef, she and her band of hired hands galloped off across the prairie on the way to Corpus Christi to "meet up with my new fiancé," Sally crowed. "I got me a young'un this time. He oughtta be goddamn easy to train."

Four of the men who had accompanied Sally Skull and Kada Garland stayed behind. After carrying the piano into the parlor, they lugged the chifferobe, the chiffonier, and several armloads of paper-wrapped parcels upstairs to Ella's room. Later, when she looked out the upstairs window and saw that they had unsaddled their mounts and now squatted in the shade of the bunkhouse as if they intended to stay awhile, Ella deduced that these four were in the employ of her mother-in-law. She wondered how anyone could live in a place that required a woman to have armed guards when she traveled. In civilized Georgia, a lady required only one male escort, their only peril perhaps the assault by a sudden rain storm or a swarm of bees. Ella breathed another of her frequent sighs of disdain, and then watched silently as Kada Garland seated Addie in the rocking chair; after which, the woman commenced tearing open the parcels and spreading out the items of clothing on the bed.

Downstairs, the children could be heard running through the house squealing with delight as they played with Francisca's, Manuela's, and Lupe's army of black-eyed, black-haired little *niños,* their presence as constant as the spicy cooking smells that permeated the house from daybreak to dark. The women's older children took care of their younger siblings; everyone had a job it seemed.

Without turning from her busy chore of unwrapping, Kada said, "When we get past this awkward silence, my dear, you can call me Kada."

"I would not be so impolite, Mrs. Garland, until we are better acquainted."

"Suit yourself," Kada said, and then smiled. "I've a feeling that *Mrs. Garland* is the last thing *you* wish to be called."

Ella did not reply, but began folding the wrapping papers as Kada tossed them aside. She silently admitted that the dresses were not bad choices.

"My son tells me you hate him. Is that true?"

Having already gotten a taste of this woman's straightforward manner, Ella's proclivity was to act in kind.

"I don't hate him. I'm angry. Angry because of what he did to me, and I intend to stay that way."

"I'm glad you don't hate him. Not for his sake, but for your own. I hope you don't stay angry all that long, either. Anger, like hate, changes a person inside and out. Harbor either one long enough and you'll be wearing it on your face and in your gut. Pretty soon, the whole world will see it, and you won't be who you think you are anymore."

Good Lord, Ella thought, as she shook the wrinkles from a lovely ecru jacket trimmed in dark-green velvet, *Kada Garland is absolutely a rural version of Beatrice Corrigan!*

"I might as well tell you, Mrs. Garland, I intend to return to Georgia as soon as possible, and I am taking my children."

Kada lifted a stylish hat from its box and flicked her fingers at the plume of colorful feathers before offering the hat to Ella. "If what was done to you was done to me, I'd be just as angry."

Ella glanced at her, allowing that the woman actually seemed sympathetic. She took the hat from Kada Garland's hands and held it out to admire it. A moment later, she watched her mother-in-law place a necklace around the blind girl's neck. Addie's hand slowly sought the necklace at her throat, and then her fingers stroked it for a long moment before she dropped her hand back to her lap.

"She seems to like jewelry," Ella said. "May I give her a pair of these earrings?"

"If you wish, but she'll use only one of them," Kada said. "Her assailant also sliced off one of her earlobes; her mother's, as well.

Ella stared at the girl in shocked silence, all her denunciations of the place reaffirmed. "I suppose I shouldn't be shocked," she finally said, adding, "Did your son tell you that I was nearly murdered when I got here, Mrs. Garland, or did you and Sally Skull hear it from Mister Grouse? I suspect it was someone other than Gentry, since he didn't seem at all concerned about it."

"I'm sure he's concerned, dear."

"It doesn't matter," Ella said, glancing briefly at her mother-in-law before replacing the hat in its box. "Anyway, one would think he'd be worried that Rabbit Jack and those other monsters would show up *here* one day when he's off with his cattle."

"They won't come here. Men like those only attack the weak and vulnerable."

"*We* aren't weak and vulnerable, Mrs. Garland?" Ella half scoffed. "We've only old man Hempstead Grouse, and a few elderly Mexicans with machetes, to defend the place."

Kada smiled. "My dear, you must be the only living soul in Texas who doesn't know what Hempstead Grouse is capable of." She laughed. "'*Old man'* Hempstead Grouse has quite a sting."

"I know he's capable of stinging ears with that foul mouth of his," Ella said.

It was then that Tessie called out that the cake she had baked was ready and they should come have a slice. But then, after a startled cry, Tessie added, "That old *Hempstead Grouse* is coming under the gate! Bet he smelled my cake all the way from that French woman's parlor in Victoria … where he surely spends most of his time!"

~

Hempstead flung his canteen onto the table and ordered Fat Lupe to fill it up. He glanced at Tessie who, unsmiling, had just remarked on his keen ability to sniff out her cake.

"No, I didn't smell your cake; but I did smell your golldamn venom, and ain't neither one the reason I'm here."

He looked at Ella and, after tipping his hat twice, once to her and once to Kada Garland, he slapped it back on his head.

"I just came from them sorry Barton's five mile back yonder." He threw up his hands. "Why Gent lets that trash heap live on the place is beyond my way of figuring," he said. Then, mumbling something unintelligible, he jerked out his tobacco pouch and papers and began rolling a smoke.

"Has something happened at the Barton's, Mister Grouse?" Ella asked, suddenly thinking of the sad-eyed girl she had seen at the dock and then again on the road—no more than a child, but whose large belly indicated that she was about to give birth.

"That gal, Molly, might be ailing. Her little peckerwood sisters and brothers—the whole kit and caboodle of them scabby little farts—come a'running at me on the trail, hollering she be needing help with her birthing."

Ella's eyes widened. "Did you see if she was all right?"

"Nope, I had my fill of puking, remember? Anyhow, I'd a'probably had to shoot Leet Barton and that crow-faced old momma of his just to get my toe in the door."

Ella told Hannah to pack a basket with everything she might possibly need to deliver a baby, and then she whirled and told Manuela to find Flaco and have him hitch up the buggy she had seen in the barn. Manuela, loudly patting a ball of dough between her wide, flat hands, ignored her. The stoic woman had been at her chore for the past hour, forming dough into perfectly round, flat disks and dropping them onto a hot skillet, browning them on each side, and then slipping them into a bowl lined with layers of cloth that she then folded around the *tortillas* to keep them warm.

"She don't understand a damn word you're saying, Miz Garland, and she ain't about to learn," Hempstead said. "It's a matter of stubborn pride. Her great-great-grandpa owned this land once upon a time. She probably thinks it got stole from him, and *her*."

"She can have it back, as far I'm concerned," Ella said. "Now please tell her to have Flaco bring the buggy."

"I'll get the golldamn rig my own self, damnit-to-hell, but I'm gonna swipe me a couple of them fresh tortillas first." He was already tossing aside the layers of cloth from the bowl.

"Take all you want, but please hurry. I'm going upstairs to change." She headed toward the stairs, and then paused. "And I wish you would not use that language in this house!"

"Now just wait a golldamn minute," Hempstead yelled. "I thought you was gonna send this old Hannah to tend the girl. You ain't got no business around them kinda folks." He glanced at Kada Garland. "You neither, Miz Kada; Gent wouldn't like his wimmen folk traipsing off to them Bartons."

Hannah bristled. "I sho ain't going by my own self!"

"I'm gonna take you," Hempstead growled at her.

"Just you and me?" Hannah cried. "I *sho'* ain't going *now*!"

"Don't worry, Hannah, I'm going with you," Ella called out as she climbed the stairs.

Kada was behind her, and Ella felt her yank on the *quéchquemitl* as she muttered, "I'll help you get into something proper."

Below, Hempstead threw up his arms and yelled up to them, "That's right, ladies! We'll *all* go! Why not the whole golldamn house and all the Meskins on the place? We'll just make ourselves a little parade and go traipsing off to help the golldamn Bartons!"

Tessie had been silent, but now she spoke quietly. "*I* am not going, Mister Grouse," she said. "You are absolutely right this time."

He gave her a sour look before he slammed out onto the porch. "That's just as well, *Miss* Peckenpaugh, 'cause you'd probably be about as useless as a doorknob on a bucket."

~

Having already determined that Gentry's mother was a slightly less elegant version of Beatrice Corrigan, Ella was not at all surprised when the woman climbed onto the driver's seat and took the reins in one hand and the whip in the other. One of her vaqueros, squatting beside the bunkhouse with his companions, opened his hands to her as if to ask if she wanted them to come along. When she shook her head, Ella wondered if Kada Garland was more worried about Rabbit Jack possibly showing up at the ranch than she let on. Regardless, Ella was glad that Kada's men were staying behind; she had a feeling her children would certainly be safe with guardians such as these watching over them.

Ella glanced at Hempstead as he trotted up alongside the buggy astride his tall horse. Dan Meaney rode up on the other side. Ella silently admitted her relief that Hempstead was there. He knew everything about this frightening land and the people who lived in it. Obviously his knowledge had kept the old reprobate alive for well over sixty years, was her guess. Perhaps Kada was right about his "sting," Ella thought, remembering that upon seeing him for the first time on that cattle boat, she had seen something in those pale gray eyes that had given her a chill.

As the buggy jolted along a beaten trail across the prairie, Ella noted the wilted landscape, trees with shriveling, brownish-green leaves, and meager patches of spiny grass that curled downward, as if wounded and on the verge of crumbling into the dust. She wondered how anything could survive in this place, scorched as it was by both sun and wind. Tessie said the Rawls told her they'd had no rain to speak of in *three* years.

As if Kada had read her thoughts, she said, "It'll rain someday, dear."

Wiping at the perspiration trickling down her neck and dampening the high collar on the comely new gray and black dress, she thought of the gentle breezes that cooled Greenpoole's verandas even on the warmest afternoons. She pulled a handkerchief from her sleeve, folded it lengthwise, and placed it beneath the band of her big straw hat to stem the rivulets of perspiration that ran down her temples and forehead and into her grit-filled eyes. "And I thought *Georgia* was hot," she mumbled, as she snatched up her fan and began fluttering it at her face.

She glanced sidelong at Kada Garland and her thoughts turned to Gentry and his futile efforts to keep his cattle from starving in this drought. Kada said he had spent weeks gathering those animals into a herd, and then more weeks driving them hundreds of miles to God knows where to find better grass ... only to have them stolen from him. What kind of life was that for a man? Why didn't he realize *"the futility of it"* the way he told her to realize the futility of restoring Greenpoole!

An hour later, they turned onto a less-beaten trail that meandered alongside the Guadalupe River. The river's unusually wide span of sandy and then muddy banks was stark evidence of the drought. Ella suddenly pictured the leering face of the man who would have murdered her in those shallows if his invisible cohort, shielded by the trees, had not stopped him. She wondered again why anyone would want to live in such a dangerous place. If there are decent people here—and there must be, she thought, as she glanced again at Kada Garland—then they were too few and too scattered to be of comfort to each other.

~

They heard Molly Barton's screams as the buggy reached the top of a small hill. The cabin was below, a short distance from the river. A large pigpen, easily recognized by its stench, connected to a sidewall of the cabin beneath a window. As the buggy neared the hovel, a small scrap of something unidentifiable sailed through the open window. The pigs, thin as sticks and squealing like the starved creatures they were, dived for it.

Closer to the cabin, the air grew even heavier with the unpleasant odors drifting from a rickety old outhouse. Only the absence of rotting fish heads scattered about the yard kept Ella from thinking these Bartons were as unsanitary as had been the white trash Shipleys back in Georgia.

Hempstead waved the buggy to halt. "Wait here. Me and Dan's gonna tell old Leet he's got company whether he wants it or not."

As he and Dan rode away, Molly Barton's four small siblings, two boys and two girls, came running up the hill. Ella felt overwhelming pity as she watched them approach. All four were as ragged and dirty as Hempstead said earlier; their arms and legs scabbed with sores. Their short hair, matted with ancient tangles, looked as if it had been chewed off rather than snipped away with scissors.

Hannah grunted. "Them chil's so caked with last year's dirt they don' even look white."

The two little girls wore tattered, outgrown dresses, the hems well above their scraped knees. Worse, as they ran, it became evident that their bottoms were as bare as the day they were born!

They gathered around the buggy, all of them talking at once.

"Molly's gonna die! She can't squeeze that damn baby out no matter how hard she try," said the tallest boy breathlessly, and then he sniffed back tears.

The older girl, no more than seven or eight, took hold of her little sister's wrist and pulled her close to the buggy, as if for Ella to inspect. "I'm scared, 'cause that's what happen to our mamma when Alva, here, was borned," she said, and gave little Alva a shove, as if to punish her.

"Molly can't ever walk," cried the boy. "She ain't walked in a week! She got a belly on her like a damn bloated cow!"

All four began to sob and wail. Ella tried to shush them, finally reaching into the basket on the seat and handing each a strip of meat rolled in a huge tortilla. "Go sit under that tree. When the baby's born, I'll call you and you can come have a good look at it. I'm sure Molly's going to be fine," she added, as one by one they snatched the tortillas and headed toward the tree to which Ella had pointed.

Leet Barton stood in the yard, glowering, as Hempstead waved Ella, Hannah, and Kada into the tiny cabin. Leet's mamma had come outside and was at an open cook fire stirring a pot of something that smelled like beans. Her flinty eyes followed the women until they disappeared inside.

Hempstead remained in the doorway, and Ella heard him growl to Leet Barton.

"If I find out from the girl the name of the scum that got her in that there fix, you better hope the sons-a'bitch's name ain't *Barton*."

Leet gave out a short laugh. "Why, shore, she'll tell ya. I can tell ya myself. He's old man Human Nature, and thet's the only name Molly's gonna give ya, 'cause it ain't none of your goddamn business!"

Sensing that Hempstead was about to explode, Ella cried out to him. "Mister Grouse! Please. You and Dan join the children under the tree … *please*." She watched him walk toward the tree, but his head craned toward Leet Barton all the way there.

Molly lay on a homemade rope bed topped with a corn shuck mattress—one of three such beds at one end of the single room. Two cots, in much better shape, were at the opposite end of the room on either side of the back door. A table and two chairs occupied the center of the room. In one corner stood a battered old wardrobe with the doors ajar and dull rags spilling from it.

Molly cried louder when she saw the women, and Ella rushed to her side.

"I'm gonna die, Ella," she hollered, and Ella did not mind that this poor child address her by her given name again.

"I've brought the next best thing to a doctor to help you, Molly," Ella assured her, as she motioned to Hannah.

Kada Garland beat Hannah there, and she pressed her hands to Molly's huge stomach, patting, feeling, pressing, and rubbing. "There are two babies in there. Seems they are ready to greet us."

"What?" Molly's eyes widened at them.

Hannah lifted the dirty sheet, pried Molly's knees apart, and took a look. "They sho is. One is 'bout to get its first peek at daylight." She straightened up and shook her head. "But them babies gonna need a wider door to squeeze through than what that poor chil' got," she said, and looked around for her basket. "Gimme my scissors, and hold her down."

Molly screeched. "What you gonna do with them scissors? You ain't gonna snip on me down there with them things! I ain't never heared of it!"

"You are a child," Kada said, as she held a small bottle of laudanum to Molly's lips. "Therefore, there are many things you haven't heard of. But I assure you, *snipping* and then *sewing* is most common for women much older than you ... or would you rather just *rip*?"

~

Each time Molly screamed, the pigs squealed, and an old hound tied to a broken wagon wheel threw up his head and howled. This went on for some time. Outside, sitting under the tree with Hempstead and Dan Meaney, Molly's younger siblings giggled wildly with each episode of screams howls and squeals.

"What's wrong with them crazy kids?" Dan asked, clearly agitated.

Hempstead chuckled. "Why, hell, Dan, thanks to Molly, this here's probably the only entertainment these scabby little farts ever had."

An hour later, Kada motioned them into the cabin.

"Two baby boys," she said. "They're mighty small, but miracle of miracles, they and their mother made it just fine."

Hempstead grunted. "Miracle or *mishap* is a hard call sometime," he muttered, as he peered briefly down at the babies then stepped aside to allow Dan and the wide-eyed children to take a turn. He glanced through the open door, but Leet Barton and his mother had disappeared.

Molly was lying flat, but she rolled her eyes first to Dan, and then to Hempstead.

"I wanna ask you fellers something," she said, and then glanced at the two bundles wrapped tightly in Ella's and Kada's relinquished petticoats—since there had not been a clean cloth of any type in the cabin. "I'm thinking to name my boys after you, Mister Hempstead, and you, Dan Meaney. I'm gonna call one of 'em *Hemp* and the other *Dan* ... cause it was you two what brung me help."

"The name is *Hempstead,* child, not *Hemp,"* Hempstead growled. "What in the hell kinda name is *Hemp* for a baby? Give the little squirt the full of it, or give him nothing," he ordered.

"All right," she said, "but I'm betting everybody's gonna call him Hemp."

Dan stepped forward. "I'm not only gonna let you name the other one *Dan,* but you can give both of them my last name, too—*Meaney.*"

Hempstead laughed. "Short of marrying her, Dan boy, you can't do that without being their pa. That there's how we tell the bastards from the rest of us."

"Ha!" Ella grunted beneath her breath, as she pressed her hand to Molly's forehead.

Hempstead gave her a long look. "You fixing to comment on that statement, Miz Garland?" he asked, grinning. When she didn't answer, he turned back to Dan.

"You gonna marry this gal, Dan?" he chuckled, as if he had voiced the ridiculous.

"I will if my daddy lets me," Dan replied, his eyes wide, his boyish face naked with sincerity.

As Hempstead guffawed, even the women chuckled.

Dan Meaney puffed up and reddened, but then his expression cleared as he clamped his hands over his big belt buckle. "On second thought," he drawled. "I ain't ever asked my old man for nothing. I ain't even seen him in almost a year. I guess I can darn well marry if I want to."

"I don't wanna marry nobody!" Molly cried, rising off the pillow. "I ain't even *thirteen* yet! I ain't nothin but a damn little *child*!"

They all stared at her for a long interval, then burst out laughing again, all except Dan.

Ella's laughter faded almost before it began, the irony of Molly's statement suddenly making her incredibly sad. Subconsciously, she raised a hand to her cheek and looked pitiably at the girl. There had been men like these Bartons in Georgia—the cruel Brunot, the slovenly and despicable Shipleys, and *Victor Faircloth*. Death had punished them all. Poor Molly's future was made hopeless the day she was born to people like these—people who would attribute their rape and impregnation of a *child* to "human nature."

With that thought, Ella glanced at the two little girls huddled around the babies. How long will it be before the glow of innocence was stripped from *their* eyes, their little bodies violated the way Molly's had been violated? Was it happening already?

"Get on outta here!" shouted Leet Barton. He stood at the door, his shotgun raised, and his scowling mother beside him with a pistol half-hidden under her filthy apron.

Ella trembled with the urge to run screaming at both of them. She wanted to tear them apart with her bare hands!

"That ain't no way to thank these ladies," Hempstead growled, and Ella saw that Dan Meaney's fingers were steadily tapping on the butts of his 44s.

"We shall leave now, Molly," Ella said to the girl, but Molly grabbed her hand and clung to it. Ella slowly pulled free. "We must go; but I'll return with blankets and clothing for the babies … for you and your brothers and sisters, as well."

"No, you won't!" Leet Barton growled. "I'll tell you right now, lady, you ain't coming back here!"

Almost before the wild-eyed man had finished speaking, Hempstead had crossed the room, struck him in the forehead with the butt of his gun, and had snatched away the old woman's pistol almost in the same move.

Leet Baron's knees folded. Dazed, he sunk to the floor in a kneeling position.

The old woman screeched, then squatted down and pressed her apron to the bloody knot growing between her son's eyes.

Hempstead tapped her shoulder. "Miz Barton, you better get a handle on that son of yourn, 'cause the more I see of him, the more I itch to shoot the sons-a'bitch. I'd done it just now, rather than hung that horn on him, but I didn't wanna harm them babies' little ears."

"You all get outta here like my boy said!" she screamed over her shoulder, still dabbing at Leet's head.

Hempstead nudged her shoulder again. "Look at me when I'm talking to you, ma'am, 'cause I don't like repeating my words. That's better," he drawled, as she glared up at him. "Now, Miz Garland here is the wife of Gent Garland, who owns this here property that you ain't got any right to be on, and wouldn't be on if not for Garland generosity. Like Miz Garland here, her husband got a soft spot for kids. Judging from the looks of them poor little shits yonder," he pointed at the children, "they be needing a soft spot as sure as dirt needs water to grow things."

Leet's mamma jutted her chin at Ella.

"The other lady, there," Hempstead continued, as he pointed at Kada, "is also Miz Garland. She's Gent's momma. If either one of them ladies shows up knocking at your door, you damn well better invite 'em in. If you don't, I'm gonna drag old Leet, here," he poked Leet with his boot, "out to that stinking pigpen out yonder and shoot him. Them hogs look might hungry."

22

What Was the Price of Them Kids?

ELLA AND KADA SAT ON THE PORCH. Hempstead lounged on the bottom step. He had spent the last hour trying to discourage Kada from returning to her Nueces Strip home.

"You ain't got no business living there now that old Kiel is gone, Miz Kada. The Nueces Strip's too dangerous for a woman."

Kada laughed, and then lapsed into her thick Irish brogue, on purpose it seemed: "Go on with ya, now, Hempstead Grouse. Are ya tellin' me ya didn't clean out all the bad from it twenty years ago, like ya been saying all this time?"

"Us Rangers was there plenty, and we cleaned out a'plenty," he said. "But the Strip's always been like a big old slobbery water trough—you can scoop the scum off but it keeps coming back."

"I haven't heard one good reason why I should up and leave my home at this late date in my life," Kada said. "I've been there forty-five years; it's a lot tamer now than it was in those early days."

"It ain't no tamer. There's still a steady stream of two-legged rattlesnakes not fit to breathe a'using that part of Texas for a slowing down place from the law—not to mention the *real* rattlesnakes and roving Meskin mountain lions," he said.

"Just like *here,* Mister Grouse?" Ella asked, unsmiling, as she swung an arm out to indicate their surroundings.

"I ain't gonna try and enlighten you, Miz Garland," Hempstead said, as he stood and stretched. "It wouldn't do a Confederate dollar's worth of good, anyhow." He ambled toward the corral, then turned and tipped his hat. "I leave her to you, Miz Kada; but if she's as stubborn as you, I *do* wish you luck."

Kada laughed again. "Oh, my dear Ella, this *is* civilization." She waved her arm in a wide circle just as Ella had. "Living anywhere on earth has its perils … whether it's at my 'big old slobbery water trough' or *here* … or anywhere else you may fancy."

Ella gazed into the vastness, and then up at a dozen or more lazily circling buzzards. She knew they waited for another longhorn to perish for want of grass. Hempstead and the others went out almost daily to burn carcasses of cattle that had succumbed to the drought. "If it weren't for the Guadalupe and San Antonio rivers, they'd be dying of thirst, as well," he had said one day after returning from such a task. "I suppose we have different ideas of what is inhabitable and what isn't, Mrs. Garland," Ella finally said. "Along with everything else, it just seems so lonesome out here."

Kada looked kindly at her. "Most of us Texans do not consider "lonesome" a bad thing when it comes to counting our acres. I once went two years without seeing a neighbor—a friendly one, anyway."

Ella glanced at her. "Your son worries about you. In Georgia, he often said how stubborn you were," she added, with another glance.

"Stubborn? Ha! That's the pot calling the kettle black," Kada said. She nodded toward the corral, where her rough-looking crew passed time by twirling their ropes over the thick corral post or over each other. "You see those men? There are more at home just like them. The danger is for anyone who comes on my property with unneighborly thoughts in their heads."

"I agree that your employees look quite capable of … just about anything," Ella said.

"Indeed they are. Not only do I have *them*, I have Gentry's cousin, Luther Garland. He's probably at my place right now helping my cowhands round up those cattle that Gentry will be driving to Abilene after he's finished with the New Mexico Territory trip."

"Gentry never mentioned a cousin," Ella said.

"You're bound to meet him one of these days. He and Gentry were educated at Yale, you know. Luther's been quite the traveler. He's been to Europe and all over the country just like Gentry's been." Luther is very much a gentleman."

"How nice it will be to meet one," Ella said then glanced apologetically at the woman, realizing that Kada Garland surely considered her own son a fine gentleman, just as *she* once had.

If Kada was offended, she did not let on. "Oh we have gentlemen *and* fine ladies all around you, my dear, in Goliad, Victoria, Beeville, Cuero, and several other towns and settlements, and all just a few hours from here."

Ella laughed. "So close as that?" This time her laughter was amiable—even while thinking that she and her children would be gone long before she became acquainted with any of those 'gentlemen and fine ladies.'

Kada poured tea. "The Rawls aren't but two hours away, and your Miss Peckenpaugh seems to have made them her dearest friends. She's been gone the entire week I've been here."

"I apologize for her absence in leaving, Mrs. Garland. Amazingly, whenever Tessie wishes to go for a visit, Mister Grouse appears from out of nowhere to escort her."

They both laughed, and Kada reached over the small table between them and patted Ella's hand. "No matter; her absence has given us a chance to get acquainted."

"Yes," Ella replied, but could think of nothing else to say. She was still a bit piqued that little Adam and Elizabeth had clung to the woman the entire week, only absent from Kada Garland's adored presence when forced to take their afternoon naps, like now.

"Anyway," Kada continued, "the Rawls are sure to visit soon, even though they are getting on in years and don't get out much."

"The only neighbors I've met so far are the *Bartons,*" Ella said, "and other than taking food and clothing to those poor children, I don't see myself getting friendly with that *Leet* and his mother."

"Oh, heaven's no," Kada said, then took a long swig from her cup. "Gentry allows them on the property because he pities the children. This, even though the lot of them, from the youngest to the oldest, curse worse than Hempstead. All of them, even the girls, steal anything small enough to get in their pockets or that can be dragged home at the end of a rope. They are on the same path as their elders, I'm afraid."

"Poor Molly. One would think we gave her a fortune when we delivered those blankets and clothes," Ella said, remembering Molly's exuberant face, especially when she saw the two blankets Fat Lupe had added to the bundle—each a liberal square of brightly weaved cloth, striped red, green, yellow, and orange, and with the edges frayed to form a soft fringe.

"I wonder how long it will be before that crazy old woman is using those blankets to mop the floor," Kada said, and both women shook their heads.

Hannah, busy ironing linens nearby, spoke up: "From the look of that floor, ain't nobody ever worry 'bout mopping it *yet,*" she said, and grunted her disapproval.

After a month-long visit, Kada guided Addie to the wagon and helped her onto her pallet. Then she and her small army of protectors departed for her Nueces Strip home. They would be back in December, Kada said. "I shall spend Christmas with my grandchildren, and *you,* too, my dear," she said, as she took up the buggy whip. She studied Ella for a long moment, then added, "I'd be fairly surprised if Gentry was back by then, but who knows?"

At sundown the next day, Hempstead brought Tessie home, and Ella could hear them snapping at each other long before they reached the overhead arch that spanned the gate. Dan Meaney followed a good distance behind, his horse moving so slowly that it was hard to detect that he was moving at all. Ella guessed that Dan was keeping out of range of their bickering.

After a brief greeting, the dusty Tessie hurried upstairs, but not before she gave Hempstead a look so pained that Ella felt a stab of pity for her. Could it be? Could Tessie Peckenpaugh actually be in love with Hempstead Grouse?

With only a nod in Ella's direction, Hempstead marched into the house and straight into the kitchen. When Ella got there, he was pouring a cup of coffee, and then was none too gentle setting down the pot. He opened the stone jar in the cupboard and took out a handful of Hannah's doughy little cakes.

Ella stood in the doorway, observing him. "Well, Mister Grouse, what did you say to Tessie this time to get her so upset? Perhaps more hurt than upset, it seemed to me."

"Hurt?" I'm the one that oughta be hurt! That is, if I was some whooshy-pants ejit open to wimmen's hurting ways."

Ella tried to hide her smile. "How on earth could Tessie Peckenpaugh possibly hurt a man like you, Mister Grouse?"

"I'll damn-well tell you how. First, she talks real nice-like to me, and when I make even the most innocent remark in reply, she turns on me like a poked skunk."

"What did you say to her?"

He took a slow drink of his coffee, his pale-gray eyes glancing at her once before retaining their steely gaze. "It's personal," he said gruffly.

"*Personal*?" Ella lightly chortled. "You actually had a *personal* conversation with Tessie? About what? How personal could it have been if you said it to *Tessie*?"

"We were talking about melons."

Ella did not hold back her laughter this time. After a moment, he silenced her with another steely glance.

"The Rawls' grandson got married a few weeks back, and old man Rawls said the boy sure could pick'um," Hempstead said. "Well, on the way here, Tessie said it was mor'n likely that it was the *girl* that had picked *him*, rather than t'uther way around … 'cause that's the way it was generally done."

"I can only imagine your reply," Ella said.

"The hell you can. I said it ain't always done that way, and if a man is smart, he'll pick a wife like he picks his melons."

"Oh, for heaven's sake, Mister Grouse, what silliness is that? No wonder Tessie got upset with you."

"She weren't upset. Not 'til she kept poking at me to explain myself."

Ella sighed in exasperation at him, then picked up a cloth and began wiping at the crumbs he was spilling on the table.

"Now lookie here, Miz Garland," Hempstead said. "Lemme see if I can explain to you the way I explained it to her." He waited for her to give him another doubtful look then continued.

"As I see it, there is just two kinds of grownup females in this here world. There's the young ones who, like melons, is still on the vine and just waiting for some unthinking fella to come along and pluck 'em loose."

"Pfff!" Ella interjected.

"Then there's the old gals like your Miss Tessie, who for one reason or t'uther, ain't never got picked, and just laid there 'til her vine just dried up and fell off."

"That usually means the melon is *sweet* and ripe for picking, Mister Grouse," Ella said, eager to correct this egregious old man's ridiculous concept of women.

"You're right, and that there's the *only* situation where melons and wimmen ain't alike. When picking a fresh, young melon off the vine, you ain't taking too many chances, 'cause you know, after it sits awhile, it's more'n likely to get sweet and tasty. But, with them old melons, you gotta be a little more cautious. You gotta roll 'em over, check their bottom, thump 'em a little bit, mebbe take a little slice to make sure they ain't too damn pithy for consumption."

"Oh, for heaven's sake …"

"I reckon the old gal thinks pretty much like you do, Miz Garland."

"As do all women with a brain in their heads, Mister Grouse."

"Well, since she was already puffed up like a fresh-killed bullfrog, I figured I might as well put the quietus on it."

"You apologized."

"I told her I wasn't planning on marrying any woman I couldn't roll over and thump first."

Behind them, Ella heard Dan Meaney snickering. He stepped into the room and went straight for the little cakes.

Ella put her hands on her hips and glowered at both of them.

Dan grinned at her. "Mister Grouse is doing Miss Tessie a favor, talking to her like that, saving her the awful fate of marrying him."

Hempstead chuckled then gave Dan one of his steely looks. He pushed back his empty cup, stood, and shifted his gaze to Ella.

"You can tell the old gal she won't be seeing me for a week or so. I'm going to Galveston to do a little business."

"Looking for another set of French pigs for that lady friend of yours in Victoria, Mister Grouse?" Ella quipped.

"Nope, I'll be looking for free Negroes for old man Rawls. He says he heard Galveston is crawling with ex-slaves looking for farming work. He hired me to find him a couple of families of them Negroes to plow and plant his corn and cotton."

Dan interjected, "Mister Rawls wants Negros that once worked on cotton plantations. He says they know lots about plantin' and plowin', and he won't have to do a lot of teaching."

"Yep, and I'm leaving for Galveston at sunup," Hempstead said. "You can tell old Tessie I'll be in the bunkhouse 'til then if she wants to apologize." He yawned and stretched. When he lowered his arms, one of his hands went into his pocket and came out with an envelope. "Your husband caught up with his cattle in the hill country northwest of San Antone. He sold a few then took off for New Mexico Territory with the rest." He tossed the envelope on the table.

Ella looked at it.

"That's for you, Miz Garland," Hempstead said. Without further explanation, he strolled to the back door and left. Dan grabbed another little cake and followed him.

~

Ella lay on her bed in the pitch black of night, wondering what time it was. She had dozed occasionally, but never so soundly that she no longer heard the yips and howls of distant coyotes. Gentalee, in her crib beside the bed, had not wakened for her nighttime feeding, indicating that the hour was not yet 2:00 a.m.

Ella sat up, lit the bedside lamp, and read Gentry's short note again.

> *This money will get you and Miss Peckenpaugh back to Georgia. If you go, you go without the children.*

He didn't even sign it! She wadded the letter and threw it across the room. If he thought she would leave without her children, he was insane!

She counted the money again. Two hundred and fifty dollars was no help at all. Even if she managed to get the children to Savannah, the money wasn't enough. They'd need funds to live on until she found a way to get her hands on more cash—enough cash to buy back Greenpoole from Banker Treadwell.

Gentalee stirred, and then began to fret and grunt. Ella carried her to the rocking chair beside the window. "You little fatty," she whispered affectionately, baring a breast for the baby's hungry mouth. "Fat as you're getting, one would think I've been feeding you every half-hour."

~

Hempstead and Dan Meaney were at the long table having breakfast when Ella stepped into the kitchen. Adam, Elizabeth, and their barking pups played nosily in the dog run. Manuela and Fat Lupe were at the stove. Manuela concentrated on slicing a huge onion into a simmering pot of beef stew while Fat Lupe flipped tortillas from the skillet to the cloth-lined bowl. In her other arm, Fat Lupe effortlessly balanced her two-year-old daughter, as the child nursed noisily at Lupe's massive brown breast. The child twisted her head away from her mother's bulging wet nipple to watch Ella sit down at the table then she quickly turned her open mouth back to her liquid breakfast. Ella shook her head, but allowed that modesty could be a luxury for a woman with so many children and so much work.

Hempstead and Dan said a unified, "Morning, Miz Garland," and Ella returned the greeting. There was no time to say more because Flaco rapped loudly on the back door, poked his head inside, and beckoned to Hempstead. The look of urgency on Flaco's usually expressionless face made even Manuela stop flipping tortillas and stare curiously at him.

Without hesitation, Hempstead followed him out back. The two men spoke in rapid Tex-Mex. Ella looked questionably at Dan. He was listening intently even as he forked Francisca's special egg dish, *huevos rancheros,* into his mouth.

"What are they saying?" Ella asked.

"Old Flaco said his cousin just got here from visiting his folks in Mexico, and said a few days back he saw some bad characters that ain't native to these parts camping along the Nueces River. Said they had a passel of little white kids with them, all trussed up like turkeys being carried off to market. One of them, a girl, saw Flaco's cousin across the river and ran along the bank hollering out to him, *"I'm Molly Barton! I'm Molly Barton!"*

"Oh!" Ella cried, slapping her hand to her mouth to partly muffle the next sorrowful wail.

"Before Molly could holler anymore, one of them sorry devils threw a loop on her and jerked her down," Dan said, and suddenly cocked his ear toward the door to listen more intently. "Mister Grouse just asked Flaco if his cousin saw an older couple of white folks with them ... and a couple of babies." Dan's eyes widened at

Ella. "Flaco said 'no,' his cousin ain't seen nothing but Molly and the other kids."

Shakily, Ella sank to a chair. "Those poor children," she whispered, feeling guilty because she had not gone to check on Molly and her siblings in almost two weeks.

"Flaco said the sheriff over in Nueces County got a bunch of men together and they're looking for them," Dan said as he stood, adjusted his six-shooters on his hips, and slapped on his hat. "I reckon that bunch is gonna sell Molly and the kids. They likely left little Hemp and Dan behind at the cabin. It's too much trouble to travel with babies, and nobody wants to buy kids that little, anyhow, since they ain't any use that tiny." He nodded, as if to reassure himself as well as her. "I reckon they left Hemp and Dan behind with that Leet and his momma."

"Thank God if that's true," Ella whispered, picturing the tiny infants, and at the same time, praying for Molly and her siblings. *How terrified they must be!*

"Being left behind with Leet and the old woman ain't a much better fate, I'd say," Dan drawled. "I reckon me and Mister Grouse is gonna be riding over there directly.

"So am I," Ella murmured. "Get the buggy Dan—I'm bringing those babies home with me until their mother is found."

"If she ever *is* found," Dan muttered, as he left to get the buggy.

It briefly occurred to Ella that it might take time to arrange care for Molly's babies, the effort slowing down considerably her endeavors to get herself and her children away from this shockingly cruel place. However, she felt an allegiance to Molly that she had not been able to explain ever since they'd both arrived on the same boat. Perhaps it was because they were two women—or a woman and a girl—imprisoned in situations that left them nearly helpless. *She* was bound to remedy *her* situation; but she knew there was little or no chance that Molly Barton would ever be able to do the same. Suddenly, Ella pictured Lupe's massive bosoms. Yes, she'd bring Molly's babies here. *They'd be fat and healthy in no time.*

~

At the cabin, Ella rushed ahead of Hempstead and Dan. Ignoring the stares of Leet Barton and his mother, she went straight to the bed to get the babies.

Leet, sporting a new bowler hat on his shaggy head and wearing a new pinstriped coat over dirty, ill-fitting trousers, jumped to his feet, his chair crashing to the floor behind him.

Hempstead stepped inside and snatched Leet's shotgun from its hooks over the door. He glowered at Leet, and then at the old woman standing beside the table. She had been kneading bread dough, and now she wiped her hands on the sides of the new calico dress she wore.

"What was the price of them kids?" Hempstead asked, looking from one to the other. "Was it them new duds?"

"You're talking wrong, Grouse," Leet said. "Molly and the kids went to town to shop a little and maybe visit a little."

"When was that?" Hempstead asked.

"Why … just this morning," Leet drawled. "Left before sunup, all five of 'em, happy as pigs in clover to be going. Gave 'em a penny each, 'cept Molly … gave her a nickel. Told 'em to have a good time."

"You liar!" Ella cried. "Where are the babies?" She was beside the bed, tossing aside the heaps of rags and old clothing.

"Molly took them two with her," said the old lady.

"No, she didn't," Dan Meaney said, as he stepped inside from the back door.

"She did!" screamed the old woman, as she hurried to the door and tried to close it; but Dan held it from her.

"Get gone from here!" Leet screeched. "They is all gone to town. Won't be back for a day or so. You can come back and see 'em for yourself!"

A fat carpetbag sat by the front door, and Hempstead nudged it with his boot. "You two planning on taking a trip somewhere?"

"That ain't none of your business," snapped the old woman.

Ella rushed up to Hempstead. "The babies aren't here, but Dan said those men would not have taken them."

Leet and his mother exchanged glances.

"All right!" Leet cried. "I'll tell ya what happened. Molly and the kids got took by Rabbit Jack and his bunch, but t'wern't our fault!"

Ella nearly fainted, remembering that Hempstead identified her attacker as Rabbit Jack, and later Sally Skull said, *"He's a killer, a rustler, a kidnapper, and a defiler of women and children … an animal so bleak of human traits I doubt he has a soul."*

Ella grabbed the woman's shoulders. "Where are the babies? I'm taking them away from here, and you can't stop me."

"Molly took 'em, I tell ya!"

"No, she didn't," Dan repeated from the doorway again, and Ella and Hempstead looked at him for the first time.

The boy's face was the color of ash as he continued to stare out the back door, a position he had not moved from since entering there.

Ella flew to him, dreading to see what so stunned him. Hempstead tried to grab her, but she was already at the door.

Only her hands clutching the door's frame kept her from tumbling through as her eyes came to rest on the two tiny bundles wrapped in the colorful striped blankets Lupe had given them. They lay on a bench next to a large washtub, their blankets dripping wet, the slow drops forming tiny dust bubbles in the dirt below the bench. Ella stared, waiting for the blankets to move, to wiggle … indicate that life persisted within the sagging folds; but no movement came.

"They're with God," Dan said in a croaking voice. And Ella tried to picture their tiny souls in a gentle heaven, but all she could think of was how helpless they had been against the evil of their world … how hopelessly caught in the cruel clutches of those who should have cherished them, protected them … *loved* them.

"Who done it!" Hempstead roared. "If you don't say the truth, I'll know it and I'll slice your goddamn gullets!" He jerked a foot-long, wide-bladed knife from the scabbard attached to his belt and pressed it against Leet Barton's throat.

Leet did not hesitate to roll his bulging eyes toward his mother. The woman folded her arms across her waist, spreading her hands over her wet sleeves, as if trying to hide them.

Ella stared at her in disbelief.

"It was the merciful thing to do!" Leet croaked. "T'wern't no way to feed 'em after Rabbit Jack took Molly! They had a high fever, was sickly and dying. They would'a died anyhow in a few more days. Ma did the merciful thing by 'em."

"You could have brought them to me!" Ella cried. "You could have taken them to anyone in town! God knows, they would have been taken in by most anyone there!" She fell to sobbing wildly, trembling so that Hempstead must have felt it necessary to let go of Leet and support her.

"I would have taken them! I would have taken them," she kept saying.

Leet eyed her in his usual hostile manner. "That would'a been *charity*. We Bartons take care of our own."

Ella pulled away from Hempstead to stare first at Leet and then his hard-faced mother. She looked helplessly again at Hempstead. "I don't understand such ..." she almost whispered. "I don't ..." she trailed off into silence, searching Hempstead's enraged face and then Dan's.

"I think she's in shock, Mister Grouse," she heard Dan say.

"Shocked, but not *in* shock," Hempstead replied. "Take her to the buggy and go on down the trail a ways. I'm gonna make sure them poor little lads gets buried."

"The grave's already dug," said Leet's momma.

"Well, that was right kindly of you, Miz Barton," Hempstead said dryly, then turned to Ella and Dan. "Get going. I'll be catching up, directly."

They had gone less than a mile when two shots, faint but identifiable, rang out in the distance behind them. Dan pulled up the buggy, and then eased it off the trail to a shady spot beneath a stand of oaks.

"Those were gunshots, weren't they?" Ella said listlessly.

"Yes ma'am. The sound of justice carries a long way in these parts, Miz Ella. We might as well wait up. Hempstead will be along directly, like he said."

Ella nodded. The pain in her heart for the dead babies … for the missing children and Molly, made those gunshots welcome. Perhaps it was wrong to feel gladness at someone's death—the same kind of gratification she had felt back in Georgia when she saw Victor Faircloth slip beneath the choppy waters of the Savannah River … saw the murdering Shipleys sent to hell by a spray of bullets. She suspected that God would punish her someday for her indifference to all those deaths. Perhaps He was punishing her now … in sending her to this hellishly cruel land.

Soon, she watched Hempstead approach at a gallop.

"That didn't take long," Dan said, as Hempstead came abreast the buggy.

"Like the old woman said, the grave was already dug," Hempstead replied. "Just had to make sure the burying was done."

"We heard shots," Dan said. "Thought mebbe you might'a laid old Leet and his mama alongside poor little'o Dan and Hemp."

"Nope. Just walked 'em into that stinking pigpen alongside the house." He jerked up his canteen, took a long drink, and then wiped his mouth hard on his sleeve. "Them damn hogs were might near starved. I left the gate open … so's they can forage for themselves … later."

23

"That's My Damn Horse!"

WITH TWO THOUSAND HEAD OF CATTLE recovered and the rustlers either dead or in jail awaiting their fate, Gentry trailed the herd and a remuda of one hundred cowponies up through central Texas across the Staked Plains to Horsehead Crossing. From there, he'd trail the herd north along the Pecos River and across Pope's Crossing into New Mexico to Fort Sumner. Due to thieving Comanches along the route, he figured he'd get to Fort Sumner with at least fifteen hundred head intact. He had twenty five men with him on this drive—enough guns in case the Indians were interested in more than stealing cattle.

The unexpected sale to the Cavalry had turned his luck for the better. Moreover, further south on his mother's land, men were busy gathering a much larger herd. By the time he reached Fort Sumner with his herd, the cowhands back home would have gathered six thousand longhorns and pointed them toward Abilene, Kansas.

The leaflet in Gentry's vest pocket advertising Abilene as a new and better cattle market, and with a "veritable sea of grass" along the entire trail—grass that would fatten his drought-starved cattle. He'd winter the herd in Kansas, fatten them in the spring, and get top dollar for them a month or two later. All he had to do was get this smaller herd safely to Fort Sumner, collect his money, then catch up to that six thousand strong *money* herd—four thousand head belonging to him.

Even while eager to be done with the New Mexico drive, Gentry left the herd with his men near El Paso to chase a rumor that Rabbit Jack was nearby. The thought that Ella had been touched by that filthy scum, her clothes torn and a knife held to her, had preyed on him to the point of sleeplessness. But after searching unsuccessfully for days, he returned to the herd. Rabbit Jack's punishment was delayed, but not forgotten.

El Paso, nine hundred miles from his South Texas home, was one of the state's hot, dry spots—the last place to get rain even when the rest of the state was getting a downpour. That's why Gentry thought it ironic that, as he got deeper and deeper into the region, the wetter it became. The rain was coming down in sheets, at time filling the gullies and making a slippery mess of everything underfoot. He and his cowhands hoped South Texas was getting the same treatment.

After crossing the Pecos River, they continued sloshing through mud for miles, and there were still heavy clouds overhead. This was Mescalero Apache country, but they had been approached only by scattered bands of Indians, no more than five or six in a bunch, and wanting food. So far, Gentry had given away twenty-five head.

They'd met few obstacles other than a close call with a tornado, and one of the vaqueros nearly drowning in the swollen Pecos River as they swam the herd across. A rattlesnake had struck at one of his wranglers by name of "Airout" Buzell. The snake got a fang caught in Airout's boot, and Airout quickly did away with the dangerous reptile. The boys teased Airout, saying the snake died after it got a taste of his sock. Airout got even by dropping his socks into the beans when they weren't looking. No one found out that Airout's smelly footwear was a part of the seasoning until the pot was almost empty. There was no guessing then as to why Airout had laughed so hard earlier when one of the boys told PeeWee Hines, the cook, "them was the best damn frijoles I ever et, Pee Wee."

~

One day, high on an orange-colored mesa overlooking his slowly moving herd, Gentry sat atop his buckskin horse watching the procession. His vaqueros kept the animals traveling in a line forty feet wide and almost a mile long, making the wild beasts easier to circle in case of a stampede. Gentry turned in the saddle to gaze behind him. A light mist fell, but he could see for miles in all directions. He wondered again if rain had blessed his homeland. Even before he finished the thought, he pictured his wife staring at him, hating him, wishing to be away from him. Had she left? In his heart, he felt she was still there. There, not because of him, but because she would never leave their children behind, no matter how much she loved Greenpoole and hated him. If he had given Hempstead a fortune to pass along to her instead of those two hundred and fifty dollars, she still wouldn't have left without the children. Maybe if he could keep her in Texas long enough to see how much better off Adam and Elizabeth were … how much better off *she* could be, she'd change her mind about leaving. He felt a tightening in his gut, his longing for her arriving unexpectedly. He could almost hate her for not feeling the same.

Realizing that he was clenching his teeth, he forced himself to relax. He didn't have time to worry about Ella. He was too busy trying to save his livelihood and his children's future.

Something in the far-off vastness caught his keen eye. Something so minute, so tiny, as to be unidentifiable, yet moving steadily at an angle toward the swollen creek that his herd had crossed miles back. He pulled his spyglass from his saddlebag and raised it, then lowered it to rub his eyes. Frowning, he quickly replaced it to focus on a speeding horse and rider.

A sudden burst of sunlight streamed between the low clouds, and Gentry stared harder. Several more riders were speeding in the opposite direction from the lone rider, and they appeared to be chasing another lone rider who pulled a string of five horses behind him. But Gentry wasn't interested in this man and his pursuers: Even at this distance, when the first rider and mount he had sighted looked no bigger than a jackrabbit, Gentry would have recognized the speeding horse's rare copper color anywhere. It was his stolen horse, *Red Man!*

He jammed the spyglass into his saddlebag, jerked the buckskin around, and descended the steep bluff at break-neck speed. He tore out across the empty landscape, his long-forgotten anger suddenly revived, and his mind on a conversation he had overheard in Fort Stockton about a traveling horse trader.

"The fellow rode a fine stud hoss of brilliant color," said the Fort Stockton man. "He and an old Mexican were leading a string of top-notch yearlings; bought one myself."

"Me too," said his companion. "The feller held a Bible under his arm … said he used to be a preacher in Georgia, but he'd give it up for the *horse* and *dowsing* business. Said, if need be, he'd swear on the Book to the sound quality of each animal."

"He was right nice. Gave me three dollars and left me these cards to hand out to folks," said the other man, as he handed one of the cards to Gentry. Already frowning, Gentry had read it.

T. Pledger's Divine Dowsing Service
If Water is below, We will know
Will Travel Texas and Beyond

"Did this Pledger say where he was going?" Gentry asked.

"Didn't say, but he did say he'd be back this way next year."

Gentry had tapped the card into his shirt pocket. On his way out the door, he tossed the man a dollar.

"What's that for? I didn't do anything for you," the man yelled after him.

"Yes, sir, my friend, you did," Gentry called back over his shoulder, remembering how, after the war, he had taken Pledger's borrowed old pet of a horse, Blackie, back to New Orleans with plans of returning him to Pledger and retrieving Red Man, but discovered that the underhanded *Reverend* had smeared Red Man with bootblack and high-tailed it out of the state. *The sneaky bastard's been in Texas with Red Man all along!* Who would have thought Pledger would go to *Texas* with a stolen Texas horse, and chance getting caught by the horse's owner? *Pledger never was too bright,* Gentry decided. He remembered thinking that day in Fort Stockton that it was too bad he didn't have time to chase Pledger down, but he had a herd he must get to New Mexico Territory, first.

Firming his mouth, Gentry spurred Buck in the direction he'd last seen that copper penny colored horse gleaming in the sunlight. *Maybe the state of Texas wasn't so big after all,* he thought.

~

Timon Pledger hunched atop Red Man's back, his coat flapping wildly in the wind, as he tossed a harried glance over his shoulder. In the opposite direction and getting further and further away, old Sandoval was not far ahead of the Mexican bandits chasing him and the string of horses. Timon swore as he took a hasty swipe at the sweat streaking into his eyes. He shouldn't have listened to the old man this time!

"We must separate, my son!" old Sandoval had said. "It is your string of fine horses these *bandidos* want. I will take them and flee south and they will chase me. You must flee north! If they catch you, they will kill you."

Reluctant to leave the old man to be chased down and possibly murdered, Timon had yelled out as they raced across the flats near the Guadalupe Mountains. "But why would they kill me if they get the horses?"

"As you *Americanos* say, 'Just for the hell of it,' my son," Sandoval yelled back.

"Well, they will kill you, too, 'just for the hell of it!' So we might as well stick together!"

"No, they will not kill me—I am *Mejicano* like them. Besides, one of them has been a guest at my rancho many times; two others are my cousins."

Timon glanced over his shoulder again to see that the bandits had caught up to Sandoval and were loping away with him. One of the bandits clutched the rope attached to the string of yearlings. *At least they had not shot the old man,* Timon thought, while not daring to slack his pace for fear that one or two of the bandidos would turn back for him.

Red Man cleared a small rise near a low creek bed and then thundered across another. When Timon looked back again, he had lost sight of Sandoval and his captors. Still, he pushed Red Man to a faster speed, not knowing where he was going … just getting as far away as he could from where he was.

A dugout in the side of a cliff caught Timon's eye and he headed toward it, intending to take refuge from the rain that had started again. With an abruptness typical of all things hazardous in this hellhole that was West Texas, lightning crashed nearby, sending up a shower of sparks that spooked both him and Red Man. The animal whirled, and then lunged into a wild run in the opposite direction.

When Timon finally regained control of him, they were nowhere near the dugout, but Timon swore under his breath with relief at still being in the saddle. If he'd had such an encounter with rampaging nature and animal a few years ago, he would have lost his seating at the first jump and hit the ground hard; but that was *then*.

As suddenly as it began, the rain stopped. Still at a fast run, Timon forced Red Man back toward the creek. Red Man was in the process of jumping a wide gulley when the thrust of his hind legs crumbled the gulley's edge, and he began to slide backward. It happened so fast that Timon had no time to panic; only to picture himself dead at the bottom of the muddy hole into which they were slipping. To his left, the drooping branch of a stunted tree caught the corner of his eye and he grabbed for it, surprised when he felt the upward thrust of his body as he detached from Red Man's back. He landed on the ground at the edge of the hole. Red Man landed on his feet in the hole, only his head visible above the muddy rim.

Timon stared at Red Man, then at the narrow pit that had the horse wedged in it all the way up to his nose. He gulped when, after a closer look, he saw that the hole was actually a washed-out grave. As dread arrived, Timon's frantic eyes stared even harder: The swiftly running creek was no more than five feet away from Red Man, and judging from the black sky, the rain would start again and the creek would flow even higher. That old grave, likely empty of bones by now, would become his stallion's burying place if he could not get him out of there fast!

He paced around the hole several times before sinking to his haunches on the soggy grass nearby. He lifted his hat, scratched his head, and then rubbed his bearded cheeks and chin.

Red Man, his muzzle barely visible above the grave's rim, nickered at him, his russet eyes rolling from side to side, as if he, too, was assessing his chance for freedom. Suddenly, Timon heard the thrashing of hooves against the inner walls of the hole, and the animal's head rose higher and higher until most of his massive chest appeared above the rim; but for only a few seconds before the animal gave out a scream of desperation and sank back down. He stretched his muzzle over the edge and, looking at Timon, nickered softly.

Flat on his belly, Timon edged closer to Red Man, gauging the earth's stability as he went. It'd do neither of them any good if more earth broke away and he wound up in there with his horse.

Close enough to slip his long arm over the side and feel for the saddle's girth strap, he grunted and groaned with the effort. If he could lighten the stallion's load by lifting the heavy saddle from his back, maybe he could help Red Man free himself. He grunted, trying repeatedly, but his fingertips barely brushed the cinch buckle. He drew his hand away and felt at the sides of the hole, discovering a slippery wall of clay all around. Red Man wouldn't be able to get a hoof-hold on that wall no matter how hard he thrashed at it.

Timon tried again to reach the buckle, and then felt for the circle of rope tied to the saddle. He found it, but his hand was crowded so tightly between the wall and Red Man's body that he had no room to untie it. He tried again, but Red Man shifted his weight and he felt his fingers nearly break against the inner wall before he jerked them free. He cursed himself, thinking that he should have carried his rope looped over his saddle horn—as old Sandoval told him to do.

Timon dropped his head, as worry for Sandoval resurfaced. Was he still alive? He wondered if he should pray for the old Mexican, even though he didn't do much of that any more. His Bible was in the bottom of his saddlebags, as was his frayed Episcopalian frock, which served no purpose other than to cushion his truly useful items, such as his cooking utensils. He removed the Bible occasionally when a prospective horse buyer verbalized doubt as to the authenticity of his claims. Swearing upon the Bible was a useful tool in his business; he could see how helpful it could be if he ever settled down and decided to run for political office.

By the time he gave up trying to free Red Man, he was drenched with sweat and streaked with mud. He crawled a few feet away and flopped over onto his back, and then stared helplessly up at a sky now bleached nearly white by an angry sun. The black clouds had traveled to a distant spot over a jagged mountain, and the new ones rolling in looked too far away to be an instant threat of the creek rising and drowning Red Man.

Exhausted of mind and body, Timon laid there, the newly exposed sun boiling down on him as hot as any he'd sweltered beneath during his travels to every nook and desolate cranny of this monstrous state. He was still flabbergasted by all that had happened to him these past five years. Seems all his life he had wondered about his purpose in life, eventually thinking there was none. His friend, Adam Corrigan, once told him that every man had a *manifest destiny* and all he had to do was find it. That he had found his manifest destiny in such a place as *Texas* made him wonder if all that searching for it had actually driven him crazy. However, like most insane people he'd met, he didn't know he was crazy but everyone else knew he was. Everywhere he traveled, folks recognized "the naked dowser" even with his clothes on. He was getting rich. He had more money in a San Antonio bank than he had ever dreamed of having. Anybody would be happy with that much money, but money was no more important to him than the gnats floating around his sweaty face. He wanted something else.

He stared up at the sky with burning eyes, knowing that more than money, he wanted forgiveness. Forgiveness for what he had done in Miz Bea's parlor almost seven long years ago. He had heard later that Ella and Gentry Garland had married after all, despite what he had done to sabotage their love. He'd been glad, in a cheerless sort of way. He guessed he was foolish to expect either of them to forgive him, especially Garland. Even so, the Corrigans would always be a part of him; the gentle Adam Corrigan, and his beautiful daughter.

Timon's face, long void of its old artless mask, hardened while thinking that Garland must be delirious with happiness ... making love to Ella all he wanted, and living a life of ease at magnificent Greenpoole Plantation. Timon gave his short beard an angry jerk. *Garland had knocked him cold once, but he'd never let him do it again!*

For some time now, he'd been glad that he was no longer overly fearful of much. He had the good sense to fear for his life when it was in jeopardy, but at the same time, the thought of death posed no discomfort. His most secret dread of all in the old days was the fear that he would die without ever having slept with a woman. He had mistaken cowardliness for virtue all those years of striving to be *Reverend* Timon Pledger. In New Orleans he'd been hooked on the habit of women after his first fornication. Consumption of alcohol—that his father called 'the devil's milk'—had finally torn aside his holy veil of cowardly virtue. He had quickly become so addicted to both alcohol and fornication that he could not have one without desiring the other.

Unfortunately, with pleasure parlors being sparse in Texas along most of the roads he traveled ... he compensated for the lack of feminine companionship with more alcohol than he could handle.

Timon reached into the deep pocket of his coat and jerked out a bottle, thinking, *Ella must be thirty by now—and probably still the prettiest woman a man could hope to look at in his lifetime.*

~

Gentry pulled up his buckskin horse and dismounted. The rain had washed away the tracks, but he'd had no trouble following Red Man to the creek. He'd been downwind of the thief and smelled him before he saw him—the rancid odor of alcohol-laced sweat, a dead giveaway that Timon Pledger, curled in a tight knot on the ground, was inebriated to the worst degree, and deep in the sleep of a drunkard. Even the loud clap of thunder as Gentry stood over him did not rouse the scrunched figure to so much as a twitch. Red Man snorted, and Gentry's eyes went immediately to him.

Gentry kneeled beside the hole, his hand stroking Red Man's muzzle. The animal responded with a deep snigger, rolling his eye to Gentry, and then pressing his nose deeper into Gentry's hand.

"Get away from my horse, you sneaky son-of-a-bitch!" said the voice behind Gentry. Even before Gentry rose to his feet, his fingers had snatched his gun from its holster. The only thing that kept him from firing as he whirled around was the sight of Pledger's empty hands waving sloppily in the air at him.

Timon stared, recognition coming into his eyes. *"Gentry Garland!*

Gentry didn't bother speaking. He holstered his gun, went to his horse, jerked a shovel loose, and threw it at Timon.

"Start digging," he ordered.

"Start digging?" Timon whispered. "You mean, you're going to bury me *here* ... in the mud?"

"That depends on how fast you get my horse out of that damn hole you rode him into, you idiot," Gentry growled, as he strode to within twelve feet of Red Man's nose and pointed to the soggy ground. "Start here." He drew a line with the heel of his boot. "Dig a wide trench, gradually getting deeper the closer you get to him ... until he can raise a front leg and get a foothold."

"It's slick clay all the way down. Wet, and too slippery for his weight," Timon said. "He'll just slide back in. I would have been in there too if I hadn't grabbed those tree branches overhead."

Gentry ignored his remarks. "When you're done digging, I'll get a harness rope on his neck and rump. Between us and Buck," he said, and nodded at the buckskin horse, "we'll pull him out." He dropped to his haunches beside Red Man and began stroking him, and calmly whispering. Red Man responded by relaxing his chin on the grave's flat outer rim, as if to patiently await his rescue.

Timon stared at the reunited pair, and then plunged to his task.

The clay was hard and sticky, building up on the shovel until he had to stop frequently to scrape it off with his hands. Intent, he did not look up until nearly three hours later, as the sun sank over the distant Guadalupe Mountains. Timon, as muddy as Red Man by now, collapsed to his knees, coughing and gasping. Gentry tossed a canteen within reach. Timon guzzled the water then vomited it up, along with the last gulps of whiskey he'd consumed earlier.

Getting Red Man out of the pit was no easy chore. The earth was as slick on the surface as it was inside Red Man's entrapment. Even after Red Man had room to lift his front hooves half way up the hole, the spongy earth collapsed against his pawing, and he slid back in. The big buckskin horse, trying to dislodge Red Man, was having no better time of it, as he slipped and slid from side to side of the trench that Timon had dug. With ropes connecting him and Red Man by their necks and saddle horns, Buck slipped to his knees repeatedly and skidded backward, even though Gentry and Timon clung to his bridle and tried to prevent it.

Finally, Gentry went to Buck, pulled a short-handled hatchet from his saddlebag, and tossed it to Timon. Timon, looking perplexed as well as exhausted, jumped aside and it landed in the mud.

Gentry nodded at the scraggly tree that had saved Timon from Red Man's fate. "Crawl up there and start chopping off the branches that have lots of thin shoots and leaves."

"I get it," Timon said, seeming to brighten. "We're going to line the front of that hole so Red Man can get a solid footing."

"Not "we", *you*. Get busy."

An hour later, the chore was done. From there, the big buckskin made easy work of pulling Red Man free. Timon once again collapsed, exhausted, to his knees.

"Now," Gentry commanded, after stripping off the saddle and examining Red Man's legs and discovering them sound, "lead him into the creek and give him a bath." He tossed a brush and tin cup at Timon. "This'll do for ladling."

Timon stared briefly at the cup, then peeled off his muddy shirt and led Red Man belly-high into the creek.

As Gentry watched the process, his eyes narrowed on the bare-chested Timon. The preacher looked just as dissipated as when he'd last seen him in New Orleans, but in a wiry sort of way. Sun-baked and nearly leathery, his neck was as red as a turkey's waddle, though somewhat thicker than the neck that had been too scrawny for the preacher's collar he'd once worn. The skinny but sinewy condition of Timon's arms told Gentry that the Reverend Timon Pledger had not lived a soft life these past years. Gentry shook his head. He was surprised that the man had survived at all.

"My friend and I were chased by bandits back there," Timon called out, waving the wet brush in a westerly direction.

Gentry did not reply, but squatted down to go through Timon's saddlebags.

"They probably murdered him," Timon said after a long pause. "He was just an old man … Sandoval was." His voice cracked, and he coughed as if to clear his throat. "They caught up to him and the string of horses that … that was Red Man's get."

Still rummaging through the saddlebags, Gentry did not look up. "You've got quite a nest egg in here, Reverend."

"You can have the string if … if you help me look for Sandoval, and if the string is with him."

Gentry laughed. "You damn right I can have the string." He arose, went to the buckskin horse, stuffed the money pouch into his own saddlebags, and then stripped off the saddle. "I'll tell you what. I'm gonna sell you Buck, here, for every dollar you've got in this pouch ... since I'm figuring it was made from selling Red Man's get all over the state these past six years or more, and also from siring him out. If you stumble over that string when you're out there looking for your dead friend, you can have them ... but only as long as you keep out of my sight. If I see those yearlings and *you* again, they're mine."

He stomped into the creek, took Red Man's reins, led him ashore, and saddled him. Timon watched until he was finished.

"You aren't going to help me find my friend?"

"No," Gentry replied. "I've got a herd near here that I think a lot more of than you and your friend." He was about to mount Red Man when Timon, abruptly red-faced, came plowing out of the creek toward him, fists raised. Gentry watched curiously as the obviously exhausted and clearly hung-over Timon lurched to his knees but then struggled up with fists still raised.

"All right, Garland! Let's have at it! That's what you been wanting, isn't it?" I'm ready!"

Gentry's look of surprise turned into a grin of disgust. "You can't hardly stand up, Pledger. It wouldn't be a fair fight."

"I don't give a damn!"

"Well, I do," Gentry said.

"Come on! Let's get at it!"

"Goodbye, Pledger," Gentry said, as he stepped into the saddle. "Buck is fast, but not as fast as Red Man. I suggest you ride away from where you last saw your friend and those bandits—or else you just might catch them."

24

"Enemies Must Join Hands, Señor ..."

THE NOISE TIMON HEARD seemed to come from all directions—a scream, voices, laughter—more screams, followed by more laughter. Was it Sandoval and the bandits? Were they torturing the old Mexican? It didn't sound like the screams of a man, but torture could make some men sound like anything but men. He drew up the reins on the buckskin gelding Gentry Garland had left him, and then pressed his hands to his sun-scaled ears. Slowly, he turned his head left and then right, dropping one hand at a time to listen; it was a trick Sandoval taught him. When the noise grew fainter or louder in one uncovered ear or the other as he rotated his head, he generally could tell which direction it was or wasn't coming from. A simple thing, but he hadn't known it. But then again, he'd not had cause to listen for much of anything during his lackadaisical days as pastor of Christ Episcopal Church back in Georgia.

He executed Sandoval's test repeatedly, always pausing longer when his open ear was opposite a stretch of low mesas to the west. He dropped his hands. Did he want to follow those sounds? Without Sandoval to clue him, it could turn out to be his last curiosity on earth; but what if it was Sandoval, and he could do something to help *him*, for a change?

An hour later, Timon lay on his belly, covered with sweat and dirt, and peered down into a clearing next to a shallow stream. The air was stuffy with the smell of man and his contrivances. For a long, thirsty moment, the shallow but cool-looking stream of creek water interested Timon more than the screams. He easily recognized the five vermin squatting around a cook fire and drinking from gourds of various sizes and shapes. Having become a connoisseur of alcoholic aromas, Timon knew the gourds contained a strong whiskey called *sotol*, made from the fermented sap of the desert yucca plant. Being downwind of the fractious little party, he recognized all sorts of smells and rude sounds. Nearby stood two small tents; one completely dark on the inside, the other lit and with the shadowy forms of two men sitting inside. The screams were coming from the darkened tent. At the campfire, Rabbit Jack, wearing the yellow bonnet that usually hung round his neck by its strings, kicked the half-naked Comanchero next to him, and then grabbed the gourd before it could reach the man's open mouth. The racket the five vermin made, laughing and cursing, was all that Timon heard now; the crying and screaming from inside the darkened tent had stopped.

As Timon watched, wondering what he could do and realizing that he could do nothing, a scrawny young girl, hugging the remnants of a faded calico dress to her nakedness, her hand pressed to the side of her head, burst from the dark tent into the revealing moonlight. The vermin laughed louder, pointing, and Timon watched her run to a tall Yucca tree … beneath which huddled four small children! Two boys and two little girls, the oldest of them no more than nine or ten! The running girl, older, but still a child, crawled in among the smaller children and hugged them around her. One of them, the tiniest girl, began to whimper.

With the abruptness of snakebite, Timon's attention shot back to the tent the girl had exited. A tall man, his hat pulled low to his face, emerged. He stood for a moment, adjusted his gun belt then tossed up a hand to the men before striding briskly to the row of horses nearby. He mounted one and rode away.

"Véale luego, Jefe," the others yelled, and then wasted no time in getting back to their drinking.

"Yes, I shall see you later, my friends," he called over his shoulder. "But first, get me a good price for the girl and those brats."

"El Jefe!" Timon uttered beneath his breath. He would recognize that voice anywhere; but the face remained a secret, just as when he'd first heard him speak from the shadows of old Sandoval's *hacienda*. He looked back down at the drunken revelers around the cook fire and realized that there was nothing he could do to save those poor children. If he tried a rescue, he'd only get himself killed.

Lying there in the dirt, he dropped his forehead into his palm, his regretful breath stirring the dirt. *Well … at least that vermin is only going to sell them, not murder them.* He pressed his knuckles hard into his scalded lips, and stared at the older girl, and then at the younger ones. *But what if selling them isn't all they do to them? And what other kind of vermin would they be selling them to?* He easily guessed what had happened to the older girl in the tent. He suspected these men would have no problem ravaging even the younger children.

With that, his trembling hand slid down to his six-shooter, and he drew it up to point down at the camp. There were *five* targets … he had *six* bullets—an *extra,* in case he missed one of the targets. Shaking as he was, he could miss them all! He pointed at Rabbit Jack, closed one eye, and gazed down the gun barrel site with the other, his finger slowly tightening on the trigger.

The hand that grabbed the pistol from behind and the other hand that closed over his mouth were as rough as *muela* stones.

"Sea quieto, my son," Sandoval hissed, his mouth tight against Timon's ear.

Sandoval released him, and Timon rolled onto his back and stared at the old man.

"Thank God! I thought you were dead," Timon whispered, moisture suddenly washing some of the dirt from his eyes. He quickly drew his sleeve across them.

"I tol' you, *esos hombres* are of my blood. They would not shed their own blood unless they have a reason."

"The reason could have been my horses."

"But I did not resist their interest in them, my son."

Before Timon could whisper back, uproarious laughter from below made them both roll onto their stomachs and gaze down.

"Remember *El Jefe,* Sandoval?" Timon whispered. "He defiled that oldest girl not an hour ago, then left."

"*Si,* I watched him leave."

"The rest of that bunch is going to sell those poor kids somewhere. Even without seeing the kid's little faces, you can tell they're scared out of their minds. We've got to do something."

"Yes, my son, we must." Motioning Timon to follow, he began scooting backward. When they were far enough away from the edge, they rose on their hands and knees and crawled to within sight of their horses, then ran the rest of the way.

"My son, I saw many men and many *ganado de longhorn* not far from here. We will go to them and ask for help."

Oh no! Timon thought. He was about to encounter Gentry Garland again, sooner than either one of them planned.

~

Gentry eyed the old Mexican man who had been staring at him ever since he and Timon Pledger rode into camp and told their story. The old man hardly blinked, his narrowed eyes on Gentry like a coyote watching a prairie dog hole.

"Do I know you, amigo?" Gentry finally asked the old Mexican, his tone none too friendly. Seeing Pledger again so soon was enough to put him in a foul mood—he didn't need a *friend-of-an-enemy* eyeing him like he'd suddenly grown horns and a forked tail.

The old man stepped closer. "Do you know a man other men call *El Jefe,* Señor Garland?"

"Mexican for *the boss … the chief,"* Gentry said, "this could be any man in authority. My own vaqueros call me jefe sometimes. I'll need a name other than that."

Sandoval squinted up at him. "That is all I know of him. I have not seen his face, but have heard his voice many times. But, Señor, he sounds almost the same as you … even the size of him." He stepped yet closer and squinted up at Gentry again. "It is very strange."

"What's he talking about, Pledger?"

"I don't know. I've never seen El Jefe either. He sounds like you, but there's a difference," Timon said, and then his frown turned angry. "He needs killing, that's all I know about him."

Gentry turned away to pour himself a cup of coffee from the huge tin pot over the fire. The only man he'd ever been compared to identity-wise was his cousin, Luther Garland. Luther was no saint, but no one had ever accused him of rape or of running with a bunch like Pledger described. He hadn't seen Luther since coming back to Texas, but Luther usually stayed close to his own property east of Laredo, and which bordered Kada's land a few miles short of Nueces County. He was a big help to Kada at roundup time. Likely that's where he was right now… helping her gather part of the herd that would be driven to Abilene.

After hearing Timon's and Sandoval's story, Gentry knew that he'd take Bones Drawgood with him to rescue the kids. Being of Indian and Negro mix, Bones was also the best tracker Gentry knew. Bones' father was an escaped slave with no last name. Maybe it was the wide, bony structure of Bones' face even as a baby that made his father name him *Bones*. Bones' Apache mother spoke little to no English, but she was proud of how Bones could sketch artful pictures on paper or in the dirt. Whenever others were around, she would pat Bones' shoulder and proudly announce, "Bones draw good." The name stuck. More useful than his drawing talents, Bones had night vision like a cat, and could shoot straighter than any man on the drive. Not that Gentry doubted his own shooting and tracking skills; but if Pledger's description of the five "vermin" with the captive white children was true, they would need to be exterminated in rapid order—a job for two expert shots armed with the new Winchester repeating rifles he'd brought along on the drive. After that, Timon and the Mexican could escort the children back to civilization on their own time—he and his herd needed to push on in the opposite direction.

Gentry threw his coffee out on his way to the supply wagon, where he pulled out two Winchester rifles. "The night's turned cool, and there's a full moon—a great night for tracking, eh, Bones?" he said, as he tossed one of the rifles to him.

"My favorite way of hunting," Bones said, without a trace of accent other than Texan.

~

Five miles down the trail, they came upon a dead Mexican bandit, and then another, and another. Sandoval identified the last three as his cousins and the man who had visitor to his rancho many times.

"Seems Pledger's "vermin" caught up with his horse thieves," Gentry said to Bones, but Timon answered.

"Sinners killing sinners," he mumbled. "Why can't that be the way of it all in this land of yours, Garland?"

"Texas doesn't have a monopoly on vermin, Pledger," Gentry drawled. "Most of it drifts in from other places … like you did."

Timon glared at him then looked away.

The tracks left by the stolen horses and those belonging to Rabbit Jack and his crew were as easy to follow as putting one foot in front of the other. Bones examined the ground and said there were eight horses carrying riders, and five without. "This last five is light-hoofed, likely the string the old Mexican had. Ain't anybody astraddle 'em," he said, adding, "All the horses are shod except three. Reckon them three are mustang ponies and they're carrying the kids."

"Looks like we're gonna get your string back, Pledger ... if we don't get killed first," Gentry said.

Timon looked away. "They're yours, Garland, and you know it—same as Red Man."

"You damn right they're mine, and I'll expect you to see them to my property in South Texas. You'll also be taking those kids back to wherever they belong if they're still alive when we find them. If so, I'm sending Bones and another good shot along to protect the bunch of you, in case you run into more low men, or Rabbit Jack himself."

Timon nodded then glanced elsewhere, but not quick enough for Gentry to miss the look of odium in the man's eyes.

Sandoval dropped the arm of one of his dead relatives and remounted his horse. "I was going to take the ring my cousin took from me, but his finger is missing," he said.

Gentry and Bones loped ahead. Bones had seen a campfire flickering in the distance, its light so small that only the two men in the group with remarkable eyesight could see it.

Minutes before Timon and Sandoval caught up to Gentry and Bones, the shooting was over. Four shots, in rapid succession, four bodies crumpled in various positions of death, sitting up or lying flat. They had obviously died without an inkling that their carefree days of murder, rape, and pandemonium were over. Upon seeing the bodies, Timon and Sandoval were not relieved, nor was Gentry—Rabbit Jack was not among them.

Just then, a collapsed tent began to wiggle and move. Gentry and Bones, with pistols in hand, flung the tarp away from the two humps that trembled beneath it.

Two well-dressed Mexican men jumped to their feet, hands in the air.

"Do not shoot! Do not shoot, Señor! We were prisoners of these rabbles ... just as *esos niños!*" The Mexican men pointed to the Barton children running toward them.

Molly Barton and her siblings recognized Gentry long before he recognized them, and they came screaming at him, calling his name.

They were starved and dirty, infested with lice and mites. Cuts, bruises, and scratches festered on their arms and legs. Molly and the oldest boy had taken a beating and, after their initial rush of excitement, could hardly stand. Molly's long brown hair hung stiff with dried blood, the left side of her head and face crusted with it. "The son-a'bitch sliced off my earlobe!" she cried, then wasted no time in telling Gentry that her uncle and grandmother had sold all five of them to Rabbit Jack.

"Rabbit Jack got away, though. Left long before you all got here, right after the son-a'bitch cut my ear!" she cried, then looked around as if he might be about to come charging out of the darkness to attack them all.

"If he's watching, he knows his men are dead. He won't be back," Gentry said. "We'll get him sooner or later."

"I guess I oughta be grateful they left my baby boys behind with Leet and Grandma," Molly said weakly, as Timon doctored her ear. "Them tiny little things would'a died for sure if I had to take 'em along. We about died our own self," she said, her enormous blue eyes flashing with remembered horrors.

"You will all be fine now," Timon offered.

"Oh, Lord! I hope little Hemp and Dan is all right! I hope Ella took 'em away from that mean old bitch and Uncle Leet!"

"Ella?" Gentry frowned at her.

"Yes. *Ella*. Your *wife,*" she said, drawing a deep breath. "Geeze, how many Ellas you know that live on your place, Gent? Ella done help me have my babies, and was mighty nice bringing them and me clothes and eats."

Timon, carrying a blanket from his saddlebags to Molly, halted in his tracks, the sudden look of interest in his eyes giving him away. "She is *here,* in Texas?"

Gentry glared at him. "Where else would my wife be but with her husband, Pledger?" he growled, while thinking, *the son-of-a-bitch still loves my wife!* Anger darkened his expression as he stared at Timon.

Timon glowered back at him. "It's hard to imagine a fine lady like Miss Ella any place but Greenpoole Plantation, that's all I meant," he said just as curtly.

Gentry turned back to Molly. "Rabbit Jack's cohorts had a hundred dollars in gold and almost as much in greenbacks—which makes me think that Rabbit Jack was planning on coming back here tonight," he said, as he handed Molly the weighty pouch.

"Wow! Is that for me?" she said, and gave out a little whoop.

"I doubt your relatives will be anywhere around when you get back, Molly. They probably lit out no sooner than they sold you kids," Gentry said.

"They wouldn't take off traveling with two little babies," Molly insisted. "They'll be there all right."

"In any case, if my wife's still there, give her the money. Tell her to find a place for you and your brothers and sisters. I'm thinking the Nun's at their monastery in Victoria will find a good home for you."

"I ain't no *Catholic!* I been baptized in the church of hot words and hard licks when I was younger than little Effie, here!" She pressed the shoulder of her smallest sister. "Them Nuns ain't gonna approve of *my* kinda religion one damn bit!"

Timon handed her the blanket and, with a tender look of understanding, spoke softly to her. "Young lady, I don't think those good Sisters will condemn you for the sins others have committed against you."

Molly looked him up and down. "What are you, some kinda preacher or something?"

"Or *something,*" Gentry said.

Sandoval stepped to Timon's defense, looking straight at Gentry for a moment before turning to Molly. "Yes, Señorita; Señor Timon is a preacher … a man of God. Not only that, God has given him a great gift. Not only can this good man speak words of wisdom, he can bring water to land that is starved for it."

Bones, standing next Gentry, chuckled. "So it was *you* who made it rain back there, eh?"

Sandoval's brown face grew darker. "Do not laugh, Señor Bones. You may need this man's gift some day when your wells have dried and your tongue becomes too fat to speak." He put up a finger and then pointed it to the ground. "It is the water below this earth that speaks to him, not the water in the clouds."

Gentry and Bones looked at each other, and then at Timon and Sandoval. Bones had gone for supplies a few days ago and came back with more information than was on the card in Gentry's pocket about a white man, accompanied by a half-crippled old Mexican—the white man *dowsing* for water *naked* as a scalded gobbler at Christmas.

Gentry laughed. "Don't tell me *you're* the 'naked dowser' we heard about at Fort Stockton?"

Timon's sun-baked face flushed even redder.

Again, old Sandoval leaped to defend him. "There is a word you gringos use, how you say … *humille … humildad …*"

"Humility," Gentry gave him the word.

"*Gracias*, Señor Garland," Sandoval said, then gazed at Timon with absolute affection. "God does not give freely His great gifts. He asks "humility" of those He honors with such power. To be naked of body and soul … this is the *humility* He asks of his servant, Timon."

"I think he means *humiliation*," Bones grinned.

"Perhaps," Sandoval said. "But it does not matter to God what you think of this man, Señor Bones … or that you laugh at him."

Bones looked embarrassed. "I ain't laughing. If you say he got a God-given gift, I sure ain't gonna buck it. My Christian daddy didn't raise no heathen."

Gentry handed Timon a few greenbacks. "It's nine hundred miles to my place, hot-as-hell every inch of the way. When you get to a town, buy a canvas-topped wagon to haul the kids in," he said, then added, "You'll bed down at my camp tonight, and leave before sunup."

Timon shoved the money back at him. "I don't need your money, Garland. You overlooked another pouch in my saddlebags back there at that mud hole."

"I didn't overlook it," Gentry said, as he pocketed the greenbacks. "I was thinking of big Buck, there ..." He nodded at the buckskin horse he'd exchanged for Red Man. "I figured you'd need money to buy Buck some grain—that is, if you ever found your way out of that creek bed."

"You'd be surprised to know the things I've *'found my way out of'* since seeing you in New Orleans, Garland."

"Well hell, Pledger, maybe you don't need my two good men at all." He nodded at Bones and Airout.

"Well hell, Garland, maybe I don't!"

"Well, let's just say I'm sending them along to watch over the kids and make sure my string of horses end up where they belong."

"Don't worry. They'll get there. Besides, I haven't seen Miss Ella in a long time. I'd like to find out if she hates me as much as you do."

Molly tossed the pouch of money at Timon. "Here, Preacher. Since we're both gonna be seeing Ella, you can give her the money. I ain't got a pocket to carry it in, anyhow," she said.

Gentry snapped the pouch out of Timon's hand and handed it to Bones Drawgood. "Give it to my wife, Bones ... or my mother if my wife isn't there," he added, low enough so that only Bones heard.

Timon stepped into his saddle, and then squinted defiantly at Gentry, as he and Sandoval led the children away on their mustangs and headed toward Gentry's camp.

Gentry yelled after him. "It's not "*Miss*" Ella any longer, Pledger. It is *Miz* Gentry Garland!"

The two rescued Mexican men had moved off to themselves, their backs to everyone, as they whispered to each other, but now they approached Gentry.

"Señor Garland, I am Diego De La Fuente, and this is my brother, Rodolfo. We are from Mexico City, and were on our way to San

Antonio when captured by those men," he said, and nodded to the dead Comancheros. "We owe you our lives, sir, and wish to repay you when we have access to our funds."

Gentry shook each hand. "No need for that. It was personal," he said, adding, "There was a man with them called Rabbit Jack; how long has he been gone?"

"Hours ago … soon after his boss, the man they called *El Jefe,* left us," said Diego De La Fuente. "He is far away by now, Señor Garland. I am afraid you could not catch him for many days."

Gentry nodded, realizing that his business with Rabbit Jack would have to wait yet longer. "Take your pick of the dead men's horses … and their weapons," he said to the De La Fuentes. "You'll need them if you're gonna get back to Mexico with your hair. This is Indian territory."

"As we know, Señor," said Diego, as he pointed to his brother Rodolfo, who had yet to speak. Rodolfo pulled down his collar to reveal a wide, jagged scar across his throat. Diego continued, "When he was a child, the Apache left him for dead after they cut him. Thanks to our Holy Father above, they took my young brother's voice, but not his life."

"He was lucky. The Apache don't usually leave survivors," Gentry said, then added, "Pledger and the men I'm sending with him will give you protection to the border. You can ride with them as far as El Paso. After that, they'll be pushing on down to South Texas."

Diego De La Fuente's bulbous eyes squinted at Gentry. "Señor, you have many men in your employ, *si*? All of them very good with their *pistolas*?"

"What's your point, Mister De La Fuente?" Gentry asked, looking around, impatient to get moving.

"I am a businessman, Señor. My business is the mining of gold. My father-in-law … one of Mexico's cruelest bandidos, has kidnapped my wife and children. He also took much of my gold—

two hundred and fifty ingots worth one hundred seventy thousand dollars in American," he added.

Gentry whistled. "With that much at stake, your father-in-law will have an army of men like himself guarding it."

"Si, he will have many like himself. I will need an army of my own."

"Good luck to you, Señor De La Fuente. A rich man like you shouldn't have any trouble hiring the kind of men you'll need for that job."

"I will pay you and your men well if you help me rescue of my family and my gold."

Gentry shook his head. "Sorry, I can't oblige. I have another herd trailing across Texas this very minute toward Abilene, Kansas. As soon as I've delivered this herd to Fort Sumner, I'm joining the Abilene herd. My men and I will winter in Kansas ... stay through spring, and into summer. We'll be gone a long time."

"Please, Señor. How long it takes does not matter. My father-in-law rules a tiny Tarahumara Indian village in the Sierra Madre Mountains of my country. He will not leave there. I know my family will be safe because he is very fond of them. If you agree, Rodolfo and I will wait in San Antonio for your return," he said. "I will pay you in gold bars, Señor Garland—*mucho oro*."

Gentry had dismissed De La Fuente's plea as soon as it was voiced, but now he looked closely at the man.

"How much gold?"

"Half of what they have stolen from me. You will earn one hundred twenty-five gold bars. These bars weigh thirty-six ounces each. You will be rich, Señor Garland. Will your cattle earn you nearly eighty-five thousand dollars, in gold, in such a short time?"

"If I were to take you up on your offer, I wouldn't argue about the price. But why would you pay as much as *half*? It doesn't make sense," Gentry said.

"My wife and children are worth much more than my gold, Señor."

~

The next morning, in the pale haze of pre-dawn, Gentry's men, whistling and yelling, got the longhorns moving again. Gentry sat atop Red Man and watched Timon, the Barton children, and the De La Fuentes, along with Bones Drawgood and Airout Buzell set out for South Texas. With Pledger on his way to Ella, it occurred to him that he had something else to worry about other than getting his herds to market. He didn't fear Pledger as a rival, but as a means for Ella to leave him. Only a lack of money stood in her way. Pledger could provide that money. When she finally figured out that he hadn't ordered his people to keep her from leaving with the children, she'd take them and be gone. He'd be away for a year. Maybe longer. She'd be gone before he could see her again … and try and convince her to stay.

Gentry's frown deepened. Even as he thought of Ella and of getting the herd to Abilene so that he could pay off his bank note and hold onto his land, the gold was never out of his mind, and another plan was forming in his head.

What if he finished the New Mexico drive then turned over the responsibility of the Abilene herd to his cowhands? He'd go straight to San Antonio to meet up with the De La Fuentes. On the way there, he'd see Ella. After that, he and the De La Fuentes could hire the men they'd need for the rescue mission. He knew Bones and Airout would be eager to earn some of that gold, as would be other of his men. Eighty-five thousand dollars in gold would solve his present money problems, as well as guarantee a future free of debt.

A mixture of anger and desperation came into his black eyes. There were not many times in Gentry's life when a decision had him so torn. If he continued with the drive, who knows what could happen? He may miss the opportunity to earn that gold … miss, as well, a last chance to see Ella right away.

Feeling a powerful thirst, Gentry headed for the chuck wagon and the water barrel. PeeWee Hines, his father's longtime trail cook, handed him a dipper full.

"You know, Mista Gent, I was thinking about that last drive I made with your daddy, Mista Kiel, 'fore he die. He done promise a man out in Montana he gonna bring him two thousand mixed herd to start up a new ranch, and we was on the way there. It was rough going, with rain and storms, and rivers wanting to drown us. We done had two bad stampedes before the first month on the trail."

"Dad told me about that one," Gentry said.

"One day, a rich man from Arkansas rode up and offered Mista Kiel twice as much money for the herd as that Montana rancher was gonna pay," PeeWee said, and chuckled. "Mos' of us hands was all stoved up and hoping he'd take it. But you daddy say to that feller, 'Much obliged, sir, that's a lot of money. But I got a *powerful intention* to finish what I started … and you wasn't no part of th' deal.'" PeeWee laughed again. "That daddy of yours was a man of th' best caliber, Mista Gent. Wasn't nothing could turn him from that *powerful intention* he was always talking 'bout—not money, not nothing."

Gentry handed PeeWee the cup. "Thanks, old friend, for the water, and the memory." With a yell and jab of spurs that made Red Man whirl and then sprint across the flat plain, he headed back to his plodding herd. There, he sent a rider to tell Diego De La Fuente he'd meet him in San Antone when he got back from driving his second herd to Abilene … if they cared to wait that long for his services.

As For Ella, he'd given up *his* powerful intention once to keep her love … he wasn't gonna do it again.

25

"'Pears to me Like Georgia Done Come to Texas …"

ELLA SAT AT THE KITCHEN TABLE chewing a fingernail. The morning hour was nearing three o'clock, and she had yet to sleep. Her mind churned with an excitement she'd not felt in a long time. Hempstead Grouse was leaving at sunrise for Galveston, and she wanted to go with him.

Earlier, for almost the entire day, she had sat at her bedroom window, staring out across her husband's vast acres and thinking of the *Rawls* and their *cotton*. Like the Rawls property, not all of Gentry's land was rolling hills; much of it was *flat*, ideal for growing cotton!

Yesterday, with that thought in mind, and with the ornery old longhorn bull, *Mean Daddy*, out of sight, she had climbed over the corral railing and walked a few hundred yards away from the house. Kada Garland said this lack of rain was a rare occurrence, and this land was usually covered with greenery.

"Droughts don't usually last this long in this part of Texas," she had said. "You just happened to show up at the wrong time, my dear; but it's bound to rain soon."

Ella rose from the table and began pacing, her mind awhirl. If she could go to Galveston with Hempstead, hire free Negroes, as Hempstead was planning to do for the Rawls, she could grow cotton as well as they! All she needed was rain and … *time*. She recalled Hempstead's words as they sat on the porch last night seeking relief from the heat.

"It's damn-well likely Gent won't be back for mebbe a year or more," Hempstead said, even though she hadn't asked. "The New Mexico herd won't take long, but he'll likely winter the bigger herd in Kansas, fatten them up before selling them at Abilene."

Later, Tessie said Mister Rawls told her that Texas planters were getting forty cents a pound for cotton if they could get it to Mexico and onto English ships without the U.S. government knowing about it. Cotton planting began in the spring, cultivation took place during the summer, and harvesting began in late August. If the drought ended, she could make good money in one season. Enough to buy back a few acres of Greenpoole and have Meshach farm it on shares. Then, with her profits wired to a bank in Savannah, she'd figure out a way to get her children away from here and back to Georgia!

Ella smiled. With rain and a little luck, and three or four Negroes to plow, plant, and pick… she could possibly harvest a crop before Gentry returned. It was worth attempting.

A scowl replaced her smile, as nagging reality joined the calculations in her head. To eventually buy all of Greenpoole from Banker Treadwell, she'd need more than one planting season … possibly more than two or three.

She sank slowly back to the chair. She was foolish not to understand that her dream would have to be long term. How long? How many cotton crops? The thought of staying here several years made her bite her fingernails again. Gentry wouldn't be able to stop her from planting the first cotton, but what about afterward, when she wanted to plant more?

She went to the window and stared out into the darkness, her mind churning again. Could she convince him that she had decided to stay, would not divorce him, and would be all that a wife was supposed to be … but would be so much happier if he would only let her have a few acres to do with as she chose?

Was she capable of such deception? Could she coolly carry out such a plot to fool him?

Her baby's piercing hunger cries jerked her back to the real world, and her shoulders slumped. *She couldn't go to Galveston with Hempstead Grouse!* She couldn't go *anywhere!* She had a hungry baby needing to be at her breast every few hours, day and night! Dejected and weighted by her depression, she shuffled across the room and slowly climbed the stairs. Midway up, the baby's cries stopped, and Ella dully concluded that she must have fallen back asleep.

The door to her room stood slightly ajar and she pushed it open, expecting to find Gentalee slumbering in her crib. Could she be so lucky that Gentalee was now going to begin sleeping through the night? But then she halted abruptly in her tracks to stare dumbly at the sight before her: Fat Lupe sat stuffed into the rocking chair, one of her big brown breasts protruding from her blouse like an oversized *calabaza*... and with baby Gentalee's hungry mouth latched firmly onto her nipple!

Ella let out a shriek.

"Pardona, Señora! Pardona!" Fat Lupe pleaded, as she came up from the chair, while jerking her blouse closed. In the process, she popped the dark, thumb-sized nipple from little Gentalee's hungry mouth. Gentalee shrieked her anger.

"No wonder she's been getting so fat!" Ella cried.

"Pardona, Señora!" Fat Lupe sobbed.

Ella opened her mouth to rant more at the woman, but quite suddenly, her furious expression cleared.

Fat Lupe, still trying to get Ella to take the baby, cried harder. She stopped abruptly when Ella, nodding amiably, gently took her free arm and guided her back to the rocking chair.

Seconds later, Lupe again nursed Gentalee, even though she never took her wary eyes off the smiling Ella, as Ella retrieved her carpetbag from the shelf and began cramming it full.

~

Hempstead was not happy. "Lookie here, Miz Ella"—he had taken to calling her *Miz Ella* when she didn't admonish him for feeding the Barton's hogs the Bartons—"I thought old Tessie was just wagging her tongue with more nonsense when she told me you been talking about the Rawls' cotton; but, *by God*!" He glowered at her, looking unaccustomedly flustered.

"Tessie wasn't talking nonsense, Mister Grouse. I come from a long line of planters. I know what I'm doing."

"I'll tell you what Gent would tell you. He'd say this is *cattle* land, ain't no damn cotton plantation, so don't even think about bringing any cottonpickin' Negroes on the place!"

"I'm past thinking about it. I'm doing it."

"Well, I ain't taking you! Even if the yeller fever ain't so strong on the coast these days, it's still there abouts. I wouldn't be going, myself, if t'wern't for old man Rawls divvying up a sum that'd just about annihilate worry over any risk to an old bone sack like me. I ain't got a soul who'd give a crap if I did catch it."

"Mister Grouse, you told me last night that the steamships were again running along the coast, the threat of fever no longer a problem. Did you lie to me?"

"I don't recall what in hell I said, Tessie was yammering so much! You damn wimmen can confuse a man quicker'n a sneaky blow to the pate!"

"I'm going, Mister Grouse, even if I must go alone and ask directions along the way."

He tore off his hat and slapped it on the table. "But golldamnit-to-hell, you got youngens to think of!"

"They are in good hands. I would not be leaving if I had doubts."

"Well, let me put it to you this way! Gent's gonna try his damnedest to skin me if I take you along. He got a pinch of Indian blood in him, you know, and that Indian blood boils up in him from time to time. It sure as hell will boil up in him when he finds out what you was up to and that I helped you with it. It'd be a damn sight worse for me if you got the fever and died!"

She picked up her carpetbag, and then handed him his hat. "I had the fever as a child and survived it. After that, I tended Negroes on our plantation that came down with it. I didn't get it then, and I won't get it now."

"You can't go, I said!"

She marched through the house and out the front door. "I do not need your permission, Mister Grouse. I need only to accompany you to Galveston."

Aware that he was storming down the steps behind her, she climbed into the buggy, settled lightly onto the seat, and picked up the reins.

His hat was in his hand, and now he used it to strike repeatedly at the seat beside her. "Get down from there, damnit!"

She stared straight ahead, unperturbed. "I think I heard you tell Tessie that you would take the train from Victoria to Port of Lavaca, then a steamer to Galveston. We'd best be on our way if we want to reach Victoria before dark."

Cursing under his breath, but loud enough for her to hear every foul utterance, he yelled out for Flaco to unsaddle Stonewall. As he waited for Flaco to appear, he shouted out to her, "Well, don't blame me for any mishaps that perchance happen on this golldamn trip!"

"I shall exonerate you from any blame, Mister Grouse," she shouted back at him, not bothering to turn around, "especially when my husband attempts to skin you."

He lit roughly onto the seat and, grabbed the reins. As if to frighten her, he let out a hellish yell before plunging at reckless speed toward the arched gate. They rode thus for a mile before he slowed down. Determined not to give him satisfaction, Ella was as unruffled by his childish antic as if she'd just been treated to a gentle waltz. She curled her lips, thinking, *if you knew of all the "mishaps" I survived long before you came into my life, Mister Hempstead Grouse, you'd feel quite foolish, indeed!*

They reached Victoria just in time to leave the buggy and horses at the livery stable and catch the train to Port of Lavaca.

~

Galveston's wharves, some of which were still in disrepair from unsuccessful bombardments by Union ships during the war, lay crowded with moored vessels. Ella and Hempstead, making their way down the pier along with the other passengers, obeyed the order of a Union officer to step aside and let pass a hundred or more Negroes that had left one of the ships. Accompanied by more than a dozen Union soldiers, the ex-slaves trotted along at a fast clip, looking neither left nor right. A second steamer began expelling an even larger number—men, women, and children, some well-dressed, others wearing the rough cloth of their past enslavement—all as silent as the first group. As Ella watched, they swarmed past, made their way off the wharf, and trudged toward the city, their Union guard trotting alongside with rifles half-raised.

"Why are those people under arrest?" she asked Hempstead.

"They ain't under arrest. They is being protected from the dangers that be, and they be plenty now the war's been lost. I hear-tell the Negro is coming to Texas by the boatload since freedom come to them. They're thinking they're gonna be safer here than deeper South, and can find work." He wagged his head. "As to the *safe* part, a good number of them's probably gonna wish they never left the boat."

Watching the Negroes move toward town, Ella's thoughts turned to home and Greenpoole plantation. She wondered where the majority of Greenpoole's people had gone when they left after the war. Some, she knew, went North; others moved into Savannah. Thankfully, Meshach, Moonbeam, and Sunbeam were still at Greenpoole in the employ of Banker Treadwell. They had a roof over their heads and food to eat—unlike these poor wretches, she thought, as the last of them filed past.

"There are so many," she said to Hempstead. "Will they find work?"

"Them that's got skills will find it ... blacksmiths, carpenters, cooks and whatnot. The rest is up Stink Creek without a paddle. They's the ones I'm after for old man Rawls—plowing and a'picking don't take much learning, just muscle."

"All right," Ella said, moving ahead of him. "Let's get them, and be on our way back on the next boat."

"Like hell we'll do it that way! I'm hungry, and I'm gonna have me a fine meal and a good night's sleep. I ain't eat right or slept tight since we left the ranch, and neither have you. We'll go straight to the Customs House in the morning ... tell them we're planning on taking some black folk off their hands, and then we'll go to the golldamn Freedmen's Bureau and kiss ass so we can do it all proper and legal."

Ella closed her eyes, struggling, as usual, to shutter her mind against his profanity. It wasn't the first time she'd felt like slapping Hempstead Grouse hard across his dirty old mouth; but for now, she had a more pressing matter; she was as tired and hungry as he. In addition, she wanted a cool bath. She'd discovered that a big tub of cold water was the only way to get a brief reprieve from Texas' heat.

~

The street leading to Galveston's Freedmen's Bureau—the U.S. government's guardian of Negro affairs—teemed with pedestrians and vehicles either going to or coming from the Bureau. Empty freight wagons moved toward the Bureau, and then departed loaded with ex-slaves.

"Them there looks like planters hauling off some workers," Hempstead said, pointing to one of the loaded wagons. "But I reckon there'll be plenty left for us to pick from."

"I'm sure of it," Ella replied, studying the crowd.

Hempstead eyed her, then cocked his head aside the way she'd seen him do when he was about to take issue with one thing or another, whether serious or ridiculous.

"Hiring hands ain't a job for a woman," he said. "You gotta look at them ex-slaves real close... make sure you don't get any that's been beat hell out of and turned mean-eyed by their old masters. It ain't no easy chore... especially for a woman."

"I'll have you know, Mister Grouse, that I ..."

He didn't give her time to finish. He stepped away, stretching his neck at something Ella could not see from where she sat in the rented hack. "I'll be back in a wink," he said, and left.

Ella leaned forward and looked from black face to black face. She didn't want anyone who looked the least bit sullen or angry. She planned to feed them well, house them comfortably in Gentry's la villa, and pay them a good wage—a fair proposition to any ex-slave looking for an honest day's pay for an honest day's work. They just must be willing to wait for the cash until the first crops were in.

Not a half-hour later, Hempstead came strolling back to her, a big grin on his rustic face.

"I got me four workers, all from the same family. They's two brothers about thirty year-old or so, and one of them's got two strappin' sons fourteen and fifteen years old, I'd say." He laughed, obviously pleased. "I'm going in to clear it with the Bureau, sign papers, and take their damn lecture. Gotta give them the boy's names and where I'm taking 'em to." He motioned to the four Negroes waiting nearby. "Soon as I get 'er done, I'll find your four workers for you, Miz Ella ... just to make sure you ain't got any regrets later."

When he was gone, Ella climbed down. She knew what she was looking for, and she could find them on her own. *Unlike you, Mister Hempstead Grouse,* she thought, *I have actually run a plantation that had nearly fifty Negro laborers. And other than carrying on the tradition of slavery, I made no mistakes.*

She stared around at the crowd of milling Negroes. Hempstead had indicated that many of these new arrivals would rue the day they stepped off the boat in Texas. Last night, in the hotel dining room, she had taken her meal at a table with three planter's wives, and their remarks gave credence to Hempstead's comment.

One of them, a young woman newly married to an East Texas planter, said white men had murdered two of her husband's newly hired freedmen last year just because they were Negroes and were now free. The killers, a couple of known rowdies, were arrested but released soon after, unpunished. Such murders and beatings were happening everywhere, she said, adding, "and if these poor darkies coming into Texas think they are going to be safe from that sort of thing, they are in for a terrible surprise."

"They most certainly are," said the second woman. "Our very own neighbor killed one of his freed slaves because the boy refused to stay on and work for him, and was not a thing done about it."

"Don't you have a Freedman's Bureau?" Ella asked.

"Of course, but what can they do when witnesses swear the boy attacked his former owner?"

The third woman spoke. "When something like that happens back home and the murderer is white, they need only his word of denial, and his statement is taken as Gospel. Why, my sister's maid was walking to town and someone rode up behind her on horseback and clubbed her in the head so hard she was senseless for days!"

The first young woman leaned close to Ella. "Why, we're all scared to death to protests such treatment of Negroes. Who wants to be called "Nigger lover" or maybe even get killed."

The second woman added: "To tell the truth, we already had enough niggers in Texas *before* the war—we don't need any more of them."

Looking into the crowd, Ella's thoughts were again on Meshach and the others she'd left behind at Greenpoole. After the war, Meshach's hulking frame and his deceptively menacing face had drawn stares of fear and hatred on Savannah's streets from men and women alike. Most of those people would never act on their impulses. However, there were those types of men that the women at the hotel spoke of—men like Victor, the Shipleys, and the constable who allowed the murder of her friends, the Nortons, to go unpunished. Ella had learned long ago in Georgia that fear and hatred bred by ignorance smothered some men's hearts and brains just as a fungus smothered an otherwise normal-looking tree. Her father once told her that the ideology of superiority over the Negro was a religion to some men, a divinity of twisted concepts and beliefs, and the abolishment of slavery threatened that religion as it had never before in history been threatened.

As Ella looked around, she could see in some of the white men's faces the religion her father spoke about, as several of them roughly shouldered their way through the black crowd. One man paused to shove a small boy off the sidewalk then touched the pistol in his belt when the boy's father glared at him. Hempstead had said that there was going to be "hell to pay" for the Negro race. Ella was encouraged to see other white men treating the crowd with respect.

She was about to step back into the hack to wait for Hempstead when an ear-splitting screech rang out from somewhere in the multitude.

"Miss Ella! Miss Ella!"

Ella spun around. The smile that suddenly appeared on her lips grew wider and wider at sight of the tall, gangling girl pushing through the crowd and running toward her, her hand clamped tightly to the bulbous red turban atop her head.

Sunbeam's shining face, still horribly scarred from the beating suffered at the hands of the cruel Brunot at Victor Faircloth's plantation, was the prettiest sight Ella had seen since stepping off the boat yesterday!

That the two women were suddenly embracing, which made them the object of stares from both Negro and white. Sunbeam was the first to pull away and look warily around at the spectators. Clinging to her mother's skirt, little Belle smiled up at Ella.

"Forgive me, Miss Ella," Sunbeam cried. "I just couldn't help myself! I thought sure we's never gonna find you in this Texas place!"

"We?" Ella cried happily, as she clamped Belle to her side and gave her a squeeze. "Is Moonbeam with you?" But before Sunbeam could reply, Ella laughed again and said, "Of course she's with you! One is never without the other, as I recall. Oh! I can't tell you how happy I am to see you!" She quickly looked in all directions. "Where is she?"

"Moonbeam ain't here, Miss Ella. She got married. She back in Savannah with her husband." She smiled, the grin growing wider and wider. "And I is here with my fine husband."

"Well, where is he? I have to meet this fine husband of yours, and tell him how lucky he is!" Even before she finished the last few words, she saw the hulking figure barreling toward them, heads taller than others in the crowd, and with a smile to match Sunbeam's.

"Meshach!"

Face to face, she could only stare up at him, laughing. When she finally thrust out her hand, he grabbed it and pumped it heartily.

"What you doing here in this here Galveston, Miss Ella? I thought you said you was going to Mista Gent's place that you sayed was the middle of nowhere. That's what you told me 'fore you leave Georgia."

"I did go there, Meshach. I'm still there, but only temporarily, until I ..." She thought better of revealing her plan just yet, even to the two persons she knew she could trust. "I am in Galveston only to find four freedmen to work for me. I'm going to plant cotton on a few of my husband's acres."

"Jubilation!" Meshach cried. "Here stand one of them hands on this very spot! That is, if you and Mista Gent will have me and Sunbeam."

Ella laughed. "What do you think?"

"Yes'sum! I mighty happy to be here, Miss Ella. Mighty happy!" He reached out and pumped her hand enthusiastically again, then released it to pat Sunbeam's shoulder. "Me and Sunbeam is mighty happy folks this day," he said, his deep, rumbling laughter turning heads. Sunbeam's exuberant nod shook the bright red turban on her head so violently that it would have popped right off if Meshach had not clamped his big hand over it, thereby causing all three to laugh.

Finally growing serious, Ella asked the obvious.

"But Meshach, why aren't you at Greenpoole? Don't tell me Banker Treadwell fired you? The fool!" she cried, thinking fool-heartedness the only motivation for firing a decent, hardworking overseer like Meshach.

"Yes'sum. He fire me and every soul on the place." He stared at his hat in his hand. "Miss Ella, I 'fraid I gots bad news. Banker Treadwell done tore th' house down, brick by brick, stone by stone. He took it all into Savannah and built him a fine house out'n it. He even take th' two staircase apart and put 'um back together in town, and most the floor, too. There ain't nothing left but a pile of trash what he burned up."

Stunned, Ella leaned against the hack to keep from falling, her hand flying to her mouth and then dropping to her throat as, fighting a well of dizziness, she struggled to breathe. How could it be? Her ancestral home of more than one hundred and thirty-five years, *gone?* Gone at the whim of a sniveling banker whose fortune was as new as baby's teeth! The man was an abysmal ass, with no past to be proud of, and a future gained only through the misery of war and death!

Watching her with pained faces, Meshach and Sunbeam remained silent.

"I … I can still buy the land back in two or three years if the crops are good. I'm sure he'll sell. Why would he not sell it now … after destroying the house? Yes, he'll sell," she murmured, nodding reassuringly, "and maybe for much less than he paid."

"Miss Ella," Meshach said, "with nobody out there tending the land, it gonna be growed over in a year. The swamp gonna take it … gonna make it just like it was before Mista Adam's great-grandpa bring slaves over from South Carolina to grub it clean, and build the house."

"Ella wasn't surprises that Meshach knew Greenpoole's history; it was likely passed down from one slave generation at Greenpoole to the next.

"Only, there ain't no more slaves to chop out all that new growth," he said. "Miss Ella, you'd have to be rich as your old grandpa was to get that land growing cotton again. Even then, it'd take more years than any of us gots left to make it like it was in the olden days."

The olden days, Ella thought, looking away at nothing in particular. Meshach made it sound so long ago … made it sound so impossible. There had to be a way to save at least *some* of the land! There had to be! She thought of the phenomenal Corrigans' Pool … its incomparable beauty … its cool waters hiding the underwater cave long ago discovered by her dear ancestor and kept secret for so long. She refused to believe that Greenpoole Plantation and Corrigans' Pool could be lost to her forever!

"Meshach, I need three more good workers. Find them for me. You will be their overseer. Make sure they know that they will work for wages, and not for shares. Tell them they won't see any money until the first crops are sold, but they will have all the food they can eat, medicines they need, and a good roof over their heads. Those are the terms. They'll be taking their chances, along with me."

"Yes'sum. I'll get tell'um all that. I gonna tell'um something else, too. I gonna tell'um Miss Ella don't truck wid no harsh treatment of Negroes. If they misbehave or don't work like they was hired to do, then they be sent off the place."

As Meshach hurried away into the crowd, Ella turned to see Hempstead Grouse leaning on a post a few feet away. She had not even seen the sneaky old thing arrive, and she wondered how long he had been lounging there listening to everything that was said. She raised her eyebrows at him as he spoke.

"'Pears to me like Georgia done come to Texas," Hempstead said. "I got all choked up seeing old-home-day twix you three, tears being shed and all." He looked from her to Sunbeam and then back again.

"Meshach and Sunbeam saved my life more than once back in Georgia, Mister Grouse. It seems they have arrived just in time to do it again."

Hempstead snorted. "Like I told you on the way here; Gent ain't gonna like what you're up to … hiring Negroes and fixing to dig up some of his good grazing land."

"Only a very tiny portion of it."

"Just the same, he gave me orders to keep things normal round his place, and bringing them cottonpickin' Negroes on his land who don't know beans about raising *cattle* ain't normal."

"What I do is none of your business, Mister Grouse."

"It sure as hell is, since your husband made me his watchdog whilst he's away."

Ella fumed. "My husband doesn't care if I stay or go. He doesn't even care that I was almost murdered getting here. He'd allow me to rot in that place, him, smug with knowing that I will never leave without my children. Well, all right. I'm staying. But I stay on *my* terms. I intend to plant cotton on some of that land of his, Mister Grouse. You, nor anybody else will stop me!"

"Gent ain't gonna be happy," he insisted.

"So what? Neither am I." She whirled to climb into the hack. "Come on, Sunbeam," she said, "before my husband's old watchdog bites you!"

26

Which Was He, Despot or Ignoramus?

ELLA, WITH GENTALEE ON HER HIP, stood on the porch, watching Adam and Elizabeth tempt a young colt around the yard with offerings of turnips. She glanced repeatedly at Meshach and the three freedmen, all busy plowing the fields two hundred yards north of the huge corral. The sounds of Sunbeam and Hannah chattering merrily as they went about their chores inside the house made Ella smile. If only she and they were back at Greenpoole, she would be much happier. *All in good time,* she thought.

Behind her, lounging in a rocking chair, Luther Garland sat sipping lemonade. Feeling his gaze on her, Ella glanced over her shoulder at him. He toasted her with his glass, then took a deep drink.

She still could not get over how much he looked like Gentry; the same hair and eyes, the same tallness, the same lean and muscular body shape—the same deep voice, except that Luther often spoke haltingly, his speech not as smooth as was Gentry's. The only other difference she was aware of was the shapes of their mouths, and the way each smiled. Gentry's lips were well-defined, quick to reflect pleasure or humor. Luther's much thinner lips twitched a bit before he allowed himself even the smallest beginnings of a smile, as if he was contemplating whether the effort would be worth it.

Tessie sat in another rocker nearby, her eyes half-closed while fanning herself with an oversized, brightly dyed *Mexican Wedding* fan weaved from raffia leaves. It was one of two such fans that a giggling Fat Lupe had presented to her and Hempstead one evening as the pair sat on the porch bantering insults. Several times this past month, as Tessie cuddled little Gentalee or returned from a romp in the yard with Adam and Elizabeth, she had lamented to Ella that, at her age, even if she married, she would be forever childless, "unless a child mercifully drop out of the blue and into my barren lap," she had said and sighed drearily.

Ella glanced at her, and felt badly at how she had disparaged Tessie so much in the beginning. Of late, she was actually *glad* that her grandmother's old friend had come to Texas with her. Their memories of home were the same. They had known all the same people, which made conversations quite nice when they reminisced; sometimes with laughter, and sometimes with tears. Tessie cried uncontrollably when told that Banker Treadwell tore Greenpoole's beautiful old manor down, brick by brick, stone by stone. Ella felt especially close to her at that moment.

This evening, Tessie was obviously preoccupied with her private thoughts, for she swallowed her lemonade in one long swill, then dug the ice from the glass and melted it against her temples. The barrel of ice had been a gift from Luther, an offering that had endeared him to Tessie forevermore. Except for today, when she seemed so listless, Luther's presence usually had her poking at her fuzzy hairpiece bun as if that pitiable appendage to the back of her head was the grand enticement that stirred him to such acts of sweetness.

Luther had ridden out from Victoria almost every day since first showing up over two weeks ago. Immediately, Ella had not liked the way he looked at her, or the overly flattering comments he made about his "cousin's beautiful wife." No sooner had she decided that he meant nothing by his teasing manner, than he surprised her by suddenly reaching out to tug lightly at her earlobe. When she jerked her head aside, he apologized, and said he was only admiring her earrings. He had done the same to Tessie, always giving her cheek a gentle, friendly pat when her eyes widened at his unexpected familiarity. Still, Tessie was quite forgiving of the handsome man who supplied the ice for her temples.

Anyone could tell that Hempstead did not like Luther. He mostly sulked when Luther was around. Ella noted that he watched Luther out of the corner of his eye, as if he expected him to do something unseemly. Not at all uncommon behavior from Hempstead Grouse, Ella thought, since the bad-mouthed old misfit appeared to disdain just about every living thing that had less than four legs.

"Where's your bodyguard, lovely lady?" Luther asked. "I haven't seen that old eagle-beaked lawman around here all day."

"If you mean Hempstead Grouse, he's gone to Port of Lavaca to take possession of some *French pigs* sent to him from France, and which he will deliver to a lady friend in Victoria—the same nationality as the pigs, I'm told."

Luther laughed, and Ella wondered how someone could laugh without cracking a smile, then she continued: "The first shipment of pigs was eaten by the reprobate that attacked me upon my arrival here. Since then, Mister Grouse hasn't stopped talking about pleasing his lady friend in Victoria with new ones."

Suddenly, Tessie surprised them with a great sob as she sprang from the rocker, threw down the Wedding Fan, and slammed into the house.

"Me and my big mouth," Ella sighed. "I'm afraid poor Tessie is..."

She did not finish, but watched Luther as he arose rather abruptly and went down the steps to his horse. He jerked a long spyglass from its sheath on the saddle and put it to his eye. Ella gazed in the direction he pointed the spyglass.

Far out on the prairie, coming over the last hill before the road leveled onto the flat plain that led to the ranch, a wagon rolled steadily along. Three figures on horseback, too far away to identify as man or woman, rode alongside the wagon. Ella counted a long string of five horses tied loosely to the back of the wagon. She wondered if the Rawls family was about to pay a visit, as Hempstead said they were liable to do any day now. Why would they bring so many horses with them? She had no idea. Perhaps these Texans traded gifts, like *Indians,* when they visited each other.

Luther lowered the spyglass, replaced it in its holder, and mounted his horse.

"Well, beautiful Cousin Ella, it's time I got back to my part of the country," he said, tipping his hat.

"You just got here, Luther. You usually stay for supper."

"I only came out today to say goodbye. I won't be back this way for a while. I'm supposed to be helping Aunt Kada gather her herd. As it is, she's gonna be pretty mad that I hadn't showed up sooner." He executed that twitchy half-smile, tipped his hat again, and galloped away.

Ella's puzzlement grew when he left the road well in front of the approaching wagon, cut off across the prairie, and then swiftly disappeared over another rise behind a stand of oak trees. Suddenly, yet *another* difference between Luther and Gentry dawned on her: Luther appeared *nervous* as he'd explained his abrupt departure; Gentry never showed such jumpiness, not ever.

As she turned her attention back to the approaching visitors, Dan Meaney came galloping up over the hill behind the wagon, caught up to it, and then, waving his hat over his head with unusual exuberance, gave out a banshee yell, and came charging to the house. Seconds later, he jolted to a halt at the steps, the dirt flying up with great turbulence and causing Ella to close her eyes and fan the gritty onslaught away from her face.

"It's *them,* Miss Ella! *Yahoo!* It's Molly Barton and the kids!"

~

Molly's arms were around Ella in a grasp that nearly felled them both before Ella finally held her at bay and expressed how glad she was that she and her brothers and sisters were safe. Molly began to cry, and Ella put an arm around her small shoulders and held tightly as she looked at the others in the party. She recognized two of the men as Gentry's employees, but she had never seen the old Mexican man on the wagon seat, or the man on the buckskin horse that hung far back from the others. A big Mexican hat was jammed so far down on his head that the brim almost touched his shoulders. The children hopped down, one by one, and Ella turned to see Tessie standing in the doorway, beaming now, and beckoning wildly to the grimy little creatures. They ran to her and disappeared inside.

"Lookie here, Ella …" Molly sobbed, pulling her hair back. "That sorry sons-a'bitch sliced my damn earlobe plum off! It hurts like fire!"

"Oh, Molly!"

"That ain't all he done to me, Ella," she huffed, screwing her lips tightly together and squinting her eyes until they were angry little slits. Then she bobbed her head slowly at Ella, as if to convey her meaning.

Dan Meaney tapped her shoulder. "Come on in the house with me, Molly, won't you? Miz Ella's got a good supply of ice wrapped in a tarp in a big barrel in the kitchen."

"*Ice*?" Molly screamed, and was half-way to the front door before Dan took a first step.

One of the men dismounted and handed Ella a folded leather pouch.

"The boss said to give you this, ma'am. He'd be much obliged if you'd take Molly and the kids to the Nuns in Victoria and give them that there money for their keep, until mebbe some family takes 'em on." Then he nodded, as if in confirmation of something. "Gent said their kin probably already high-tailed it outta here, and he was right. We went by the cabin. Guess they took Molly's babies with them. Ain't nobody there but a bunch'a hogs running wild and rooting up the place."

"Yes, Leet Barton and his mother are long gone," Ella replied, looking at the pouch. "I doubt they'll be coming back, Mister ...?"

"Drawgood, ma'am, Bones Drawgood," he said, removing his battered hat and pointing it at his companion. "And this here feller—dirtier and dustier'n me—is Airout Buzell. We call him *Airout* 'cause he's always in need of airing out."

"*Thaddeus* Buzell, ma'am," Airout said, as he doffed a hat that looked as if it had been dipped in a mixture of grease and dust, then kicked across the prairie.

Ella nodded politely to them both. They were like every *cowboy* she had seen since arriving in Texas, whether Anglo, Mexican or Negro; all of them overly ripened by the sun, their skin in various stages of processed leather—even that of the young men. Common among them, too, were the faded red bandanas that most wore tied around their necks like a bib. It seemed to Ella that almost every bandana in Texas was cut from the same bolt of red cloth.

Even as she nodded to Bones Drawgood and Thaddeus Buzell, Ella was oddly aware of the man on the buckskin horse. There was something familiar about him. Something almost sad in the way he sat there with his head down at an angle to his shoulder, as if he expected a rebuke of some sort. She wondered why this man did not dismount and introduce himself. It was the respectful thing to do ... extend the same courtesy shown her by Gentry's two cowhands. His silence was puzzling in that she had discovered that even the most ignorant of Texans were genuinely polite—that is, those that had not proved to be despots. Which was he, despot or ignoramus?

Standing so long in the boiling sun and getting no response was enough to nourish the ill temper she had developed lately. Feeling a surge of that crossness, she was about to call out for him to step down and introduce himself ... when a loud, tortuous scream from the house made even the horses toss their heads and neigh.

Poor Molly! Ella thought, as she hurried toward the steps, *she's been told about her babies.*

On the porch, she turned briefly to point at the strangely behaving man on the buckskin horse and the old Mexican on the wagon seat.

"Mister Drawgood, those two men can sleep in the bunkhouse until they are ready to leave in the morning. I'll send supper out to all of you as soon as it's ready."

She paused, thinking of the extraordinarily long table in the kitchen with all its chairs and benches, and where Hannah said Gentry and most of his cowhands dined each night.

"On second thought, Mister Drawgood, you and Mister Buzell can dine in the kitchen with me … those two as well," she added, with a tight nod toward the wagon and horseman.

To her surprise, the old Mexican on the seat immediately thrust his hand high in the air, and called out.

"*Un minuto, por favor,* Señora Garland. My friend has come for your forgiveness."

"What did you say?" Ella asked, surprised.

"He will pay for this forgiveness with a gift so precious that money cannot buy it … prayers cannot bring it … faith cannot provide it… except through …" he twisted around on the seat and pointed at the slumped figure astride the buckskin horse, "this man."

Ella moved to the edge of the porch and stared curiously at the pair. The man on the horse reined up close to the wagon and seemed to argue with the old Mexican. He made a move as if to turn his horse around and ride away, but the old man grabbed the bridle, and held him there.

"That was an interesting statement, Mister …"

"My name is Federico Menchaca Ruiz Sandoval, Señora Garland."

"As I was saying, Mister Sandoval, it is an interesting statement you made. Please explain."

Still holding onto the buckskin horse's bridle, he climbed down and slowly bent over to scoop up a handful of dirt. "We have been told, Señora Garland, that the well that cures the thirst of this rancho will soon be as dry as this." He let the dirt pour from between his fingers. "But it does not have to be so," he added, as he wiped his hand on the tattered poncho draped across his chest.

Ella's curiosity grew. Several times since her arrival, she had watched Gentry's Mexicans dig for water, and then refill each cavernous hole when all they produced was more dirt and clay. She nodded at Sandoval.

"Whoever gave you that information told you the truth, Mister Sandoval; but I doubt your friend can dig any deeper than has already been dug on the place. The people here carry water from the river for most needs," she said, thinking of yesterday when she and Sunbeam gathered up all the dirty clothing and linens in the house and rode down to the river with Manuela and Francisca. When they found a spot that wasn't so muddy, they had followed the pair's ancient example of rubbing lye soap into each piece of laundry, and then slapping it on a flat rock until they felt as if their arms would fall off. Next time, she'd insist that they haul the wash tubs down there … and the benches to sit them on.

The old man gazed all around before he spoke. "It is foolish to dig holes if one does not know if water lies beneath." Standing next to the buckskin horse, he clamped his hand over the rider's knee. "This man, Señora Garland, will find this water. If it is there, he will find it, and his debt will be paid."

"His debt? What debt is that? Does he owe my husband money?" *I shall be happy to collect,* she thought.

"No, not *dinero*. This man's greatest debt is owed to *you*, Señora."

"He owes me nothing. He's Mexican. I don't know him. I am not from Texas." She turned away, deciding that the old man was leading up to asking her for money in exchange for digging more waterless holes.

"It's me, Ella … Miss Ella," the man on the horse quickly corrected himself. "It's me, Timon Pledger." Under Ella's stunned gaze, he dragged the huge hat from his bowed head.

"For heaven's sake!" was all she could say. The once-pink-faced Timon, with the spattering of peach fuzz on his soft cheeks, and with hands as white as her own … was now as parboiled and weather-beaten as Airout Buzell and Bones Drawgood!

He crawled down from the horse, as hesitant in doing so as little Adam was whenever in trouble for some boyish misdeed.

Ella felt the old anger from the past tighten her throat. This man had ruined her life! Had stolen from her! Had kept silent when he had information that would have kept her from marrying Victor Faircloth! However unfairly, she could even blame him for the loss of her parents. He had promised to bring them home from New Orleans, but in the end, had only written a letter saying they were dead! Timon Pledger was the last man on earth she ever expected to see again … especially in *this* God-forsaken place!

What on earth was he doing here? And looking so … so uncivilized! His eyes were so red-rimmed and turbulent that she wondered if this man was not someone only pretending to be Timon Pledger. Grandmother Corrigan always said a person with eyes like that was more than likely as crazed as a mange-tortured hound.

Despite her anger, she quite unexpectedly pictured the Timon of her past—the distant and *pleasant* past when they were children, and then young adults … before the war, before Victor Faircloth … before Gentry Garland. Timon had been the sad, silent little boy with no mother, and she had been his only friend. Even now, as she stared at him with fury in her eyes, she saw that tormented little boy.

"Come here, Timmy!" she heard herself saying, while pointing rigidly to a spot on the steps in front of her, just as if she were summoning a naughty child to his punishment.

27

Was He a Man Driven Crazy?

IF TIMON HAD TOLD ELLA that he would be wandering around the grounds *buck-naked* when he performed his *water witching*, she might not have refused to go into the house that first day. However, he had stammered so much that she thought he only meant he would be self-conscious with her watching. Therefore, when he disappeared into the bunkhouse and came out long minutes later shirtless and pantless, and with only a small Mexican blanket wrapped around his hips, she thought she might have been correct in thinking earlier that he had lost his mind. Stunned, she quickly turned her head aside.

When she finally dared look, her mouth dropped open; Sandoval, dogging Timon's steps like a shadow, now had the blanket, and the former preacher of Christ Episcopal Church in Savannah, Georgia was as naked as the day he was born. The sight, though shocking, was mesmerizing.

As the old Mexican made a half-hearted attempt to shield Timon Pledger's bare buttocks with the colorfully striped blanket, Ella stared after them. The incessant cruelty of this land, so far away from her cherished Savannah home, had likely driven poor Timon crazy. What other explanation could there be? Would it do the same to her?

Watching the two men—the battered, sunbaked Timon and the crippled, old Mexican—she suddenly recognized her own feeling of nakedness in this strange, treacherous place in which she had been forced to reside. She knew then how Timon must be feeling as he moved testily along, constantly glancing over his shoulders, but helpless to do anything about the prying eyes taking in his nakedness. Like him, she was a *naked dowser*, unsure of herself … searching for something that, even though present, could be unattainable…

Just then, Timon stumbled and went down hard on all fours. A moment passed before he used his hands to push himself up, stiffening his knees as he did, and causing his bare backside to raise high into the air. The blanket shot up, but not fast enough to spare Ella further knowledge of Timon's anatomy. However, like Gentry's snickering *Mejicanos* watching from the porch, she was incapable of looking away.

Laughter arose from the scattered onlookers working around the grounds and hanging around the bunkhouse, but Timon trudged on, the forked dowser stick held horizontally to his bare groin.

Ella knew she should turn away, shield her eyes, and go into the house; but she could not make herself do so. Would he find water? Was Timon truly blessed with a special gift, as Sandoval said he was? Or had he actually been driven mad?

She whirled as, from behind her, she heard a string of curse words that could have only come from Hempstead Grouse! He must have come home in the night from his French pig expedition. He was stalking forward, a bullwhip raised high over his head, his pale-grey eyes on Timon in a homicidal stare that set Ella to waving her arms frantically in an attempt to stop him.

"Get in the house, Miz Ella! There's a crazy man tromping 'round the place *naked* as a golldamn *jaybird*!"

Ella ran to him, her arms spread. "Stop, Mister Grouse! Stop! I know the man! He's from back home in Georgia! You don't understand what he's doing!"

He halted and stared at her. "Ain't gone crazy your own self, have you?"

"Not yet. That man is famous for finding water in the nude. They say he never misses," she said, and clamped a hand on the upraised whip.

"I heared of such a man, but I was drunk at the time, and so was the kicked-in-the-head cowboy what told me about him. I thought the floppy-jawed ijiot was a'pulling my leg."

"Well, he wasn't," Ella said. "That's Timon Pledger from back home in Georgia, and he is the famous *naked dowser*."

Hempstead lowered the whip, while continuing to glare at Timon. "He sure as hell is *that*, ain't he," he muttered.

Just then, Sandoval halted and dropped the blanket. Shocked by what she saw, Ella spun her back to the sight, but not before she witnessed Timon's somatic reaction to the dowser stick bouncing in frenzy at his groin!

"Son-of-a-bitch …" Hempstead said on the slow expulsion of breath that he had been holding since the blanket dropped.

Seconds later, Timon trudged past on his way to the bunkhouse, with the blanket wrapped tightly around his hips again.

Sandoval was hammering a stake into the ground and shouting something in his own language to the Mexicans. When he finished hammering, he tossed the mallet aside and made a shoveling motion with his arms, still shouting at the Mexicans that had ridiculed Timon from the porch. Ella could tell by the sharp tenor of his voice that he was chastising them for having no faith.

Still a bit stunned, Ella and Hempstead went to the house—her, wanting to sit down, and him, wanting to know, "What other kinda per'verty nuts you know in Georgia?"

That evening, she sat on the porch and watched Meshach and the Negroes take turns with the Mexicans at digging the well. Was there water down there? *Had poor Timon finally discovered his calling in life?*

"Agua! Agua!" shouted one of the Mexicans at sundown the next day as he shimmied up the ladder. Ella smiled. *Yes! Timon had*

discovered his calling! She hurried with the crowd to peer down into the bubbling water, as the dozen grimy diggers danced around the hole in wild celebration.

~

Timon laughed with genuine happiness at getting his old "pet of a horse" back. It was then he told Ella about his encounter with Gentry, and how they had gotten Red Man out of that muddy grave, and then rescued the Barton children. Between Timon, Bones Drawgood and Thaddeus *Airout* Buzell politely giving each other a turn at talking, Ella heard the whole story.

The next morning at sunup, Bones and Airout rode up to the porch to tell Ella they were leaving and to thank her for the bags of vittles Hannah had packed for them.

"We heard the preacher was gonna be dowsing for some more wells on the place, Miz Garland," Airout Buzell said. "This'll be the only ranch in these parts that'll have more'n one or two wells. That's gonna be mighty good news to them thirsty cattle Gent's got."

"Why yes, Mister Buzell, and with so much water and so much land, I just might plant ... well, let me think ... perhaps a huge patch of petunias," she said, smiling as the two men glanced at each other, looking almost shy in their discomfort. She had already guessed that they had seen the sacks of cottonseed in the barn.

As she watched them gallop away, she wished that they hadn't seen the cotton seed ... and that she hadn't made the pointed remark about the petunias. They'd have much to tell their boss when they got back to him and his longhorns. *Who cares,* she thought. She refused to think that far ahead. For now, Gentry was the least of her concerns.

She shivered as she recalled everything they had told her about the rescue of Molly and her siblings. Rabbit Jack's cohorts were dead, but Rabbit Jack still roamed freely, as did the mysterious white man known as *El Jefe*. Suddenly, Ella was once again glad to have

Hempstead Grouse underfoot … as well young Dan Meaney and his pair of 44's.

~

Ella had already learned that Gentry's Mexicans worked hard and, with reason, celebrated even harder. Timon's discovery of water was supreme of all reasons for merrymaking, and this time the *fiesta* that took place in la villa included every living soul on the property. Music and dance was the theme, food and drink the fuel. The tables were loaded with aromatic dishes of traditional Mexican food, rich in flavor, and as colorful as the fiesta garb worn by almost everyone, even the children. The adults toasted with a glass of *mescal,* an alcohol beverage that old Flaco made from the *maguey* plants he grew with unusual success behind his hacienda.

At a small table decorated with bright paper flowers, Ella sat across from Timon, and accepted his explanation that he had never found water when clothed.

"As God is my witness, I have tried many times," he murmured. This time he looked her straight in the eyes … something she could not recall him doing in all the years she had known him. He then dropped his gaze to his glass of *mescal.*

"Sandoval says it is God's will that I be *humbled* in my service to mankind. At first, I said 'to hell with God's will! I won't do it!'"

"It's not like you to say such a thing, Timon."

"It *is* like me, Miz Ella," Timon said, twirling his drink around in its glass. "The *Reverend* Timon Pledger hasn't shown his face in a long time. Even so, I should not have needed Sandoval to remind me of God's will—not *I,* who once preached to others that the Lord moves in mysterious ways."

Poor Timon, Ella thought, while sensing that he was still as confused as ever about his place in the world—even though he seemed to have found it. Aside from the animals that had stripped him naked and would have killed him, she could only wonder at what else he had gone through after arriving in Texas. Who would ever imagine that the timid, stammering preacher she had known back in Georgia would discover his true calling in life while amidst the worst elements of humanity imaginable?

She gazed at Timon, as he turned up his glass to drain it dry. He looked so much older. The babyish features she remembered had turned rather sharp-chinned and angular; his cheeks deeply sunken. It felt odd to think of Timon as the person he now was. Although he still was not handsome, there was something appealing about him—if one ignored his hair, which was much too long and shabby, and concealed most of his profile. She guessed that his ears were still big and red behind those stringy brown, sun-bleached, curtains. Those ears had been only one source of the ridicule he'd received from bullying children when a little boy; his confused shyness another. Her eyes softened on him, and she began to drum her fingers on the table in beat to the cheerful melody played by the six Mexican musicians, all ranch workers.

The music, created by two fiddles, three strange looking guitars, and a single trumpet, was like none Ella had ever heard. At first, the tunes stirred her to enjoyable laughter as the men, women, and children whirled to a fast polka, swishing their colorful skirts and stamping their feet. Then, when the polka ended and Fat Lupe's surprisingly beautiful voice, throaty and seductive, sang a slow, plaintive song, interpreted by Timon as a song about ill-fated lovers, Ella could not stop the tears that suddenly streamed down her face.

When Fat Lupe finished the last mournful note, Ella, with help from Dan Meaney and Molly Barton, slowly carried her sleeping children along the beaten path to the house. Timon stayed behind, having earlier switched his drink to *tequila* supplied to him by one of the revelers. Tessie, ahead of Ella on the trail, busily steered her new charges, the four little Bartons, spreading her arms as if she were herding baby chicks into a coop.

The next day, Ella made certain that she, as well as all children on the place, were indoors and not within sight of Timon ... as his dowser stick quivered frantically again, this time in the Mexican's village. Then, after several long days of digging, shouts of "Agua! Agua!" carried all the way up to the house. Standing at the back door, Ella nodded her pleasure at the cry. With Timon in mind, she mused aloud, "What irony there is in this world."

Ella saw firsthand that Timon had fallen into the same addiction to liquor that had weakened her father, and yet he was self-reliant in a way that no one who had known him *in the old days* would have ever expected of the faint-hearted Reverend Pledger. In later conversations while sitting on the porch late evenings, he sounded like an old sage, wisely reviewing the life and errors of a departed relative, rather than his own life, as he told her of his early rearing in Arkansas as a lonely, beaten boy and later in Georgia at the mercy of bullies. He had never seemed to please anyone, he said. One failure followed another, one of which was his parishioners' dissatisfaction with his lackluster sermons at Christ Episcopal Church. He told her about his dreaded encounter with Gentry in New Orleans in '64 when Gentry was about to hitch a ride to Savannah on that Union frigate. He confessed his fear, at first, when he thought Gentry was going to punish him … possibly severely enough to kill him. "He had every right a man has to kill another," he said, then quickly switched to telling her more about his labors since coming to Texas. The money he had earned off of Red Man stunned her. She was even more astounded by the small fortune he had made dowsing for water all over Texas.

At the end of that conversation, Timon stared sadly off into the distance, saying, "No matter what I do, for the rest of my life, I can never make it up to you for what I did. To say I am sorry … so *very* sorry … is not enough… will never be enough. If I could only help you in some way…"

Ella was not ashamed to take the cash he then offered. After all, he said an apology was not nearly enough. That he could repay her, in this small way, with *greenbacks,* pleased him … and delighted her.

28

A Hanging, a Memory, and Bitter Decision Renewed

WITH HER RETICULE FULL OF TIMON'S MONEY, Ella bought more farming tools and lumber. She had promised her newly hired Negroes a good roof over their heads, and so the Mexicans helped build two small houses in la villa across from the Mexicans' own haciendas. Meshach, Sunbeam, and Belle occupied one house; the three additional workers shared the other. Timon's money also convinced Gentry's loyal old Flaco and a few of the other Mexicans to help the Negroes plow the two hundred acres she's mapped out for growing cotton.

The idea of fencing in her crops to protect them from straggling longhorns like old *Mean Daddy* came to Ella when she discovered rolls of dust-covered slick wire in the barn's loft.

As the workers dug post holes and strung the wire around the sections that she had marked off, she pushed aside a sudden rush of apprehension. Gentry would not be happy to see even these small sectors of his land fenced in … even though there was plenty room for his cattle to go around each division.

Kada Garland said as much, but said it so nicely that Ella felt almost as if she had an ally… especially when Kada added, "You'll have to tell me about your plantation back in Georgia someday, my dear, where you grew all that cotton. I'm afraid I don't know how to produce anything from God's earth other than little patches of herbs and vegetables." They were standing in the yard, and she picked up a cotton seed that had fallen from one of the bags being hauled out to the plowed fields. She turned the seed over and over in her hand. "To be able to grow acres and acres of that beautiful fluffy stuff from this unimpressive little seed is quite a monumental thing, I would say."

With that, Ella had sat down on the porch and spilled out the manuscript that was forever imprinted in her head. She began with Greenpoole Plantation, relaying every facet of life there, including Corrigans' Pool and its secret cave. She told Kada Garland about her parents, and that the matriarch of the Corrigan family, Grandmother Beatrice Corrigan—a martinet for personal cleanliness—handed out handkerchiefs like other old ladies handed out prayer cards. "Spare the sleeve and spoil the handkerchief," was one of Beatrice's favorite admonishments, Ella said, and both women laughed.

After a while, it seemed quite natural to Ella that she was telling Kada Garland *everything* about herself ... her parents, her sweet sister, Honor ... about Victor Faircloth, his Moss Oak Plantation and the cruel activities that had taken place there. He and his radical cohorts had violently hung her friends, the golden-haired Norton youths, for helping Victor's brutalized slaves escape—fifteen year-old Amber Norton, her brother Herman, and the baby of their family, twelve year old Purcell.

Lastly, she told her about her precious little boy, Seth. She had never talked about that dreaded day at Moss Oak plantation. But now, as she quietly told Kada how and why her little boy died, she was anything but quiet on the inside. She felt herself begin to tremble as, unexpectedly, that day began to play over in her mind's eye, and she saw Victor Faircloth standing in the row boat, legs straddled, as he shifted his weight from one foot to the other. Ella tried again to dispel the picture, but failed. *"No! No! Please, God, No!"* she had screamed that heart wrenching day when she saw the two tiny forms huddled together in the bow of Victor's boat ... saw the boat flip onto its side, saw Seth and Adam dumped, like the garbage Victor Faircloth thought them to be, into the murky water. With her agonized cries shattering the early morning silence, she splashed into the numbing river. Her sodden wool skirts tugged at her like an anchor. She went under time after time but struggled to the surface, her strength coming from the desperate need to reach her sons. From behind, voices yelled for her to come back. *They were insane if they thought she would watch her sons die!* In her heart, she knew she would never reach them in time; she knew only that she would join them. The boy Cricket swam past her toward the overturned boat. Someone grabbed her. *Meshach*! She screamed with rage and fought to pull free. *Meshach mustn't stop her! Mustn't keep her from her sons!* But she was no match for his strength, and he dragged her, sobbing and screaming onto the bank.

Kada Garland was looking pitiably at her, and she knew her face must be showing the horror of what she was seeing in that darkest recess of memory, even though she was not wording it. "Oh, my dear, don't think about it," Kada was saying, but it was too late. She was still at the river.

"Look! Lookie there, Miss Ella!" Meshach cried. "Little Adam swimmin' like a hound pup! He gonna make it, for sure!" Ella's heart soared then sank. *But where is Seth?* She waded back into the river, searching, trembling with dread.

"That boy Cricket gonna find him, Miss Ella," Meshach said over his shoulder, as he ran back into the water to help Adam. "He been mighty good in th' water ever since he be eyeball high to a gander goose. He swim on the bottom much as he swim on the' top!" But nothing could stop the horror building in her mind's eye of the weighty metal brace on Seth's crippled leg! Was he wearing it? Had Victor strapped it in place, knowing that…!

Staring at Kada Garland, she clenched her eyes shut, horrified by the vision of tiny Seth slipping silently through the murky depths of the river, and then swaying lifelessly on the sandy bottom, anchored by the steel brace encircling his leg.

Ella felt Kada Garland squeezing her hands but could not pull herself into the present; her frantic eyes were on Victor, as he kicked away from the tipped craft and began to swim. Was he going to find his son? *Yes! Yes! Oh, please…!* Instead, he continued toward the river bank with strong strokes, and never looked back. Her hatred welled, violent and rushing, like the river that would snuff out her sons' lives with such ease. Victor's slave, Lenny, dashed past her and splashed into the river, his thin arms slapping the water with wild, artless strokes, going to his master's aid, she thought. Meshach emerged carrying little Adam, and she ran to them and tore the child from his arms. The boy sobbed, pointing at the river.

"Seth, Momma … Seth!" And then Cricket burst to the surface … *clutching Seth's tiny, still body.*

Ella opened her eyes to discover that Kada had a tight grip on her hands and was shaking them, as if to awaken her from a nightmare. Ella drew a deep breath, as did Kada, as she loosened her grip.

"The man I was married to before I married Gentry, murdered our child—his own son, Mrs. Garland. Too cowardly to go through with his plan to kill himself after he thought he had killed me, he was swimming to shore when one of his abused slaves swam out to him, and drowned him," Ella said shakily, then paused to regain a calmer voice. "I was glad to see him die—drowned by his own half-Negro son, Lenny. Lenny was simple-minded, but he had sense enough to know that Victor Faircloth did not deserve to live another second on this earth."

"You poor child," Kada whispered. "But my dear, you must not let those memories consume you. At some point, all of us must leave the past behind; it is not disloyal to do so. Time will help with this. You will see."

Ella reached up to dash away a fly that was tickling at her cheeks, and then discovered that what she had thought was a fly was actually trails of tears.

Kada smiled kindly at her. "Like your Grandmother Beatrice, I don't have any prayer cards, my dear—but I'm always good for a handkerchief," she said, and handed it to her.

After that day, it seemed quite natural to call her mother-in-law *Kada*.

~

Timon's *divining gift* made possible another of Ella's ideas that if water wells, with pumps, were placed strategically amid those two hundred acres, water could be trenched to her cotton when finally planted, drought or no drought.

Timon tackled her request with enthusiasm. "This time," he said, "there won't be any manual digging. We'll build a drilling platform, and I'll get auger machines, powered by horses that will walk on a circular path around the platform, to do the drilling."

He went to Galveston and bought two auger-boring machines, lumber, pulleys and pumps, and four wagonloads of pipe at a cost of eighteen hundred dollars. A fortune to Ella! Guilt nagged at her this time. *I shouldn't let him do this. He has done more than enough already.* However, by the time she thought to say so, he, Meshach, and the freedmen had a platform built atop a flat wagon bed, the augers were set, and the horses were plodding along.

~

Hempstead Grouse continually spouted fury at all the activity around the place that had "nothing to do with running a ranch."

Ella suspected he was extra grouchy because Tessie, content to shower her attention on the Barton children, and still incensed about the French pig assignment, now ignored him.

Thoughts of Gentry sometimes came from out of nowhere; filling her with apprehension. She suspected that Hempstead was wise to her plan to fool Gentry into thinking she had finally given up her desire to return to Georgia. But how could he know? For certain, she knew Hempstead didn't think she should take money from Timon.

"Gent ain't gonna like it," he growled each time he drove her to town to spend more of Timon's cash on the needs of her crop. The old pest complained about the "dirt farming junk" taking up too much space in the barn, and the sight of Negroes and Mexicans plowing the fields set him to grinding his teeth.

"Aside from Gent being madder than a swatted-at hornet," Hempstead said, "I don't like to see nobody get gulled the way you're gulling that per'verty jaybird feller."

"If you mean I am *cheating* Timon, Hempstead Grouse, you could not be more mistaken," Ella shot back. "Timon and I have a friendship that you don't know anything about. I know what I'm doing, and so does he."

"*He* ain't doing *you*, is he?"

"Mister Grouse!"

"No, I don't reckon he is. The poor feller moons after you like the sick-in-the-head jackass he is, but the only mooning I see in them eyes of yourn is when he pulls out his poke of greenback dollars."

Ella's eyes snapped. "That is not true! If I told Timon that you dared say such a thing to me, he would shoot you!"

"Then you'd be gulling him out of his life as well as his money, 'cause I damn well ain't never let no man draw down on me without killing him for it."

That horrible conversation with Hempstead had taken place two weeks ago, and they had avoided each other ever since. She never knew where he was at any given time day or night … until one day he came riding through the gate with two strange men. They rode up to the porch where she stood talking to Timon.

"Since this is a cattle and hoss ranch and not no damn *cotton* plantation, there's bull calves that need cutting and hosses that need breaking."

"No one's stopping you, Mister Grouse," she shot back.

"Damn right they ain't," he said, and then swept an arm toward the two rough-faced men with him. "This here is Baldy Hall and Alvin Hornletter. They bust broncs and tend cattle for a living, and do whatever else is necessary on a *cattle ranch,*" he growled, again emphasizing the words. "And since there's a new bunch of hosses that need breaking … and you got Gent's Meskin cowpokes plowing your damn acres all day alongside them cotton pickin' Negros, I hired Baldy and Alvin to do the Meskins' work."

She thrust her hands to her hips. "Like I said, no one is stopping you. Looking after those cattle is what my husband hired you to do, wasn't it? Or was it only to spy on me?" She didn't give him time to retort. "Whichever, you've been neglecting both duties for quite some time, Mister Grouse. I suggest you get busy." She gave a quick nod of greeting to Baldy Hall and Alvin Hornletter then went into the house, but she didn't miss Hempstead's remark to the two men.

"I told you she might not be too friendly. Likely mad cause she missed me so goddamn much.

~

Christmas came and went. Kada stayed until late January, and then took Tessie and the Barton children to live at her home in Victoria, where Tessie could send the children to school each day. No one mentioned taking them to the Nuns in Victoria. They were *Tessie's* children now, and she made that clear when she screeched that she would borrow Hempstead's guns and shoot anyone who tried to pry them away from her. Tessie was now so happy she looked almost handsome … *if she would only get rid of that fuzzy bun,* Ella thought each time she saw Tessie poking at it. Worse, even Hempstead had begun walking up behind Tessie to poke at the snarled little fake chignon, just to make Tessie whirl around and furiously slap at his hands, as he guffawed.

To Ella's surprise, Sally Skull and her solemn-faced fifth husband—that she called *Horse Trough,* likely because his name was *Horsdorff*—dropped by several times in the past months. Each time, the pair camped by the river, and Sally left him behind at camp while she visited Ella for long hours. Surprisingly, when Adam and Elizabeth were present, Sally never uttered a single curse word, but cooed over them as if she couldn't get enough of their giggles and cute chatter. However, the last time she showed up, she was not happy with *Horse Trough,* and Ella sent the children out of the room after her first sentence.

"The sons-a'bitch don't take no direction a'tal," she said to Hempstead who had followed her into the parlor where Ella sat sewing, while Molly rocked Gentalee to sleep.

"Even my blacksnake whip don't make him no more savvy than a goddamn bump on a punkin!" Sally railed. She sat for an hour telling them what a "half-brain sons-a'bitch" her young husband had turned out to be.

"Uh-oh," Hempstead mused after she left, "if history repeats itself, seems like young Hoss Trough might not be long for this world—just like a couple other of Sally's uncherished mates."

Ella laughed. Sally Skull was shockingly coarse, her language sprinkled with words that Ella had never heard but knew by the very sound of them that they were the vilest of vile. Even so, she didn't believe that Sally could be a husband killer; then again, nothing would surprise her anymore.

Molly, unsmiling, spoke up after Hempstead's remark. "I think an awful lot of men *do* need killing—the ones I knowed all *my* life, anyhow. Then she added, "Not you, Mister Hempstead."

Wherever Molly was, Dan Meaney was only a few steps away; which meant that Ella and her children scarcely had a moment to themselves. Adam and Elizabeth loved having Molly and Dan constantly in attendance, for the older pair romped and scampered about with them as if they were all the same age. However, much of the time, Molly and Dan sought Ella out at every turn and corner, it seemed to Ella. Molly had even laughingly called her "Momma" a few times and then fell awkwardly silent. Dan said he was waiting for Molly to turn thirteen, at which time he would be fifteen, and said they would marry. Molly only gave him a look and thumbed her freckled nose at him. Ella noted that they often rode out on the prairie together late in the evening, but she didn't have time to worry about the feral pair. They both proved to be beyond anyone's guidance—Dan, wild by his own volition, and poor little Molly by her worthless family's abominable theft of her childhood.

Timon dropped by whenever he was in the area. In addition to his dowsing, he now owned and operated a water well drilling business. He traveled with an entourage of workers, augers, mules to pull his platforms, and a big draft horse to do the hard work of turning the auger. This time, Ella refused Timon's offer of money, even though he said he was getting richer by the week and could never spend it all. More than once these past months, she had thought of borrowing enough to buy a few acres of Greenpoole, but finally decided against it. Besides, she didn't know if she would ever be able to repay all she'd already borrowed. Upon refusing his offer, she laughingly told him that if he wanted to continue his charitable ventures by helping ladies in distress, he could talk to Tessie about her dream of opening a dress shop on Victoria's town square. He promptly did so, but the dress shop dream had happily ended when Tessie latched onto the Barton children. Ella wondered if there was anything the repentant Timon would not do simply because she mentioned it.

~

Baldy Hall and Alvin Hornletter proved not as dastardly as she'd first thought when Hempstead brought them on the place. The two rough-looking cowboys often performed chores for her and ran errands into town, bringing area newspapers, hard candy for the children, and sometimes a mail order catalog they thought she might enjoy. She depended on them to run old Mean Daddy away when he roamed too close to the ranch yard.

"Old Mean Daddy shoulda been shot long time ago, Miz Ella," Alvin said to her on one such occasion. "He got it in his head he owns the place. He been chasing the wild mustangs and gouging 'em with them sharp horns," he said, and shook his head at the severity of it. "I'd shoot him, but he ain't mine to shoot."

Ella agreed, but Hempstead wouldn't have it. "It ain't gonna happen," he almost yelled. "Old Mean Daddy's too fine a bull to get shed of just 'cause he's doing what comes naturally to a bull!"

The two cowboys quickly became a part of Ella's daily comings and goings. Baldy pricked her memory one day when he shyly reported that he and Alvin had tipped their hats to her on the sidewalk in Port of Lavaca the day she arrived in Texas. All three laughed when she told them that she had thought them quite frightening upon first glance.

Baldy and Alvin told her that the horizontal scars parting the facial hairs down Hempstead Grouse's long cheeks were actually Apache carvings inflicted upon him when he was "a young Ranger and a'clearing the state of it undesirable sorts." Apache Indians chased Hempstead and his two brothers, shot arrows into them, staked them down and disfigured them, and would have done more "if Kiel Garland hadn't come a'shooting at 'em." Baldy said.

Alvin nodded, "Hempstead was barely alive but a'holding onto his earthly soul like a buster hugs a mean bronco. Sad to say though, them two brothers of Hemp's was already in the misty beyond."

The two men had gentled a golden mare for her, and which she had named *Gaia* after the beautiful little filly she owned back at Greenpoole, until Sherman's army took all her family's animals. Each day, the two cowboys led Gaia up to the porch for her to pat and feed turnips. She liked both men, enjoyed their soft-mannered politeness, their almost comical shyness when she invited them to "sit, and talk a spell." Usually she did all the talking; but when they spoke, she enjoyed the novel pungency of their speech, the picturesque rawness of their phrases. Like when Baldy pointed at old Mean Daddy one day, saying,

"When it comes to that mossy-horned old bull out yonder, if I was to try and rope him, I'd first hafta hunt up something I could use for a backbone."

Alvin had nodded in agreement. "I'm downright cold-footed when it comes to him, my own self."

~

On a chilly February morning, Ella had Meshach saddle her horse. The amiable Baldy and Alvin, who usually saddled Gaia for her, had ridden off to visit relatives in Cuero for a few days, and Ella knew they would return with sweets for every child on the place and perhaps something for her, too. She was riding over to visit the Rawls who now came once a week to visit her. She and Mister Rawls talked *cotton*, and although she was knowledgeable on the subject, Mister Rawls' comments and advice on growing "South Texas cotton" were valuable. Dan Meaney, with his two six-shooters strapped to his boyish hips, rode beside her on the way to the Rawls. There had been no crimes in the area since the Barton children's terrible ordeal, and Ella was daring to hope that the attack against her upon her arrival was a rare occurrence. She allowed that perhaps violence was not as prevalent here as she once believed.

She and Dan were less than a mile from the Rawls' when he stuck up his hand and halted. Far ahead, and off the trail, a dozen or more horsemen gathered in the shade of a huge old oak tree.

"One of them fellers is Hempstead," Dan said. "I'm gonna ride over and see what's going on, Miz Ella. You best wait here."

Ella ignored him, and when Dan spurred his mount forward, she was right behind him.

Out of the dozen or more solemn-faced men, Ella recognized only Hempstead, Mister Rawls, Baldy Hall, and Alvin Hornletter. Alvin and Baldy were motionless in the center of the crowd, and to her horror, Ella watched Hempstead ease his horse up beside Baldy and drop a knotted noose over his head. Another man did the same to Alvin.

"What are you doing?" she screamed.

Hempstead, looking both surprised and angry to see her, yelled back, "Go home, Miz Ella! This ain't no place for you to be today!"

"But … that's Baldy and Alvin! They work for us! Get those ropes off their necks!"

"They earned a hanging, Miz Ella. You'd best not watch," Hempstead growled.

"What could they have possibly done to deserve *hanging*? They would not hurt a fly, and you know it!"

"No ma'am, they wouldn't hurt a golldamn fly, that's for sure. But they'd damn well steal mor'n twenty of Gent's hosses and sell 'em to Mister Sandell here, from over in DeWitt County." He nodded to the man who had slipped the noose over Alvin's head.

"That's true, ma'am," Mister Sandell said. "I recognized the Garland brand, even after they tried to burn through it, and they didn't have a bill of sale."

Ella stared at Baldy and Alvin's downtrodden faces, feeling the panic they were obviously concealing.

"But … how do you know for sure they stole those horses? Maybe they got them from someone else! Did you even give them a chance to explain?" Then she cried out: "Baldy … Alvin! Tell them you got those horses from somebody else!"

Hempstead tapped Baldy on his shoulder. "Did you and Alvin steal them hosses, Baldy, or—which ain't likely—did you get 'em from somebody else? If you got a story to tell, spill it. It might not save you from hanging, but it might get you a few days in the hoosegow whilst I track down the truth."

"I ain't no dadblamed liar, Hemp. We stole 'em."

Hempstead nodded, patted his shoulder, and then addressed Alvin.

"You go any last words, Alvin?"

Alvin, sweat pouring down the creases in his face despite the chill in the air, grinned. "If I'd knowed I was gonna get fitted with this here Meskin necktie today, I'd a'rode a little'o donkey instead of o' Big Boy here," he said, nodding down at the horse he straddled.

Soft tittering came from the circle of stern-faced men. A few only smiled.

"You would'a just been making it hard on yourself, Alvin … with having to stand on that little feller's rump to get hanged," Hempstead said.

Mister Sandell spoke up. "I have a Bible if you boys would like me to read from it."

"No sir, not me," said Baldy. "I have me a long talk with the good Lord most every night. When it's all over, I reckon He's gonna be a lot easier on me and Alvin than you fellers were, Bible reading or not. Much a'bliged, though."

"That there's my way of seein' it, too," Alvin nodded, then glanced shyly toward Ella, and nodded again. "Give them sweets in my saddlebag to Miz Ella over yonder, won't'cha?"

Both men closed their eyes as Hempstead and Mister Sandell raised their whips.

Ella wanted to turn away, but her intention did not match the speed of Hempstead and Mister Sandell's whips. The squeal of the horses as they shot from beneath Baldy and Alvin sent a shock wave through Ella that made her thoughts scatter like dust in a sudden wind. Suddenly she was seeing a different scene, one from the sorrowful past. Now, as then, the cry that tore from her throat did not sound human to her own ears. Rather than Baldy and Alvin, she saw Amber Norton and her brothers, Herman and young Purcell … their eyes clenched tightly closed in death, their necks twisted queerly by the ropes from which they dangled. Amber's shiny gold-rimmed spectacles dangled from a golden curl over her ear. Hanging from the high branches of another oak were the two slaves that Amber and her brothers were helping to escape, one of them a woman heavy with child ….

Ella saw Dan Meaney's blurry hands dart out to grab her, and then blackness swept everything away.

No one spoke as Ella rode home flanked by Dan and Hempstead. Her mind flashed from one horrific scene to the other—the horses beneath Baldy and Alvin jumping out from under them … her Norton friends swinging gently in the breeze, half-turning, then stilling, and then drifting round again in peaceful irony to the anguish below them.

"You should not have killed them!" she cried aloud, her red eyes turning to Hempstead. "Why did you do that? They were not bad men, and you got the horses back!"

Hempstead pulled up and grabbed her reins.

"Now lemme get something straight with you, Miz Ella. If a man steals only *one* hoss, it shows he's lacking of any shred of moral decency. A man's most valued property is his hosses, 'cause they is what gets him from one place t'uther so's he can make a living or get help when there's danger and help's needed. Without his hoss, he might as well give up the ghost."

"But you got them back!" she cried.

"Well now, that ain't the point, is it?" he growled, then spurred his mount and shot on ahead, leaving Dan to escort her home.

"Miz Ella," Dan said, "Mister Grouse don't feel good about what he done. Nobody wanted to hang Baldy and Alvin, but they did a crime that can't be ignored."

Ella dropped her head. "It ... it was so violent, Dan."

"Yes ma'am, I reckon hanging is violent."

Ella rubbed her stinging eyes. "But Hempstead knew those men for years. He knew all their kin. He told me he'd known Baldy since he was born. How could he hang them? How could he?"

"Sometime the folks who mete out the justice have got to be hard-willed," Dan said. "Especially these days, since the war ended and things is getting so bad for them that's law abiding. Folk have got to stay primed and cocked ... ready to do what's needed to hold on to what's theirs." He paused, and when he next spoke, there was an unusual sadness in his voice. "It's getting mighty hard for some men to make an honest living. My pa's one of 'em. Ain't much telling what he's been up to lately. He rode off with a bunch of fellers that go gallivanting 'round the country doing whatever."

Ella glanced at him, expecting to see the face of a boy who missed his father and worried about him; but if Dan was feeling those emotions it didn't show, for he was as straight-faced as every other cowboy she'd met so far—*just like Gentry Garland,* she thought. If he felt anything other than toughness, he'd choke it down and never bat an eye doing it!

Ella stared out across the rolling prairie seeing none of it, and still unable to understand the brutality she had just witnessed. She knew Dan was right when he said things were getting worse since the war ended. Area newspapers were full of vicious acts, blamed mostly on the war's aftermath. Across the entire state, fights and killings happened regularly among whites, Negroes, and Mexicans. Mexicans and Negroes got the worst of it. Everyone wanted their rightful place in society, but very few wanted to be closer than a surveillance distance from those different from themselves. Newly formed outlaw gangs were a scourge that roamed freely wherever they wished. "Many of their members are area good old boys," Hempstead had said one day. "The crimes going on in East Texas and other parts ain't happening so much in our neck of the woods. Maybe some but not a lot," he had said, then added: "We don't tolerate it."

Ella rubbed her eyes as a gust of wind filled them with gritty dust. She should have taken Timon's last offer of money and found a way to get her children away from here. She wanted to go home! But how could she? Her beautiful old home was demolished … and the land was no longer hers.

Suddenly, she pulled Gaia to a halt, dropped her chin to her chest, and cried out her frustration, not caring that Dan Meaney was staring at her like a boy with a toothache.

After a while she straightened up and wiped her face on her sleeve, taking the reins when Dan urged them back into her hands. *I mustn't let this place get the best of me, or I'll lose my mind,* she thought. *I'll do whatever it is I must do … and then, one morning Gentry Garland will wake, as I did … and find me and his children gone!*

"Miz Ella …" Dan said, interrupting her thoughts, and still eyeing her worriedly. "Remember the day we met, and Hanna told me I better behave myself this time … then Fat Lupe shot daggers at me with them big eyes of hers … and then everybody laughed like what I done was the funniest thing they ever saw?"

Ella nodded.

"You wanted to know what I did, but I didn't get a chance to say. I'm gonna tell you now."

She glanced solemnly at him.

"Me and the boys was horsing around one day, roping this and that, and I swear I didn't see Fat Lupe go inside that little privy behind the bunkhouse to do her business. I rode hard past it and threw a wide loop … jerked it plum over," he said, and chuckled. "Fat Lupe crawled out of there cussing in Meskin, her skirts gathered up under her arms where they ought not to be, and her big hind end showing and just a'bouncing, as she ran past us all the way to the house," Dan finished, laughing hard.

Unsmiling, Ella only made a small sound, as if to acknowledge that he had spoken.

Dan stopped laughing. "I guess I shoulda told you a lot sooner," he said glumly.

"Why?"

"You might have laughed."

Part Three

29

Rain

THE FIRST HEAVY RAINS CAME IN JANUARY, the second and third in February and March. After each downpour, the days of slow, constant drizzle that followed closed the cracked earth as if a healing elixir had been poured into millions of gaping wounds. After a few weeks, one might have thought there had never been a drought, had they not suffered through it. The trees in the oak motts stood plush with leaves and twittering birds, and the once scorched prairie was now a gently swaying green sea, from which peeked millions of wild flowers in colors of yellow, red, purple, pink, white, and blue. Although the heat was still unbearable at times, the air seemed fresh and new, as if the rain had pushed it through a sieve and cleaned it.

Ella smiled, as she gazed appreciatively at the rows of green and white fluffiness rippling gently in the breeze. The first harvest from those plants lay under tarps behind the barn; today, a second picking had begun. In a few days, the bales would join Mister Rawls' cotton and be on the way to Mexico … and then England.

With the drought ended, there appeared to be more cattle than ever grazing on the prairie lands. It seemed to Ella that every time she looked out her bedroom window or rode out to the fields, she saw cows with new calve; yearlings romping like kittens, and young bulls ramming each other with their ever-lengthening horns. *Do these Texas longhorns proliferate like rats?* She wondered.

No one had heard from Gentry, which Hempstead said wasn't unusual. "Gent's been known to gather strays on his way back or pick up a second herd, as a favor to a friend and for a profit, turn smack-dab around and head right back to market with it." Ella hoped that was the case.

Meanwhile, Ella was making the best of her delayed departure, had even begun to welcome the restful solitude of ranch life after so many busy months of putting her crops in the ground, and then watching them grow.

Even Tessie appeared to be happier, and Ella marveled at the woman's transformation. The *old maid of Savannah* and the little Bartons merrily tended each other's needs in Victoria, and rarely came out for a visit that lasted longer than a day or two.

"Soap and the Bible do wonders for a child," Tessie said. "Why, my little darlings have almost stopped cursing," she whispered to Ella on her last visit.

Molly had turned thirteen and gone off with Dan Meaney somewhere to get married. Ella tried to convince them that they should first take time to enjoy their childhood. Dan only stared dumbly at her, and Molly laughed. "Too late for that, Ella," she said, and Ella had to silently agree.

Kada came for a visit and said Sally Skull's dour-faced young husband, Horse Trough, was seen in several locations without Sally, and flush with money. He told folks Sally went to West Texas to visit kin. Soon after, he left for parts unknown. Hempstead had his suspicions, as did others: "'Pears like we ain't likely ever gonna see old Sally and that blacksnake whip of hers again," he said.

Late evenings, Ella looked forward to sitting on the porch, rocking Gentalee, and with Adam and Elizabeth playing games at her feet and asking questions children are wont to ask. She answered, loving their quick smiles and infectious laughter. Only when they talked about their "Daddy" did Ella quickly change the subject. The less said about him, the less they would miss him when the time came to leave.

Elizabeth now called her "Momma," and Ella wondered if the child had any memories at all of Honor. The thought filled her with sadness. Honor must never be forgotten. Greenpoole, and the family that lived there and were now buried there, must never fall from memory. She could never let that happen. Never! She had a responsibility to keep Greenpoole alive in her children's hearts, because it was to Greenpoole that all three of them would return with her someday. She often showed Adam and little Elizabeth a large, hand-drawn picture of Greenpoole's mansion that she had sketched from memory.

"The house is gone," she said, "But Momma will build another almost as big, and just as pretty." She pointed out the body of water that was Corrigans' Pool. "This picture is like the one your mother once drew for me, Elizabeth," she said. "Your mother's name was *Honor*, and she was very beautiful, and very talented with pen and paper." She pointed to the pool. "Wouldn't you like to swim in that pool every day when the weather's hot like this?" she asked.

"Yes!" they both cried.

"I like to swim," Adam chirped. "Is Daddy gonna come with us, Momma … and Aunt Hannah?"

"You don't think Aunt Hannah would stay in this awful place when she could be with us at Greenpoole, do you?" she said, and laughed playfully.

Adam frowned. "It ain't so awful," he said. "What about Daddy?"

Ella searched for the right words. "Well … I suppose he will be happy to know we are having so much fun swimming in that lovely pond, and will surely join us."

"Yeah! I bet he will," Adam said, cheerful now.

"But you mustn't say anything to anyone about going to Greenpoole —especially not to Aunt Hannah or your father when he comes home," Ella quickly added. "We want it to be a surprise.

Besides, Momma has lots more cotton to plant before we go there and swim all we want."

She didn't doubt that Banker Treadwell would sell her family's property back to her. After all, even before she left Georgia, he had the reputation of a land speculator, buying cheap and selling high. She'd worry about building another house and returning the property to its former condition *after* she had the deed in her hands. Perhaps she and the children must live in Savannah for a while … just for a short while. She had friends in Savannah who would surely provide temporary lodging for her and her little family … if only because she was the granddaughter of the towns departed but highly revered benefactress, Beatrice Corrigan. In any case, she'd find a way.

Nights, while the children slept, all that distracted her from her plans were the distant refrains of the Mexicans' guitars that came from la villa and drifted in through her open windows. The tender strands, soulful and passionate, affected her as no music ever had. She anticipated the gentle and plaintive sounds coming from la villa with a heart raw with loneliness, welcoming the Mexicans' emotional music as she once welcomed the sound of cool spring water slipping down the mossy boulder into beautiful Corrigans' Pool. Most nights, sleep came late, as she lay in Gentry's big bed estimating her future profits after all the cotton was in … and then going over her plans for Greenpoole. Sometimes her rampant thoughts exhausted her so much that even the distant howl of coyotes and noises of other night-prowling animals no longer disturbed her slumber when she finally fell asleep. Come morning, the rapid-fire language of the Mexicans, laughing and teasing each other as they went about their chores gave her a secure feeling … especially upon hearing Hempstead and the cowhands out by the corral … or Meshach giving instructions to his crew as they headed for the fields. For the time being, all she had to do was be patient until she had finally earned enough money to leave.

~

As usual, Hempstead was quick to rile her. As they sat on the porch one day, Ella wondered aloud about Luther Garland's long absence. No one had seen him since that day he rode away just before Timon and the rescued Barton children arrived.

"Mebbe Luther thinks Gent's come home," Hempstead said. "Them two ain't got no affection for each other. The only thing that's kept 'em from brawling, so far, is Gent's mamma. Miz Kada's right fond of Luther, despite himself. Luther was always a rascal, but Gent tolerated him when they was growing up. They was passable friendly at times, 'til one day, it was over, just like that." Hempstead snapped his fingers. "I reckon Gent finally got a belly full of Luther's natural meanness," he said, and then pierced Ella with those pale-gray eyes. "I wouldn't encourage Luther's visits, if I was you. I been suspecting a long time that he's the sorry snake that's been taking pot-shots at ..."

A loud shotgun blast echoed across the prairie, where Ella knew Meshach and the freedmen were in the cotton fields. She was off the porch well ahead of Hempstead, and running toward the sound.

As she rounded the barn, she slid to a halt, fear weakening her knees. Coming toward her at a slow but deliberate trot was a snorting, drooling, wild-eyed *Mean Daddy!* Meshach was running hard behind the massive bull, clutching his shotgun. She was about to turn and run when Hempstead stepped in front of her, then continued forward at steady stomp toward Mean Daddy, his six-shooters in his hands and firing simultaneously.

The old bull stumbled to his knees, dropped his nose into the dirt, and then collapsed only scant yards in front of Hempstead's firmly planted boots.

Ella could not move. She watched Hempstead and Meshach approach the bull warily, shotgun and pistols pointing.

"Meshach, you blew a hole in old Mean Daddy's damn belly big as a dishpan with that shotgun," Hempstead said, "and the sons-a'bitch still kept a'coming."

Meshach ducked his head and wiped the sweat from his brow with his shirt collar. "That bull lift five of them fence posts right out'n the ground, tromped over the wire, and come right at me," he said, then turned to Ella. "He kilt that fine hoss you give me to ride, Miss Ella. I shore sorry, but I couldn't get him off that poor hoss."

Ella, though trembling, gave Hempstead an angry look. "Well, Mister Grouse, I guess poor Baldy and Alvin were right! That animal should have been shot a long time ago," she cried. She had been mentioning Baldy and Alvin to Hempstead every chance she got—remarking on how kindly they were, and how the children, Mexican and white, loved them.

Hempstead grimaced at her. "Well, thank you very much, Mister Grouse," he mimicked, "for keeping old Mean Daddy from gutting me!" He stormed off, yelling over his shoulder, "If you think old Mean Daddy didn't like that golldamn fence, just wait 'til your husband sees it!"

~

Today, Ella smiled with satisfaction as she nudged her mount toward where Meshach and the others were picking cotton. She dismounted, and led her horse along the fence line. A good distance from the workers, she paused to tighten the knot at her waist where she had tied the tails of her shirt. She'd drawn a few stares at daybreak this morning when she walked out on the porch wearing pants and knee-high boots. She was stubborn enough now, and tired enough, not to care what anyone thought of her garb. Lady-like attire blowing in the wind was a nuisance when she spent so much time outdoors overseeing the hard work going on in the fields. She felt quite comfortable today, it being so windy and she not having to grab at her violently flaring skirts and petticoats. *Why, I haven't had on a pair of pants since …* She didn't want the memory, but couldn't stop it. It was a sparkling spring day back home when she lay on her stomach atop the old tree trunk that hung over the Savannah river bank … and watched a family of swans drift placidly by. Then, from behind her, came the deep, masculine voice of a stranger. *"Pardon, ma'am,"* Gentry Garland had said, and she had sprung to her feet and whirled around, her heart pounding with the panic of utter surprise. That innocent day had been the beginning of both love and overwhelming despair … and then love again when she and Gentry had finally wed.

She forced the memory aside. She would not remind herself that they had been happy once, and that she had loved him so. He had stolen her son and deserted her! How could she forgive such treachery? She could not. She only hoped that when he returned, she could convince him otherwise … then she'd show him that Greenpoole was not "over and done with!"

As she neared Meshach, he looked up from the bulging cotton sack he was dragging to the wagon and then removed his hat.

"This second picking might near be good as th' first, Miss Ella," he said.

Ella nodded. "It is a beautiful sight, indeed."

Meshach pointed northwest, in the direction of the Gulf of Mexico. "But look at them low black clouds over yonder. Look like to me we's gonna get a big rain … maybe a storm."

"Well, you know what they say, Meshach, 'look for rain when the crow flies low'," she replied, "and there is not a crow in sight."

She'd learned a thing or two about Texas weather, and having seen black clouds like these that melted into clear blue skies in a matter of minutes, she wasn't worried. Besides, those clouds were miles away and would likely move off in another direction soon. Above her, the sun was white hot and glaring, and that's the way it would stay until her crops were in.

She smiled. Behind the barn, under tarpaulins, she had the first cotton from these fields. By late tomorrow, she'd have the second picking under tarps and ready to haul to the Rawls'. Nothing was going to ruin her contentment today.

Meshach was still gazing northwest. "Them clouds sho' is mean-looking," he said, as he emptied his cotton sack onto the wagon bed.

Caught up in calculating the dollars this crop would bring, Ella paused to stroke Gaia's smooth neck. When she looked again at Meshach, he was still squinting off into the distance, one big hand shading his eyes. Ella's gaze followed his.

"Miss Ella, like I said, them clouds don't look good. They look more like bad, *storm-coming* clouds than they is rain clouds."

But Ella's stare had locked on something else—the men and cattle coming up over the hill and moving slowly along directly *beneath* Meshach's storm clouds.

"El Jefe!" Flaco cried happily from the shade of a nearby huisache tree from where he periodically hauled drinking water to the cotton pickers. "Your husband is home, Señora!"

Ella drew a deep breath in an effort to stem the rapid pounding in her chest. Like Meshach, her hand went up to shade her eyes from the sun's glare. She squinted, trying to make out the faces of the men that skirted the advancing small herd of longhorn cattle. She supposed Hempstead was right, and Gentry had picked up strays on the way back.

Moments later, Meshach said something to her, but she did not hear him. Her eyes were growing wider and wider. The herd was heading straight for her fenced cotton at the far end of the field!

With an enraged shriek, she sprang into her saddle and pummeled Gaia's rump. Meshach jumped back as she shot past him and took off across the prairie, screaming like a crazy woman!

30

"What Are You Up To, *'Actually,'* Ella?"

BONES DRAWGOOD EDGED HIS MOUNT UP alongside Gentry's Red Man. "Well I'll be damn, Gent; looks like we ain't gonna get through to the north range from here," Bones drawled. Then he added, "Unless my eyes is playing tricks, that looks like a three-string wire fence stretched from here to yon, and I ain't even gonna mouth what's growing inside it."

Gentry's eyes were two narrow slits in a sun-baked face as he jerked the kerchief from over his nose to stare at the sight before him. The thought struck him that this land no longer belonged to him, but he knew that wasn't the case; he still had a full month to pay off the note he'd made at the bank in San Antonio. He'd taken time to gather up a small herd of unbranded strays on the way back from Abilene, but he knew he had not lost track of the months he'd been gone.

"Craziest thing I ever saw," Bones Drawgood continued. "I guess your missus wasn't fooling about …" He snapped his mouth shut and stared off in the other direction, as if he hadn't spoken at all.

Gentry's eyes locked on him, narrowing even more. "My wife wasn't fooling about *what*, Bones?"

"Well … I told you about the water wells what that feller, Pledger, was finding," he drawled, and then paused to wipe a crusty line of wet dust from inside his bottom lips. "I didn't say nothing about the cotton seed in the barn 'cause planting it was just something I overheard the Mexicans talking about. It weren't anything that Miz Garland said to me that she was gonna do, and I didn't think it'd be fair to the lady to say something she ain't said herself to me. I ain't a man to put words in nobody's mouth, Gent. I especially ain't a man to speculate about a man's wife. You been knowing that much about me long before now."

"Who in hell did you think was gonna plant that cotton seed, Bones, if not my wife?"

"Well … I don't rightly know…," bones replied, reddening.

Thaddeus Airout Buzell, grinning, rode up beside Bones. "Wonder where Miz Garland laid out that *petunia patch* she said she might plant?" Then he motioned to the back of the herd. "Hempstead Grouse is back yonder saying 'howdy' to the boys. Said he saw our dust from a hill outside Goliad and come to meet us."

They were approaching the fence now, and Gentry's face was like granite as he glared up and down the fence line. Hempstead and the rest of the cowhands rode up. Gentry had seen enough, but the men raised themselves in their saddles, craning their necks at the unfamiliar sight.

"Welcome home, Gent," Hempstead said, and shook Gentry's hand. "I see you gathered up quite a herd of strays on your way home," he added, then nodded at the cotton and fence. "I was riding like hell to reach you before you got here and laid your eyes on *that.* But I reckon ain't nothing I could say would'a eased the sight of it."

Gentry did not reply. He jerked the rope from his saddle horn and shot forward, his loop swooshing through the air to flop heavily around one of the fence posts. He ordered his men to do the same, but before any of them had time to obey, a frantic, angry scream, high above the low bawling of the cattle, jerked every man's heads toward it.

Gentry's upraised arm, poised to jerk the post down, froze in mid-air, his hard jaw suddenly going slack.

Hempstead, who had been swallowing his curse words around the ladies lately, now let loose a blue string of them. "If that animal steps in a gopher hole, the hump straddling that saddle is a dead'un!" he said. "He won't quit rolling 'til he hits the Guadalupe." He leaned forward for a better look, and then swore again. "Well, I'll be damn if it ain't the guilty party, Gent. She's gonna kill herself for sure. I ain't never trusted the footing of a hoss that was broke with turnips and kisses like she done that one."

Ella's hair, glittering in the sunlight, stretched wildly on the wind of her speed, her terrible screams growing louder and louder, each shriek interlaced with words that widened the seasoned cowhands' eyes. Then, a collective *sucking-of-wind* among the onlookers followed the loathsome title with which she christened their stone-faced boss.

Before her mount could come to a full stop, Ella was on the ground, landing on both feet. Her tangled hair nearly covered her face before she swung it aside with an aggressive toss of her head. She stood wide-legged, defiant, and glaring up at him, her hands clasped tightly to her hips, her chest rising and falling in anger.

While she glowered up at him, Gentry's stare slid over her. Her cheeks were flushed bronze under the golden peach color of her once-milky skin. Her blue-green eyes glittered like gems in the stormy excitement of her face. There was fierceness about her, an aliveness that he had never seen before—not even back in Georgia when they had been happy for a time.

"What have you been up to in my absence, Ella?" he said, realizing it was a silly question. The wide field of cotton growing on his land made *what she had been up to* obvious.

"Perhaps what you should have been up to instead of chasing those mangy beasts all over God-only-knows where," she said, tossing her head contemptuously at the herd.

He almost laughed, but his hard expression did not change even as he took in the remarkable sight of her. There were slight hollows beneath her high cheekbones that had not been there before. Her face was thinner than he remembered, making more profound the fullness of her mouth—tempting even now in her anger … even now in *his* anger. He had always thought she was the most beautiful woman he had ever seen, and he was thinking it again, even while being taken aback by the odd changes he saw in her. Or had he been on the trail too long? He glanced around at his dirty, trail-worn men. All but Hempstead seemed to be waiting, with half-opened mouths and appreciative eyes, for whatever she would say next.

"Get that rope off my fence post," Ella yelled through gritted teeth, but then whirled and flipped it from the post herself.

He didn't realize he had been smiling until he felt the smile leaving his face.

"*My* fence, you mean," he growled. "It's *my* land and it's *my* fence, and so is all that damn cotton you've planted on *my* land. I'm taking my herd to that meadow yonder," he pointed over the cotton field, "and *my* fence and *my* cotton is in the way." He twisted around in his saddle. "Pull it down, boys!"

Bones Drawgood, looking miserable, spoke up. "Are you sure, Gent? Maybe it can wait a little…"

"Do what you're told," Gentry said, his hard eyes not leaving Ella's enraged face.

Hempstead raised an arm. "Hold on, fellers," he said, stopping the men, and then turning to Gentry. "Now Gent, why don't you and the missus talk this over in private … *sleep* on it. Tomorrow's soon enough to tear it down, if that's what you still want. She ain't fenced it *all* in. You still got plenty grazing land. We can bed the cattle down back there near the river for the night, then move 'em tomorrow."

"Tear it down," Gentry growled, his eyes still locked on her.

"No!" she screamed, backing up against the post and stretching her arms out along the wire. "You'll have to tear me down with it!

You'll have to let those beasts run me right into the earth! I'm not moving!"

"Go get her, Hemp, and take her home," Gentry growled again.

"Go get her your own self. She's *your* wife. I ain't ever been dumb enough to own one."

Gentry cursed beneath his breath and was about to dismount Red Man when, with a cry of rage, Ella scooped up a large dirt clod, and let it sail. The instant it struck his chest and shattered into a dozen tiny pieces he was on the ground and moving toward her, his mouth set. He has seen and heard more than enough.

If Gentry, or any of his men, expected her to retreat, they were mistaken. She came at him at a fast run, her arms upraised, her fingers curled into claws. The thought struck him that she had changed in more ways that had been obvious. She was behaving as if that damn cotton was the core of her existence!

She slammed into him with a scream and a grunt, and before he could prevent it, she had clawed his cheek. In her wild attempts to maim him and his attempt to avoid her kicking, slugging, and scratching, their entangled bodies toppled into the dirt. It all happened in a matter of seconds: With a flaming face, because he knew his men were gawking at their boss and his wife like schoolboys at a circus sideshow, he instantly secured her wrists and scrambled to his feet pulling her up with him. There was no way to make it look dignified.

"Don't let her hurt you too bad now, Gent," Hempstead said, and laughed, motioning to his own scarred cheek to indicate the bloody scratch on Gentry's.

Still holding her at bay—although she was tensed but no longer flaying away at him—Gentry yelled to his men. "Get out of here! Take the herd down to the river! Get going!" he added, when they were not fast enough to turn their mounts. Even then, as they obeyed, they craned their necks over their shoulders.

With the men and the herd moving away, he released her, then watched while she took her time vehemently slapping the dirt from her sleeves and pants.

"Why are you still here?" he finally said. "I sent you the money to leave."

"Leave without my children? You knew I wouldn't!"

As he scowled at her, memories of a happier past flashed across his mind. That same memory had snuck up on him many times since the day he left her in Georgia nearly two years ago and then later when she showed up in Texas. Suddenly, staring into her furious eyes, his hands tingled with the desire to take her in his arms and caress her the way he had back then; but knowing that she would push him away, he could only continue to stare.

"So you got even with me by using that money to turn my range into a cotton farm," he growled, swinging an arm toward the white-capped field.

"The money you sent wasn't near enough to accomplish what I've done! Timon Pledger offered the cash, and I took it."

"I had a hunch your drunken preacher friend would wheedle himself back into your good graces. I reckon he was happy as a mangy pup that's finally coaxed somebody into scratching his belly."

"Yes, he was happy. *Very* happy!" she spat.

"Your forgiveness was *all* it took to get that money?"

"Don't be ridiculous!" She glared furiously at him, but then, in the time it took him to blink, her eyes softened, and then batted downward. "I didn't plant that cotton to get even, Gentry," she said, surprising him even more. "Your mother told me about the note you owe the bank in San Antonio. She said you'd lose your land if it wasn't paid." She glanced up at him and then down again. "I … I was *actually* trying to help pay it off."

His shock came and left in the same instant, and then he laughed. "What are you up to, *actually*, Ella?"

"You said you didn't want me to leave. You said you wanted us to forgive and forget." She turned her back to him, and spoke so low he almost could not hear her. "If I had really wanted to leave, don't you think I could have asked Timon for the money? I … I've had all this year to think it over and …" she turned and looked him squarely in the eyes, "I am not leaving you, Gentry. But I would be so happy if … if you allowed me keep my cotton." She paused, as if waiting for his reaction. When he didn't say anything, she continued, "It's only a few acres, and you have thousands for your cattle. I know you don't like the idea of a plantation, but it really wouldn't be one. You would simply be a cattleman who has given his wife a very tiny patch of soil to do with as she pleases. Why, any man with all your land would happily do the same for his wife if …"

"Sold," he said, interrupting her.

She stared at him, and her cheeks darkened. "But I'm not *selling* you anything … especially not … our future together."

"Yes, you are, and I'm buying."

He strode to Red Man, stepped into his saddle, and galloped off toward his herd. A sudden streak of lightening flashed across the sky, followed by an earth jarring clap of thunder that rolled and rumbled across the prairie like a celestial warning of what was to come.

He'd have to get his herd settled down before the storm struck full force, he thought—a man never knew what to expect from a Gulf hurricane … *or a woman.*

31

A Night of Twin Storms

ELLA FOUGHT DOWN HER SWIRLING SKIRTS as she stood on the porch and watched Felipe, Flaco, and their sons turn the cows and horses out of the barn and corrals and then shoo them onto the open prairie. Pellets of rain spattered the dust, stopped, and then sprinkled lightly again.

"The animals must be turned loose, Señora," Felipe said in answer to her question. "I have seen skies *como este* many times before. It is, how you say, *el viento del Diablo*—'wind of the Devil,' Señora—*mucho* wind and rain."

"A hurricane," Ella said.

"*Si,* the animals will be safe on the prairie where nothing can fall upon them or strike them down, Señora. Perhaps the barn will not fall, but one does not tempt el viento del Diablo by being careless, no?" Then he pointed at the chicken and turkey pens. The fowl, though, must be locked in the barn. It is the only place for them, for the winds will blow them and their pens away.

She nodded in agreement, then sat on the porch steps and watched as he and his sons boarded up the windows on the house and outbuildings. Behind the barn, Meshach and the freedmen were hammering stakes into the giant tarps that protected her cotton from the rain. The second picking was still in the fields, and although Ella feared that it would be lost, she was relieved that the first picking was safe and dry under the tarps.

Every now and then she looked at the low black clouds hovering over the road and wondered if Gentry had decided to keep company with his herd down by the river rather than come home; if so, she was glad, since she had no idea what to say to him. She was not so sure that he believed her explanation this morning after that disgraceful tussle in front of his gawking cowhands. If Gentry didn't believe her, why had he agreed to her request so quickly?

Felipe came to tell her all was secure. She thanked him.

"De nada, Señora," he said, and motioned to his sons while mopping his wet face with a big orange handkerchief. "We go now to prepare *nuestras casas* … our own homes," he explained, and they all marched off toward la villa.

With a last look up the road and the low hills beyond, Ella went into the house to check on her little family. She found the entire household in the tiny cellar beneath the kitchen—Hannah and the children, Manuela, Francisca, Fat Lupe, and the three women's entire brood of wide-eyed little *niños*—all squeezed together on a cushiony pallet on the dirt floor. Above them, the glow from a lamp glimmered against jars of preserved fruits and vegetables that lined the walls. A few jars were open on a small table next to a loaf of bread and a stack of tortillas. Clearly, there was no room on the pallet for anyone else to squeeze in among them unless they sat on the table … or crawled under it. Standing midway on the cellar stairs, Ella took in the crowded situation, and realized she would have to weather this storm alone. She retreated up the narrow stairs.

Alone in the parlor, she wished that Sunbeam had not gone to town for a few days to help Tessie with the orphans. Perhaps she'd go back down and sit on the cellar steps, she thought nervously. Then, feeling such cowardliness was absurd, she raised her chin and made the decision not to be afraid. She had sat through many storms back in Georgia. Besides, this sturdy old cypress house was miles inland from the Gulf waters. This storm could not possibly compete with the dangerous coastal hurricanes she had weathered.

Peeking through the boards over a front window, she searched the rolling black clouds again. Below those dark blankets, the wind swished and howled across the prairie like a team of berserk ghosts. She jumped as one of the blustery apparitions lifted a bucket from the porch and then kicked and rolled it across the yard.

She watched from the window for a long time, as the storm increased to blow much stronger than she had believed possible this far inland. Though only four o'clock in the afternoon, there was scarcely enough light to see to the next hill. The brunt of this tempest would arrive in the pitch darkness of night, and that frightened her—she preferred to *see* danger as it arrived.

Just then, she was startled by a loud, insistent knocking on the front door. She took a moment to calm herself before rushing to pull the door open, then struggled to keep the wind from snatching it from her hands.

Seeing no one, she exhaled loudly at the sight of an old black and tan hound dog contorted into a big ball and scratching a floppy ear with a hind leg while his long, thick tail and his other hind leg drummed loudly on the porch boards. Suddenly, he stopped thumping and rose up with an alert slowness, the hair on his back rising in cadence with his low growl, as he stared toward the road.

A lone rider was passing under the gate, plodding slowly and easily along as if *el viento del Diablo* wasn't whirling all around him. As he drew closer, Ella knew right away that the gangly, slumped figure was not Gentry. Only *Hempstead Grouse* sat a horse as if he was straddling a corral gate on a lazy afternoon. Hempstead's long, relaxed frame, swathed in a rain slicker and topped with a hood over his big hat, did not so much as sway, but seemed to be a permanent part of the horse beneath him.

"Howdy, there," he called out. "I see you shucked them damn breeches you was wearing."

She raised her chin and stared coolly at him as he leaned forward and patted his horse's neck before he dismounted.

"We made it, didn't we, Stonewall?" In a few quick moves, he stripped away Stonewall's saddle and bridle, then slapped the horse's rump. "Get on out to the low prairie, boy, and keep your head down," he yelled, as the animal bolted away.

"I need some hot coffee," he said, as he slung the saddle and bridle onto the porch.

"There is always a pot ready in the bunkhouse," she said frostily, standing stiffly in the doorway as if to block his entry, one hand braced on the door frame and the other restraining the door.

He shook his head as he clumped up onto the porch, removed her hand from the frame, and strolled past her. The old hound dog, seeing his opportunity, shot through the opening, his long paws slipping and sliding on the wooden floor on his race to the kitchen.

"I worry like hell about what the world's coming to when I see a lady in men's trousers," Hempstead tossed over his shoulder at her as he followed the dog. "Hell, even old Sally Scull had more sense than to wear pants. She may have worn a man's coat and vest, even a tie sometime, but she never wore no damn trousers."

Ella followed him, oddly itching for a fight. Suddenly, everything about him aggravated her more than ever. *He would have loved to pull my fence down! Why, it was written all over his ugly old face* … even when, to her surprise, he had stopped Gentry's men from doing it. She thought to accuse him, but knowing that anything she said to this man would get back to Gentry, she held her tongue. Whatever his motive for stopping the men, she mustn't forget again that Hempstead Grouse was her husband's friend, not hers—as she had been so foolish to almost believe a few times these past months. She watched him take a cup from the cabinet, pour his coffee, and take a deep slurp before he sat down at the table.

"The gullblamed Guadalupe's rising higher than a son-of-a-… Anyhow, we liked to got drowned when the herd got spooked and started swimming across the river before we could turn 'em. Loss a couple of steers when lightening fried 'em. That nigger kid, Cricket, got swept away in the chuck wagon."

"What?" Ella cried.

"He's all right. The wagon got hung up on a golldamn beaver dam, and he crawled out across them sticks on all fours all the way to the bank, just like a damn beaver himself." Then Hempstead yawned. "I need an eye opener. Got any whiskey to put in this?" He indicated the cup.

"Where is your boss, Mister Grouse?"

"If you mean your husband, who knows? That was a hell of a home-coming you give him. If I was him, I'd be sitting in a saloon in Victoria getting drunk ... mebbe talking to some sweet thang that wudn't so mean and mouthy."

"You should have followed him to that saloon for your whiskey instead of coming here or, better yet, gone to that parlor where your French pig-loving lady friend plies her wares."

He laughed, slapping the table. "I don't see her all that much. I just make Tessie think so."

She slammed the cupboard door shut. "What do you want, Mister Grouse? You didn't ride here in a hurricane just for a cup of coffee."

"All battened down? It's gonna get a lot worse, you know."

"I'm aware of that. This isn't my first story. And yes, we are prepared. Felipe, Flaco, and the others took care of everything." She snatched up a rag, squatted to the floor, and began wiping up the water dripping from the rain slicker he had tossed onto a wall hook. Without looking up, she added, "If my husband sent you, he needn't have bothered."

"He didn't bother," Hempstead replied.

She felt a tingly sensation in her cheeks, and knew they had suddenly turned red. Rising abruptly to her feet, she slammed the soppy rag into the corner next to the wood box.

"Since you have the coffee you came for, Mister Grouse, I shall join my children. If you're hungry, there are beans and tortillas and a rack of beef ribs on the stove." She moved stiffly toward the door.

"I thought you might like to jaw a little."

"Excuse me?"

"*Jaw* a little. You know … *talk*. Tell me about 'the storm within' … as the poets say."

"Don't be ridiculous," she said icily.

"It might be easier if you stopped calling me *Mister Grouse* and call me *Hemp* or *Hempstead*."

"Good night, Mister …" she began, then finished with, "and please take that dog with you before he loosens all his fleas in the house." She pointed at the hound that was again rhythmically scratching his ear while his other hind leg drummed the floor.

"How about *I* do a little jawing about your husband then?"

Ella turned at the door. "I doubt you could tell me anything about Gentry Garland that I haven't discovered for myself."

"It'd be mighty nice if you'd dish them beans up for me, since I'm as tuckered out as a blind woodpecker in a copper kettle, and then sit a spell."

She drew an impatient breath, but went to the stove. After placing a bowl of beans in front of him and pouring more coffee into his cup, she sank into a chair and folded her arms across her chest.

He attacked the food in his customary manner, elbows on the table, both hands working in sync with his mouth, a rolled tortilla in one hand and a spoon in the other. She wondered if Tessie had ever seen him eat.

She looked away, agitated by her mix of feelings for this old despot. He had hung poor Baldy Hall and Alvin Hornletter … had dropped that noose over Baldy's head as coolly as she had seen him drop his loop over a stray calf—even though he'd known both men and their families all their lives. She wished she knew what gave him and so many of his fellow-Texans their "cut and dried" attitudes. Educated or uneducated, their rural sense of justice left no room for reflection, their principles "primed and cocked" as Dan had said to her the day Baldy and Alvin were hung. How readily Hempstead had done away with Leet Barton and his cruel mother in that pigpen was another example, though no two people ever deserved it more. She recalled what he had said to her on the long, grueling trip to Gentry's ranch: "For a long spell, life was mighty cheap in these parts, and death was even cheaper—some folks still think so." However, *r*ather than only "some folks," Ella supposed that Hempstead's remark applied to the majority of these people … these *Texans* … especially him.

"Gent tells me you ain't gonna leave him," he said, interrupting her thoughts.

"Does my husband confide everything to you, Mister Grouse?"

"I asked if you was leaving, and he said no."

"*You*, of all people, are well aware that even if I had not decided to stay, leaving would be impossible—with you, and everyone else around here, ordered to prevent it."

He guffawed as if she had just said something hilariously funny. "Hell! Wudn't nobody told to stop you if you made to leave." He laughed again. "Gentry was just a'saying what he had to say to keep you from taking off with his kids. Guess he did the right thing … beings you come to your senses and is gonna stick it out with him."

Ella was surprised at how calm she remained. "Unfortunately, with no money to speak of, I couldn't have left anyway," she said.

His eyes narrowed at her. "But you'll sure as hell have enough money just as soon as you sell that cotton, won't you?" he drawled.

She felt a flush of guilt and hoped it had not traveled to her cheeks. "I've yet to have a conversation with you, Mister Grouse that didn't turn ridiculous on your end. I can see now why Tessie scarcely speaks to you anymore."

"Oh, she's speaking to me all right. Speaking to me the way you females always do when you're trying to get your way." He tore off a hunk of tortilla and dipped it in his beans. "She figures if she keeps her mouth shut and keeps on snubbing me, I'll miss her dammed pestering so bad I'll give up the ghost and drag her to the preacher." He leaned over the bowl and stuffed the dripping tortilla into his mouth. "I got a feeling being married to that woman would be a mean piece'a business."

"For *you* or for *her*?"

"For us both, golldamnit!"

"I'd say Tessie would be the one to suffer."

"You do, do you?" he said then made an agitated sound. "You know what she done gone and done now? She done took in a batch of them yeller fever orphans. Six of them whiney little farts," he railed, then added, "two of 'em still pooping their drawers!"

"Tessie is a compassionate and generous woman, Mister Grouse, and deserves the affection of a *gentleman*. She would be wise to keep *you* far, far away from those children, so that you cannot influence their vocabularies with your vile discourse."

"Like I done influenced your vocabulary, eh? I heard them monikers you hung on Gent when you come charging at us like a damn Comanche on the warpath."

In reply, she only glared at him, and then blinked rapidly.

He pushed back his empty bowl. With elbows still on the table, he balanced his chin on both fists. "How 'bout I tell you something shocking about the Garlands that Gent don't know about."

"Trying to get on my good side, Mister Grouse?"

"Don't tell me you got one!"

"Pfff..." she uttered.

"That little blind Addie LaPonte is really Addie Garland ... Gent's sister."

Ella's mouth dropped open. "Gentry never said he had a sister," she said, while puzzling over what Kada had told her—that Addie was left for dead and her mother murdered. "I don't understand, Mister Grouse. Why would Kada Garland deny to me that she was Addie's mother?"

"You ain't really that green, are you, Miz Ella? Kada ain't her mother. Old Kiel had a town woman. Had her at least once, anyhow."

"Why, Mister Grouse, on top of everything else, you are a gossip. If you're planning on giving me the details, I'm not interested."

"Miz Kada never told Gent that his pa sired another kid with the LaPonte woman. She didn't want to betray old Kiel even after he betrayed *her*. She didn't want Gent to think bad of his father."

"Well ..." Ella said, drawing a deep breath, and rising, "I admire Kada Garland. Not many women would take in her cheating husband's illegitimate child."

"Nope, most wouldn't," he agreed.

She took Hempstead's empty bowl to the dishpan. "The storm's getting louder. I suggest you go to the bunkhouse before it gets any worse, Mister Grouse. Goodnight."

He didn't move. "When Gent finds the man who shot his father in the back, he'll also find the man who did them bad things to little Addie, and then shot her and her mamma."

Ella stopped washing his bowl, and turned. "Is there more to this secret of yours, Mister Grouse?"

"Ain't there always more to a secret than what's leaked out?"

"Most always," she replied, her manner toward him still cool.

"Gent thinks his pa was bushwhacked out on the prairie by some of his enemies from the old days when they tried to run him off his land; but that ain't the way he got it. He was shot whist he was leaning over the half-dead little Addie. Miz Kada and me figured he got to the house mebbe just seconds after the attack, and the killer hid when he heard old Kiel coming. Miz Kada was in the buggy outside waiting for old Kiel. Him and her went by the girl's house every few months to leave money for the child's care. They'd been doing it for years."

"What?"

"Yup. Miz Kada found me in town that day. Me and her carried the old man out the house in the black of night. We thought the girl was dead as her mamma ... her head was so bloody. We brung old Kiel straight here to Gent's ranch, where it took him a goodly while to die. Gent was in Georgia, but made it home before the old man give up the ghost."

Ella nodded, while remembering well the terrible pain Gentry's unannounced departure caused her. When weeks passed with no word from him, her inconsolable bitterness unwisely drove her into Victor Faircloth's clutches.

"The girl was sitting on her mamma's porch the next morning, bloody, and dumb-eyed as a stunned rabbit. She ain't uttered a sound since … just stares at nothing with them blind eyes of hers."

Ella breathed a sigh of sympathy, but then returned her frosty gaze to Hempstead. "If you know all these details, Mister Grouse, I don't see how it's such a big secret."

"Don't nobody know what I just told you except four people—me, Miz Kada, *you* … and the murdering bastard who done it."

"Certainly you don't think I'd be flattered to be included in this group, do you?" Before he could reply, her eyes snapped at him. "Well, I'm not! Why on earth did you tell me?"

"Well, golldamnit!" He stood, slapped his hat on his head, and grabbed his rain slicker off the hook. "Mebbe I was just trying to make you feel to home!" He stomped through the house to the front door, jerked it open, and then struggled against the hellacious wind to pull it closed behind him, expletives spewing from him even above the maddening roar.

Feeling a bit conscience-stricken that she had not asked him to ride out the storm in the house, Ella tiptoed down the cellar stairs to check on her family. Seeing the children asleep, and the women nodding off, she retraced her steps. How could anyone sleep at a time like this? The wind had increased in the last hour, assaulting the house until it was alive with noise. She jumped as something struck the house with a pinging sound—likely that loose bucket she'd seen flying through the air earlier. She drew a calming breath. Apparently, she was the only coward in the house, she thought, as, hearing a shutter bang upstairs, she hurried up to close it.

~

Standing at the window, Ella sensed his presence rather than heard him, and she spun around.

He stood leaning in the open doorway, hatless, his wet shirt slung over one bare shoulder, his gun belt over the other. His black hair, long now from months on the trail, glistened wetly in the soft glow of lamplight. When she finally realized that she was staring at the sleek, animal-like elegance of him, she snapped her mouth closed.

"You ... you are wet," she heard herself say.

"The weather was so pleasant Red Man and I decided to take a little swim in the Guadalupe," he said matter-of-factually, then straightened himself and moved across the room, his wet boots and dripping trousers leaving a trail behind him. He flung his shirt across a chair, dropped his gun belt over the bedpost, and then turned to her.

Glancing into his moody eyes, she wondered frantically if he had seen through her this morning and knew of her scheme. Her heart began to pound, and she jumped when he spoke.

"Where are the children?"

"In ... in the cellar with Hannah and Fat Lupe ... asleep as if they didn't have a care in the world," she said, and tried to sound calm.

"But *you* do, don't you, Ella? *You* have a care in the world."

"Storms make me nervous," she said hurriedly, picking up his wet shirt. "I'll get dry clothes for you."

"Is that a part of the bargain?"

"I don't know what you mean."

"You'll fetch my clothes, fix my meals, and maybe even polish my boots, if I want, eh?" His grin was not pleasant. "I've got people here who do those things for me, so that job's taken. What else have you got to bargain with?"

She felt a rush of anger, but spoke calmly. "I'm not *bargaining* for anything, Gentry. I said I wasn't leaving. I assumed you would know what that meant. I only asked if you would let me have a few acres to plant. You said yes."

"To be precise, I said *sold*."

"Have it your way then. I'm going downstairs in case the children wake and need me to comfort them."

He stepped in front of her. "Hannah's done a pretty good job of comforting them in your absence, and I'm damn sure they're content and cuddled up to her right now. You'd best turn your efforts to comforting the one who holds your bill of sale," he muttered, as he pulled her solidly up against him and kissed her hard.

She had no idea that she would kiss him back, but she did ... memories of how they had made love so many times in the past sweeping her along, carrying her to another place. In Georgia, in their conjugal bed, he had instilled desire in her that she had not known a woman could possess much less *feel* the pleasure that grew from it. She had felt those remarkable moments of bliss in her husband's arms time and time again; she was reminded of those times, now, with his lips on hers. The ladies of her society back in Savannah would have described Gentry Garland's lovemaking and her reaction to it as scandalous, had she whispered it to them.

Her ardor must have shocked him, for he paused only a moment, and then began to struggle impatiently to defeat the stubborn strings of her corset. She wasn't aware that her hands had deftly released the buckle on his belt until she had done it.

Finally, as the hurricane swelled, its powerful roar surrounding the house and rattling the windows, and the chimney across the room beginning to whistle, screech and bellow like an orchestra tuning up for a concert, they fell onto the bed, aware of nothing other than their unabashed eagerness to explore territories long denied.

32

The Morning After…

WITH GENTALEE ON HER HIP, Ella stood at her bedroom window fighting back tears, as she stared out at the destruction left by the hurricane. The tarps that had protected her cotton were gone, the bales ripped to pieces, the muddy shreds of her first crop scattered for as far as she could see. And there would be no second picking; the cotton that only yesterday stood plush and ripe in the distant fields now lay flattened, unrecognizable as anything other than mud-spattered vegetation. Her anguished thoughts cried, *Ruined! An entire year of hard work ruined!*

Weak with loss, she stumbled to the baby's crib and laid her down, then sank to a nearby chair. Last night, as she lay in Gentry's arms worrying about her ripe second crop, he had softly reminded her that she had all the time in the world to plant more cotton next year, and the year after that … and the year after that. She had nodded in agreement, glad that the room was dark and he could not see her face, for if he had, he would have seen that her heart was still intent on growing cotton at Greenpoole. Suddenly, she slumped over, and buried her face in her hands.

Sometime later, she heard voices in the yard. She rose slowly and went back to the window. Gentry had been gone when she woke, but she saw him now, along with Meshach, the freedmen, and the Mexicans clearing the grounds of debris. She spotted Hempstead, carrying a horse bridle, trudging across the soggy field and calling out to Stonewall. The horse came to him at a fast trot. The animals Felipe and Flaco had set loose could be seen scattered in the distance, all apparently unharmed. Unfortunately, the chickens and turkeys that had escaped the barn did not fare as well; a few lay dead and those that survived were stripped of almost all their feathers. Even so, they wandered about pecking at the sodden ground for morsels, as if nothing had happened.

Adam and Elizabeth followed Gentry around the yard, frequently straying off to zigzag among scattered roof shingles and splinters of wood that must have come from the damaged bunkhouse. A litter of playful hound pups yapped at their heels. Gentry ordered the children to the safety of the porch and when they lagged, he escorted them there, slinging little Elizabeth up on his wide shoulder. He looked up, saw her in the window, and smiled.

Struggling against her depression, she smiled weakly back at him before her eyes darted elsewhere. That woman in her bed last night was not her! That woman had clung to the man responsible for her misery … clung to him as if he were all that she needed in this world. He wasn't! Shame swept over her. Even though dreading to face him, she forced herself to get dressed and go below.

Hannah met her at the bottom of the stairs, and reported that Gentry and Hempstead left to check on his men and the herd, and then the old servant executed her most exuberant smile.

"Mista Gent say pack some clothes to last a few days, and you and the chil'rn be ready when he come back."

"What for?" Ella asked, already searching for an excuse not to go.

"He ain't say what for, but he taking us all to Victoria with him. He seem mighty pleased about something."

Ella flushed, and Hannah continued.

"I ain't never seed Mista Gen'te in such a high mood. Why, when him and me got to Texas with them babies, he all th' time was like that bad tempered ol' *Mean Daddy* what hang round pawing th' ground and snorting at all he see, 'til Mista Hempstead shoot him. But today I gots a feeling th' Mista Gen'te we first knowed long time ago is back for good." She paused to cast a sly smile at Ella. "Mista Hempstead done say to me that you and Mista Gent is gonna *'make a go of it'* right here in Texas."

"I do not want you discussing my personal business with Mister Grouse, Hannah," Ella said, agitated as she realized that Hannah might not be the ally she expected her to be.

"I ain't th' one what do th' talking, Miss Ella," Hannah said. "Mista Hempstead th' one. He say he hope Mista Gent ain't no fish that done swaller th' hook you toss him and is gonna wind up flopping in th' dust." Suddenly, she frowned, and tilted her head at Ella. "Why do Mista Hempstead say such a thing, Miss Ella? You ain't gonna leab Mista Gent flopping in th' dust, is you?"

"Hempstead Grouse is a ridiculous old fool," Ella said over her shoulder as she headed upstairs to pack. Obviously, now was not the time to let Hannah in on her plan—nor was it wise to say no to her husband's plan for a trip to Victoria.

Packed and waiting for Gentry, Ella walked out onto the porch and watched the mud-covered chuck wagon roll under the arch. When it came to a stop, Cricket, looking a foot taller than when he left, jumped down and sauntered up to the porch, his spurs jingling and his hat pulled down tight over his ears like the cowboys she had seen chasing madly after stray cattle. Worn over his trousers was a pair of scarred and scuffed leather chaps that looked as if they had lain around for years before he found them and put them back to use. Dangling from one skinny hip was a six-shooter that looked to be two feet long.

"Howdy, Miss Ella!" he called, tipping his hat then raking it off.

"I'm glad to see you've returned unharmed, Cricket, especially after spending last night on the prairie in that storm," Ella said.

"Shucks," he said, and he almost sounded *Texan,* "after we got the chuck wagon out'n the river, me and the boys sit it out in a old Indian dugout in the side of one of them hills."

Ella almost smiled at the change in him. "You'd better go in and let Hannah see that you are still in one piece."

"Shucks," he repeated. "Me and them other *vi'karoes* been through a lot worse on the trail than that hurricane, Miss Ella. On the way to Abilene, a *twister* pick up some of them longhorns and then drop 'em smack dab in the Red River. They swim out with nary a scratch on 'em. It happen so fast, when it was over me and that there chuck wagon was facing the other direction from where we was first headed." He laughed. "It sho' enough been something trailing them longhorns wid Mista Gent. I ain't ever had so much fun!"

"I'm happy for you, Cricket," she said, smiling through her gloomy mood.

"Mista Gent say we gonna be leaving again real soon, and this time, I get a rifle to go with this here gun." He patted the butt of the six-shooter.

Ella's ears perked, some of her depression lifting. In his absence, she could mark out even more acres for the next planting season. Also, without him around, there'd be less chance of him getting wise to her plan. She blushed. After her wildly accommodating behavior last night, he'd need the powers of a prophet to see through her!

~

On the way to Victoria, Ella gazed about, surprised that the rolling prairie showed little evidence that a hurricane had passed over it. The only indications that a storm happened at all were a few small tree branches scattered about, and pools of water here and there: That her cotton hadn't have fared as well almost made her angry.

Gentry stopped the buggy to let a rafter of turkeys, trailed by dozens of recently hatched poults, cross the road. While they silently watched, a large black and yellow butterfly fluttered persistently near Ella's face. Gentry gently waved it away.

"Away with you, Mister Monarch," he said, "that's *my* nectar you're trying to get."

Ella felt her face burn and knew she must have turned as crimson as the scarlet tatting on her black and gray striped dress. When he laid his hand over her knee, she jerked it aside.

"What's this? *Shy* all of a sudden, my darling wife?"

"I'm still angry with you for wanting to tear down my fence, Gentry," she said, turning away in a pouty fashion.

"Oh, yeah? If last night was any indication, you can stay angry," he said, and chuckled.

"Shussh!" She turned back to him, and then dared a look over her shoulder at Hannah and the children, all of whom were closely watching the turkeys. Then she felt her color deepen yet more when he laughed louder and leaned close to whisper in her ear.

"Just don't get any madder—you almost crippled me."

She snatched up the whip and slammed it against the horses' rumps. The last of the turkeys scattered. Why, oh why had she agreed to this trip, she wondered nervously, *and why did everyone, even Adam and little Elizabeth, seem so secretive?*

She had her answer the instant she walked into Kada's Victoria home and was met with the high tenor of children's voices mixed with the varying tones coming from the adults gathered in the room—all boisterously singing:

"For she's a jolly good fellow, for she's a jolly good fellow
For she's a jolly good fellow … which nobody can deny!

Instantly, Ella's face clouded. She didn't like the song, and she didn't like the occasion; it reminded her too much of another surprise birthday party back in Savannah. She was the wife of Victor Faircloth and, like now, harboring another secret that she feared would be exposed, all to her detriment.

As Adam and Elizabeth ran off to play and Hannah carried the sleeping Gentalee upstairs, Ella shook off the reminder of that Savannah birthday, and tried to smile as she examined the room full of people. Tessie stood front and center, a baby in one arm, and the other stretched out behind the immaculate, well-dressed Barton children and six others of varying ages. Almost as if he were posing for a family portrait, Hempstead Grouse sat stiffly in a chair to Tessie's right, a baby on his knee. He glumly shrugged his shoulders when Ella looked at him. Like he had said last evening, Tessie had taken in another family of orphans, and Ella did not doubt that even *more* was Tessie's intention.

The Rawls, along with their son and daughter-in-law, waved gaily to her. At least forty people crowded the spacious room; men and women, old and young—most all of whom she'd never seen before. As her eyes met their curious gazes, they converged, each waiting their turn to grasp her hand and introduce themselves—so many names that she knew she would never remember even one.

Over their shoulders, Ella saw Addie LaPonte, wearing a pink satin gown and sitting on a long brocade sofa beside a magnificent marble fireplace. Ella's smile faded to one of pity as she looked into the girl's sightless eyes, and thought of the secret Hempstead had thrust upon her. She could not help but examine Addie's head … well-covered with hair as black as Gentry's, and so beautifully coiffured that none would ever guess that beneath that glossy mane was a scarred-over bullet hole and a disfigured ear without its lobe.

Ella put on her social face and shook each hand, even as disturbed thoughts about Addie, her mother, and the unknown brute responsible for those horrifying crimes, lingered on. Soon, she had met each guest and, with a fake smile hurting her lips, she gazed amiably about. All of a sudden, her sociable observation turned into a surprised stare: Near the parlor entryway and standing with his back to her, a tall, thin, one-legged man leaned on wooden crutches.

All other thoughts flew from her mind. Jack was here! Her dearest friend on earth had come all this way to surprise her on her birthday! She was about to cry out his name when he turned and she saw the face of another stranger. Her shoulders slumped. She should have known better. Jack was in Missouri, married to his brother's widow by now. Or perhaps he had succeeded in dying by his own hand, as he had once intended. Suddenly, she wanted to run from the room. She did not want to meet all these strangers! She would not be around long enough to make a friend of any of them!

She looked up and saw a smiling Kada Garland coming toward her with outstretched arms.

"My dear," Kada said, hugging her. "You look lovely."

Before Ella could reply with a greeting, Gentry walked up and put his arm around her waist. She didn't pull away. If she were to succeed with her plan, her thoughts must never show in her eyes, her words … especially not in her actions. She smiled up at Gentry. The way he looked back at her caused another twinge of guilt: Hannah was right; he hadn't looked this happy since long before the problems with Greenpoole came between them.

"You did a fine job with all this, Mother," Gentry said, looking around at the handsomely decorated room. "Thank you."

"Yes," Ella said, while taking a quick look at the vases of fresh flowers, garlands, and festive streamers. "Thank you, Kada. It's kind of you to want to celebrate my birthday. I had forgotten it."

"It isn't only to celebrate your birthday that brings you and Gentry here today," Kada said, and laughed happily. "There's also to be a wedding, with cake and champagne to follow."

"A wedding?" Ella said, looking this way and that for sight of a bride and groom. Surely not Hempstead and Tessie—although he did look quite subdued with that baby on his lap. Suddenly, she spied Dan and Molly strolling in from the dining room, arm in arm. Molly had announced weeks ago that she was with child, and she seemed to be sporting her rounded little tummy with pride. Seeing Ella, she waved exuberantly and then threw her a kiss.

Ella turned to Kada. "Why, I thought Molly and Dan married months ago, Kada," she said.

Gentry took her hands into his. "Not Dan and Molly, Ella … *us*."

"*Us?*" Ella echoed him, momentarily stunned.

Kada patted her shoulder. "Excuse me, dear. There's the Reverend Trout. I shall show him to the food tables. He says it's bad luck to perform a wedding on an empty stomach," she said, and left.

Ella stared up at Gentry. "We *are* married, Gentry. Surely, our Georgia wedding meets *Texas* standards," she said, trying to keep the sarcasm out of her voice.

He smiled, and led her out onto the wide porch.

With each step into the moonlit darkness, her alarm grew. She was not willing to stand before a minister of God and swear to something she knew was false! In her belief, Gentry's abandonment of her while stealing her precious son had released her from the sanctity of that *first* vow, even without the legality of a divorce. Despite her anger with God in the past when the cruel demise of loved ones had left her senseless with grief, she *still* would not have sworn falsely on the Bible. Renewing wedding vows in a religious ceremony… swearing on the Bible to *love, honor* and *cherish* Gentry, when she knew she planned to leave him, would be sacrilegious!

"A second ceremony is not necessary, Gentry," she said, sounding resolute, as she braced her hands on the porch railing.

"Yes, it is necessary, Ella. We've both been through hell. I admit, *you* more than me. I'm sorry for all of it. I wish I could undo it." He turned her to face him. "Ella … I want this to be a fresh beginning for us." He took a ring from his pocket and slipped it on her finger.

She stared silently at it, recalling the day he left her and she ran down to the pier and threw that first wedding ring into the Savannah River. She looked up as he spoke.

"There'll be times when I'll be away from you for months, my darling; but each time you look at this ring I want you to hear my voice saying *I love you … I love you … I love you."*

His black eyes moved so tenderly, so lovingly, to every part of her face that she quickly covered it with her hands, as an unexpected sadness, and then guild, swept over her—she had never known Gentry Garland to be so vulnerable!

He pulled her hands away. "What's wrong, Ella?"

"I … nothing, Gentry," she finally replied, and managed a smile. He kissed her, and then wiped her wet cheek with his thumb; until then, she had not realized that she was crying.

"I'm going to San Antone tomorrow, and I'm taking you with me," he said. "I'm meeting two gentlemen from Mexico to discuss some business, but it will also be the honeymoon we never had."

"San Antonio? But I can't leave the children. They need me."

"Hannah will take care of them. It's only for a week. When we get home, I'll be leaving again, for a while."

She frowned and started to speak, but he interrupted.

"The railroad between here and San Antone's been rebuilt. We'll enjoy the ride," he said.

Ella nodded, knowing it would not be wise to decline. Kada beckoned to them from the doorway and he took her arm and led her back into the house.

In the parlor, standing before the preacher, as old vows were renewed, Ella forced herself to remember the morning she awoke and found him gone … forced herself to remember her misery at finding her precious son stolen from her … remember the heart-pounding despair that followed the loss of all she had ever loved—Greenpoole plantation among them. She glanced sidelong at Gentry's serious face, and then down at the gold ring he had slipped on her finger minutes earlier. Then, unexpectedly, his deep, warm voice filled her head. *I love you … I love you … I love you.*

She raised her trembling chin, and then stared straight ahead … still as determined as ever to leave Texas and return to her treasured Greenpoole—she just wasn't going to enjoy her revenge as much as she had thought she would.

33

A Dowser, a Killer, and a One-legged Ghost

E STOOD AT HER SECOND-STORY WINDOW in the Menger Hotel in San Antonio, and watched for Gentry to return. Occasionally, she shaded her eyes from glints of fading sunlight that filtered through a grove of laurel and huisache that bordered the ancient old mission called *The Alamo.*

No sooner had Gentry unloaded Red Man from the train, he had followed her rented buggy to the hotel, settled her in, then gone off to "tend to business," he said, but did not elaborate. She had been in the hotel room all evening waiting for him to come back, the noises from the plaza seeming to grow with each passing hour.

In her observations of San Antonio, the town seemed in constant celebration. Even at daybreak, the plaza below echoed with brassy Mexican music mixed with the shouts of teamsters and cries of Mexican vendors. They were selling everything from fresh vegetables and spicy cooked stews to tall stacks of straw hats, blankets, baskets, furniture, and leather goods. Raw beef and plucked chickens hung on hooks above it all. Everywhere, the colors were brilliant, lending an air of gaiety to the plaza—the food with garnishes of red and green peppers, and the Mexican women in their multicolored skirts and bright fringed shawls. Pink and white honeysuckle and bugle-shaped yellow Esperanza trailed along the fences of almost every impressive home or impoverished hovel. Roses were everywhere; in pots, in yards, carried in the hands of children selling them to passersby. Bulging vines of thorny but stunning red or purple bougainvillea hugged the hotel walls, as well as the low adobe parapets surrounding a beautiful old mission they had passed when coming into town. Now, nearing the supper hour, the music was louder, and the air saucy with the accents of several dialects, mostly Mexican, German, and Irish mixed with vernaculars purely Texan or otherwise Southern.

Ella gazed across the plaza at the old Alamo mission. During the train ride, Gentry had told her about the tragic battle that had taken place there in 1836 during the fight for Texas independence from Mexico. The survivors of the battle were later executed to the very last man by Mexico's General Santa Anna—close to two hundred men in all. A month after the Alamo fell, Goliad, near Gentry's ranch, was the site of another hated massacre by the Mexican army. Short weeks later, the Alamo and Goliad massacres drove Texans to victory at San Jacinto near Houston, with *'Remember the Alamo! Remember Goliad!'* echoing from every man's lips.

Gentry told her that seventeen men avoided death at Goliad when a Mexican general's wife pleaded that they be shown mercy.

"Proof that if women, not men, made decisions in matters of war and peace, there would be no wars and senseless killings," Ella said, thinking he would surely assert a different opinion.

Gentry had smiled softly at her. "You're probably right," he said, and she had looked away. It seemed that she could say or do nothing that he disagreed with. He was indeed happy. His contentment showed in his walk, his manner of speaking, and the expression on his handsome face when he looked at her.

As Ella thought about the change in him, the panicked sadness returned, and she could not stop his voice, repeating in her head, *I love you... I love you ... I love you.*

Each night in the room above the plaza, when she turned out the lamp and slid between the linens, she tried to concentrate on anything but Gentry's lovemaking; but success was a far reach. She wondered sometimes at the person she'd become—embittered, and set on leaving him—and yet able to willingly open her arms to him.

Near sundown, Ella grew tired of waiting. Dressed in a new frock of mauve silk with filmy lace at the neck and sleeves, and a wide, black streamer flowing down the front, she went downstairs to wait for Gentry outside, and to watch the sights. The vast lobby was filled mostly with men. Some were distinctly *gentlemen,* in coats, vests, and shiny shoes … others patently *cowboys* in big stained hats, gun belts, and trail-scuffed boots. All tipped their hats and gazed at her with appreciative eyes, their manner courteous. Though she would never respond outwardly to such attention from the opposite gender, she was flattered, for she had not felt *pretty* in a long time.

As she walked out onto the wide hotel steps, a drumbeat coming from up the street caught her attention, as well as the curiosity of everyone in the crowded plaza. A young man, beating on a huge bass drum, led an enormous canvas-covered wagon, followed by a line of smaller wagons, into the plaza and rolled toward the hotel. Yipping and yelling children of all ages and sizes ran alongside, grabbling at items slung at them from the lead wagon. Many adults emulated the children, darting back and forth to grab up the diminutive objects. A small boy ran past Ella with his pockets bulging. As he ran, he tore a paper wrapper from one of his prizes, stuffed the contents into his mouth, and then let the wind have the little square of paper; Ella grabbed it as it threatened to land against her face. Noting that the paper was printed upon, she smoothed it out and read it.

Dowsing and Mechanical Well Digging Service
If Water is Below, We Will Know.
T. Pledger, Divine Dowser

Handing the scrap of paper to a man who was politely trying to read it over her shoulder, Ella smiled. *A good way to advertise,* she thought, since the town's children would be dropping those candy wrappers all over town and at their homes. As the wagons rolled past, she saw that every vehicle advertised Timon's lucrative business, the sideboards brightly stenciled, and the canvas tops draped with banners. From the number of wagons, and the equipment aboard, Ella supposed that Timon's business had likely tripled since she'd last heard from him.

She watched from the crowd as Timon, Sandoval and, of all people, *Luther Garland,* trailed slowly behind the last wagon. Sandoval rode directly behind Luther. The old horse, Blackie, trotted at Timon's side. As they neared, it was obvious that they did not see her in the crowd. All three riders showed the dust and dirt of a long journey. Ella's attention settled curiously on old Sandoval. His usual kindly, but droopy demeanor seemed uncharacteristically rigid ... almost *wicked,* the way his eyes never left Luther's back. *How strange,* she thought.

Before she could wonder more about the old Mexican's stealthy behavior, one of the wagons rolled to a stop in the middle of the plaza. Though the sinking sun was in her eyes, Ella saw the blurry figure of a man drop to the ground, and then drag down an enormous leather bag. She squinted into the sunlight as he limped across the plaza toward the hotel. She did not feel that she knew this man, but for some reason entirely unknown to her, she could not take her eyes off him. Then, as he emerged from the blinding sun and plopped a brown beret at a cocky angle on his head, Ella screamed like a child presented with a long-desired gift.

But it couldn't be! It couldn't be Jack! This man was walking on *two good legs,* albeit it with a limp so meager that it could have been the result of a sprained ankle. But yes ... it was Jack!

"Jack! Jack!" she cried, as she pushed her way through the crowd.

Recognition halted him and then hurled him forward, his left leg swinging outward a bit, as he all but ran to her open arms. They met midway in the plaza, and she did not resist when he wrapped her in his arms and planted a kiss directly on her lips.

When they finally parted to stare happily at each other, both speaking at the same time, moments passed before she realized that they were not alone. She glanced to her right to see Timon Pledger silently staring down at them from atop his buckskin horse, his eyes on Jack as if he could kill him; but she had little time to concern herself with Timon's silly jealousy. Behind her she heard Gentry's voice, and she spun around to see him standing between two extremely well-dressed Mexican men.

"My wife, gentlemen," Gentry drawled, as he extended his hand in her direction, "and our mutual friend, Jack Kearney. Ella ... Jack, these gentlemen are Diego and Rodolfo De La Fuente, friends of mine from Mexico City." He turned to Jack. "That was some greeting you gave my wife, old friend," he said.

Ella's cheeks flamed as she nodded politely to the two men.

Jack grinned. "You know me, Gent. When given the rare chance to kiss a pretty woman, I grab it."

Ella looped her arm through Gentry's. "... and I was so overcome with happiness that Jack was alive and I wasn't seeing a ghost, I simply could not help myself," she said, and laughed.

Still grinning, Jack glanced at the hitching rail nearby. "I see you are still riding that fine red horse me and Malbone raced and beat in Savannah before the war."

Gentry grinned back at him. "As I recall, that race was a tie."

"So it was," Jack said, as he and Gentry at last pumped hands in a friendly greeting.

Just then, Diego De La Fuente called out to Timon, "Ah-ha! We meet again, Señor Pledger, but this time, in not so much danger, *si*?"

Timon solemnly agreed, and Ella recalled that Timon had told her about these two men. They had been captives of *El Jefe* and Rabbit Jack, along with Molly and the siblings. She nodded as the De La Fuente brothers turned politely to her, took their leave, and departed.

Remembering that Luther Garland had ridden into town behind the caravan, Ella looked around for him. He was nowhere in sight. *How strange,* she thought for the second time. Then, reminded that Hempstead said that Luther and Gentry harbored a bitter dislike for each other, she understood why he had left.

Sandoval, standing a distance away and still looking mysteriously angry, called out to Gentry. Then, with his arm folded clandestinely across his chest, the old Mexican beckoned with a single motion of stiffly curled fingers.

"I'd appreciate it if you'd escort my wife to the dining room in the hotel, Jack. I'll join you as soon as I can," Gentry said, then immediately went to the scowling Sandoval.

Seconds later, Gentry beckoned to Timon and, to Ella's puzzlement, the three conversed in low, rapid tones … then walked swiftly across the plaza and disappeared among the crowd of Mexican vendors and shoppers.

Ella was already wondering why Gentry made her wait so long for him in their room, and now he was leaving *again*. She took Jack's arm when he offered it.

"As important as my husband claims I am to him, apparently there is something else more important," she said.

"Now, Ella …"

"Come along, dear Jack. We shall dine. I can't think of anyone I'd rather sup with than you anyway. Besides, we have a million things to catch up on."

~

In the Menger Hotel's elegant dining room, Ella could not get enough of looking at Jack. He was no longer the gaunt, spiritually broken, one-legged man who rode up to Greenpoole's steps on a dilapidated mule, in rags, and with only a musty old bedroll and rough wooden crutches to call his own. She didn't know what to ask him first.

"But Jack, I thought you went to Missouri to marry your brother's widow? What happened? What are you doing here? Are you working for Timon?"

He laughed, and reached across the table to pat her hands. "I shall try to answer your questions in the order you threw them at me," he said, then picked up the cup of coffee that a Negro server in an immaculate white tunic and breeches set before him. As if to tease her for her impatience, he gazed at Ella over the rim while he blew on the coffee to cool it.

"Oh, Jack..."

"All right." He set the cup down. "When I got to Missouri, my brother's little widow, with the great personality, decided she didn't want a one-legged sad sack like me. She had her eye on a neighbor fellow who, fortunately for him, missed out on the war," Jack said, then grinned. "And there I had been thinking that luck had passed me by for the rest of my ever-loving life," he said, grinning, then sipped his coffee.

"And?" she prodded.

"And one day in town, I met a one-legged man who wore one of these." He pulled up his pant leg and revealed an artificial leg he called a "Jewett's Leg," named after the man who invented it. "It's a little complicated to explain, but the foot has hinges at the ankle and at the toes ... makes it a lot easier to walk once you get used to it, not to mention that I can wear two shoes now instead of one."

"Oh, Jack, that is so wonderful! Is that new leg the reason you look positively beautiful?"

"Maybe. I kinda like being on two legs again. I haven't tried dancing yet, but I might."

"I'll bet you can," she said, and laughed. "But go on, tell me the rest."

He nodded at the huge leather bag he had set on the floor to one side of the table. "In that bag, there are half a dozen Jewett legs, all sizes. I work for the company that makes them, and I travel about looking for one-legged fellows, hoping to interest them in going to the North Carolina factory to get fitted for their very own." He grinned again. "I'm a walking, talking, advertisement."

She laughed. "And a very good one, I imagine," she said, so happy that tears came into her eyes. But then she grew serious, almost afraid to ask the next question. "But Jack, in Georgia you received word that your mother and sister were ill. Did they … oh, Jack, I hope they didn't…?"

"They're both fine, and so are my two little brothers," he said, then tapped his Jewett's leg, adding, "Thank God those little scamps were too young to join the Confederacy. It was hard enough on Ma losing Ike, Radford, Shelby, Anton, Pa, and then Andy. She couldn't take losing *all* her wild brood." He smiled sadly.

Ella returned his smile. She knew why Jack recited all their names so slowly. She did the same when speaking of those close to her who had perished: To speak their names was to keep their memories alive, recognize that they had existed, and that they had given and received love.

"Is your mother still in Missouri?"

"She and the little folks travel with me. Right now, they are in Galveston, at a boarding house. That's where I saw Timon and hitched a ride with him rather than take the stage," Jack said, and then laughed. "Can you believe the change in that fella? On our way here, I had the rare pleasure of witnessing our shy former minister of Christ Episcopal Church in Savannah prance around buck naked with that dowser stick of his."

"I know," Ella said. "Isn't it the oddest thing you've ever seen?

"Not the *oddest,* but probably the most obscene. Don't tell me *you* saw him do it," he said, and laughed.

She blushed, but rushed on as if she hadn't heard him: "I would love to see your mother again. I remember how she went to Savannah twice a week to teach the children at Bethesda orphanage to read."

"She still teaches from McGuffey's Reader whenever she can get students with parents willing to pay a few pennies. If not, she teaches them anyhow. We'll probably make Galveston our home."

Ella observed him a long moment. "Jack, is it important that Galveston be your home?"

"Well ... no."

Ella leaned back in her chair and smiled so long and confidently at him that he narrowed his eyes at her.

"As I recall, dear Jack," she began, still smiling, "your mother and Miss Tessie Peckenpaugh belonged to all the same clubs in Savannah, and were very good friends."

"Ah, yes. The *peahen* society, better known as *the tea and cakes brigade.* I say so with all due respect, of course."

"Tessie lives in Victoria. A fine town near Gentry's ranch, and she has blissfully taken in two families of orphans. Knowing Tessie, there will be more." She reached across the table and took Jack's hand. "Tessie would be so happy to have you and your family move to Victoria. Your mother could teach the orphans ... have a wonderful place to raise your little brothers and sister, and you could make Victoria your home base for selling those legs. Why, Texas is just *full* of one-legged veterans!" she cried. Then they both laughed at her misplaced jubilation.

"Timon told me that Miss Tessie was in Victoria. He told me your whereabouts, too," he said, and paused as if thinking it over. "I know Ma would shout *hallelujah* to be with old friends from back home again. I think of home a lot myself, even knowing it isn't the same there anymore. Do you ever miss it, Ella?"

"Oh yes, terribly. My heart breaks each time I think of Greenpoole. The house is gone. Banker Treadwell tore it down to build himself a fine home in Savannah," she fairly spat the last words.

"Jesus Christ!" Jack rubbed his mouth. I can't imagine it gone." He shook his head sadly. I'm sorry, Ella."

"Yes ...but ...," she began, then hesitated, wondering if she should tell him her plan. Then without further thought, she blurted, "Jack, I'm saving up money to buy Greenpoole from Banker Treadwell, and someday I'm going home for good, and I'll build another house."

"Ella ..." he began, but she continued,

"We'll talk about my plans later. But for now, I just need you to be my friend, like always. I haven't had a true one since you left." She smiled affectionately at him, her eyes again brimming over, as she added, "And now, in the midst of all my misery, here you are! Big and bold, and every bit the Jack I have loved all my life."

It was then she noticed Jack's troubled eyes were looking past her rather than at her. She glanced over her shoulder, stunned to see Gentry leaning against a pillar not four feet away.

A sick feeling, worse than any she recalled ever having, crawled over her. Gentry's black eyes stared into hers like shrewd oracles digging into her exposed brain; yet, she could not look away.

Finally, she dropped her gaze to the coffee cup clamped tightly between her palms, and waited for the brutal words he surely must have for her. She waited ... the moments crawling with unbearable slowness, and then his deep voice shattered the silence.

"Good luck to you, madam," he said, and walked away.

Jack stood. "Geeze, Ella, he thinks I'm involved in this little scheme of yours. I'd better go set him straight," he said, but she waved him back into his chair, and hurried after Gentry.

It was a bit late for truth, she thought, but she felt the need to voice it—all of it. Just as important, she did not want him thinking there was anything but friendship between her and Jack.

When she entered the room, Gentry was emptying a drawer of his belongings, and stuffing them into his saddlebags. He didn't turn around. She forced herself to speak.

"I can't let you leave thinking there is anything between Jack and me, Gentry. I love him only like a sister loves a brother."

Gentry still did not turn around. "I can't say I give a damn."

She felt her cheeks burn. "About the other thing you heard me say; I did plant that cotton hoping to earn enough money in a few years to buy Greenpoole back from Banker Treadwell," she said, pausing as he turned to face her, "and then I … I planned to take my children and leave you."

"I discovered your intentions a few minutes ago, remember? So what's this after-the-fact confession supposed to accomplish?"

"I … don't know. Nothing, I guess. I still want to take my children and go home. After we married I thought you and I would always be there, Gentry. I never let myself imagine that you would want me to leave Greenpoole forever."

He kept packing. "We've said about all there is to say on that subject. Anything added to it is just wasted breath."

She opened her hands to him, tears of frustration filling her eyes. "I hate the danger of living here, Gentry! I want my children to be safe!"

"You want *Greenpoole*. That's all you want, or ever wanted, and that's the everlasting fact," he said.

"I was almost murdered just hours after I arrived here! I'm afraid for Adam and Elizabeth and Gentalee! I don't want what happened to the Barton children to happen to them! Those men could come back…"

"Most of them are dead. Bones Drawgood and I killed them."

"You didn't kill Rabbit Jack."

"Not yet. Nor his leader, the white man called *El Jefe* … more commonly known to you, and everyone else, as …"

"It doesn't matter if you killed them," she cried. "There are too many others here just like them!"

Gentry waited to see if she would say more, then began again with the sentence she had interrupted: "… the white man called *El Jefe* … more commonly known to you and everyone else as Luther Garland."

Ella stared at him.

He turned his back again, but continued. "Seems Luther operates incognito—heard, but never seen by his victims. He and his crew came close to murdering Pledger and old Sandoval a few years back. They never got a look at his face, but they heard his voice. The day we got the Barton kids back, Pledger heard him again when he saw him exit a tent right after Molly ran out bleeding, and minus an earlobe," Gentry said, tossing his shaving mug into the saddlebag. "When Luther joined then on the road today, he and Sandoval recognized his voice."

Ella tried to digest the news even while her mind raced with the knowledge that the killer of Gentry's father had also severed the ear lobes of Addie and her mother. She shivered, remembering how interested Luther had been in *her* ear that day on the porch.

Gentry threw his saddlebag over his shoulder. "Sandoval says that Luther knows he and Timon recognized him, but couldn't kill them on the spot because of too many eyewitnesses on Pledger's wagons. I'm gonna find the son-of-a-bitch and send him to hell. But first, I have to find your preacher friend and tell him to hide somewhere. Luther's probably looking to kill him, and I doubt Pledger's got the guts to shoot first."

"But Gentry, what if ..."' She was going to say, *what if you are the one killed,* but she closed her mouth. Such words of concern would ring hollow after the way she had been scheming against him.

"After I've finished with Luther, I'm going to Mexico. I'll try to be gone long enough for you to make your cotton money."

"You mean I can still use those acres?"

"Go ahead. Plant away. Why in hell not? Plant all the cotton you need to buy your precious Greenpoole. I'll *help* you buy it when I've got the money. I wouldn't want you to remain 'in the midst of your misery' any longer than you have to." He stalked to the door. "Tell my children that daddy will come see them in *Georgia* someday. They'll never do without anything as long as I'm alive, I'll see to it."

As he gripped the door latch, Ella cried out to him. "Gentry, please wait! I have to tell you something … something else about Luther that you have a right to know."

"What?" he drawled coldly. "Tell me that he visited you at the ranch every chance he got? Did you grow to love him like a brother, too, like your friend Jack Kearney?"

She ignored his sarcasm. "That poor girl, Addie LaPonte, and her mother …" she faltered, and could not go on.

"I don't need *you* to tell me that Luther did it. Seems collecting female earlobes is a pastime he enjoys. Knowing him, he probably has them pickled in a jar somewhere." He turned and jerked the door open and was leaving when she cried out again, her tone even more frantic than before.

"It's about your father, Gentry! Your mother said he was bending over little Addie's body when someone shot him in the back!"

Gentry halted and stood dead still.

Ella continued. "Your mother and Hempstead carried your father to the ranch. They didn't tell you he had been in Addie LaPonte's house when he was shot because … because …"

Gentry turned around. "Because *why*? What are you talking about?"

"Gentry … you must speak to your mother about this. I … can't say more. I *won't* say more."

He stared hard at her, and then left, not bothering to close the door.

Ella pressed her hands to her face and sank to the bed, sobbing too loudly, she knew. Hempstead had said Luther Garland was Gentry's match in every way when it came to shooting, fighting, "or just plain gut toughness." Had she sent Gentry to his death by telling him the secret that his mother had been keeping from him for so long?

Suddenly a chill of foreboding weakened her so thoroughly that she could not have stood if she tried. Fear for the father of her children grew, as she realized that Luther possessed something that

Gentry did not possess—*the heartless cunning of a child-rapist and a murderer!*

34

Justice

GENTRY SEARCHED SAN ANTONIO for Timon and old Sandoval. But even though aware of the importance of getting to them before Luther did, he could not get Ella out of his mind. She had wounded him in a way he'd once believed no woman ever could. He was a fool to tell her she could continue using his land, when he knew she'd never be happy until she could plant her damn cotton in *Georgia* dirt! Well, if that was the thing that was making her so crazy, let her hang that 'rotting albatross' back around her neck ... and good riddance to her!

As for him, he'd never had an interest in growing anything that didn't pitch, buck, or bawl, and never would. There was a hard-earned pride in being a cowman, or even a roving, landless, cowhand—*independent*, no matter what. He'd always believed that cotton farming took away a man's independence. From what he'd seen of that occupation, nothing had changed his mind. Before Ella's nonsense, he'd felt sorry for his planter friends who had to watch their crops wither and die in droughts, or get demolished by storms, as had happened a few days ago. At least *his* commodity was on the hoof, *sellable* in any weather, and *moveable,* in most instances, to where the grass was greener—as long as the range was wide open and without *fences*! It was his father's way of life and it was *his*, and it galled him that the woman he had wanted to share it with hated it.

Gentry's frown deepened as he thought of his father. In the six years since Kiel's death, the need to punish his killer burned in the pit of his stomach like a slow poison, a poison curable only by ending the life of his father's murderer—and now he knew who the murderer's identity.

With that, Gentry refocused on the powerful intention that had sent him searching the town: He'd find Pledger and Sandoval, tell them to hide, and then he'd give Luther the justice he'd needed for years.

Timon's wagons stood lined up at the livery stable behind the hotel, but Timon and Sandoval were not in the stable or the hotel. After searching San Antonio until well after sundown, Gentry wondered if Luther might have already killed them. He thought so for sure when old Blackie, alone, trotted from an alleyway and then wandered aimlessly along the street to graze on sparse patches of grass.

With his hand on the butt of his pistol, Gentry rode slowly into the alley, which led him to a public bathhouse and barbershop behind the plaza. Pledger's and Sandoval's horses stood hitched nearby. Another horse nickered from the darkness a few yards away, and Gentry rode up to it for a closer look. Luther rode many horses, but his highly tooled black and tan Mexican saddle was a dead giveaway.

Slipping through the back door and treading softly down a long adobe-walled corridor that led to the barbershop's back entrance, he quietly peered into a room with four trough-like iron bathtubs. Two tubs were in use, steamy vapors rising off the half-submerged cowboys, as an old Negro poured hot water over first one, and then the other.

Gentry moved on, stopping at a door at the end of the hall. Without making a sound, he stepped up on a chair and looked over the transom. His eyes hardened. Luther, alone in the room except for the barber, sat with eyes closed as the barber snipped at his thick black locks.

Gentry's stare settled on him, hatred for his murderous cousin tensing every muscle in his body. At the same time, he wondered where Pledger and old Sandoval were. If in the building with Luther, it wasn't likely they were still alive.

From his vantage point, he kept vigil on Luther. He would wait until the barber finished and Luther was on his two feet before he killed him. He wanted the bastard to know why he was about to die. The more Gentry thought of how his father died, the more enraged he became. Luther had come to the ranch nearly every week as his father lay dying. Death had taken a slow and torturous three months in coming. The son-of-a-bitch had brought gifts of ice and brandy nearly every week … had sat deathwatch alongside him and Kada the night old Kiel finally passed from this life. Had offered a prayer over Kiel's grave! Had escorted Kada back to her ranch the day *he* left for Georgia intending to marry Ella …

Gentry pressed his forehead against the transom. He should have never left Texas in the first place. His father would still be alive, and he would not have a wife about to leave him and take his children with her. His marriage was over, he knew; but there was a part of him that didn't blame Ella for wanting to hold on to her family's ancestral plantation—he felt the same about his own land. That she no longer loved him, and yet had made unbound love to him in order to fool him, disgusted him.

The tiny bell over the barbershop's front door jingled, and Gentry raised his head to see *Timon Pledger* enter, *empty-handed,* and then head straight toward Luther … a nervous grin on his face.

"*Damn*!" Gentry swore under his breath, as he wondered what the sheepish-looking idiot thought he was going to do … and where was old Sandoval?

"Do you remember me, *Jefe*?" Timon asked Luther as he halted directly in front of Luther's chair.

"How could I forget the naked *pendejo* who discovered water for me on my new rancho?" Luther said, then smiled. "I see you've expanded your business. How about I become your partner?"

"No, thanks."

"Well ... how about I let you live and I become your partner?"

Gentry swore under his breath again as he drew his six-shooter and aimed it over the transom. Sandoval had said in the street that he and Pledger has a *cuenta,* a *score* to settle with Luther; but Gentry knew Luther would kill them so fast they wouldn't have time to say *amen!*

Suddenly, out of the corner of his eye, Gentry saw Sandoval move from behind a curtained door in the darkened corner of the room directly behind Luther's chair. The Mexican barber stepped smoothly and quietly aside as Sandoval took his place. Gentry frowned. *What the hell is he ...* Gentry slowly cocked his gun.

"I already have a partner," Timon replied to Luther's last question.

"*Si,* Jefe," Sandoval said softly, as he plunged his knife into Luther's spine just below the back of his neck. "Señor Timon *has* a partner."

Gentry burst through the door as Timon whipped out his pistol and fired, the bullet entering squarely between Luther's bulging eyes.

Gentry's stunned look shot from Timon to Sandoval, then back to Timon. He was thinking that Pledger snapped that gun out like a man who knew what in hell he was doing! Gentry frowned, reluctant to admit that his old enemy could have become so adept.

"He was mine to kill," Gentry growled through gritted teeth, his glare going to Luther's dead face. "The son-of-a-bitch murdered my father ... shot him in the back!"

Sandoval touched his sleeve. "This man was of the same blood as you, *si*?"

With his brooding stare still on Luther, Gentry nodded.

"Then it is good you did not kill him, Señor Garland. It is a curse for a man to kill his own blood … even if he is evil like this man, El Jefe," Sandoval said, pointing at Luther. "The killer of your father is forever quiet, and the king of hell is feasting on his soul."

Gentry, still angry, turned to leave, but was stopped by Sandoval calling out to him.

"Señor Garland, we have done you a *favor* killing this man, *si*?"

"I didn't ask you to kill the son-of-a-bitch," Gentry growled. "I planned on doing it myself."

"Ah, *si*, Señor, but we have saved you from the blood curse."

"*Your* superstition, not mine," Gentry said.

Timon spoke up. "You wanted him dead, and so did we. If you killed him, we would have considered you had done us a favor, and thanked you."

"Thank you," Gentry said blandly. But as he reached the door, Sandoval called out again.

"You are very much welcome, Señor … but we wish to have the *favor* instead."

"You *what?*" Gentry's patience vanished.

Just then, the barber motioned to them. "You must go, Señors! The sheriff will come soon!"

"*Muchas Gracias*, my cousin," Sandoval said, as the barber pointed to the curtained door. All three men quickly left through it.

As they made their way down a dark corridor, Timon stayed on Gentry's heels.

"Sandoval was told by a cousin that works in the livery stable that those two Mexican gentlemen told you they needed ten or eleven wagons for your trip to the mountains, and twice that many men," Timon said.

"Is that *compañero* of yours kin to every Mexican in Texas, Pledger?"

"Is it true you want those wagons?"

"You got a reason for wanting to know my business?"

"I've got eleven of the sturdiest wagons a man can own, and I can supply drivers for each vehicle … plus me and Sandoval, and all of us with our own firearms and ammunition. Sandoval said you would be hauling flour, corn, and beans—lots of it, to trade for something important."

Gentry turned, but before he could speak, Timon continued.

"I also know that you haven't been able to find that many wagons and drivers—not for a fair price, anyway."

Gentry narrowed his stare at him, the look in his eyes registering his unending dislike for the man who had once messed up his life so thoroughly.

"Two questions, Pledger. What's your price, and why in hell would you and the old Mexican want to go? I doubt where we're going if anyone could pay for your dowsing talents—even for the added entertainment of laughing at your skinny naked ass."

"Sandoval's three sons are in those mountains. The very village you're going to. He once told me that all he wanted before he died was to see his sons again. Sandoval saved my life. He's been like a father to me. I want …"

Gentry interrupted him. "Okay, so you think a lot of the old man. I get it. What's your price?"

They were outside now, the orange glow of a nearby torch light flickering on their faces, and intensifying the look of disdain on both.

"Not a stinking dollar, Garland," Timon said, as he stomped away. "Just consider it another of my cockeyed attempts to get your goddamn forgiveness!"

~

The De La Fuente brothers had the sacks of beans, flour, and corn stacked to the rafters in a rented warehouse. Once Gentry had Diego De La Fuente reaffirm their deal, in writing, of one hundred twenty-five gold bars payable to Gentry after completing their journey, Timon's eleven wagons were loaded. Gentry sent a rider to tell Bones Drawgood, Airout Buzell, Dan Meaney, and five other of his *vaqueros* to load all the provisions, guns and rifles into PeeWee Hines' chuck wagon, and then join them on the trail. They would be crossing the remote West Texas bad lands with twelve heavily loaded wagons—Indian country again, since the government in Washington had called an end to reconstruction and was pulling the U. S. Cavalry out of Texas. In absence of the Cavalry patrols, there was no buffer between roving bands of hostile Indians and law-abiding travelers, the latter thinking twice before venturing westward these days. Once across Mexico's border, they would be in even more danger—outlaws and Mexican bandits, along with the Indians—and in a foreign country that hadn't been too fond of visitors from North of the border since Texas' battle for independence.

With luck, Gentry figured that he and his men could be in and out of Mexico in less than four months. The steep mountain trails to the tiny village of *La chica de Lágrimas* high in the Sierra Madre Mountains would be slow-traveling and dangerous, but worth the risk once he'd received his gold.

The wagons were about to pull out when, at the last minute, an additional wagon, with Rodolfo De La Fuente on the seat, rolled from the warehouse. Riding alongside the wagon on horseback, Diego De La Fuente insisted on stationing the unexpected wagon midway in the convoy. He explained to Gentry the reason for its central placement.

"*Por favor*, Señor Garland. My brother is not a coward, but he is fearful for a very good reason, of which I told you previously," Diego said, lowering his eyes sadly. "Rodolfo does not forget what the Apaches did to him when he was a boy. The experience with Rabbit Jack has made him more cautions I think." He shook his head sorrowfully again. "He has become nervous; that is all, Señor Garland."

"I reckon a man knows what he can handle and what he can't," Gentry said. "No one will fault him for it." As he spoke, a public carriage rolled past and he saw Ella, pale, looking at him through the canvas portal. Her luggage was strapped to the back of the vehicle, and he knew she was headed to the depot to catch the train back to Victoria. Jack Kearney, sitting on the opposite seat, cordially tipped his beret. Unsmiling, Gentry did the same, and then turned his back.

As Diego De La Fuente rode away, Sandoval again motioned to Gentry, as if he were about to deliver important information. "Señor Garland, did I hear you tell Diego De La Fuente that you had the twelfth wagon waiting at your rancho?"

"Yes, my men will have a chuck wagon filled with supplies and guns, and a cook."

"Then this new wagon upon which Rodolfo De La Fuente rides, is the *thirteenth* wagon, Señor," Sandoval whispered.

"There'll be thirteen wagons," Gentry agreed, growing impatient, and wanting to be on his way.

"But Señor Garland, that is *mala suerte! Mucho* bad luck. *Un rato malo!* How you say … a bad spell."

Gentry stepped into his saddle. "Haven't you got a *curación* for bad spells, old man … a raw egg under the bed, or something?"

With that, he spurred away to the head of the wagons. They'd meet up with his men at his mother's ranch on the Nueces. From there, they'd set out for Mexico. But first, he wanted his mother to answer the question that Ella had refused to answer.

35

Superstition or Intuition?

KADA PALED WHEN GENTRY TOLD HER that Luther was Kiel's killer. She had raised Luther alongside Gentry after Comanches killed his parents. He and Gentry were both thirteen at the time. Luther had never been affectionate or obedient, but Kada treated him with kindness. Luther had been a bully even before his parents died so brutally. Many times before, and after their deaths, Gentry had fist-fought him for bullying the Mexican children on the place. He was yet crueler to animals, even his own. Gentry, though tough, was kind and peaceful as a boy; but Luther did something one day that sent him into an uncontrollable rage—the day he found his aging dog Boone dead, hanging by his neck from the barn rafters, and Luther sauntering from the barn, laughing. Gentry had Luther on his back and was in the process of giving him the beating of his life when Kada and Kiel came running from the house to stop him.

Brooding and angry on the trek to his mother's Nueces Strip ranch, Gentry wished a thousand times that he had killed Luther for that heartless act—if he had, his father would still be alive … and who knows how many others.

He waited until after supper to ask the question that prayed on his mind all the way from San Antonio. Kada did not hedge; she told him everything.

"I was protecting your father," Kada said. "I would do it again."

"I wouldn't have thought less of him if you'd told me about her, Mother," Gentry said, nodding at Addie. "I would've been mad as hell at him, but I wouldn't have thought less of him."

"What's done is done," Kada said, still unapologetic. "As far as I'm concerned, your father made one mistake in his entire life—the LaPonte woman. The child that resulted was blameless. I forgave him, and that was the end of it."

Addie, sitting beside Kada, had not moved, and now Gentry reached down and lightly grasped her chin and lifted her face. "So you're my sister," he said softly. Her small hand went slowly up to feel at his, and then lowered to her lap again.

"How old is she, Mother?"

"Fifteen," Kada answered.

"Then she was only nine when it happened. He did more than this to her, didn't he?"

Kada hesitated a long moment, then nodded.

Gentry's black eyes glinted. "You cried many a tear over Luther, Mother, but don't shed another. He deserved a worse death than he got. I wish I could have obliged him," he said, his voice filled with the hatred he felt for his murdering cousin. He suddenly envisioned the young cowboy he'd found near Horsehead Crossing on the Pecos River a few months ago after the Comanches had finished with him. The boy lay spread-eagled, his manhood mutilated, hot coals burning deep into his chest and stomach—all obviously done while he was alive. *A man like Luther warranted such a death, not some lone traveling cowboy trying to get back home to his family and friends after a long drive*. Luther's death had been too quick ... too painless!

"You should have told me he was shot in the woman's house, Mother. The truth would've kept me from going back to Georgia ... maybe led me to the killer a lot sooner."

"You might never have learned that you had a son if you hadn't gone when you did."

"Ella's leaving with the children after she's made enough money from another cotton crop or two."

"What did you do this time, Gentry?"

"I discovered her scheming ways sooner than she planned, is all."

"Oh, Gentry," she said, drawing a deep breath. "That young woman has been through much sorrow in her lifetime. It's that very sorry that causes her to cling so to the few *good* things from her past. You should have been patient."

"I was patient. In fact, I made a damn fool of myself being patient," he growled. "I'd give her the money to leave if I had it, but I'm broke again. I paid off the bank note in San Antone, and it took almost every dollar I made at Abilene." He took a sip from the glass of brandy she had poured. "But now I have a chance to make a small fortune. All I have to do is get those supply wagons to Mexico, and help Diego De La Fuente retrieve valuable property that was stolen from him."

Kada glanced out the window at the wagons that had rolled onto her property behind Gentry. "I have a feeling it isn't horses or cattle you will be retrieving."

"No. It's Diego De La Fuente's wife and children stolen from him by his father-in-law. He's holding them in a remote village called *La chica de Lágrimas* in the Sierra Madre Mountains. He also stole two hundred and fifty gold bars, and De La Fuente wants those bars back, along with his family.

"Don't go, Gentry," Kada said, suddenly looking worried. "The Mexican government rarely bothers with those isolated mountain villages. Surely, there is no law there, and if you get into trouble..." She laid her hand on his sleeve. "I have a bad feeling about this."

Gentry smiled for the first time. "That's the *Irish* in you, Mother. Ignore it. What I'll be doing is a lot less dangerous than trailing cattle. I'll get back to that business, but first, I'll make us solvent."

"We're solvent enough. What on earth induced you to do this?"

"One hundred and twenty-five gold bars worth eighty-five thousand dollars was all the inducement I needed."

"I am now more worried about you than ever," she murmured.

"And I'm worried about *you*. What are you doing back here? I thought you promised me before I went to San Antone that you'd stay in Victoria."

"I'm going back. I only came home to get the next batch of horses I plan on selling."

"That's another thing, Gentry said. "When I get the gold De La Fuentes is paying me, you won't be traveling around selling horses anymore."

"Oh, is that right?" Well, let me tell you, I'll be doing it as long as I feel like it, fortune or not!"

He grinned. "You're a stubborn woman."

"True. So don't think I'm moving to Victoria just because *you* say so. There's something within a few hours ride from that town that has a lot more influence on me than you do, dear boy. I'll spell it out for you—g-r-a-n-d-c-h-i-l-d-r-e-n!"

They both laughed; but then Gentry grew glum. "She'll be leaving with them someday, Mother."

"Well then son ... I guess I'd best hurry on to Victoria."

The next morning, Gentry was eager to catch up with the wagons and his men, all of which had left an hour before dawn. He stayed behind to watch Kada, Addie, and their escort of *vaqueros* leave for Victoria. As he took a departing look over his shoulder at his mother, he saw that she was doing the same, the look on her face more troubled than the evening before. He smiled to reassure her, even while agitated that for that brief instant she had transferred her hereditary sense of premonition to him. He shook off the feeling. *It's the Irish in her*, he thought, as the *powerful intention* he'd inherited from his father pushed him onward to the remote Sierra Madre Mountains of Mexico.

~

When Gentry caught up with Timon and his wagons, the De La Fuentes had a third man with them, a belligerent-looking slant-eyed character with a beaded headband worn low on his long forehead and plainly visible beneath the brim of his *gringo-type* Stetson hat. The man's distinct eyebrows slashed straight across his forehead like a pair of arrows, and his pug nose was too small for his basket-sized face, a face that looked like it belonged on a fat man rather than the tall, flat-bellied giant he was. When he turned to the side, Gentry saw the long, black pigtail that hung to his waist. He must have been what Diego De La Fuente considered an inferior, because he did not bother to introduce him.

"He ain't no full-blood Meskin," Airout Buzell said. "That mean-looking feller looks more *Chineezy* than anything else."

"I suppose you're right," Timon said. "I heard them call him *"Chink,"* and he stepped right up."

Rather than push on to El Paso, as Gentry thought would be their point of entry into Mexico, the De la Fuentes opted to cross the border two hundred miles east of there. They forded the Rio Grande River at *Presidio del Norte,* where the Río Conchos and the Rio Grande merge amid a rock-strewn terrain of deep mountain gorges and arid ranges of prairie and desert. Diego explained that Chink brought them word that his father-in-law's *hombres malos* were watching for them at the El Paso crossing, since that was where the De La Fuentes were chased when they narrowly escaped being caught the first time they tried to rescue Diego's family. Gentry never liked last-minute changes, but accepted their reason.

The tiny border village of *Ojinaga* in the state of *Chihuahua* welcomed them *con una fiesta,* accordions and trumpets competing in a fast and fierce *norteña* or *conjunto* style polka that quickly set the men in the caravan to *Mejicano*-style yipping and yelling.

Gentry halted Red Man and gazed around. *Seems we were expected,* he thought, not pleased at what looked like a small army, in various forms of Mexican and native Indian attire, pouring from a cantina at the end of the dusty street. Banded together, they stood as if waiting for the caravan to reach them. The De La Fuente brothers reined up on either side of Gentry.

"Señor Garland, we thought it best that we have more protectors for our journey to *La chica de Lágrimas*. Chink has gathered this fine band of guardians for us. After all, we will be in possession of much gold when we leave there," Diego De La Fuente said. Then, as the music grew louder, he added, "Perhaps the town's musicians decided to give us a fine welcome, also." He laughed. "Come! Let us drink and enjoy the music! We shall rest tonight and leave at dawn."

Gentry glanced calmly at the grubby bunch at the end of the street. Rather than "guardians," they looked more like the types he and his men sometimes had to protect themselves and their herds from on their long cattle drives.

For the second time since leaving South Texas, Gentry felt the uncomfortable presentiment of his mother's Irish nature. He estimated that the disparate gang at the end of the street outnumbered, five to one, his ten armed men on horseback, including him. Other than Cricket, PeeWee, and old Sandoval on the chuck wagon, Timon's eleven drivers didn't look like they'd be much use, even with the rifles Timon supplied them.

"If you hadn't told me a different story, Señor De La Fuente," Gentry said, "I'd think, judging by the number of your *protectors*, that you were planning on starting another revolution."

Diego De La Fuente laughed loudly. "No. No, Señor Garland, *esos hombres nos mantendrán seguro*. They will not only keep us safe on our journey through the mountains, they will keep *you* and your men safe until you have crossed the border back into Texas. After all," he added, "you will be in possession of much gold."

Rodolfo De La Fuente, though a mute, slapped Gentry's shoulder, his big mouth spreading into a fawning smile. For the first time Gentry noticed the gold crowns that decorated every visible tooth in the man's head.

Diego delivered another bit of news. "Their women will, of course, follow them. It is their way."

Gentry looked into the crowd at the scattering of females, some wearing big sombreros, serapes, and gun belts like the men they clung to, others in shawls and skirts. Common on all their faces, male and female, was a look of shared obstinacy.

Sandoval whispered to him, "I do not like this, Señor Garland."

The next morning, Gentry, Timon, and the others waited for Rodolfo's wagon to rejoin the other wagons. Gentry had thought it strange that the De La Fuentes drove Rodolfo's thirteenth wagon into a barn the night before. Obviously, De La Fuente had given its load of beans, corn, and flour to the locals ... because now it contained only a thick pile of old clothes, which were tied down to keep them in place. Rodolfo maneuvered the wagon back into its central position among the line of wagons.

Dan Meaney scratched his head as the wagon went by. "Guess them mountain folks is mighty poor if they'd wear *them* rags," he said.

Airout Buzell made a disgusted sound. "Don't ride too close to that there wagon, boys. Damn pants rats is jumpin' off them rags onto anything that moves," he said, and then nodded at De La Fuentes extra men, as he added, "The whole pile smells like some of them mean-looking water shy fellers yonder musta sweated in 'em 'bout ten years before they finally peeled 'em off."

Bones nudged Gentry. "That same wagon's the only one that got bogged down in the creek and river crossing on the way here, Gent. Did you notice that? And it's wasn't hauling any more sacks of grub than the other twelve."

Gentry nodded. "I noticed," was all he said, but his eyes were on the tracks the wagon's wheels were leaving in the dirt as it rolled past—*still* far too deep for the light load of rags it now carried.

He also noticed that the cook, PeeWee Hines, was now riding Sandoval's horse and Sandoval was riding the chuck wagon with Cricket ... and had stationed the chuck wagon at the very end of the convoy this time.

~

The Sierra Madre Mountains in northern Mexico proved a challenge for the laden wagons and the men driving them. Wind-swept rains pounded them to a standstill for almost a week. When they finally got moving again, burning days followed by cold nights made the grueling, slow ascent a miserable undertaking.

After climbing at a snail's pace for three more days along a narrow trail on the edge of a cliff, the caravan entered a high canyon surrounded on three sides by precipices and plateaus dotted with ancient cave dwellings, some of which, judging by the lean-tos attached to their rocky walls, appeared inhabited. Below, in a valley surrounded by mountainous cliffs, the tiny village of *La chica de Lágrimas* stood, as it had stood for centuries. Huts of grass and sticks hovered among low rock dwellings with thatched roofs, most all of them with lean-tos hung with gourds, baskets, strings of dried peppers, beads, and colorful masks carved of wood.

"These Tarahumara Indians are half-pagan, half-Christian, but very peaceful," said Diego De La Fuente, "except for my father-in-law. He is only *half* Tarahumara. He lives in the only fine house in the entire village." He pointed to a tall building constructed of large adobe blocks. Two carved pillars stood on either side of the front entrance. A balcony swept across the second floor, behind which were a set of French doors and windows.

"We will ride into the village like we owned it," Diego said. "We are too many for them to resist."

As they entered the village, Gentry was aware of De La Fuente's *protectors* bunching up around him and his men.

"Something funny's going on, Gent," Bones said, and then Gentry heard Timon, to his left, swear, "Oh, hell!"

Gentry's six-shooter was already in his hand, but he knew it would be foolish to act: The cocking sounds of more than sixty guns and rifles—plus those held by the grinning De La Fuente brothers—broke the silence, as they aimed at him and his vastly outnumbered men. Coming toward them from one of the huts, and with a wide grin on his face, was *Rabbit Jack,* the last living member of Luther Garland's gang of cutthroats ... other than the De La Fuentes—as was now made obvious.

Gentry cursed his heedlessness: If he'd paid attention to his gut back at *Presidio del Norte,* he wouldn't be sitting here with the De La Fuente brothers' guns in his face ... and with him and his men in grave danger of being murdered.

Diego De La Fuente dismounted and strolled to the wagon that contained the rags. He dropped the tailgate and thrust his hand beneath the pile, then drew out a glittering gold bar.

"Señor Garland, you and your men made a fine escort for me and my gold. I was beginning to think I would never get my fortune out of San Antonio and safely back to Mexico without being murdered for it by the rabble that roams freely between your country and mine," he said, and then smiled sadly. "Unfortunately, you cannot leave here. If I let you go, I fear you would be very upset at not receiving the gold I promised you, and then you would cause me much trouble."

"You goddamn right we would, you greaser sons-a'bitch," Airout Buzell shouted from behind Gentry.

Chink raised his rifle at Airout, but Diego De La Fuente stopped him from pulling the trigger.

"No, no, Chink. Let him be. His death will come soon enough."

"Go ahead and shoot, you Chineezy bastard," Airout yelled, glaring at Chink.

"Quiet, Airout," Gentry said, his black eyes locked coolly on Diego De La Fuente. He had found a small bit of encouragement in that he and his men hadn't been gunned down immediately. It wasn't likely that they would live through this, but every minute that passed and they weren't being murdered, was all good. "Keep your hands off your guns, men," he ordered.

"That is very wise of you, Señor Garland—your cousin Luther said you were a smart man," Diego said. "Perhaps you do not know just how smart you and your friends were in killing Luther. His plan was to be here to greet you, and then kill you. After that, he had only to see to the demise of your heirs." Still smiling, he added, "You see, Señor Garland, as much as I love my gold, my friend Luther loved the idea of owning every acre of Garland land, and all else he could come by. It was his idea to promise that outrageous amount of gold to you."

Gentry grinned sarcastically. "Guess he figured he'd get lucky the third time he aimed a gun at my back, but at a closer range this time."

"Ah, yes, your shoulder wound. He was a very bad shot, wasn't he?"

"Very," Gentry said. "Look, De La Fuente, my men are no threat to you. Kill me if you're worried that I'll return and blow your head off. I give you my word these men will leave and won't be back."

"Now wait a minute, Gent ...," Bones Drawgood said.

Diego De La Fuente's laughter incited his snarling crew to do the same.

"I take no *gringo's* word for anything, Señor Garland. Why would I let even one of you go when it is so much easier to just to shoot all of you?" His bulging eyes hardened. Now, tell your *compañeros* to hand over their pistolas and rifles!" You will have a short reprieve in our fine *cárcel* while my friends and I celebrate the successful completion of our journey."

Gentry turned in his saddle and ordered his men to relinquish their weapons ... noting, as he did, that among the number of wagon drivers coming forward with their hands in the air, two were missing—*Cricket and old Sandoval.*

36

"We're All Naked Dowsers, of a Sort..."

CRICKET AND SANDOVAL LAY FLAT, WAITING FOR DARK. The narrow cliff that held them suspended over the village of *La chica de Lágrimas* was so high that the men and horses below looked like toy figures. A wild celebration had begun earlier, even as Gentry and the others were dragged from their horses and marched to the end of the village, and then herded beneath a thatched roof without walls and supported only by a circle of poles.

"Why they taking 'em in there?" Cricket whispered.

"It is a jail," Sandoval replied, not bothering to lower his voice. They were too high up to be overheard.

"A *jail?* But it ain't got no walls," Cricket said. "Don't look like no jail to me," he added, staring down as if he expected to discover something.

"I was in that jail one time many years ago when I came to see my sons," Sandoval said. "It is a big hole, with its wall of bricks rubbed so smooth that hands and feet cannot climb out."

"*A hole?* You mean they put Mista Gent and the rest of 'em down in a *hole*?"

"*Si,* very deep. The devil's hole. But we must be grateful they have not killed them ... as I believe they plan to do."

Cricket let out a mournful groan. "But … but if they gonna kill Mista Gent and all them others, what you reckon they waiting for?"

"They will celebrate the end of their journey first," Sandoval said. "Celebration *es más importante* to those pendejos, and they will get drunk now, and then, if God is with us, they will sleep."

"What we gonna do?"

"We must make a plan," Sandoval said, and then pointed to one of the many caves on the opposite cliff. "*Mira,* the wagon with the filthy rags is there beside that cave. That is strange, do not you think so?"

Cricket nodded, as the Mexicans beside the wagon began tossing the garments aside then loading the waiting arms of Tarahumara Indians with objects that they lifted from the bed. The natives disappeared into the cave with their loads, returning for more.

"There is something of much value they are putting into that cave," Sandoval said. "Did you not notice how many bandidos rode beside that stinky wagon all the way up the mountain?"

"I never give it no thought … these folks is crazy-acting, anyhow," Cricket replied.

"I believe it is the gold," Sandoval said. "It was in the *thirteenth* wagon under the sacks of beans and corn. In *Ojinaga, t*hey replaced the beans and corn with the old clothes to lighten the load up the mountains. The gold, as we can now see, has been in that wagon all the way from San Antonio, mi chico."

"You mean *that's* the gold we come here to get?"

"*Si.*"

"But if we had that gold with us all the way from San Antone, then why they want Mista Gent and all us men along?"

"Perhaps they feared they would lose their gold to men as bad as themselves who roam the many miles between Tejas and Mexico. Two Mexicans traveling alone can be in great danger even without the burden of gold."

"But how did the gold get to San Antone in the first place?"

"This, I do not know. We have only to concern ourselves with Señor Garland, his vaqueros, and my son."

"Your son? I thought you said you had three sons here."

"I have three sons here in this village. I will see them if I can. But I speak of my gringo son, Señor Timon."

"What we gonna do?"

"I will walk into the village as if nothing has happened."

"What?"

"I will tell them that I left the wagon when I discovered you had fallen off while you slept, and that I found you and you were dead."

"What?"

Sandoval pointed down to the cave again. "*Mira, t*hose pendejos are leaving. They are so drunk they have put the gold in the cave and left no one to guard it."

"Who's gonna take it, anyhow?" Cricket said, and scoffed.

"You are, mi chico."

"What?"

"When darkness comes, you must steal a cart and a big goat."

"Wha-!" Sandoval's hand went over Cricket's mouth.

"You cannot do this, mi chico?"

"Why ... I ... I reckon I can, I guess. But why? What we gonna do with all that gold?"

"We will use it to ransom our friends. It will buy their freedom."

"But..."

"Say no more, mi *chico.* If we are to save them, then you must do this. Load the gold onto the cart. I will help you when I return."

"*If* you return," Cricket grumbled.

"*Si,* if I return. If I do not, God be with you on your journey back to Tejas."

~

Diego De La Fuente's bulbous eyes burned into Sandoval's innocent ones, holding the stare for what seemed much too long to Sandoval.

"I am trying to determine if I believe you, old man. You are telling me that Señor Pledger has two hundred fifty thousand dollars in a San Antonio bank?" He squinted at Sandoval. "He has *more* in greenback dollars than I have in gold bars?"

"Señor Timon is blessed with *mucho dinero*. For his freedom, and the freedom of those with him, Señor Timon's riches will be yours. He will give me a letter to his bank."

"Humm ..." Diego De la Fuente frowned, seeming to ponder.

"You have many amigos waiting for a share of your gold, Señor De La Fuente," Sandoval said softly. "Once you have paid them, your gold will have melted to not so much fortune, si?"

Diego was still frowning, still thinking.

Sandoval continued: "But of course, you would not have to tell your amigos about Señor Pledger's great fortune; it could be yours alone ... if you spare the lives of the gringos."

Diego De La Fuente's response was instant: "I want his two hundred fifty thousand in United States greenbacks."

"*Si.*"

Diego wrote something on a slip of paper. "This is the address of my hacienda in Mexico City. You will deliver the greenbacks there."

"*Si, si,* it shall be done," Sandoval assured.

"It is a long journey to San Antonio; I will be generous and give you sixty days to deliver Señor Pledger's money to my hacienda," Diego said. "Freedom will come to the Americans when I have word that the money has been delivered."

"*Gracias*, Señor De la Fuente." Sandoval said, and then, looking painfully sad, added, "I have one small request. I am a crippled old man, and, as you said, the journey is long. I ask that you let me choose one of the prisoners to accompany me."

Diego laughed. "That is a reasonable request. I see that you are more like an old woman than a man, and will need the strength of another to help you along. But if you say the traveling companion must be your Señor Timon, I will know that you take me for a fool.

Nor must he be Señor Garland. He is an angry man. Much too dangerous to let loose … until the time comes, of course," he added.

Sandoval clasped his hands as if about to pray. "If you will be so kind, I must speak to your prisoners. Only I can convince Señor Timon that he must write the letter and give up his fortune if he is to live to make another."

"Yes, Yes," Diego growled impatiently. "Here is pencil and paper. Be on your way! I am certain when you see your *compañeros*, you will be inspired to complete our bargain with all haste," he said, and laughed again. As Sandoval hurried away, he called out, "I want to read his note. We do not want his bank to make any mistakes, do we, old woman?"

As Diego dismissed him by turning his back, Sandoval rolled his eyes upward and crossed himself, thanking God for this man's greed. Diego De La Fuente could have more gold than found in all of Mexico … and still, he would want more. He would take the money, and would then kill everyone. The loss of his gold, when he discovered it stolen from him, was all that would stop him from murdering every man imprisoned in that pit.

~

Sandoval held a torch above the pit and tried to see to the bottom, but it was too deep. An uproarious barrage of cursing came from below.

"My friends, it is I … Sandoval."

Young Dan Meaney's voice rose up. "We thought it was them Bandidos' whores come back to empty their pee buckets on us again. I smell like a dern slop jar!"

"Yep, if we ain't stepping in our own juice, we're dodging theirs," said someone who sounded like Airout Buzell.

Bones Drawgood added, "These damn tortillas got a tang to 'em that ain't too tasty, neither."

One of the vaqueros cried out angrily, "*¡Si salgo de este hoyo, yo cortaré las gargantas de estas putas!*"

"Count me in on that, Beto," Airout replied to Beto's threat against the whores. "I'll *help* you slit their sorry damn throats!"

Sandoval waved the torch. *"La calma, mis amigos. Calma.* We have much to discuss, and I do not have time to waste."

All went silent.

"Timon, my son … Señor Garland … are you well?"

"Your *son* has a broken leg," Gentry growled. "Fell off the rope ladder on the way down."

"I … I'm all right, Sandoval," Timon said. "Garland fixed me up… used our belts to hold the bone in place."

"I will throw down some sticks. Sticks are better to hold a broken bone. First, I will throw down a pencil and paper, and candles I took from Señor De La Fuente's house."

"Good," Dan Meaney said. "We got matches and a few smokes, but they ain't much for giving off light."

After Sandoval explained his bargain with De La Fuente, Timon agreed to write the note. But he feared out loud what they all feared; De La Fuente would take the money and kill them anyway. "So it really doesn't really matter that I don't have two hundred fifty thousand dollars in the San Antonio bank," he said.

Gentry spoke to Sandoval: "I take it you're doing this to bide for time, thinking to get a rescue party together?"

"No, Señor Garland, but I cannot tell you my plan. This is for your safety if they question you in a cruel way. You cannot tell them what you do not know. A rescue party could come, but I have *ventaja, a*n advantage that Diego De La Fuente does not know about. He will know in good time, and will release you. That is my plan."

A low chuckle came from below, and as Sandoval readied to leave, he heard Timon speak in his defense.

"Don't laugh, Garland! Sandoval is a wise man … probably a lot cleverer than any of us."

"You might be right about that, Pledger—we're in this damn hole, and he ain't," Gentry muttered.

~

Timon, sitting straddle-legged against the smooth rock wall, moaned as Gentry unwound the belts from around his broken leg.

The bone is poking through the skin, Pledger, but not much," Gentry said. "You keep wiggling, and it'll poke through a lot worse.

"I ... I thought you snapped the bone back in place before you strapped on the belts," Timon said, his voice quivering. "I think ... I passed out from the pain of it."

"I did, and you did. But the belts didn't hold," Gentry said, while examining the sticks Sandoval had thrown down to them.

"Christ Jesus!" Timon cried. "A man should be drunk out of his mind at a time like this."

"Anybody got any whiskey?" Gentry jokingly called over his shoulder, and the thirsty men laughed despite their misery.

As Timon yelped at a fresh stab of pain and then opened his mouth for another comment, Gentry's fist flashed out and popped him hard in the jaw. The blow propelled Timon's unconscious head to a second collision against the brick wall.

"That ain't whiskey, but it'll do," Bones Drawgood said, as he braced Timon's knee while Gentry gave his foot and calf one swift jerk, popping the shattered shinbone back into place.

Timon slowly regained consciousness as Gentry bound the splints, using the belts and the sleeves Bones had ripped from Timon's shirt. Timon watched, gritting his teeth in silence, as Gentry worked on his leg.

"Awake, Pledger?" Gentry asked. "From here on out, you'll have a nice scar, maybe a limp, to detract from your skinny ass when you're prancing around naked like a superstitious idiot."

Timon rallied. "Damnit Garland, it isn't superstition! Whether a blessing or a curse, dowsing was laid on me like a bolt from the blue when I was seconds away from being murdered at the orders of your sorry, devil-of-a-cousin, Luther Garland!"

"Maybe you have Luther *and* the devil to thank for your blessing," Bones Drawgood interjected. "Ever think of that?"

"The devil doesn't save lives like mine was saved," Timon said, and then looked back at Gentry, who had finished with his leg and was sitting, crowded against the wall, beside him. "I had been beaten, stripped bare by Rabbit Jack and those other stinking animals. They were going to cut my damn throat. I was naked when my life was saved by me finding that first water … and I found it with nothing but a prayer and a damn mesquite stick. Since then, I tried a hundred times doing it with clothes on, and it never works."

"The workings of an irrational mind," Gentry drawled, and the men chuckled.

Timon hunched forward to glower at him in the candle light, then cried at the top of his shivering voice: "You think I like stumbling around like a dammed naked *mental* just to get by in this world? I'm forced to it! *Commanded* to it, I tell you! A man shouldn't have to …!" his voice broke, and the chuckling stopped just as abruptly.

A long moment passed where only Timon's pained breathing was heard, and then Gentry's deep voice, sounding less indifferent this time, broke the silence. "I reckon, Pledger, we're all forced by one thing or another to do one thing or another … some of it begging to be explained or justified in some way but can't be. I guess that makes us all naked dowsers, of a sort."

After another lengthy quiet, a voice in the darkness that sounded a lot like Airout Buzell, added, "…and I reckon you can't rightly judge a man by the clothes he don't wear, neither."

37

A Stink Worse Than Death

CRICKET THOUGHT IT THE BEST LUCK HE'D EVER HAD when, in the bright moonlit night, he watched a lone drunken bandido stagger into the cave leading a big, brown and white goat attached to a goat cart. The cart, with high sideboards and huge wooden wheels, was loaded with large rocks. Cricket squatted in the bushes near the cave, and waited.

A while later, when the bandido left the cave without the goat and cart and weaved his way back down the steep trail to the village, Cricket scratched his head in puzzlement. Why did the bandit leave with the other bandits earlier, then return *alone* with a rock-filled goat cart, and then just leave it, goat and all, there in the cave? Whatever the reason, Cricket had a feeling the bandido would return for his cart, so *he* had better get busy. He'd switch the rocks in that cart for the gold, but first, he had to find the gold.

He used almost his entire tin of matches before his hands stopped shaking long enough to light a small torch he found next to the cave opening. He again felt truly blessed with good luck when, after searching only a few minutes, he found the goat cart tied next to a shallow hole partially covered with a tarp.

Cricket had never seen a gold bar before, but he knew the objects glittering in the torch's glow were not molds of clay bricks. Not wasting another second, he jerked the tarp away, jumped into the hole, and as fast as his arms and legs could move, he threw the bars out of the hole and replaced them with the rocks from the cart. That done, he spread the tarp over the rocks. Soon, the gold was loaded onto the cart. He scratched his head: He knew how to count and there wasn't but half the gold Mista Gent say they had come to rescue. He scratched his head again. *Guess somebody can't count,* he thought.

After retrieving some of the smelly old rags and covering the gold, he stood back and observed his accomplishment. *That was too easy*, he thought. And it was. The goat would not budge.

"Oh, Lawd, I'm gonna be kilt for sure when that bandido come back," he mumbled, as he tugged at the goat's harness. "How much could one hundred and twenty-five gold bars weigh? It don't seem like this cart outta be so heavy," he mumbled. *Mista Sandoval should been back by now*, he thought, trying not to panic. At the same time, he worried that the bandido would be coming up the trail any second, and his cowboy days would be over quicker than he could say *vi'karo*! He tugged harder, pleading, as he pulled the goat from the front and then pushed the cart from the rear. Finally, the animal took slow, halting step, until they had exited the cave and started along the narrow path, opposite the direction the banditos had taken.

They had gone only a few yards when Cricket heard the fall of horse's hooves on the rocky trail. He jumped behind nearby bushes and squatted low, his head almost between his knees.

"It is I, *mi chico.* Come, we must hurry."

Sandoval gazed down at him from his perch atop the Reverend Pledger's old horse, Blackie. Behind them was Dan Meaney on Mista Gent's *Red Man!*

"Oh, Lawd, we gonna be kilt for sure when they find them hosses gone!" Cricket cried.

"Señor Dan and I have permission to leave, and to take these horses, so that we can deliver a letter to Señor Timon's bank."

"What letter?" Cricket asked Sandoval.

Dan answered. "It don't matter what letter, because we ain't going to no bank."

Sandoval was more obliging: "The letter giving Señor De La Fuente Señor Timon's great fortune in Texas."

"Mista Timon got a great fortune in Texas?"

"Only a small one. The great fortune Señor De La Fuente will bargain for will be his own gold once he discovers we have taken it, and he reads the ransom note one of my sons will slip into his *hacienda* after we are too far away to be caught by them."

"But where we gonna take it?

"Back to Texas."

"What!"

"Si. We must leave right away, while darkness is still upon us." He laid his hand on the goat's rump. "The black horse and I will lead this goat down the mountain, and then this black horse will pull the cart. You and Señor Dan will ride Señor Garland's fine animal. We are in God's hands. If He wishes us to complete our mission, He will keep us safe."

"Yeah," Dan Meaney said, "and you can ride tail, Cricket. I get the saddle—and I'll have that six-shooter you're wearing, because I'm a better shot than you, for sure."

Cricket frowned, but unbuckled his gun belt and handed it over. Dan grinned obligingly, and gave him a hand up.

"We better hurry," Cricket said, "'cause there a *bandido* gonna be coming after this cart."

"No he ain't," Dan said. "He came up on me and Sandoval back yonder …," he pointed down the trail. "We got in a little tussle with him. As his bad luck would have it, that poor feller wound up taking a fatal leap right off the cliff."

"I'm sure glad of it," Cricket said, then twisted around to look at Sandoval. "But what about Mista Gent, and them others? Did you see 'em?"

"Yes, I saw them," Sandoval answered. "Señor De La Fuente is not anxious to kill them now that he waits for Senor Timon's fortune; but we must hurry on our journey, for they are not treated well. They live in filth and must eat the foul scraps thrown down to them."

'That ain't all that's thrown down on 'em," Dan said, as Cricket pulled his bandana up around his nose to ward off Dan's stench, which was near as bad as that coming from the filthy rags covering the gold bars.

Suddenly, three Tarahumara Indians, in drooping loin cloths, their dark-brown skin painted all over with big white dots stepped out of the bushes. They had green and red sashes looping their waists and necks, and wide headbands fanned with dozens of turkey feathers.

"My sons have come to help us," Sandoval said. They have brought a harness for Blackie, and goatskins to cover the gold."

Cricket and Dan stared. Sandoval's three sons were a fearsome sight.

Later, as Sandoval's sons, herding a flock of goats, led them down the mountain on a route rarely used by anyone other than the Tarahumara Indians, Sandoval explained his sons' attire. "It is how they celebrate *Semana Santa* ... the Holy Week before Easter. Many years ago, the Jesuit priest made them Catholic.

"Is it Easter already?" Cricket asked.

"No. It is a long time until then; but the criminal who rules the Tarahumara is without God. He makes them wear their Holy costumes because it pleases him."

"Them get-ups and that paint don't look Catholic to me," Dan said.

"The new faith has joined the old faith, and the old faith is what you see," Sandoval gestured to his sons. "Mankind does not cast away so easily that which has molded him."

"Are your sons coming away with you?" Cricket asked.

"No. This is their home. Perhaps I will not see them again. They honor me as their father, but they do not know me. They are their mother's sons."

"Well … at least you got to see them one more time," Dan said.

"*Si*. I am pleased."

"*I'll* be pleased when we get deep into Texas," Dan said.

At the bottom of the mountain, Sandoval bid his sons goodbye. After telling Cricket to drive the cart, he began herding the goats.

"Hey! We ain't got time to worry with no goats!" Dan cried.

"We must take the time, for these goats may save our lives," Sandoval called back to him.

"How so?"

"Tonight, when we rest, we will kill four of these goats and cover the cart with their meat and bloody hides."

Dan looked stunned. "Geeze! What for? It's gonna stink to high heaven in a day or two and draw every damn blowfly in Mexico!"

"*Si*, and no one will come near such a cart with so much stink and so many flies. We are passing through the land of the Apache soon. We must take all … how you say… *defense?*"

Cricket was happy to drive the cart. Dan's stench had just about set him to *"airin' his paunch"…* as old Mister Grouse always said when something sickened his stomach.

~

Eight days later, as Sandoval, Cricket, and Dan Meaney crossed the border into Texas at a desolate part of the Rio Grande River away from town or village, a small band of Apache Indians, their bodies and faces striped with paint, appeared from behind a low hill and moved stealthily along at a parallel angle from them. Suddenly, Sandoval ran up beside the cart and began to undress.

"Take off your clothes, mi chicos! All of them!" he cried.

"No, sir-ree!" Dan Meaney roared.

Sandoval was busy smearing his naked body with the rotting goat flesh from the cart. "They are coming! Take off your clothes and do as I do! If you do not, they will kill us!"

Cricket had already jumped down and disrobed in record time, and was gagging as he smeared his body with the putrid mess. Dan soon joined him.

When Sandoval began to stagger around, dancing, hollering, and screaming, Cricket and Dan did the same, but always with a wary eye on the Indians … and Cricket's eye on his six-shooter dangling from Dan's hand.

"Booga-booga! Ba-aaa! Ba-aaa!" Dan cried, while waving his arms over his head, and shooting off Cricket's pistol.

The Indians halted, and sat staring at what they must have thought was a bad omen—three crazy men, naked in a haze of blowflies, all three screaming and twisting their bloody bodies like demons from the white man's hell. Suddenly, they turned their ponies and galloped away.

"Do not stop," Sandoval yelled. "If we stop, they will know that we are not crazy and will return."

The few live goats in the herd went wild, and, bleating and bucking, stampeded in all directions.

"I stink like death!" Dan screeched.

"Me, too!" Cricket cried, wiping with disgust at the slimy chunks of bloody debris that covered every inch of him.

"*Si, mi chicos,* as do I," Sandoval replied. "But which would you prefer, to only stink like you are dead … or to be dead?"

38

Burying Things …

ELLA STOOD AT THE WINDOW AND WATCHED Hempstead Grouse drive Tessie and her orphans back to Victoria. The flatbed wagon, fitted with two bench rows behind the high driver's seat had been Hempstead's idea, and worked perfectly for transporting Tessie and her growing brood. Ella was glad to see them leave this time. Their conversation had been quite taxing while the three of them sat in the parlor, *she* mending rips in Adam's pants, and the two of them bantering back and forth as if she wasn't there—especially when Hempstead pulled out his tobacco pouch and rolled his nasty smoke while dribbling tobacco all over the carpet. Tessie had been lamenting about never having children of her own. She said now that she had taken in her orphans, she realized, more than ever, what she had missed all these years.

"So you ain't had any kids of your own, Tess. It don't do you no good to moan over it though," Hempstead drawled. "You got plenty of 'em now," he added, nodding toward the noise coming from outside as the children played. "If you'd had kids of your own when you was young, you would'a been putting a shameful cart before a disgraced horse … since you never was able to trap a husband."

As if she had not heard him, Tessie went to her knees to pick up the tobacco, piece by piece. "If I had a child for every salty tear I cried over *not* having one, the little darlings would be crowding the entire population right over the ends of the earth—if the earth were *flat*, that is," she said.

"Yup, and if I could make salt out'n every *happy* tear I shed in gratitude for *not* having any, you could season every pot'a beans in South Texas."

"You? Cry? I doubt it," she said.

"It was just a picture of speech, Tess, that t'wern't meant to be factual," he growled. "And just to keep the story straight, I ain't got nothing against kids as long as they're somebody else's."

"Well, anyway, Hempstead, there are not but *twelve* children in my care, counting the two babies," she said, firming her cheeks defensively, and looking for a place to put the retrieved tobacco that now decorated her open palm. "The children are no problem at all," she continued, "since my dear friend Mildred Kearney has come to live with us. Jack is a tremendous help, too, when he isn't off selling his legs."

Hempstead held his tobacco pouch beneath her hand and then used a slow forefinger to leisurely sweep the flakes into the pouch. Tessie glanced at Ella as if she wanted to bring her into the conversation, but then left her completely out of it by pointedly addressing Hempstead.

"What about our dear Ella, Hempstead? She is so quiet lately. Do you think she is all right?"

"If she ain't, it ain't affected her damn cotton planting any," Hempstead replied.

"I am very worried about her, you know," Tessie said, her eyes darting upward to the ceiling and then at Ella. "She hasn't been to town since … when was it, dear? Four months ago, wasn't it? The day sweet Jack Kearney escorted you back from San Antonio, wasn't it?"

"That long?" Ella replied stiffly, growing more hostile as Hempstead joined Tessie's silly game.

"Mis Ella's too dern busy to come to town, Tess," he said. "Four or five months ain't long if you're busy as a hound with a tick in his ear, and she is *that,* with having them Negroes plowing the fields again, and a'getting ready for her next cotton planting, ain't'cha, Miz Ella?" He turned back to Tessie. "Them cotton patches is her only damn fret, it seems like to me." He eyed Ella briefly. "You'd think she'd be fretting over the fact that Gent ain't come back, even if she ain't got any use for him."

Steaming, Ella slammed her sewing into the basket at her feet, excused herself, and said she must help Hannah prepare dinner. However, wondering if Hempstead would say anything else about Gentry… or have an idea why he wasn't back yet, she had stood outside the parlor door, listening, and watching the pair in the big mirror directly across from them.

"She has not once mentioned Gentry's name to me, Hempstead, not once," Tessie was saying, her tone one of disapproval. "Molly Barton—excuse me, Molly *Meaney*—now comes to town to do Ella's shopping. Molly's had her baby, you know, a girl."

"I know she's had her baby," Hempstead said. "Where you think I been, Tess, under some damn rock?"

"Who knows where you've been?" Tessie shot back, then continued. "Molly comes by to see her brothers and sisters, and tells me that Ella is fine, though she admits she's a bit short-tempered," she said and sighed, adding, "But you know *Molly;* Ella can do no wrong in her eyes. Still, four months is a long time to let someone else do your shopping."

"I used to stay away from town longer than that when I didn't have nothing to go in for," Hempstead said, and winked.

Still on her knees, Tessie smiled demurely up at him, which was an odd look on Tessie Peckenpaugh's aged and haunted face.

Obviously mistaking the look, Hempstead leaned over and helped her to her feet.

"Don't get on your knees if you're too damn old to get up by yourself, Tess. I may not always be around to help them old creaking bones of yourn get to moving."

"Oh, hush. They don't creak any louder than yours," she scolded half-heartedly.

"I got a remedy for us both," he said, and winked again. "If we could get them old bones to creaking and popping together … you know, up real close like … it might be a cure."

"If you are proposing marriage, Hempstead Grouse, the answer is…"

"No!" he bellowed. "I'm answering for us both."

"Exactly!" she said, and picked up his coffee cup and saucer with the half-eaten slice of buttermilk pie. He reached for it, but she held it away. "Go home, Mister Grouse … or go wherever it is you go. I am quite busy today. I will be quite busy the next time, too. So please don't bother coming by."

"Are you losing your senses, Tess? I *am* home! *You're* the one who's visiting, golldamnit!" He slammed on his hat. "You Georgia women is about as tetchy as a bucket of poked rattlesnakes! I guess I might as well mosey on out to the kitchen and expose my tender feelings to that other contrary Georgia female. She's even meaner than you lately. If Gent's smart, he'll get himself shot or scalped."

As Ella dashed toward the kitchen, she heard Hempstead stomp across the floor and then halt to yell out to Tessie, "And quit poking at that damn squirrel you keep pinned to the back of your head—it makes my pate crawl!"

After the wagon containing Tessie, her brood, and Hempstead disappeared over the hill, Ella continued gazing out the window at the empty road. Tessie was right. She had not mentioned her husband's name; but she had wondered, from time to time, if he and his men were all right, especially since Kada was so worried about him. Kada visited weekly, always with a new fret about her son … unable to shake her "dire premonition." But Ella wondered what could happen to an army of more than twenty well-armed men, counting Timon's wagoners. Gentry's men, especially, were experienced with the treacherous ways of this land.

Sunbeam interrupted her thoughts.

"Fat Lupe sayed she gonna need more wood for the cook stove come supper time, Miss Ella. But she can't find Flaco what 'posed to bring it," she said. "Fat Lupe say Flaco been moping 'round long enough over his old '*mamacita*' passing on to glory like she done. Fat Lupe sayed that ol' woman was near one hundred year old. She couldn't walk, wouldn't talk ... and she mess her drawers just for meanness if no one come real fast when she holler for 'em."

"I'll find Flaco," Ella said, and then watched Gentalee toddle off to the kitchen with Sunbeam, followed closely by the frolicking Adam, Elizabeth, and Belle. How they were growing, especially Adam. He looked more like Gentry every day, and she had no doubt he would be as tall.

Her thoughts were on Gentry again. Kada said he should have been home by now. A strange feeling swept over Ella as she glanced down the deserted road. Even though she planned to leave for Georgia and divorce him as soon as possible, she did not like to think that Gentry could be injured ... or even dead. *I love you ... I love you ... I lo-!* She forced the deep, velvety voice to stop, then went out onto the porch and stood in the pale twilight of late evening.

Soon, she pressed a trembling, curled forefinger against her lips—a habit she had subconsciously picked up lately from unrelenting memories of Beatrice Corrigan. Curling a finger over her upper lip was something Beatrice always did when she pondered over something. Sometimes Ella felt as if the woman was standing over her shoulder, admonishing her, telling her what a blind fool she was. Grandmother Corrigan had *loved* Gentry ... thought he was "the best thing since peach cobbler" as Honor said. Ella's eyes hardened. *Grandmother must have loved him a lot,* she thought, *since she gave him every dime of my money!* Moments later, she took a deep breath to calm herself as she remembered what Kada had said to her the day they met: *"Anger, like hatred, changes a person inside and out. Harbor either one long enough and you'll be wearing it on your face and in your gut. Pretty soon, the whole world will see it, and you won't be who you think you are anymore."*

Ella relaxed her tense mouth. She didn't hate *anyone*. She wasn't even that angry anymore. She *did* continue to despise the terrible thing that was done to her under the erroneous belief that it was for her own good. She supposed she could credit her grandmother for thinking she was doing the right thing in selling Greenpoole and giving Gentry the money. Then, while being so benevolent toward her grandmother, she could then credit Gentry for putting the money away for the children instead of spending it on his debts. Fine. She'd give credit to those who has schemed against her. However, to her own credit, she had written to Banker Treadwell and he agreed to sell her the Greenpoole property. He'd set up a mortgage once she'd made a substantial down payment, which she knew would take another crop or so. The future was looking brighter.

She slapped her wind-blown hair away from her face and headed for the barn to look for Flaco and tell him to bring wood for the cook stove. She stepped into the semi-darkness of the barn, and called out to Flaco. Receiving no reply, she supposed that Fat Lupe was correct, and he was still down at the Mexican cemetery kneeling beside his mother's grave.

Ella sighed in sympathy for him. She was about to retreat when a horse whinnied in the far end of the barn. Thinking that no one had fed the children's horses, she headed toward the stalls, but then drew back in shocked surprise when she got there. Gentry's horse, Red Man, was in one stall; Timon's *Blackie* in another!

Before she could collect her thoughts, three figures slowly emerged from behind a stack of hay bales and into the shadowy light streaming from the rafters—a bent old man in a filthy poncho, a ragged Negro with huge, haunted eyes, and a grimy white boy, slight of build, and with a long six-shooter strapped to his skinny hips.

Moments passed before she recognized the three, for they were as scruffy and wild-looking as the half-dead coyote she'd found in the chicken coop yesterday after the hounds had gotten hold of him. Dan Meaney shushed her with a finger thrust to his lips, then went to look out the barn door as if to see if someone had followed her. Satisfied she was alone, he turned to her.

"You think we look bad now, Miz Ella ... you should'a seen us 'fore we rinsed off in the Guadalupe."

They had been traveling for forty days, mostly at night, for fear of being robbed and murdered by outlaws and Indians during the day. The story the three told left Ella aghast and strangely silent, as she stared at the one hundred twenty-five bars of gold. Each bar had '*36 onzas puro oro*' stenciled into it. Ella knew enough to know that "onzas' meant ounces, and she was good enough at figures to calculate that one hundred twenty-five bars added up to over three hundred seventy-pounds of gold ... *worth over eighty-five thousand dollars!*

Dan explained further. "When the De La Fuentes get the note I wrote—and that old Sandoval here dictated to me because I'm the only one of us three who can write—he's gonna want that gold back more than he wants to kill Gent and the others. Our note tells 'em he ain't gonna get the gold unless he sends everybody home first," Dan said, grinning. "Then, we'll hand it over to whoever he sends for it. '*Word of honor,*' I wrote. And that's the way it's gonna be."

Ella clasped her hands tightly together to stop them from shaking. Nothing could happen to Gentry. Why, he was practically infallible!

As she watched them laboriously push the cart into the stall, groaning and grunting with each slow advancement, she realized just how much their unspeakable journey had exhausted them; three hundred seventy-five pounds of gold should not have been almost more weight than the three of them could handle.

Cricket mopped his face. "Phew! If it hadn't been for Blackie and Red Man taking turns pulling that cart, we never would'a made it."

Ella dragged a tarpaulin from across the barn. "Help me spread this over the cart," she said. "I'll fasten it down while you rest." They drug the canvas into place then the three of them dropped onto a pile of hay.

Ella worked steadily, tucking, and then securing the canvas with rope. When almost finished, she noticed something unusual along one side of the cart. One of the long panels nailed to the side had pulled loose and she saw something wedged between the floorboards and what appeared to be a second bed beneath the first. She squeezed her hand through the opening, her groping fingers discovering one bar-shaped object after another! She stopped breathing.

She hovered beside the cart, staring at nothing, her body perfectly still, but her mind whirling like a tornado from one thought to the next. Cricket said he had stolen the goat cart from a drunken Mexican bandido. Obviously, neither Cricket nor Sandoval nor the De La Fuente brothers knew that the bandit—unable to forego the temptation of making himself rich—had stashed some of the gold under the floorboards of his cart.

She straightened up, and as she did, she pressed her knee against the cart's sagging panel and pushed it back into place, her thoughts still churning: Sandoval, Dan and Cricket knew only about the one hundred twenty-five bars; once Gentry was home and those bars turned over to whomever was sent to retrieve them, the De La Fuentes would not be able to do anything about the bars they *didn't* get back. Suddenly, she shivered with the knowledge that only *she* knew the whereabouts of that second load of gold bars.

What wonderful luck, she thought. From what she had been able to feel with her probing hand, there appeared to be as many gold bars crammed into that secret compartment as was on top! There would be no mortgage on Greenpoole! She could buy her family's ancestral property outright, and never have to worry again!

Just then, Sandoval stepped to her side, and whispered, "Señora Garland, we must find a better hiding place for this gold."

"What?"

"The gold, Señora. We must hide it."

"I ... I'll take care of it, Sandoval," she said, and took a deep breath. "For everyone's safety, I think it's better if only one of us knows its location ... until ... it's time to hand it over to De La Fuente." She stepped away from the cart, and motioned to the three of them. "Come into the house; you must be starved."

As they made their way across the yard, she pondered on a hiding place. Suddenly, her face brightened. She'd *bury* it! *Yes!* She'd bury it in the ground. But she'd have to find a plot of soft, easy-to-dig earth where no one would ever think of looking...

Deep in thought, she paid no attention at all when Molly, apparently after looking out the window and seeing Dan, came screaming down. Soon, the yard filled with welcomers. Ella, nearly knocked off-balance by the army of little niños that raced from around the corner of the house, recovered without so much as a blink of her glittering eyes, her thoughts still on the gold.

She glanced furtively toward la villa and at the Mexican cemetery where old Flaco still knelt beside his mother's freshly dug grave, *with its soft mound of black earth ...*

But who could she trust to help her? Cricket? No. He was one of *them* now, one of Gentry's *"vi'karos."* She would not even consider old Sandoval or Dan.

With that thought, she followed the trio to the house, her head swimming with anticipation of the wee hours of night when all would be asleep—except for her and *Sunbeam.*

~

Forty-eight days later, Ella stared down at Timon Pledger lying on a litter attached to a dusty mule—and her plans of riches fizzled like a spatter of rain on a hot desert rock. With him were his eleven well-digger employees who had driven his wagons to Mexico. All of them looked like scarecrows, starved, scaly of skin, and red of eye, injured of body and soul by their former imprisonment, and then further tortured by their horrific forty-eight day journey. Timon said Diego De La Fuente was furious when he found the note and discovered that he had been fooled and his gold stolen for ransom. Timon reluctantly handed a letter addressed to Ella from Diego De La Fuente.

My dear Señora Garland,

With haste, you and you alone will take my gold, by steamer, to el puerto de Veracruz.

In good faith, and to show that I am a kind man, I have forgiven Señor Timon for his false claim of riches, and have freed him and his empleados. If you follow my instructions, I assure you we will be done with this unpleasant business, and your husband will be freed. He and his men are in Veracruz awaiting their rescue. They will be freed the instant my gold is handed over to my trusted mensajero, the man who will meet you as you depart the boat. You and your husband will then leave Mexico on the next vessel.

I urge you, Señora Garland, do not be slow in arriving in Veracruz.

If you do not return my gold in 15 days, your husband and his men will be taken to the outskirts of Veracruz and executed.

Your humble servant,

Diego De La Fuente

After reading the letter, and then reading it again, Ella told Hannah and the Mexicans to take care of Timon and the others, and then she went straight to her room. Once inside, she stood trembling just inside the door. The letter terrified her! The very notion was ridiculous! There was not the remotest possibility that she would go to Mexico *alone,* and carrying a fortune in gold! She'd probably be murdered for it long before she got there! She closed her eyes and envisioned the beautiful *civilized* streets of Savannah where a woman's only danger was the wagging tongues of the *tea and cakes brigade* if she failed to commit to her social obligations. Risk her life in Mexico among the thieves and murderers who had possibly already murdered her husband? Dear God! She'd have to be insane!

If she was ever going to get away from here, now was the time: She was rich! All she had to do was pack up *her* one hundred and twenty-five bars of gold, along with her children, and take the next boat home! The other half of the gold could ransom Gentry … if he was still alive. She sank to her knees then doubled over, sobbing.

~

Later, as Hannah scrubbed Timon's festering leg, then packed it in a thick poultice of raw potatoes she had shaved to a squishy pulp, he stared forlornly up at Ella.

"De La Fuente was pretty mad when I told him I didn't have two hundred fifty thousand in the bank like Sandoval told him, but he cooled off when I told him the true amount. Forty thousand … and he could have it," Timon said, his voice dry and raspy from illness and hardship.

Ella gazed incredulously at him. "Oh, Timon, why did you tell that thief he could have your money? Why, oh *why*, did you do that? You should have simply assured him that he'd get his gold back. After all, that's all he really wanted until you so foolishly revealed your life's earning to him."

"But, Ella, what if getting that extra forty thousand all to himself means he really will let Gentry and the others go? I can get more money the same way I got that forty thousand, but I think maybe you and Garland's children think there ain't but *one* of him."

Ella dropped her head, and then looked away.

Timon continued. "De La Fuente said to put my forty thousand in a carpetbag, one that you must carry off the boat. I gave Mister Grouse a letter to my bank in San Antonio. He took the train to get it. *I'll* take my money and the gold to De La Fuente, not you."

"You look half-dead, Timon. I doubt you could stand another trip, even by boat. Besides, the note instructs that *I* and I alone must do this," Ella said then frowned. She hadn't realized she was going, until she heard herself say it.

Trembling, she went out onto the porch to be alone. Ringing in her ears were her grandmother's words, spoken that dreadful day back in Georgia when she revealed that she had sold Greenpoole: *"You stupid woman! Your husband and your son and the child that you carry, is your life! This..." she had swept her arm out, indicating Greenpoole, "is not your life! It is the rotting albatross around your neck!"*

She clung to the porch column, stunned by how easily that rotting albatross had fallen away … but was it too late?

~

Three days later, Ella watched a wagon come under the gate. Hempstead was on the seat, and on the bed was a shiny new casket.

"It's polished oak. Ain't it purty?" he said.

"Who … who is in it?" Ella asked.

"Nobody, yet; but that gold you hid from everybody is gonna be." He hefted a big carpetbag from the seat beside him and dropped it to the ground. "I got the jaybird's money. Me and you is gonna catch the first boat to Mexico, Miz Ella."

"You are not going, Hempstead Grouse! With so many of Gentry's men captured with him, and only old Flaco, Felipe, and their families left on the place, Gentry would want you *here*. Regardless, that is what *I* want. Of course, I know Meshach and Sunbeam will be looking out for Adam, Elizabeth and little Gentalee, but …" she took a deep breath, and softened her voice. "I would feel so much better knowing that you were also watching over my children … Hempstead."

For the first time he had nothing to retort. She glanced sidelong at him, thinking: *It couldn't have shocked him that much that I called him by his first name.*

"I shall go with you, Señora," Sandoval said quietly. "I know these men. I do not trust Señor De La Fuente, but I will not be as noticeable as Señor Hempstead."

"Going unnoticed into an enemy camp ain't my way of doing things," Hempstead growled.

"No, Señor; but a man who is not important in the eyes of his enemy has many weapons." He looked at Ella. "No one will know that I am there, Señora."

That night, when everyone was asleep, Ella and Sunbeam pulled a cart down to the Mexican cemetery and parked it beside the grave of Flaco's *mamacita.*

"You sure you wanna do this, Miss Ella?" Sunbeam asked, as she sunk the shovel into the mound and wiggled another load onto it. "I don't think it a good idea. What if ...?"

Ella, on the opposite side of the grave, removed another shovel full. "When we're finished, Sunbeam, we must make certain *mamacita's* resting place looks exactly as it looked before."

"But Miss Ella, what if them bad folks open that casket and see it ain't got but *half* their gold!"

"Shush! Let's not talk about it anymore, Sunbeam. I get sick to my stomach just thinking about it. Judging from what Sandoval said about not trusting Diego De La Fuente, this may not be the smart thing to do, but I must keep on believing that it's the *right* thing to do... or I'll go crazy!"

39

"My *Cuchillo* Had a Very Large Target, Señora ..."

STANDING ON THE WHARF IN VERACRUZ, Ella watched two Mexican boys pull the casket, atop a single-tongued cart, down the long wharf to the darkening street. Sandoval, obviously remaining *no importante* to anyone who might be watching, lagged far behind, shuffling among the last passengers to disembark. Timon's money was in the bottom of her carpetbag beneath items of clothing, and Ella clutched the handle so tightly that her hand had begun to cramp. She released a quivering breath. She doubted that old Sandoval would be of any help to her should she need protection. She thought of her children. *Oh God!* If she were to die ... and Gentry, too, then what would happen to them? Would they end up orphans under Tessie and Kada's care ... and with the dastardly Hempstead Grouse constantly coloring their vocabularies?

A half-hour later, she looked nervously at the dwindling street crowd. They stared back at her, perhaps out of curiosity of the lone, pale-haired *gringa,* dressed in widow's weeds, her hand resting on a shiny oak casket, her long black veil rippling in the breeze.

Soon, with darkness falling and the crowds dispersing except for the stevedores far down the wharf and a vendor selling fish on the corner, she was alone. Was this the right place? Should she just stand here and wait? Her nerves were so taut she felt as if she would hear them crackle if she took another step. The letter said a man would bring Gentry to her, and then she would hand over the gold and the carpetbag containing Timon's forty thousand dollars.

After waiting an hour in which her wide eyes darted from one dim corner to the next, she motioned the boys to follow with the cart, and then moved haltingly along the street. At the end of the block, she stood in the glow of a flickering torch that extended from a pole on the side of a building. Up ahead, she saw a gaping black entry to an alley. Shivering, she looked over her shoulder, hoping to catch a glimpse of Sandoval. Where was he?

When she looked straight ahead again, her heart gave a frightening leap, then thudded like a rabbit's as she watched a shadowy figure step from the dark alley.

The man was like a giant; thickly built, and wearing a big, Texas-style hat like those worn by Bones Drawgood and Airout Buzell. He stood perfectly still for a moment, then stalked toward her at a pace unmistakably purposefully. She took a step backward as he halted and the torchlight fell across his wide, slant-eyed face. Visible beneath the brim of his hat, a beaded headband rode above black eyebrows that slashed straight across his forehead. He stared menacingly down at her, then at the casket. He turned to look up and down the street, and she saw a long, black pigtail hanging down his back all the way to his hips. He swung back around.

"That Mister De La Fuente's gold in there," he said, as if he already knew the answer.

She swallowed hard and placed a protective hand on the casket. "Where are my husband and his men? You can have the gold as soon as I see them." She was so scared she could scarcely keep her knees from trembling.

He looked at the carpetbag clutched tightly in her hand. "Is that the forty thousand?" he asked, at the same time jerking it from her with such force that she was dragged to her knees. Then he said something in Mexican to the two boys, and they began pulling the cart toward the alley.

"Wait! Where is my husband?" she cried, as she scrambled to her feet.

He kept going.

She screamed her protest, grabbed the back of the cart and held on. "Stop! You cannot have this until you give me my husband!"

He whirled around, his hand going threateningly to the huge knife in his belt. He did not have to unsheathe it. Abruptly silent, she released the cart. He turned away and motioned the boys down the alley then paused to give her a final threatening look before following them, the carpetbag clutched in his monstrous hand and swinging lightly at his side.

Ella was sobbing hysterically, her cheek pressed to the wall of the nearby building, when Sandoval limped silently past. She called out to him but he ignored her. Stunned, she watched him disappear into the murky alleyway.

Confused and scared, she retreated to the edge of the wharf. What was she to do now? The gold was gone, Timon's money was gone, and she had nothing left with which to bargain! Suddenly, she doubled over, as a feeling of tragic mourning swept over her so completely that she cried out with the pain of it. *Gentry! Gentry! You can't be dead! You can't!*

She did not know how much time passed before the familiar sound of squeaking wheels made her whirl and look down the street into the darkness. Her heart pounded as she waited for the torch light to reveal the source of the noise. The terrifying thought struck her that Diego De La Fuente's *'trusted mensajero'* had looked into the casket and was returning to bludgeon her to death with his wicked dagger. But then, just short of whirling around and running for her life, she stifled a yelp as the two young Mexican boys emerged into the torch's glow, pulling the cart. The casket was still there. Behind them limped Sandoval, carrying the carpetbag! She ran to them.

"What happened? How did you get this away from him?" She looked frantically over Sandoval's shoulder, fearful that the brute would appear, and they would be murdered! "You are hurt, Sandoval," she cried, as she noticed smears of blood on his hands.

"It is not my blood, Señora," he said, and touched the hilt of the knife that dangled in a scabbard around his waist. "My *cuchillo* had a very large target, Señora, but it was very hard pulling it out of Chink's back."

"You knew that man?"

"Si, he was very bad. That is why I did not give him a chance to turn around. Like I told you, it is good not to be noticed by one's enemies."

Still shaking, Ella nodded, but then burst into tears again. "But … but what are we to do now? Gentry must surely be dead! He *must* be, or he would have been here!"

"I believe Diego De La Fuente would wait until he saw his gold before he killed them," Sandoval said.

"If only that were true and he is still alive!"

"We will not know this, Señora, until we go to Mexico City and speak to a man who will be interested in capturing these thieves, and will send men to the village of *La chica de Lágrimas.*"

"But who will do this?"

"Have you not heard of Presidente *Benito Juarez*, Señora?"

~

El Presidente Juarez finished assessing the casket, and then gathered up the clothing that had covered the gold bars and extended them to Ella. She declined them; she couldn't open the carpetbag and put the clothes inside for fear he would see Timon's money.

"Those are only old rags, sir. I don't need them," she said.

He spread them over the gold and lowered the lid.

Ella fidgeted under his gaze. It had taken her and Sandoval all day to get here from Veracruz once they hired a man and his wagon to bring them. Then, another day passed before they were allowed into the National Palace, there to wait yet longer while they convinced an aide to look into the casket; after which, he hurried away to speak to his *Presidente.*

Ella tried to look unruffled now, as President Juarez ran his hand over his hairless chin as if stroking an invisible beard. Then he strolled slowly back to his massive mahogany desk and sat down.

"An informant who knew about this gold said two hundred fifty ingots were taken, Señora Garland, each weighing thirty-six ounces," he said. "There is only half that much in your casket."

"Obviously, Mister President, your informant lied to you about the amount," Ella said. "If there ever was that much gold, perhaps *he* would know where the rest of it is."

"Perhaps," he said. "But he was one of the thieves, and is no longer with us."

"I assure you, sir, this is the gold that was on top that cart when it arrived to my husband's ranch," she said, trying to keep her voice from shaking. After that horrible encounter in Veracruz, it hadn't taken her long to realize how dangerous it was of her to assume that she and Gentry would be safely out of Mexico before Diego De La Fuente opened the casket and discovered only half his gold—and now, she was lying to the President of Mexico about it! It was possible that she might never see her children again!

Benito Juarez was unsmiling. "I am curious as to why the informant would lie, Señora. Did I tell you that my government already knew that two hundred and fifty bars were taken? We knew because it was taken from our own treasury."

She succeeded in looking him in the eyes as she spoke. "I have no idea what that man was talking about. The gold in that casket is all that was atop that cart when it arrived at my husband's ranch."

Benito Juarez's frown deepened, and she knew that he did not believe her. She forced herself to gaze calmly at him while wondering if she was about to be arrested.

"The gold was stolen over five years ago, Señora Corrigan. At first, we suspected it was taken by persons who wished to aid your country's Civil War," he said, watching her face as if he expected a revelation.

"My husband fought for neither North nor South, and he abhors politics."

"Even so, how do I know, madam, that your husband was not involved in this crime against Mexico?

Her anger leapt into her eyes "Because, sir, my husband is an honest and honorable man! He has never wanted any more to do with thieves and murderers than you have!"

Clearly, she had surprised him with her furious reply. He continued to study her, his expression one of displeasure. She had read about this man and his refusal to give clemency to the hapless Maximilian of the House of Hapsburg—a nephew of the Austrian emperor, and whom the French had tried to make Emperor of Mexico. Maximilian had ended up facing a Mexican firing squad. Would the same happen to her and Sandoval? Ella jumped when he finally spoke.

"As you wish, Señora. A company of my *Rurales* will go to the village of *La chica de Lágrimas.* Your husband and his men will be freed ... if they are still alive."

Relieved, Ella could only whisper her thanks, and then bowed her head respectfully.

"My Rurales will leave immediately. You will stay in Mexico City to await their return."

"Please, sir. I *must* go, and Sandoval with me. It was he who rescued your country's gold."

"My Rurales travel by horseback, Señora. It is a long trip. You would not be comfortable," he said before she could speak.

"The fact that I am a woman does not mean that I cannot ride a horse as well as your Rurales, Sir. I won't slow their travel, nor will I expect special treatment simply because I am a woman."

He remained unsmiling, and his dark, slightly bulging eyes showed a flicker of impatience. "I have known *Tejas* women to be braver than smart, but ... almost always very good with horses."

"I am not a Texas woma-" She stopped herself.

"Very well, Señora Garland. You may go; your *compañero* as well. I will pray that you do not fall prey to your own valor," he said, still unsmiling.

She bowed again, and this time, performed a curtsy befitting the acknowledgment of a king.

He gave her a slight bow, and then sat down and wrote something on a sheet of paper. Finished, slipped it into an envelope then jangled a bell on his desk. The doors abruptly opened, and four aides rushed in and carried the casket away. Another aide entered behind them and President Juarez handed him the letter. "Deliver this to Captain Roca and tell him a lady will be accompanying him."

"Excuse me, Señora Garland, but I must finish some work," he said, sat down, and began shuffling through a stack of papers on his desk. "Be seated please. My Rurales will come when they have prepared for the journey."

She obeyed. After a few moments, she wondered if she should attempt friendly conversation. She decided against it. *"Do not speak unless El Presidente speaks to you, Señora,"* Sandoval had warned on the road to Mexico City. By the look on the president of Mexico's face, she decided Sandoval had given her good advice.

A half hour later, he arose, offered her his arm, then led her through the wide doors and out onto a tiled terrace surrounded by tropical beauty that spread in every direction. Fruit trees—peach, pomegranate, orange, avocado and lime, stood among great plots of tropical flowers. The flowers, most of them nameless to Ella, spread like bright gems from huge, decorative pots as colorful as the plants that cascaded from them. Almost immediately, Ella's eyes diverted to the large band of horsemen now charging into the courtyard below the mansion's back gate.

"My *Rurales*, Señora Garland," Benito Juarez said, and his open hand swung out as if to introduce them to her.

They rode in a manner reckless with confidence, straight up in their saddles, the reins held loosely in one hand, a rifle raised high in the other. Their sombreros were huge and gray, some black. Their distinctive gray uniforms, braided in silver, hugged their bodies beneath crisscrossed rows of rifle cartridges across their chests. Black or red kerchiefs were tied around their necks. Ella had never seen men so well armed. As well as the carbines in their upraised hands, pistols, knives, and sabers hung from their hips. Those who were not clean-shaven sported long, drooping mustaches—regardless of which, all wore the solemn look of dangerous men.

The Rurales parted, making way for a tall, barrel-chested man on a black horse and leading a second high-stepping animal with a ladies sidesaddle strapped atop him. As Ella looked out over the treacherous mountains ahead of them, it occurred to her that riding astraddle a horse would be better suited to the travel ahead. But from the stern look of this man, she knew better than to protest. Another man stepped up and presented her with a heavy wool shawl and a palm leaf hat—"the shawl for the cold mountain nights, and the hat for the blistering hot days ahead, Señora," said the man, while giving her a slight bow. She thanked him then turned to the barrel-chested man who, by his air, she knew was in charge.

"Sir, thank you for what you are about to do. I am most grateful."

"I am Captain Roca. You and your Mexican *sirviente,* Señora, will keep up with my Rurales, or you will be left behind," he said coldly, then added, "A woman belongs in a house with women's work, not in a saddle among my *Rurales."*

40

"Good as Gold"

ONCE PAST THE MOUNTAINOUS RANGE around Mexico City, they crossed the central plateau and then began to climb the mountains of the Sierra Madre, a high region of deep, impassable pits and fog-obscured valleys lying between the snowcapped peaks in northern Mexico. The Rurales traveled fast, slowing only for rough terrain or short intervals to eat and sleep. Exhausted after a few days, Ella kept up, and sometimes raced her mount past the seventy-six man army of *Rurales* to ride silently beside the somber Captain Roca, if only to prove that she could. Her carpetbag did not leave her sight, nor did Sandoval. When the carpetbag was not tied to her saddle as she rode, it served as her pillow when she rested. And always, her hand gripped the handle.

"Tarahumara," said the captain one hot afternoon when they had been traveling for days.

Ella dared to glance away from the steep gorge that dropped off scant feet from the narrow mountain trail they plodded cautiously along. The captain was pointing to a small, dark-skinned man in a white loincloth and white, tunic-style shirt. He was watching them from his squatted position on a cliff high above the rocky trail. His thin, brown legs were bare to the crotch; his shoulders rounded and hunched forward as if his study of them was intense with aggression. He appeared to be balancing himself with a long object that Ella immediately assumed was a spear.

"*Indians*!" she cried beneath her breath to the captain.

"*Indian*," the captain corrected her. "A Tarahumara Indian … more peaceful than my old grandmother. *Un pastor de cabras* … a herder of goats." He pointed to the goats that Ella had failed to notice in her fright. The long object she thought a spear was actually a shepherd's staff.

She sighed with relief. "I thought our luck had come to an end," she said.

He glanced at her with a look of disdain. "It is not '*luck*' that you are safe and will remain so, Señora. Have you not noticed that no one has dared accost my brave *Rurales* these many miles?"

"I'm sorry, Captain Roca, I didn't mean …"

"No! They have not!" he raved. "And we have seen many *criminales* along the way who would have no mercy on an *estúpido gringa* were it not for me and my Rurales*!*"

"For heaven's sake, I said I'm sorry! Are *you* so '*estúpido*' that you don't understand that I meant no insult to you and your Rurales?"

His affronted eyes raked her up and down, then slowly returned to their usual look of superiority. "The village of *La chica de Lágrimas* lies in a high canyon up there," he said, and pointed.

Three hours later, the trail widened, and the terrain changed to scatterings of pine and oak trees, and then a tropical forest where the travelers crossed a cool stream. Ella watched a pair of red crested parrots sweep past to light in a low tree with thick dark green leaves that must have been two feet wide and twice as long.

Captain Roca ordered her and Sandoval to dismount. "You will wait here until I send for you, Señora."

She started to protest, but he thrust a finger to his pursed lips. "Believe me, Señora Garland. Until our business is complete in *La chica de Lágrimas*, you will not want to be there." With a tip of his sombrero, he shouted an order to his seventy-six Rurales, and they thundered away at a full run.

Ella sat on a stump beside the stream and drank coffee that Sandoval had boiled over a small fire, her hands shaking. "Do you think my husband is all right, Sandoval?"

"I do not know God's wishes, Señora," he said. "You must be brave."

"I don't know if I should be here," she murmured. "My husband may not want …," she clamped her hand to her mouth, and spoke from behind her hand. "I don't know *where* I should be!"

"I believe, Señora, *today* you should be in México …for it is where your heart is, si?"

She stared at him, tears welling in her eyes. Finally, she nodded. "But I'm afraid it's too late," she whispered, then jumped to her feet, as gunfire and screams echoed across the mountain, the loudness of it ricocheting through the deep arroyos and canyons, making it impossible to judge the direction from which the terrifying noises originated. Then, as abruptly as it had started, it stopped.

An hour passed, and she was pacing back and forth, when another volley of loud shots rang out, many rifles, firing all at once, it seemed. Then, complete silence again. She sank back down on the stump to wait and worry.

Minutes later, an escort of Rurales rode up and motioned for her to follow. She grabbed her carpetbag, tied it to her saddle, and Sandoval boosted her up.

"I believe there has been much bloodshed," Sandoval said as they rode along. "You must prepare yourself, Señora Garland."

She gave her mount a sharp jab, soon catching up to the Rurales that led them.

~

The first thing Ella saw were dead bodies—women among them—being dragged away from a blood-spattered adobe wall by white-clad natives like the one she had seen on the mountainside. They piled the bodies onto several goat carts.

"My God, Captain Roca! You have killed women!" she cried.

"*Banditas,* Senora. They were no better than the men they followed. They would have slit your throat for the hat on your head had they the opportunity."

Fearful of whom she would see among the gory dead, her eyes darted from one cart to the next, her dread easing only a bit when Gentry was not among them, nor were any of the men she knew to be with Gentry when he left Texas. Captain Roca answered her question before she asked it.

"The *bandidos* that held your husband have been executed, Señora," he said, nodding to the bodies—except those three," he added, pointing.

Ella gasped at the sight of Rabbit Jack and the De la Fuente brothers, their faces so bloody they were almost unrecognizable. With their hands tied behind their backs, they stumbled along, their eyes rolling wildly with fear, as the Rurales prodded them to the wall. Ella shuddered, realizing anew that Luther Garland had been the leader of these beasts.

"I see, Señora Garland, that you recognize these men."

"Yes, I met the De La Fuentes in San Antonio when they hired my husband. The other is Rabbit Jack." Once, he was stopped from cutting my throat."

"It is a bad man who would murder a woman without good cause," he said.

"Remembering what Sally Skull had told her, Ella said, "Someone once told me that Rabbit Jack is killer, a rustler, a kidnapper and defiler of women and children—an animal so bleak of human traits I doubt he has a soul."

"Ah, then the pleasure of his death shall be ours," Captain Roca replied.

A church bell rang, and Ella looked up to see a tiny rock church high on the side of the mountain, with a wooden crucifix atop it that looked twice as tall as the structure. Around the church were dozens of women and children, some of them with babies slung in shawls across their backs. Obviously, they had fled the village as soon as the shooting started.

"The church bell rings because we have freed this village of its devils," Captain Roca said, smiling and waving pompously up to the women.

Still looking frantically around for Gentry, and knowing that any moment now Captain Roca would order the firing squad to shoot the De La Fuentes and Rabbit Jack, Ella grasped his arm. "Before you shoot them ... did they tell you what they have done with my husband?"

"They told me if they had not believed that you would return the gold, they would have murdered your husband and his *compañeros* weeks ago. However, this morning they grew tired of waiting ..." he said, slowly drawing out each word.

"No!" she cried.

"*Please*, Señora Garland," he scolded. "You do not let me finish speaking."

She knew by his smile that he enjoyed tormenting her.

"As I was saying, they grew tired of waiting and today, at noon, was to be the time of your husband's death." He smiled ruefully at her again, then pulled out his watch and showed it to her. "Had I and my *Rurales* not gotten here in time, you would now be a grieving widow."

"I am grateful to you, Captain Roca, very much so. But where is he?" Her worried eyes scanned the village again. *Was Gentry in one of those huts? Was he in one of those caves up there on the cliffs?*

"Come with me, Señora, to the *hacienda*," said the captain. "Your husband will be released to you as soon as the arrangements have been made."

"Arrangements? What arrangements? The bandits are dead and you have taken control of the village. What else is there to do?" Ella asked, and then flinched as the rifles cracked and she heard the sickening thud of bullets slam into Rabbit Jack and the De La Fuentes at the wall. She did not turn to look.

"Yes. But still, there are preparations, Señora, and these things take time," Captain Roca said. "Come. We will have a meal, and then you will see this husband of yours from that balcony up there as he comes to you. You can wave down to him," he said, and laughed lightly. "He will be surprised, no, to see that his beautiful *esposa* has risked her life to save his?"

With his hand at her back urging her along, Ella crossed the piazza, cautiously looking around. The village's entire perimeter was visible from one end to the other on a flat plain no larger than her smallest cotton patch back in Texas. It consisted of a spattering of stone or grass huts, at the edge of which stood a tall, two-story adobe building—the *hacienda* to which Captain Roca was taking her. The building, with a high balcony and elaborately carved columns, looked out of place amid the raw poverty that surrounded it. In center of the piazza spread a huge, circular fountain with a tall, iron pump. Across from that was the bloody adobe wall. She quickly averted her eyes from the wall as natives trotted up to drag away the crumpled De la Fuentes and Rabbit Jack.

"Well! Well!" Captain Roca cried, as they entered the second-story room facing the piazza, and saw two young Tarahumara women, wearing embroidered white blouses and brightly dyed skirts, cowering in a corner. One of them held a large platter of roasted meat surrounded with fruit and vegetables; the other clutched an unopened wine bottle and glass. Ella wondered if the terrified women had been standing there ever since the shooting began. Captain Roca tipped his sombrero to the women, then waved it toward the table, indicating they should deposit their burdens. They did so, and hurried from the room. The captain held a chair for Ella and she sat down. She stiffened as he stood behind her a bit long before going to his chair.

He reached over to touch her shoulder often as they ate and as he talked about himself, mostly about his career as a revolutionary soldier and then a Rurale. His father had died at the Alamo, his three uncles at San Jacinto—"*all* in proud service to Mexico, and killing *Texans* like those we have now come to rescue," he said, his large eyes abruptly glittering with hostility.

She only nibbled at the food. After listening to him for what seemed like more than an hour, she swallowed her fear, and met the

Rurales captain's bold gaze with a smile, as she lightly shrugged her shoulder from beneath his pressing hand, arose, and strolled to the window. Careful to keep her movements casual, she gazed down at the piazza. Except for the gory barrier and the reddish-brown pools of blood drying in the dirt, the scene was remarkably placid. Village women and young girls surrounded the tall fountain in the center of the plaza, chatting as they filled their buckets and gourds, then stood aside to chat yet more. They seemed in no hurry to return to their huts on this sultry afternoon, Ella thought.

Sandoval and three Tarahumara men sat on the ground in the shade of the fountain, and seemed quite at ease with each other. *But where was Gentry?* She closed her eyes to keep from crying, as she twisted the wedding ring on her finger. *I love you … I love you … I love you,* she heard that deep, unstoppable voice say again. Forcing another smile, she turned back to Captain Roca.

"Captain Roca. I appreciate your hospitality, but I was told that my husband and his men would be released right away. Did not the letter from President Juarez give those instructions?"

"*Si,* I have the letter from *el presidente* here." He touched his vest. "His orders will be followed. Your husband and his comrades will be free to leave Mexico. *You,* with them, Señora Garland." With a low laugh, he rose, and came to join her. He pushed open the French doors, and motioned for her to step out onto the balcony. "But first, there is something I wish for you to see." He waved his arm, and yelled to the plaza below, "*Traiga a los presos*!"

Before she could wonder what he had said, she stared, speechless, as Gentry and his men, blindfolded, filthy almost beyond recognition, and clinging to a single length of rope evidently meant to keep them moving in the same direction, stumbled from the shadows between two buildings. Laughing Rurales tugged the roped men across the plaza, and then shouted them to a halt against the bloody wall. Behind them trotted the *Ru*rales firing squad that had executed the others.

Ella screamed, and clutched at the captain as her knees buckled. He bolstered her roughly against him, grasping her jaws, and forcing her face around until she stared down into the plaza again. He raised an arm high over his head and shouted an order. The firing squad took aim. Ella continued to scream at him, cursing him, condemning him and his *presidente* to hell … the whole of Mexico to hell! She stared at his upraised arm, knowing that at any second, he would drop it and Gentry would be dead! *Dead*! The man she loved would be dead! Gone from her forever! She grabbed his upraised arm and, with all her might, tried to keep him from dropping it, but the effort was feeble against his monstrous strength. He pulled her tighter against him with his free arm, the other still held high.

"What will you give, Señora … to save your husband's life?"

"Anything! I'll do anything," she cried, staring frantically into his bold eyes. "I'll do anything you want!"

Squinting, he stared hard at her, and then shoved her down, forcing her to her knees.

"I want you to watch!" he laughed.

Kneeling, she grasped the iron balcony railings as he pressed her face between them. Her mouth tore open as he dropped his arm, but the agonized scream building inside her never came out.

Rather than the fatal sound of rifles cracking and bullets thudding into bodies, the sound of women's laughter filled the plaza as the women by the fountain charged the wall and, with great gusto, splashed their jugs and buckets of water over the men.

As Ella stared, a murmur of obvious surprise went up from the men as the women untied them. With their hands free, they tore off their blindfolds … just as another crowd of laughing women ran from the fountain with more water, this time wielding large slabs of soap.

Ella stared, still unable to catch her breath as the women tugged at the men's filthy clothing until, at last, they—Gentry included—voluntarily disrobed, and cheerfully guided the women's soapy hands over their filthy bodies.

Laughing wildly at his joke, the captain pulled Ella to her feet and squeezed her in a bear hug. Too weak to pull free, she laid her head on his big, smelly chest and sobbed.

~

Waiting alone in the room for what seemed like hours, Ella went to the window. The piazza looked as she imagined it might have looked on any normal day, villagers going about their business, children playing, and old men squatting or sitting in the shade of their hats. The exception was Captain Roca's seventy-six Rurales milling with their horses near the wide barrier wall, as if waiting for orders. She had almost stopped thinking that Gentry would seek her out. He had seen her on the balcony, had heard her scream … knew that she had come here because of him. She could have sworn he repeatedly looked up at her … even as he stripped and then scrubbed himself with the women's soap.

Feeling a familiar tightness in her throat, and with a sinking feeling that he had stopped caring about her the day he left her in San Antonio, she retreated to the chair in which she had spent long hours waiting. Growing more dejected, she thought at least he would want to thank her, if nothing else.

"A man don't like to be fooled," Hempstead had said. He had suspected all along that she was *"playing Gent like a snake-oil salesman plays a hick—something you don't do to a man like Gent Garland,"*

A tapping on the door brought Ella to her feet. *Gentry!* She raced across the room to open it, but when she did, only old Sandoval gazed solemnly up at her.

"El capitán says we must be ready to leave, Señora. His Rurales will escort us to the border. El capitán said we must leave Mexico and do not come back."

"But … but what about *Gentry*… his men?" Ella cried.

"Us, too," said a deep, familiar voice, and then Gentry stepped into view from around the open door. Sandoval departed.

Once inside the room, he looked her up and down. "Wearing widow's weeds, already"?

"Only because I delivered the gold in a casket …" she hurried to explain.

"I know. Sandoval told me. It was a dangerous thing to do, Ella."

"Well … it … turned out fine in the end," she said, then could only stare at him in search of some indication of how he felt about her being there.

"Sandoval is a lot smarter than I gave him credit for. Stealing De La Fuente's gold kept us from being murdered. I owe him and Cricket a debt."

"I … I was beginning to think you'd already left," she lied.

He rubbed his jaw, and it was only then that she noticed the bruises on his face and the small cut an eyebrow.

"Captain Roca thought I might be able to tell him where the rest of the gold is. His methods were less than diplomatic," he said, then chuckled dryly. "Unfortunately, I never got a glimpse of any of it, and I'll sure never lay eyes on the gold bars De La Fuente promised me and my men. I guess some other greedy thief found the opportunity to grab it up."

Ella felt her face redden.

Gentry walked past her and went to the window to look out. "Sandoval told me how the gold got to Texas and how the ransom idea fell apart in Veracruz—I'm surprised Chink didn't cut your throat, hanging onto that cart like you did," he said, and then turned to her. "So," he growled, "you've made the acquaintance of the *presidente* of all of Mexico, eh? Did Captain Roca treat you well getting here?" he asked, before she could reply.

"Yes, and I see he was nice enough to give you fresh clothes," she said. She hated the sound of her nervous voice.

"Courtesy of Diego de la Fuente's ample wardrobe, since he won't need it anymore."

"I know. I saw them shoot him and his brother, as well as Rabbit Jack," she said. She glanced down at her own dusty attire. "You are cleaner than I, for sure," she said, then felt silly for saying it.

He looked at the carpetbag. "That belongs to you, doesn't it? It looks too crammed full not to have a change of clothes inside."

"It … it does, but they are yours …a shirt and pants, and socks."

He looked at her a long moment, his black eyes unreadable, as always, and then he opened the bag. "Much obliged. I think I'll shed

De La Fuente's duds and wear my own." He pulled them out, and then stared into the bag. "What the dickens is this?" He picked up a stack of Timon's money.

"It belongs to Timon Pledger. Forty thousand dollars. All the money he has in the world, to the very last dollar. He thought it might convince Diego De La Fuente to free you."

Gentry continued to stare at the money for a moment then dropped it back into the bag.

Ella waited nervously while he stepped behind a screen and silently changed into his own clothes. When he came out, he was shaking his head.

"So he was gonna give every last dollar to his name for my return, and quite a fortune at that. I guess this means the *naked dowser* is due a little forgiveness on my part."

"Yes," Ella said. "He truly deserves our forgiveness, Gentry. You can tell him so when we get home and give him back his money."

"What home is that, Ella?"

"Pardon?" she said, as if she had not heard him, and now stalled while trying to figure out what to say and how to say it. The last thing she expected was for him to touch her, and she gasped when he abruptly pulled her up close.

"Where your heart is, eh? And where exactly is that?" he asked.

She stared at him in surprise. Had she spoken? Had she answered his question and been so out-of-her-mind happy that she had not heard her own voice? She knew she had been thinking it, but had she said it? Sandoval must have told him everything she said. She'd say it again and again if she had to!

"Oh, Gentry, I remember that you told me once that *home* is where the *heart* is. It's true. I just forgot it for a while."

"So, this means you're gonna be a Texan now? You sure you can handle it?" he said, smiling.

She pursed her lips thoughtfully for a moment, and then smiled back at him. "I can be a *Texican* as well as you or anybody else. There's nothing particularly difficult about it," she said then added impatiently, "Aren't you going to kiss me, Gentry? You haven't even kissed me hello."

Before she could utter another complaint, his lips were on hers, and he was holding her so tightly she could scarcely breathe.

Long moments later, he raised his head. "Too bad we have to leave right now... I'd like to show you how glad I am to see you," he said, nuzzling her neck. "But your Rurales friends are waiting impatiently to escort us to the border."

"We'll have the rest of our lives to show how glad we are to see each other," she said, as she handed him Timon's carpetbag and picked up her shawl and hat.

He draped his arm around her shoulders as they went out the door. "As soon as I trail another herd to Abilene, we'll try again for that honeymoon trip ... maybe New Orleans this time."

"Rather than traveling off with your longhorns no sooner than we get home, I hope you'll stay awhile and build a nice, shady porch all the way around the house ... perhaps help me decide on a few other improvements to the interior," she added, smiling."

"I'd like to build that porch for you, sweetheart. I'd like to give you the world. But your husband is now more broke than ever. So broke, we'll have to borrow a few bucks of Pledger's money to get home on. I thought I'd come away from this trip a rich man, but a land-poor cowboy is all you'll have for a while, until I can get another herd together."

"Oh, I think we can dig up enough money to see us through for a while, Gentry—maybe quite a long while."

He grinned at her. "Your cotton is gonna be that good this year, eh?"

"Good as *gold*," she said.

www.ingramcontent.com/pod-product-compliance
Lightning Source LLC
Chambersburg PA
CBHW020259030826
48979CB00026B/1536/J

* 9 7 8 0 9 8 3 1 1 9 7 3 9 *